Avarice

Anita Burgh is the author of *Distinctions
of Class*, *Love the Bright Foreigner*, the
Daughters of a Granite Land trilogy,
Advances and *Overtures*, as well as the
Tales from Sarson Magna series.

Also by Anita Burgh

Distinctions of Class
Love the Bright Foreigner
The Azure Bowl
The Golden Butterfly
The Stone Mistress
Advances
Overtures

TALES FROM SARSON MAGNA:
Molly's Flashings
Hector's Hobbies

Anita Burgh

AVARICE

PAN BOOKS
In association with Macmillan London

First published 1994 by Macmillan London

This edition published 1995 by Pan Books
an imprint of Macmillan General Books
Cavaye Place London SW10 9PG
and Basingstoke
in association with Macmillan London

Associated companies throughout the world

ISBN 0 330 33884 6

9 8 7 6 5 4

A CIP catalogue record for this book is available from
the British Library

Typeset by CentraCet Limited, Cambridge
Printed and bound in Great Britain by
Cox & Wyman Ltd, Reading, Berkshire

For John, Prue, Rachel and Rupert with love

Acknowledgements

I would like to thank the following, Prue Willday and the Huntington's Disease Association, Valerie Coral and Baron Stefan-Ulrich von Kaltenborn-Stachau for their invaluable and generous help and advice during the preparation of this book. And to Billy and Kate Jackson my gratitude for their constant encouragement and support.

The previous evening Dieter von Weiher had beaten his mistress. This morning, before setting out on his journey, he had hit his wife. The Countess had been shocked as well as surprised – her husband was never normally violent with her. His mistress was taken less by surprise. Dieter was like that with her. Both forgave him for both loved him.

At six forty-five a.m., across the world on the East Coast of America, Walt Fielding had awoken, feeling randy, but had not sought out his wife, in her room, for relief – he never did. Instead, at one-fifteen p.m. he visited his mistress and then found that he really couldn't be bothered to perform sex with her, a frequent occurrence recently. His day was full as he closed a deal which he had been nursing for a good year and which would net him several million dollars. At eight he called a dating agency and by nine had again felt too lethargic for sex – but he tipped the girl well for her trouble. Between then and midnight, to keep his mind off this worrying state of affairs, he kept busy making phone calls, setting up deals, clearing some papers out of the way before catching his private jet for Europe. All these times were accurate, Walt kept a diary and noted down such things. He was like that.

*

About eleven a.m. James Grantley, known to the world as Jamie Grant, regretted the night before as he awoke with a hangover in his London apartment. As he studied his handsome face in the mirror he could not ignore the signs of the havoc his lifestyle was wreaking on what had once been his greatest asset. He vowed not to repeat the exercise, as he did most mornings of his life. He lunched at his club and spent a worrying hour with his bankers and an even more worrying one with his agent before travelling to Heathrow to catch his flight for Nice. He would have liked to make love to his wife if he had known where she was. She had disappeared again. She was like that.

Cannes – autumn 1992

The Mediterranean sea, gun-metal grey from the overcast sky, lapped languidly, as if exhausted from the exercise of last night's storm, on to the deserted beaches and the jagged rocks along the coastline. The sands were littered with the flotsam the sea had spewed upon them. It looked as if a giant waste-paper basket had been tipped on to the streets, scattering paper, wood, used condoms. The fronds of the palm trees hung tattered and limp. A blue and white municipal dust cart trundled slowly along the Croisette, attended by a scurrying entourage of blue-overalled aco-lytes who were clearing the street of the debris. There were few people about, it was not a day for walking or parading for rain had begun to fall. From the doorways of the seafront restaurants anxious proprietors peered up at the ominously leaden sky and made quick calculations on what to cut from the day's menus to minimize their losses, for business would be bad today.

A deep depression had settled on the area, not just meteorological but the sadness more commonly found in an English seaside town when winter sets in. Cannes should have been basking under a gentle winter sun with kinder temperatures than this. Today it was no different from Morecambe when the crowds have departed, the sun doesn't shine, the white buildings look drab, and business is non-existent. Then the inhabitants creep into their winter carapaces of melancholy and wait for summer and trade to return.

From the bedroom window of his suite in the Carlton Hotel Dieter watched a small elderly figure plodding purposefully along, head bent against the rain, well wrapped in Burberry and scarf, and holding the leads of two Yorkshire terriers with bedraggled red bows which kept their topknots out of their eyes, looking as if they would prefer to be anywhere but on this damp walk.

'Must be English,' Dieter decided, and allowed himself a rare genuine smile at the sight of the intrepid old lady battling with the elements below him. He turned at the discreet tap at his door. The valet he had asked for sidled into the room, each muscle of his body moving as if in apology – Dieter had that effect upon subordinates. He gave his instructions to the man with neither a please nor a thank you, as he dialled a number on the telephone. 'Over there,' he ordered the valet with marked irritation, waving his hand imperiously in the direction of his luggage. The bags were of finest black leather but were neither Vuitton nor Hermès, no one else's initials but Dieter's were upon them. 'Dieter von Weiher here,' he finally said into the mouthpiece. 'Is that you, Toto? How are you and your beautiful wife and children?' His oily smile matched the tone of his voice, speaking impeccable English with a slight Germanic accent – the sort of clipped accent which made even the most respectable of English women think of sado-masochism with an excited frisson. 'If you would please tell His Excellency that I shall be with you by late evening tomorrow, I should be obliged?' Dieter cradled the telephone and spoke softly into it. He would, for Toto was important to him. As the powerful personal assistant to his client, Dieter had to be polite for His Excellency listened to Toto and saw only those of whom his aide approved. Toto was the entrée to a deal which should net him a clear couple of million after expenses. Even though it was illegal money, its purchasing power was the same. He teased Toto, hinting at the present he had for him. Toto was like a child where gifts were concerned – the gold Patek Philippe watch was probably one of countless others he had received but he always liked the latest model – a gift and his sizeable commission, of course.

Dieter was aware of what a filthy occupation the 'toy' business was, something he preferred not to think about if he could help it, and certainly not about the innocents, wiped off the face of the earth by such arms-dealing. He'd rather concentrate on the money it could make him far more easily than his legitimate concerns.

His calls completed, he stripped, pausing to admire his tanned and firm muscular body in the full-length mirror. He knew that with his unlined face he looked ten years younger than his actual mid-fifties. He had the beautiful clear blue eyes of one with Teutonic blood, but his hair, far from the expected blond, was dark brown with only a slight scattering of grey at the temples. He had to stand straight – ramrod straight – to compensate for his lack of height – something which pained him and for which, sadly, there was no cure.

He stepped into the shower cubicle and turned the water full on and as cold as he could set it. He gasped as the icy water struck him, tautened at the pain on his body, writhed with pleasure. Then he looked down at his flaccid penis, picked it up in one hand and hit it hard with the palm of the other. He leaned his head against the tiles and wept with frustration at the problem for which there also appeared to be no cure.

Walt Fielding was angry. He had shouted at the pilot of his private jet as if it was the man's fault that a malfunction on the instrument panel had forced them to fly to Nice airport instead of pressing on to Cairo.

'Didn't you have the goddamn thing checked out in New York?'

'Yes, Mr Fielding, I did.' Josh Nightingale spoke calmly, looking at his employer with a level stare. Walt had once been the fairest and most equable of bosses but just recently there had been a change in him, he'd become unpredictably irascible. Most of his employees cringed at his sudden bursts of temper. Not Josh, for he was one of only two people in his employ not to be afraid of him.

'Who checked it? The usual company who do our servicing?'

'Yes, this is the first time . . .'

'Then fire the lot of them. Find a more reliable servicing agency.'

'Yes, Mr Fielding,' Josh agreed, while resolving to do no such thing.

'You sure we can't press on? You sure you're not being over-cautious?'

'No, Mr Fielding, I am not. That temperature gauge bothers me.'

'I could always get another pilot.' Walt glared at him from under his thick blond eyebrows.

'Of course you could, Mr Fielding. And if you intend continuing this flight I advise you to do just that – I'm not going up in it until it's fixed.'

'What if I order you to?'

'Then possibly you'll die without me.' Josh shrugged his

shoulders in his smart blue jacket edged with gold braid which always secretly embarrassed him.

'You're an insubordinate bastard, you realize?'

'No, sir, a wise one.' Josh grinned.

Walt's temper was not helped when, upon arriving at the discreet and luxurious hotel he always stayed in, it was to find his usual suite taken by someone else. And no amount of bullying and shouting on his part could make the manager budge the incumbent, a notoriously bad-tempered female Hollywood star, who the manager knew would not even countenance such an idea.

'The Carlton,' he ordered his driver instead.

He looked moodily out of the window at the rain-swept promenade. What a God-awful place to be on a night like this, he thought. No one worth anything would be here, that was for sure.

The Carlton management and staff were more than pleased at the unexpected arrival of Walt Fielding – one of the richest men in the world and one of the best tippers. Clients like Fielding who, if they liked a place, would return year in year out and would book in clients and friends, were always welcomed effusively.

In his suite overlooking the Croisette, Walt explored, checking every detail – the comfort of the bed, the size of the bathroom and more importantly, the size of the towels; the lighting; the closet space; the cleanliness.

'Okay,' he eventually said to the hovering duty manager who clicked his fingers at the porters in the hallway, summoning them in with Walt's baggage. A maid and valet were with them to sort out his luggage and unpack. A bottle of Jack Daniels was ordered and delivered – courtesy of the management. Only when he'd had a glass poured, the ice clinking comfortingly, and he was settled in a chair with his secretarial assistant hovering close by did he allow himself to smile.

'This will do me,' he said to everyone's relief. 'Call

Baroness Conteil for me,' he ordered Beth Lovell, his secretary of many years' standing.

'She'll be in Paris.'

'Did I ask you where she was? Just call her.'

'Here or in Paris?'

'Jesus Christ – I don't know – just call her, will you?'

But the Baroness was at neither number nor was Cecilia Stern, one-time film star, now a high-class call girl. Nor were the half-dozen other women Beth tried to contact.

'Shall I call Madame Bartelli's?'

'I've never paid for it and I'm not about to start now.'

'No, Mr Fielding,' said Beth, allowing herself a quiet smile at the barefaced lie. 'What would you like me to do for you, then?'

'Nothing,' he snapped.

'Yes, Mr Fielding.' Beth picked up her briefcase.

He watched the secretary's neat figure as she collected her pad. 'Maybe I should sack you, get one who could oblige on nights like this.'

'What a good idea, Mr Fielding. So much more convenient for you. Will that be all, then?' answered the second person in his employ who was not afraid of him.

'Sassy, aren't you?'

'I hope not, Mr Fielding. Am I free for the evening?'

'Once you've telephoned Cairo and told them we're delayed and why.'

'Very well, Mr Fielding. I'll dine in my room.'

'Too bloody right you will – think you can gad about at my expense?'

'Of course not, Mr Fielding.' She turned to leave.

As she reached the door Walt called out, 'Beth, I'm sorry I snapped.'

'Your prerogative, Mr Fielding.' She smiled as she let herself out of the room. She had worked for him for nearly twelve years and knew him better than most. He was testy these days and for no reason that she knew of. But he was fair, and when, as now, he had no cause, he invariably apologized and no doubt would follow it up with a small gift.

Finally alone, he shifted one foot out of his handmade loafers and eased his toes and rubbed his ankles. Strange, he thought, his ankles always felt swollen after a long flight these days, something that never normally bothered him. He pulled himself up out of the chair and lumbered towards the bathroom, drink clutched in his hand. Shower or bath? Bath, he decided, more relaxing. He turned on the taps and stripped off his clothes, dropping them on the marble floor. He stretched and as he did so caught sight of himself in the three-way mirror. 'Friggin' gut,' he mumbled. He sucked it in but still it protruded slightly. What did he expect with the life he led? Too much desk work, too many limousines, not enough sex. He peered at his face: it had never been his fortune but the rugged features suited him better now, in his late forties, than they ever had as a young man – that was one good thing about getting older, but it was the only damn thing he could think of. With a sigh he sank into the warm water of the gargantuan bath-tub. In a way he was quite pleased that no woman he desired was in. It would be nice to take it easy. He wasn't sure why he'd even bothered to contact anyone – habit, he supposed. Strange how he of all people appeared to be losing interest in sex. Must be getting old, he thought, as he slipped down the bath and allowed the warm water to cover him.

James Grantley had arrived at the Carlton the day before and should have left by now. He looked moodily out of the window at the gathering storm and hoped tomorrow's flight would not be cancelled as today's had been. He frowned, not with irritation but with concern: he had not budgeted for this extra day. He suddenly grinned. 'Budget' was an odd word to choose for himself but he supposed this plan of his had been as near a budget as he was likely to get.

When he had booked in by telephone he'd been asked if he wanted his usual suite. His initial reaction had been to decline and ask for a simple room with bathroom but then he remembered what his Uncle Frederick had told him years ago.

'Take my advice, boy. If you're ever on your beam-ends never let anyone know. The more financially embarrassed you are the more you must pretend to be flush. Not that you'll ever need this nugget of information.' Uncle Frederick roared with laughter at such a ludicrous idea.

Good old Fred, closer to him than his cold, precise and ordered father had ever been. Chaotic-living Fred had been a greater influence than he had ever known. But Fred had had too much faith in Jamie and had not realized just how easily he could wade through a fortune.

Jamie had booked into the suite. But now he was faced with having to pay for two nights instead of one. Still, he'd been careful – he hadn't used room service once. If things had gone as he had planned, he wouldn't have been worried about money. But, just recently, anything Jamie planned went awry. When Andy, his cousin, had called this morning to tell him he'd lost the wodge of money Jamie had entrusted him with he had hardly been surprised. His apparently calm acceptance of the situation did not, however, alter the fact that things looked bleaker than they had for a long time.

Jamie took a notebook out of his pocket and studied it carefully. This system should have been foolproof – what had gone wrong? For months Jamie and his trusty Apple Mac had been working out a surefire system to beat the roulette wheel. It must be Andy's fault – he must have failed to memorize the numbers correctly. Stupid berk, he'd told him not to attempt it unless he was sure. Silly sod had probably been too idle to bother. He should have tested it himself.

He was glad Uncle Fred was dead.

'Roulette's for the mugs, boy,' he'd told him. 'Bank always wins. Stick to chemin de fer – use your skills, boy.'

Aunt Thomasina's death could not have come at a more opportune time. But she was the last of his great-aunts to pop her clogs, there'd be no more handouts from that quarter. And what had he done with his legacy? Blown the lot. He'd paid off what he considered his most pressing debts – a decision not necessarily shared by his other creditors. He'd bought Mica a new car, himself a couple of new suits. Last night's effort saw the last of it gone. And yet . . . he banged his fist into the palm of his other hand with frustration . . . it should have worked. If only he'd been able to go to the casino himself it might have been a different tale. Now he was still left with the unfortunate business of the debt he owed his favourite haunt in London, the Elysium, not a vast sum but embarrassing all the same – then there was the rather unpleasant business in Las Vegas – first and last time he'd go there. Worst of all was the awkward matter of the cheque he'd given Busty Mortimer at the club when he'd lost rather heavily against him at backgammon; the damn thing had bounced like a giant rubber ball. No, the word was out on Jamie, no casino or game would welcome him at the moment. Things should have been different, *if* it had worked.

'Shit!' he muttered, and took out his wallet. He counted the contents and then counted them again just in the faint hope he'd miscalculated. Maybe if he could get a game of backgammon – play for cash . . . or if only he could get a decent part. These days all he was offered was mindless crap. Not like the old days when he'd played Peter Ascot, private eye, in the series of films by old Forrest Ellingham. Brilliant producer, Forrest, until he'd got himself flattened in that stupid car crash – a crash that shouldn't have happened – rich as Croesus Forrest driving on retreads – the man had been mad! Five films they'd made and the money had rolled in and, in Jamie's case, out again. Now he could muse on what might have been if he'd been sensible like other actors he knew and had invested it in restaurants, shops, apartment blocks. Still, he grinned to himself, the spending had been fun.

He looked critically at himself in the bathroom mirror as only one whose face is his fortune can. It was still there, the rakish charm, the sardonic smile, the quizzically lifted eyebrow. He'd still got it in spades. If he laid off the booze for a bit he'd be right as rain and would still be able to knock them in the aisles when the right part turned up.

He turned away from the mirror. Fat chance of that with the British film industry in the state it was. And all the TV mini-series seemed to be tightly buttoned up by the same group of actors so that you were never sure if you'd watched a particular one or not.

No point in getting depressed. Hell, he was only forty-four, early days even for his profession. Thank God he was male, he added to himself.

He quickly showered and changed. He'd not go out to eat tonight. He'd go to the bar here, he might meet someone, with luck he'd be invited to dine with them. With even more luck he might find a game . . .

Yet another storm which had been flirting all day with the inhabitants on the high ground of Haute Provence gathered its force and roared down the Var valley with the speed of an express train, gleefully tearing up trees by their roots, causing mud-slides, hurling cars and caravans about like toys, ripping off chimneys and roofs, and slammed on to the Côte d'Azur, joining forces with the unsettled weather still hovering over the Mediterranean. Winds of hurricane force, lightning that lit the sky in cobalt-blue and thunder that deafened with its ominous roar hit Cannes at eight.

The sea whipped up into angry waves and lashed the pavements, hurling stones and debris at the elegant buildings, drenching the palms, destroying the carefully planted municipal gardens. Nothing moved in the streets. Shutters were closed, windows slammed shut, and doors bolted.

There would be no venturing out tonight.

Or would there? Nestling in the hills behind the Côte d'Azur stood a large, white and luxurious villa, shuttered tonight against the storm. In the garden of exuberant and exotic vegetation the plants were tossed, swayed and bowed by the vicious wind. As the lightning flashed the normally red-tiled roof appeared almost black, a shutter broke loose and banged rhythmically and the telephone rang in a study of a stark simplicity that could only be achieved at great expense.

'You wanted to know about certain gentlemen?' asked a voice which had neglected to identify itself. But it was recognized by the owner of the villa who had taken the call.

'Most certainly.'

'They're at the Carlton.'

'Who?'

'Both of them.'

'Good gracious, you're not joking?'

'A Mr Fielding and a Count von Weiher booked in late this afternoon and as I told you last night, Jamie Grant or Lord Grantley – whichever name you prefer – is also here.'

'What luck! Tell me, have they ordered cars, booked into restaurants?'

'No, sir. Not surprisingly. It's hardly the night to venture out, is it?'

'But it most certainly is, my good friend.' And as soon

as the call was disconnected Guthrie Everyman ordered his chauffeur to be ready in an hour. He heaved himself out of his specially strengthened Louis Quatorze chair and lumbered across the room towards his dressing-room. He was rubbing his hands with apparent glee.

'How fortuitous. All three under the same roof. Tonight's the night, Guthrie old fruit,' he told himself, and giggled almost excitedly. 'Time to set things in motion.'

He padded into his sumptuous white bedroom and clapped his podgy hands together. 'Chico,' he called. 'Run my bath, there's an angel,' he said in passable Portuguese to the flat-faced, large-nosed small man who answered his summons.

Walt looked out at the ferocious weather and decided to call room service, but as he picked up the phone he changed his mind. Whoever was staying in the hotel was trapped by the storm. It might be amusing to see who was here. He'd dine in the restaurant – he called Beth to tell her, he did not invite her to join him.

Dieter wondered if he should not call Toto again and say he might be even further delayed, this storm looked set for days. He decided against it. He hated ditherers himself. What if he called with a delay and then needed to call again tomorrow to say he'd be arriving? No, best to leave it. Tomorrow would do. But he'd dine downstairs, one never knew who might be here.

The shutters and heavy curtains in the bar slightly deadened the racket which was going on outside. The room was not crowded – the hotel was not busy, but there was a respectable gathering.

Walt and Dieter arrived almost at the same time.

'Count Dieter von Weiher, now this is a pleasant surprise!' said Walt, savouring the use of the title, quite unnecessarily since they knew each other of old.

'Fielding, my dear chap.' Dieter smiled as he clicked his heels in greeting.

'And isn't that Lord Grantley over there?' Walt said, pointing to where Jamie sat alone, moodily picking at the olives in front of him, aware they might be all he would eat that night. Jamie was not in Walt's money league but then he didn't have to be. As an English lord and with his reputation as a famous movie star, Jamie had an entrée to many different strata of society. 'Let's ask him to join us, Dieter. I like Grantley, he's an amusing Limey.'

Walt, Dieter and Jamie, while acquainted with each other, did not know each other. They belonged to that exclusive group of people who travelled the world endlessly, and wherever they were could meet up with others similar to themselves – if they chose.

Membership of this select group carried certain unspoken rules. Money was one – to be rich was important, not modestly so but seriously so. Breeding was useful and gained immediate entry even if one's wealth was somewhat depleted – hence Jamie's welcome. Without breeding the wealth had to be just that bit greater. Women were only on the periphery and were there because of their menfolk, either as wives or mistresses. Most were stunningly beautiful, for this circle of men tended to trade in their females as they passed their best and replace them with younger, fresher ones.

Also on the periphery, but tolerated, were men who were amusing and could entertain them – actors, singers, pop stars fell into this category. But should their fame slip, the invitations quickly ceased. It was his title more than his profession that ensured Jamie's invitations these days.

They had dined at each other's tables. Shot each other's game. They had got drunk together and sobered up together. They had shared stock-market tips, and women. They admired each other, did not necessarily like each other, and none of them would trust the others one inch.

'I should enjoy dining with you, Walt,' Jamie said, looking pointedly at his watch. 'It would seem this storm has delayed my friends,' he lied smoothly, but he knew that in this society it did one's standing no good to appear to be alone and at a loose end.

'No one with sense will be out and about tonight unless they need to,' Dieter advised. 'And I gather the phone lines are down.'

'I thought I was in for a damned dull evening but things are looking up.' Walt grinned at the other two and flicked his fingers imperiously, which was not necessary since a waiter was already standing at a slight distance ready to take their order.

Once their drinks were in front of them each looked around the bar. Walt was disappointed by the poor showing of celebrities; he collected famous people as other people collected works of art. It wasn't just to amuse him, he felt strangely secure in knowing them. 'No one of great interest,' he said.

'The storm no doubt – and not the right time of year. What are *you* doing here yourself?' Jamie asked.

'I was en route to Cairo and then India,' Walt said.

'More herbal remedies?' Dieter smiled as they all did at Walt's habit of scurrying about the world looking for herbal cures to add to the many his pharmaceutical company already produced alongside more conventional drugs. He employed hundreds of able chemists but he invariably did this field-work himself.

'Anti-balding cures. Ever seen a bald Indian?' he announced proudly.

'Well, no,' Dieter said.

'Exactly.'

'Ben Kingsley?' added Jamie.

'Anglo-Indian, doesn't count.' Walt waved his hand in dismissal.

'Gandhi?' Jamie grinned.

'He was different in all things. No, the man who discovers a cure for bald men will be the richest in the world.'

'Unless someone else finds a product that can cure impotence or one that will keep *it* up for hours. Now, *that* man really would be rich!' Jamie laughed. Dieter looked at him sharply to see if he meant anything but saw Jamie was genuinely laughing at his own idea.

'Who knows?' Walt was tapping the side of his nose.

'Cairo?' Jamie leaned forward with interest.

'Maybe.'

'Do let us know the results of your expedition,' Dieter said in as relaxed a manner as he could muster.

'And you, Dieter, usual business trip?' Jamie asked pleasantly enough, hiding his true feelings expertly. There was a very strong and persistent rumour that Dieter, behind his fine art and auctioneer businesses, secretly dealt in arms. Jamie normally had little time for people who traded in death and destruction and then, as if to cover the truth from themselves, insisted on referring to their products as 'toys'. But, along with everyone else, he tended to give Dieter the benefit of the doubt, for he was so rich and well connected that he was too useful a person to alienate.

'I've contacts to make,' Dieter replied smoothly. 'And you, Jamie, what brings you here, out of season?'

'A deal.'

'Successful, I trust?' Dieter, while smiling, managed to make Jamie want to hit him.

'Very,' Jamie lied.

'I'm so glad,' said Walt. Jamie was a fool, and there was no greater fool than a gambler, was Walt's opinion. Word was already out about Jamie's latest foolishness with Busty of all people – one of their group's biggest gossips.

He was obviously teetering on the brink of losing everything, and then where would that leave him in the group? Maybe his rank would save him, maybe he'd still be welcome; Walt hoped so, he liked the guy. He'd have to see which way the wind blew for the young English lord. Walt was not one to buck the system, he might even help him out – he might, but he'd have to give up the gambling first. 'Say, isn't that Guthrie Everyman?'

They all looked towards the door where a tall and obese man, a red satin-lined cloak half-flicked over his shoulders, stood and surveyed the bar with an amused expression, as if he had just heard a particularly good joke, allowing himself a half-smile at the interest his appearance had evidently caused.

Guthrie Everyman was a billionaire, courtesy of his steel manufacturing father, and a world-class celebrity courtesy of his own talents. He had written twenty brilliant plays and it was a rare month that one of them was not playing in London and New York concurrently. He wrote novels which bridged that impossible gap between literary and popular fiction and which unfailingly entered the charts at number one on their week of publication. He had dabbled in music, and songs he had written and long since forgotten were played on radio stations around the world. The royalties rolled in.

He was rarely seen in public – hence the frisson of interest in the bar this evening. He had homes here and in Paris where he stayed when the smart people had left.

He need never have worked but when asked why he did his answer was invariably the same.

'To keep boredom at bay, darling.'

Lauded and applauded, he always appeared to be mildly surprised at all the fuss. He was a homosexual, and one who had made no secret of his proclivities even when it was an offence and therefore dangerous to admit them. It was rumoured that the Nobel Prize and a knighthood had been denied him purely because of his penchant for younger men but Guthrie didn't '. . . give a fart, darling'.

'Guthrie Everyman!' exclaimed Walt. Guthrie, since he so rarely appeared in public and tended to mix with his own exclusive group, was anyone's dream social catch. 'Anyone know him?' he asked.

'But of course.' Jamie smiled. 'Guthrie, my old fruit,' he called out amiably. 'Over here . . .'

'Grantley, my poppet. How are you?' Guthrie boomed across the bar and began to trundle towards them on his gargantuan legs. 'Sweetest little fag I ever had.' Guthrie popped a moist kiss on the top of Jamie's head.

'I'd no idea . . .' Walt blustered. He was none too happy with fags – unless they were mega-stars.

'He means I was his fag at school, Walt. Nothing else.' Jamie grinned.

'But a fag . . .'

'I know, I know, but in the English public school system it means I had to fetch and carry for the old bastard, doesn't it, Guthrie?'

'Those were the days! But he kept the tightest arse of any fag I had – or didn't as the case may be . . .' Guthrie laughed loudly, his strange, high-pitched laugh which would have better suited a small woman rather than someone as large as he.

'Perhaps you'd care to join *my* party for dinner?' Walt asked, for here was a queer whose fame made his preferences, if not acceptable, easy enough to ignore.

'Bless you, dear boy, bless you. I was afeared I was in for a tedious night but things are looking up. And how's the family, Walt?'

'Very well, thank you, Guthrie,' Walt replied with a surprised expression since as far as he knew Guthrie knew nothing about him, or was he just being polite?

'Such a relief for you that must be. Poor you . . . such a strain.' Guthrie smiled sweetly and Jamie looked at him intently: what was Guthrie up to with his reaction to the apparently innocuous question and answer? He had heard the light sarcasm in Guthrie's response which the others evidently had not.

'And dear Dieter,' he held his arms apart expansively, his cloak slipping as he did so. 'Blown up any good aeroplanes recently?' he asked with a sudden sharp hard edge to his voice, at total odds with the broad smile he directed at Dieter.

'I beg your pardon?' Dieter said stiffly.

'Semtex, old fruit. Got any handy?' Guthrie's eyes fairly twinkled with mischief. Jamie and Guthrie laughed immoderately at this and Dieter finally joined in. Maybe it was an *English joke*, he thought, giving them the benefit of the doubt. Jamie looked from Guthrie to Dieter and wondered what it was that Guthrie knew.

'Are you normally here out of season?' asked Walt.

'It's the only time to be here – I can't stand riff-raff, and the Côte has a special charm in winter, I find. And Paris will be *bloated* with people.' Guthrie shuddered at the thought.

'But what are you doing here on a night like this? I'd imagined you cosily tucked up in your villa.'

'A little bird told me you were all here. I simply had to come and see my dear old friends and hopefully make a new one.' Guthrie bowed in Walt's direction and Walt felt overwhelmed by his charm.

'Really?' said Jamie with marked cynicism, for Guthrie was not one to put himself out for anyone. Jamie sensed there was something behind his sudden appearance, and was even more sure when he saw Guthrie wink at him in a conspiratorial way.

It was a good dinner and a merry one. By the end of it Guthrie was prepared to invest heavily in the latest pharmaceutical plant Walt had acquired. 'Anyone dedicated to work on the phallus gets my money,' he announced to the consternation of the other diners who, for the most part, pretended not to hear.

Guthrie had agreed that he might try wild boar-hunting on Dieter's estate, provided he could find the energy; he'd picked up the hint that Jamie might be interested in letting him see his remaining Romney. Both knew that he meant to sell it and Guthrie would buy it but since the conversation was conducted in that languid, throwaway style of the English the deal was missed even by Dieter despite his excellent knowledge of the language. And everyone had accepted a surprise invitation to a ball Guthrie was to give in the New Year, the invitations for which were about to be sent out.

'Think, I could have brought your three and saved on the postage.' This idea seemed to amuse him greatly.

'A ball doesn't sound like your bag at all, Guthrie,' Jamie commented.

'Normally, no. But I feel I should celebrate managing to totter to the great five O, don't you?'

They lingered over brandies and it was on the fourth that Guthrie made a suggestion – and changed all their lives.

'Fancy a treasure hunt?' he asked nonchalantly.

'What sort of treasure hunt?'

'Something to relieve the tedium of winter. To amuse you, dear boy.' Guthrie smiled his mischievous smile at Jamie. 'I'll arrange it, the clues . . . all that. You put up an ante each. If you lose, I'll take your money. If you all fail you double the ante. We can finalize the details when you come to my ball – I'll have worked it out by then.'

'How much?' Jamie asked cautiously.

'Two and a half million – doubled if you all fail.'

'Sterling?' Walt asked, interested – big sums always interested him.

'Good God, no, dear boy. Swiss francs if you don't mind.' Guthrie grinned.

'About a million sterling, then?' Jamie asked.

'If you say so, poppet. Sums always confused old Guthrie here — I was always more of an artistic bent myself.'

'What on earth could be the prize that would be worth an outlay of that size?' Dieter asked. 'I mean, we've all got everything we want.'

Guthrie looked at them one by one, amused by their eagerness. He did not reply but allowed his gaze to travel over them again, prolonging the moment — he knew all about timing. 'Well . . .' Guthrie steepled his fingers. 'Now, what would you chummies think if I told you that old Guthrie here has found the Elixir of Life?' He smiled at their dumbfounded expressions. 'Now that's what I call a rare turn-up, what do you say, dear hearts?'

1 Dieter

1

En route for Spain – autumn 1992

In the night the storm had swept on across the Mediterranean. It had left the towns which circled the coastline battered, with fallen trees, torn-off roofs and wrecked cars. At sea it had capsized any boats foolhardy enough to be out; had successfully sunk a yacht, drowning four with six still missing; had damaged countless other craft and so had ensured that it was a storm which would be long remembered and talked about.

Dieter had breakfasted early and by eight had booked out of the Carlton. He had left Walt a note thanking him for the previous night's hospitality – Dieter was not one to forget the niceties of life. He had written a second for Guthrie merely saying what fun it had been to meet him, hopefully ensuring that the promised invitations to the ball would materialize but with no mention of the bet – he would have to think about that first.

As his powerful Mercedes slid through the almost deserted streets of Cannes – as if the inhabitants were afraid to venture out for fear of the damage they might see – Dieter was thinking about the proposed treasure hunt. Fifty miles further along the motorway which would lead him to Spain he was still thinking about it. He was bothered.

It wasn't the size of the ante which deterred him – today's deal alone would easily cover that – he had bank accounts scattered throughout the world as a precaution against the volatility of money. He had deposit-boxes galore filled with gold and cash, plus a share portfolio sizeable even for the rich circle he moved in; he had a castle in Germany, a flat in Vevey and one in Munich, as well as an estate in Scotland which he visited once a year. He had a collection of porcelain which was world-renowned and a personal art gallery of importance. No, the money was not his problem, Guthrie was.

If Guthrie had discovered the Elixir of Life – and it was a big if – why should he be willing to let it go when its ownership would make him the richest man in the world?

Elixir of Life, Dieter smiled to himself, it sounded more like fool's gold. Such a thing could not possibly exist. It was a joke, it had to be. Guthrie was planning an elaborate charade at their expense.

The key to it all was Guthrie's background. A million pounds to him was nothing. Never having to worry about where his money was coming from; never having worked for it – why, he himself admitted that his play-writing was a lucrative hobby – Guthrie was blissfully uninterested in it. He would not want to be the richest man in the world – it would not attract him. Dieter banged the steering-wheel. That was it, it was the game that mattered. His hands tightened on the wheel – Guthrie was the complete opposite of himself. Dieter was hungry for money, always had been, always would be . . . and Dieter was always afraid that one day it might all disappear in a flash but then neither fact was surprising . . . not when one thought about it . . .

Germany – autumn 1944–spring 1945

The little boy, a toy rifle slanted over his shoulder, was drilling earnestly on the large lawn at the foot of a long flight of steps, guarded by stone lions with benign faces, which descended from the terrace in front of the small schloss south of Munich.

Such was the incline of the bank and the steepness of the steps that he could not see the activity on the terrace as lorries were loaded with furniture and paintings from the castle. Nor did he hear the noise of the engines, the heavy footsteps of the soldiers, the shouted commands, the loud curses, for he was too intent on his drill. He concentrated totally, his dark-haired head held rigid, his clear blue eyes looking neither to right nor left. Back and forth he marched in his highly polished black riding boots – polished by him so that he could see his face in them. Up and down, counting silently to himself as he swung to the left and retraced his steps. He had to be perfect for he felt certain his papa would come today.

For six months he had been waiting to see the father he adored and for six months his pretty mother had promised him, 'Maybe tomorrow he will come.'

It was the lorryloads of soldiers who had appeared this morning that had convinced him he would come today. Where there were soldiers, there would be his papa.

'He's coming today, I'm certain,' he said to his mother in the French they always used to each other.

'I don't know, my darling,' she had replied and burst into tears. Dieter hated it when his mother cried, which she did often. Usually he preferred to ignore the tears but this time for some reason he had tried to comfort her. But each time he put his small arm around her, it only made her cry more, so he was quite relieved when she told him to run away and play.

He had watched the soldiers for a while but soon became bored for they were not doing what he expected soldiers to do; they were more like removal men as they trudged back and forth carrying the contents of his father's house and stowing them in the lorries.

He had run upstairs and changed out of the pale blue knitted suit and white shirt which his mother had dressed him in and which he hated. From his cupboard he took the box his father had given him last Christmas, containing one of his most prized possessions – a miniature soldier's uniform. Dressed in that, with his boots and his gun, he had run back and down to the terrace.

'What are you doing with my father's things?' he asked a soldier politely.

'Fuck off,' he was told.

'I beg your pardon, I don't understand. What does fuck off mean?'

'Then piss off,' the Gefreiter said instead.

He knew what 'to piss' was, he'd overheard the stable lads talk. The irritated expression of the soldier told him there must be another meaning.

'I hope my papa gave you permission,' he shouted from a safe distance before jumping down the stone steps two at a time, his polished boots neatly together.

He did not mind being alone for he had never known it any different. There were children on the estate but he was never allowed to play with them. His father was far too grand a man for his son to play with ordinary children – his mother's maid had told him that, and he rather liked the idea that he was so different.

He found amusing himself easy enough. There was a fine collection of books and since he had learned to read at the early age of three he could often be found in the library studying a book with stern concentration as he grappled with ideas and theories way beyond his years.

He loved the books, but perhaps he loved the paintings and the porcelain even more. His father owned a Brueghel, a wonderfully muted painting of skaters with windmills in the background which Dieter had studied so carefully that he knew the face of every child as if they were his kin and had given names to them and imagined families. His father also had an early Picasso of a small boy and girl with hoops – he called them Stefan and Stefanie and talked to them by the hour. These children were his playmates.

He spent hours by the great glass cabinets staring intently at the Dresden figurines, the Delftware, the Meissen; filing away in his child's mind the exact depth of colours, the proportions, the lines used so that by the age of seven he was able to tell which pieces had been fashioned by the same man.

'He's going to be a connoisseur,' he had heard his father say proudly to his mother. 'Already he has a fine eye.'

'A pity, then, they won't be his,' his mother had said softly enough, but his father had frowned, looked annoyed, had turned smartly on his heel and walked out of the room quickly. How silly his mother could be, he had thought. Everything here was his father's and so, therefore, it was his too.

To anyone watching, the seven-year-old marching back and forth across the lawn had an almost mesmeric effect. It was as if the child was in another world of his own. He wasn't. He had not been aware of the noise of the soldiers simply because it was of no interest to him. But he was listening all the same, listening for the one voice he longed to hear.

'What the bloody hell is going on here?' that voice shouted.

Dieter looked up. 'Papa!' he yelled and raced back up to the terrace. 'Papa, you came!' He hurtled himself towards the tall, muscular figure in the uniform of a colonel, the sun glinting on his blond hair. Dieter longed for his own dark hair to turn that colour, magically, in the night.

'Not now, son,' his father said in the German he always used to him, and pushed Dieter away. 'Who's in charge?' he asked the rude sergeant.

'Of the loading? — Schmitt.' The sergeant nodded towards the open door of the castle.

'Unload that stuff,' he ordered.

'I can't do that, sir. Orders.'

'And I'm ordering you to unload it . . . now.' Such was the authority of his manner that despite their misgivings the men, with disgruntled expressions, began the laborious task.

'Papa . . . please . . .' Dieter caught on to his father's uniform jacket and tugged it.

'In a minute, Dieter.' With an irritated gesture he shooed the boy away and leaped up the steps to the door two at a time, Dieter in hot pursuit.

By the time he caught up with his father it was to find him in the long salon already in a furious argument with Oberfeldwebel Schmitt.

'I've orders — papers signed by the Reichsmarschall himself.' Schmitt opened his black leather briefcase. 'Satisfied?' He smirked as Count Heinrich von Weiher und Scharnfeld snatched the papers from him and scanned them rapidly.

'But this is stealing!' he objected loudly.

'Hardly, sir. Your possessions are being taken to a place of safety, sir. Just a precaution in case of bombing. No doubt you'll be able to reclaim them later. Everything is itemized and numbered — there can be no error.' The man spoke as if by rote, as if he had learnt the speech and was used to repeating it.

'If you believe that, you'll believe we can win this war.'

'Sir?' the young Oberfeldwebel said, his face deadpan.

'Heinie, thank God you've come . . .' Dieter's mother raced into the room, her face, as Dieter would have expected, tear-streaked.

'Why the hell didn't you stop them?'

'How could I! With what?' she said with surprising spirit.

'*Speak French*,' he ordered her, switching into that language. '*When did they come? Did you check their papers?*'

'*I did, but I sensed they meant business and I was afraid. And the other man . . .*'

Heinrich had been watching the young officer's face as they spoke, and seeing the blank look of incomprehension he relaxed slightly.

'*Well, they're not taking my belongings, thieving bastards . . .*'

'*Heinie . . .*' Sophie held out her hand as if to stop him.

'*Don't worry, he doesn't understand what we're saying. I know what this is. They're stealing my family's treasures so that those fat sods can have something to live off when this damn catastrophe ends – as it will, any day now, thank God.*'

'Not exactly what one could describe as loyal sentiments to the Führer, my dear Count.' A short and corpulent man in the black uniform of the SS emerged from the depths of a large wing-chair which had been turned away from them. 'Seditious talk even if in a foreign language, which, unfortunately for you, I studied at the Sorbonne in 1930.' The officer smiled, but Dieter shivered: it was not a pleasant smile at all. 'I think we should talk, don't you? And in private.' The man looked at Dieter and his mother.

'I don't know of any jurisdiction which can order my property to be removed,' Heinrich said shortly.

'Don't you? How unfortunate for you, then. If you don't mind . . .' He nodded at the woman and child.

'Best take Dieter upstairs, Sophie.'

'No, Heinie . . . no . . .' and to Dieter's mortification his mother began to cry and then – worse – to hurl herself at his father and to cling to him, screaming. The man in the SS uniform nodded at the officer who marched to the door and barked out an order, and three armed corporals entered. Unceremoniously Sophie's hands were forcibly wrenched from Heinrich's jacket and she was dragged still screaming from the room by one of the soldiers.

'Dieter, go and take care of your mother.'

'Yes, Papa.'

Dieter ran towards the door though he would have preferred to stay with his father.

'And Dieter . . .' Dieter, his hand already on the door-knob of the tall door decorated in green and gold, turned back to see his father standing in the middle of the room, a soldier either side of him, the unpleasant SS officer languidly offering him a cigarette.

'Remember your honour and look after your mother, always, you promise?'

'Of course, Papa, I promise,' he said unthinkingly.

The next months in the schloss felt strange to the child. The best pieces of furniture had been reloaded into the lorries, the best paintings taken down, boxed and added to the cargo with large packing-chests containing all the porcelain. With rooms half-furnished there was now a strange echo as he wandered about. He hated the patches on the walls where the pictures had hung and could not bring himself to look at the empty china display cabinets.

His mother had taken to her bed, so he could not look after her as he had promised he would. At first his mother's maid did that, and when she left suddenly, the cook took her trays to her.

He had heard the officer tell his father the furniture must go because of the fear of bombing but no raids came and he was disappointed. He thought he might have enjoyed being bombed. Throughout his lifetime there had been few members of staff in the castle. His father had told him how in the past they had had many servants but that with the war the men had gone to fight and the younger women to work in the factories. Soon there had been only the middle-aged and elderly left. Then those of middle age had also gone and by Christmas even the elderly were required to go and fight – Dieter would have loved to go with them.

Dieter and his mother were left with a couple to care for them, the wife, Maria, cooking and the husband, Willi, doing odd jobs around the house and tending their vegetable gardens. Though only in their fifties, and old in Dieter's eyes, Willi was exempt from service because of wounds suffered in the Great War.

Food wasn't a problem because they had their precious vegetable plot and they could barter with the villagers for rabbits, fish and game birds. Dieter did not suffer but he knew his mother longed for coffee more than anything and spurned the brew of acorns and maize that Willi and Maria drank.

Eating a plate of potatoes and rabbit at the kitchen table – it was too cold in the dining-room – Dieter listened to the pair as they talked of invading armies and who would get here first: the Americans, they hoped – for coffee, they joked – then the English, but most feared were the Russians.

'You should not speak such nonsense, my father would not like it.' Dieter felt duty-bound to admonish them. 'Of course we shall win. Of course our Führer will be triumphant. Germany cannot fail.' He spoke with the conviction and sureness of one who from his cradle had been told by his father of the importance of duty to the Fatherland above all else. Of how duty and honour were intertwined. He'd watched his father and learnt how a gentleman and an officer should behave, and aped him whenever possible.

So it enraged him when they laughed at him. He kicked back his chair and marched stiffly from the room, their laughter following him, fuelling his anger that they should treat him with so little respect.

'Peasants!' he said angrily as he put on his hat and coat. He eased his rucksack on to his back – it held his thermos, clean socks and pencil and paper. From a shed he got his wheelbarrow and made for the woods to collect kindling for the fire. He did so every day now, there was no one else to do it.

There had been a hard frost in the night and it still lingered at midday – white rime was on the trees, the earth covered in a crystal-white sheet. His breath vaporized as with effort he pushed his barrow across the ploughed field – ploughed but with no crops sown, as there had not been time before the last of the farm workers were called away. He was making for the Higher Wood for several reasons – firstly because he hadn't been here for some time and there should be a good load of kindling to find; then because it was far from the house and the old couple and he hoped the distance might dissipate his anger; and lastly because he had a den there in an old disused hunting-lodge. He wished to check it for he rarely went there in winter when the weather was too cold to enjoy.

This den was his favourite secret place since it had also been his father's when he had been a boy. In fact it was his father who had shown him it and had given him the few sticks of furniture with which he had furnished one room.

He missed his father in a way that he could not put into words. There was a dull ache in him that he knew would only go when his father returned. He had hoped he would come at Christmas but was disappointed; the same at New Year. Now he was pinning his hopes on Easter.

He made straight for his den; he could pick up the wood on the way back, it would be pointless to push a laden barrow into the wood and then out again. He stopped as he reached the clearing where the old timbered lodge stood. It reminded Dieter of the gingerbread house in the fairy stories with its curling roof, latticed windows and timber beams. Over the front door – oak and studded – an antler hung but it was askew – he'd get a hammer and nail and mend it next time he came.

He trundled the wheelbarrow round to the back and hid it in an outer shed. He never let any sign of his presence show – he was always afraid the boys from the village might come and take his den away from him.

It was pleasantly dry inside the little house, only a thin layer of dust which he would sweep up when spring really came – not long now, he reassured himself, chafing his hands to try to get some warmth into them. Maybe he could light a fire, no one would see; it was so cold, surely the village boys would be safely at home? Maybe he could even move in here alone – he'd like that, away from the stupid prattling of the servants, away from the mournful face of his mother. He could boil potatoes, boil rabbits – he knew how to set a trap . . . he could . . . His head jerked up. From outside he could hear the unmistakable purr of a powerful engine. Quickly he climbed the stairs and entered a small bedroom and crossed to the window.

Beneath him he saw a large black Mercedes car; bumping along the forest track that led to the road, another car approached, then stopped. The doors opened and soon the small clearing seemed full as six officers hastily began to unpack the boot of the car, until the ground was covered with wooden boxes, canvas holdalls and sacks.

'You sure this place is safe, Helmut?' one asked.

'Undoubtedly. If it was safe enough for the Count, it's safe enough for us.'

'He really buried stuff here and he told you?'

'He did. Some family silver and matters sentimental.' The man laughed dismissively.

'What if he told someone else?'

'But he didn't – only a servant killed at Leningrad – no one else knows, not even his family.'

'He told you all that?'

'A very obliging gentleman, the Count.' And when the man laughed this time he looked about him and Dieter, with an unpleasant pumping of the heart, saw that it was the SS officer who had ordered him and his mother from the room the last time he had seen his father.

He ducked down as the men turned and entered the lodge. He tiptoed silently to the small landing but he need not have bothered for the men were making a great deal of noise as they transferred the baggage across the hall and down the cellar steps. He craned over the banister to try to hear what they were saying.

'Gentlemen, the Count . . .'

He heard a great cheer and laughter and he smiled, that was nice of them he thought, maybe they were having a drink, maybe they were toasting his father. Perhaps he should join them as his father's representative. Maybe . . .

At that point the cellar door opened and the men emerged. Each carried a bag. And there in the hall, laughing, they stripped off their uniforms and changed into the field grey uniform of the ordinary infantry soldier, for to have changed into civilian clothes would have meant risking being shot as deserters. Dieter was shocked by the way they were discarding their uniforms on the dirty floor — such disrespect for their position. His father would never do anything like that. Then one of them picked up the uniforms, boots and daggers and hurled them into the cellar. Dieter noticed that they kept their guns.

One man appeared with a hammer and a box of nails and deftly nailed up the door. Then all six of them heaved a large oak dresser from across the hall and pushed it in front of the door — no one would know the cellar even existed. Hurriedly they bundled out of the lodge into their cars, and with a roar were soon bumping back the way they had come.

Dieter rubbed his eyes. It had all happened so quickly it was almost as if it had not happened. He waited a few minutes to make sure they were not coming back. Then he raced down the stairs, through the dining-room, into the kitchen to the pantry. He lifted a sliding panel and lowered himself on to a wooden platform. He took hold of a rope, swung a wooden lever and slowly lowered himself on what had once been a produce lift down into the cellar, something he had often done in the past.

It was dark in the cellar but Dieter had a candle and matches in his pocket. He lit the candle and gave himself a few minutes for his eyes to acclimatize to the gloom.

It was the uniforms which attracted him the most. From each he carefully unpinned the medals he found – he was lucky. There was an iron cross and another with the oak leaf, and best of all, one flashing with a bright, sparkling stone.

Several other medals he did not recognize. With no scissors he tore off the men's SS flashes and cap badges and slipped them into his pocket. Then he looked at the boxes and bags. The boxes were nailed down – he would have to return another day with a crowbar. The bags proved uninteresting. Most were filled with silver wrapped in cloth, none as ornate as their own which had been taken to safety. But then a dagger glinted in the light of the candle and he saw that the hilt was studded with shiny stones, the same as on the iron cross, which winked at him. He found three like that and three that did not shine, and stowed them in his rucksack. At the bottom of one bag was a tin which opened easily and it too was full of shiny glass stones. He liked the pretty lights that flashed from them – green, blue, aquamarine. It was a small box, easy enough for him to carry, he thought, as it joined the daggers.

He lifted the candle high above his head to see if there was anything else of interest and saw his father.

'Papa!' he called out with surprise and then, less sure, 'Papa?'

For it was his father, and it wasn't, for this man was slumped against the wall. His face was a strange colour, his eyes were wide open but were not smiling at him. There was dried blood on his cheekbone and shoulder. Dieter stepped towards him. 'Papa, is it you?' He touched him gingerly and his father slumped forward and then the child saw he had no back to his head.

2

Germany – spring/summer 1945

Dieter raced up the wide marble staircase of the main hall. His boots clattered as he ran, his heart thumped painfully. The fat maidens and baroque knights in the great painted fresco that lined the walls and ceiling were the only witnesses to his panic.

At his mother's bedroom door, taller than two men and heavily decorated in gilt, he had to stand on tiptoe to reach the latch.

'Mama, Mama, come quick!'

'Really, Dieter, what do you mean by clattering about in those boots? You'll mark the marble.' His mother was standing in the midst of chaos; clothes were spread on every surface, including the floor; cases, bags and trunks stood open and Sophie was stuffing them unceremoniously full. In the corner, Maria was systematically folding underwear, neatly lining each crease with tissue paper and reverently placing the garments in a case, while tears flowed down her face. Why did all women cry so much? Dieter wondered.

'Mama, it's Papa . . .'

'Yes, darling, I know. We're going to find him.'

'But, Mama . . .'

'Run along and pack a case of toys. Maria has done

your clothes. You can have one small case, you understand? No more.' She turned from him and distractedly
tried to push more clothing into an already over-full case.

'Please, Mama. Listen to me.'

'I haven't time to listen to you.' Sophie's voice was
rising dangerously. 'Go and pack. The Russians are coming
– just our luck it's not the Americans. Maria, can't you
hurry up?' she added with such marked irritation that
Maria stopped crying silently and began to howl. 'Oh, my
God . . .'

'It's Papa. I've found—'

'Don't you listen to a word I say? Your father is in
Berlin and we are going there to find him; we'll be safer
there, Berlin will never fall. Now Maria, pull yourself
together.'

Dieter shrugged his small shoulders and went to his
own room and began to sort through his toys. If no one
wanted to know where his father was then he wouldn't
tell them. The lodge deep in the wood had been his secret
with his father and he'd keep it that way. He'd tell them
when they got back. Meanwhile his grief was his alone,
something to hold to him which, in the hiding, made him
feel as if his father was still with him. His throat ached as
he fought back the tears he would have liked to shed. But
he couldn't cry – must not – what would his father think
of his son crying? 'Officers and gentlemen never cry,
Dieter, remember,' he could almost hear his father say.
And so he swallowed hard, clenched his small fists, bit his
lip until it was sore – but he didn't cry.

He wasn't sure what to take but packed his collection
of Prussian lead soldiers. Then he ran to the library with
its depleted shelves and from the secret hidey-hole his
father had shown him at the back of one of the bookcases,
he took a first edition copy of Schiller. His father had
loved this book since his mother had given it to him when
he reached his majority. Dieter had not met his grand-

mother and did not know if she was nice or not but he felt it would please his father if he kept the book safe. In his father's dressing-room was another secret place. Dieter had once walked in to see only his father's legs – the rest of him was up the chimney. His father had sworn him to secrecy about the guns he had hidden high up there. Dieter pulled a chair on to the hearth to stand on. He felt for the ledge on which were two hand-guns – a Luger and a small one with a pearl-encrusted holster which had belonged to his grandmother, and a tin containing ammunition. He thought his papa might like him to take them for safe-keeping too. He added them to the contents of his rucksack.

While feeling for the guns his hand had brushed against something hard and metallic. He put some books on the chair and clambered back up, felt around and emerged, slightly sooty, with a silver tray. 'So that's where it was,' he said aloud. He rubbed the surface with his sleeve and carefully read the inscription upon it. He did not need to, he knew it by heart. The tray had been a present to his grandfather, a mess-tray, engraved with his regimental coat of arms, its name, '2nd West Prussian Field Artillery Regiment no 36', and the signatures of his fellow officers. He was glad his father had thought to hide it. He knew it had been one of his proudest possessions. 'Not that valuable, you understand, Dieter. But priceless for senti-mental reasons,' his father had told him. He had nodded, unsure then what his father had meant, but understanding now. He wrapped it carefully in a shirt and pushed it into the almost full rucksack.

An hour later the old car was loaded – though over-loaded was a better description. Sophie had cases strapped on top, poking out of the boot where they rested on large drums of petrol, and also stacked on the back seat. Dieter sat in the front, his small case and his rucksack at his feet. Sophie finally emerged from the castle, swathed in furs, followed by Maria carrying a large picnic hamper. Sophie fussed about the car, checking the cases were secure. Maria stood stoically in the late February cold, holding the basket.

'Well, put the basket in the car,' Sophie ordered.

'I can't, there isn't room.'

Sophie pushed and pulled at the bags and then came round to her son's side. 'You can't take that filthy old thing.' She tugged at his rucksack.

'No, I need that.' Dieter hung on grimly.

'You can't take both – we'll need the food.'

'Then take the case.' Dieter manoeuvred the small case out from between his feet. He balanced it on his knees, opened it, and took out the book and shoved it into his bulging rucksack. He was sorry about the soldiers but he needed the guns, he was sure of that – with guns they would be safe. The book he had to keep since his father loved it so.

Seeing his sad expression, Willi stepped forward. 'I'll look after the case for you, Dieter. Don't worry.'

It seemed an age of waiting before Sophie, after prolonged and tearful farewells plus two more trips back into the house for essential forgotten items, settled behind the wheel.

'But, Mama, you can't drive.'

'Of course I can. The time I've spent as a passenger I've picked it up, and your father gave me lessons once,' Sophie said confidently. She turned on the engine, lit a cigarette and hung out of the window for a last farewell.

'Do you think you should smoke with the petrol in the boot?'

'What a dumb cluck you are. Of course I can if I keep the window open. What an exciting adventure this is!' She laughed gaily, let out the clutch and the car wove from side to side down the long drive. Dieter turned in his seat but his view was blocked by the packing. So he opened his window and hung out for a last glimpse of his home.

"Bye, house,' he called. 'We'll be back soon . . .' He waved. Maria and Willi waved in return. The crested and crenellated castle faded from his view.

The journey had been easy initially, despite Sophie having forgotten to pack any maps. They drove along deserted minor roads – with little petrol available there was no traffic. This at least enabled his mother to learn to drive as she went along without inflicting any damage on them or others. But within a short time they began to meet people – people in cars, buses, carts – all fleeing but in the opposite direction. This trickle of humanity soon became a flood as citizens, in panic, deserted the towns and cities and made for the country.

They had given up the car a few weeks into their journey or, more truthfully, the car had given them up. There was a grinding noise in the engine with black smoke seeping from the bonnet, and they had initially fled for their lives convinced it was about to explode. It didn't, however, and they had returned to collect their baggage, the quantity of which had diminished. Unknown to them as they bounded along, heading north, some cases had fallen off the roof soon after they had left the schloss, others had been stolen one night as they slept in a wayside inn. After that they had taken to sleeping in the car in fields and washing in streams and rivers. And it was then that the car had died.

Faced with too much luggage, Sophie began to repack. It was the first time Dieter saw the contents of the cases. He could have cried with rage at the space taken up by ballgowns, tea gowns, smart Parisian suits, shoes, hats, photographs in silver frames and make-up.

'I know, don't say it.' Sophie looked up at him and grinned. 'I've been incredibly stupid but then I didn't know it would be like this.'

The car had died in the early spring, but even so, Sophie now had the sense to repack heavy winter clothes. 'Just in case things get worse,' she said. 'And the silver frames might come in handy.' She paused long enough to stroke the image of Heinie, handsome in his uniform, before laying the photo frames in the base of the largest case.

It was Dieter's brainwave to remove a wheel from the car and the spare in the boot to make a makeshift trolley for their cases. It was he who thought to remove the exhaust to join them; it took him a long time to saw a piece off with the silver bread-knife his mother had packed. Together they ripped the back off her cabin trunk and Dieter lashed the whole together with silk stockings and scarves.

When the trolley was finished and their cases strapped on, his mother looked ruefully at her broken nails.

'Ah, well, they'll grow again, I suppose,' she said, forcing optimism into her voice. 'And I can replace my stockings when we get to Berlin.'

In answer Dieter clambered back into the car and retrieved her large leather make-up case.

'Is there room?' Sophie asked, brightening up at the sight of her beloved cosmetics.

'We'll make room, Mama. Whoever heard of a French lady without her make-up?'

'Such a clever little gentleman you are.' She kissed him on both cheeks, which always annoyed him, but he let her all the same.

After they had given up the car, their progress was more difficult, fighting as they were against the stream which only parted for an army vehicle, its horn blaring importantly. But as the days passed, such sightings became rarer. Instead they began to come across tanks and armoured cars which, as they broke down, had been abandoned by the fleeing Wehrmacht. These were quickly stripped of anything useful by the refugees, so that these great machines soon looked as if they were the discarded broken toys of a giant's petulant child.

Dieter, who had often thought his mother a silly woman who spent too long in bed and never wanted to do exciting things, and was always having headaches and crying, had to revise his opinions of her.

Over the months he had watched her change from an elegant woman interested only in fashion and entertaining into a resourceful and tough survivor. Young as he was, her resilience surprised him. She had become stoical, never complaining, and from doing nothing walked for miles each day without protest. She who had slept in the softest feather-bed with the finest linen sheets sank into a pile of straw – if they were lucky – or hastily gathered moss if they weren't, with as contented a sigh as if she were back in her own fine rococo bed decorated with gilt cherubs in the magnificent bedroom in the schloss.

When Dieter was lucky and had caught a rabbit in a snare she had happily cleaned and cooked it over an open fire – she who had never been seen in the kitchen back home. And when she bartered a necklace of gold and cornelians for a dozen eggs and a live chicken he had watched amazed as she wrung its neck.

'You paid too much, Mama,' he complained.

'When you're as ravenous as we are, what is a silly necklace worth?'

Miraculously she managed still to look clean and smart. Her dark hair was always neatly pinned into a chignon, her face was clean – she never wore the make-up Dieter had saved for her, which puzzled him. And her clothes, limited though they now were, always matched. Whenever they camped near a stream she would wash her precious silk underwear, sparingly using the bars of scented soap she had, with unusual foresight, thought to pack. He was proud of how beautiful she looked. In his innocence he was unaware that it was a beauty that could lead them into trouble.

She would often tease him about his rucksack, wanting to know what it contained. He would never tell her, afraid she would be angry with him for taking his father's guns and stealing the soldiers' daggers and badges. This action weighed heavily on his conscience. He knew it was wicked to steal, something his father would not have approved of. Several times he thought about burying the bag in some out-of-the-way forest but he could never bring himself to do so. He sometimes liked to hide up in a tree where his mother would never follow and look at his shiny things and play with them. And it was during these times that he allowed himself to think of the father he loved. He knew that the ache inside him, of longing for the man, would never disappear now.

In April, still halfway to their destination, they heard rumours that Hitler was dead, others that he had fled and, more fearful, that Berlin had been taken by the Russians. 'What rubbish!' declared Sophie. 'As if the Allies would allow the Russians to take such a prize all to themselves. I don't believe a word we hear.' And they pressed on.

Frustrated by their lack of progress, they took to the fields and byways but the roughness of the terrain impeded them just as much as they pushed and pulled at their trolley. It had moved well on metalled roads but was difficult to manage across fields and through woods.

They didn't discuss leaving the trolley, they both knew

that if they were to get anywhere it had to be ditched. One morning they repacked, and the car-load of over a dozen pieces was finally reduced to one case each, Sophie's make-up case and Dieter's rucksack. They had learnt a lot about survival now and didn't just abandon the luggage but knocked on cottage and farm doors and bartered the contents for food, each of them carrying a bag of provisions in the other hand.

In May they learned from a tearful farmer's wife that Germany had surrendered. They could not believe what they heard until the woman invited them to hear it on the radio. This news Sophie could not simply brush aside.

'Still, there's a good side . . . at least I'm French and so a visitor – they can't harm us,' she said quite cheerfully.

'Oh, Mama, how can you joke?' admonished Dieter, who was deeply depressed at the thought that the great German army was no more.

'At least your father will now be safe,' Sophie said more seriously this time.

Dieter turned away, he hadn't the heart to tell her the truth and witness her despair.

They made better speed now, finding their way by heading east and asking directions on the way.

'Look after your pretty mother, young lad,' a man who in another time might have been a professor, advised one day. 'If you're aiming to go through that forest, keep your eyes and ears open, there's deserters in there – desperate fellows.'

'Germans?' asked Sophie.

'No, Russians,' came the reply, to Dieter's great satisfaction. It was beyond his comprehension that a German soldier would desert even when beaten.

They debated whether to go round the forest but it was large and would add many miles to the journey and they decided to take the risk and go through it. That night while his mother slept Dieter took the precaution of loading both guns. He knew what to do, he'd seen his father load guns countless times. He felt happier when he had; he put them under his rucksack which he always slept with and was soon asleep under the warm night sky.

When he awoke he was immediately wide awake. He looked across to where his mother slept but she was not there, just her fur coat which she had hung on to grimly through everything. He did not call out but sat quietly listening – he was unaware that, in the past months, he had acquired the instincts of a wild animal. He heard a rustling and muffled noises away to the left. He took his guns and with bare feet crept silently on the forest floor towards the sounds.

What he saw filled him with such anger that there was no room for fear. His mother was lying spreadeagled, her clothes rucked up, her knickers down at her ankles. Above her a filthy-looking man was pulling his trousers down while his mother watched with terror in her eyes, her hand over her mouth as if suppressing a scream. Dieter did not have to think.

'Scum, get off my mother!' he ordered, stepping into the clearing. His hands were shaking as he lifted his guns, one in each hand, and aimed. More by luck than judgement he shot the man in his stomach with one gun and in his groin with the second.

The recoil knocked Dieter off his feet, his arms tingled from the power unleashed from the weapons. His body reacted but his mind felt nothing as he watched the man arc backwards, almost gracefully, and flop dead even as the sounds of his guns echoed and ricocheted through the forest, the noise bouncing from one great tree to another as if playing tag, and waking the birds and animals as it went, creating a great scuffling noise of panic in the forest.

His mother was on her feet, rapidly pulling up her underclothes – she did not speak but put out her hand to her son, a gesture of pleading with a hand that shook as if she were old. He grabbed hold of her and led her quickly back to their camp. They still did not speak as they hastily packed their possessions and silently disappeared into the trees, walking as quickly and quietly as they could to put as much distance as possible between themselves and the corpse. Both had thought the same thing – what if he had companions?

They did not stop until dawn and then rested by a stream.

'Thank you, my darling. You were very brave, your father will be proud of you,' she said.

He thought to tell her then that Papa was dead but decided against it, feeling, with a wisdom beyond his years and comprehension, that she had been through enough.

'Why didn't you call for me when that man came?' he asked instead.

'I didn't want you frightened, I didn't want you to see,' she answered, looking away with an embarrassed expression. 'I love you, Dieter,' she added simply.

'Oh, Mama!' It was his turn to look away with embarrassment.

'Well, at least I now know what you keep in your rucksack.' She laughed, aware of his discomfort, changing her tone of voice and her expression.

And now, five months since their adventure had begun, they had finally reached Berlin. Weeks of extreme cold in the early days, followed by excessive heat. Pride and optimism had changed to degradation and fear. And when they arrived it was to a Berlin that barely existed in a country that had been defeated. Standing in the street, in the swirling dust of this overbombed, destroyed city, they saw the reality of that defeat.

They arrived sitting on a small cart squashed in among boxes of fruit which rotted in the summer heat as they

made their laborious way. Sophie had swapped her diamond ring for this cart, horse and fruit. She had reasoned
that with food shortages such as there were she could sell
the fruit in the city on the black market – there must be
one, surely – and it would set them up to start a new life.
But in her urban sophistication she had no idea that food
must reach market quickly. The difficulties and delays of
travel were undoubtedly the reasons why the farmer fifty
miles or so back had agreed to her deal with such alacrity.
Now, as they inched their way cautiously through what
had once been proud city streets, the horse, old, underfed
and underwatered, lifted its head, whinnied and collapsed
in the shafts of the cart. Neither Dieter nor his mother had
time to react to this before people emerged from the
bombed buildings, raced towards them and began to scoop
up the rotten fruit with eyes ablaze with lust for food. The
horse was still twitching while the first blows were rained
upon it as men with axes and knives began to dismember
it for food. Blood shot into the air, raining down in
crimson droplets, filling the air with its sweet smell.

Dieter, tired and dirty, turned away with disgust and
sadness and despair – he had learned to love the ugly old
horse. But Sophie reacted differently.

'No you don't,' he heard her scream. 'That's my coat!'
And from the grasping hands of another woman tore back
her precious fur coat. Dieter leaped forward and just in
time grabbed his mother's case and the smaller make-up
one. He was too late to save his own but at least he had
his rucksack.

'You are funny about that coat, Mama,' he said, as they
wearily made their way through the city, trying to identify
the streets, searching for his father's house – a difficult
task when everything had changed out of all recognition.

'It looks as if life is going to take a little longer than I
thought to get back to normal. We'll need this coat for the
winter.'

She marched on resolutely. 'If your father's not at the house I don't know what we shall do.' Or if it's no longer standing, thought Dieter, looking at the devastation around them, but he kept such ideas to himself.

They eventually found the house. Once it had been a great mansion, now only the outer walls remained.

'What now?' Sophie asked, her whole body slumped with fatigue, her face suddenly full of despair.

'Perhaps the basement survived,' Dieter suggested brightly, wanting to take that look from her face, and he led the way through the gap where massive iron gates had once stood.

The basement door was boarded up, a notice that trespassers would be shot was chalked on it.

'Well, we're hardly that, are we?' Dieter said, looking about him for a piece of metal to tear the boards down.

Inside it was dark and Dieter thought it smelled of rats and rotting things. Rubble was everywhere and little furniture remained.

'We can soon clean this up,' said Sophie, their discovery having made her mood optimistic once again. Then she giggled at her own foolishness as she flicked the light switch on and off.

'There's a trickle of water,' Dieter shouted from the sink beneath the boarded window.

'There. We shall be snug and clean tonight,' Sophie said, and for the first time in months began to sing as she started hurling rubble out of the door. 'When your father gets here we can really get organized. I expect he's moved out to somewhere nice and secure.'

'Mama . . .' Dieter paused. 'Mama, there's something I must tell you . . .'

'Yes?' She looked up expectantly, smiling at him, standing in a shaft of sunlight which pierced the gloom.

'Papa's dead . . .' And then he told her of his grisly find in the hunting lodge. He told her in an expressionless voice as if he was devoid of feeling. Speaking thus was the only way he could put into words the horror he had seen. If he let his true feelings out he knew he would wail and rant with misery and that would make his mother's suffering worse. Sophie clapped her hands over her ears and sank to the floor as if in slow motion and crouched there, rocking back and forth and making a strange keening noise, and for the first time in months Dieter saw her cry.

Awkwardly he put his arms about her and rocked with her.

'I'll look after you, Mama. I promised Papa I would. Don't cry, I'm here.'

In the dark, dank basement he comforted her, a small, undernourished child of eight who was already becoming a man. For in that five months, during that journey, Dieter, though unaware of it, had left his childhood behind.

3

France – autumn 1992

Guthrie Everyman was blessed with the need for only a few hours' sleep a night. He would rarely awake later than six, refreshed no matter what excesses he had pursued the night before. He was a considerate employer and would never expect any of his servants to be up at the unsocial hours he kept, as he was very fond of repeating. However, most mornings, he stomped about his villa slamming doors, dropping things, making as much noise as possible on the off-chance that he might wake a servant or any guests who were staying. Then, if successful, he would be full of profuse apologies at his thoughtlessness, pretending that any noises had been quite accidental. Guthrie was rather like a large puppy who needed constant attention and the distraction of someone to play with.

This morning, after the dinner at the Carlton, he awoke at five and for once crept about the villa for today he needed no diversions. After a quick wash he glided silently down the white marble staircase on his soft, rich red moccasins with his crest embroidered in gold on the front. His fine lawn nightshirt flapped gently and was all he needed to wear in the highly heated house. In the pillared hall he paused by the large urns of white flowers and stopped to deadhead a bloom, before passing in front of the ornate Chippendale mirror to realign a candlestick on the console table, to match its pair. He then pushed open a door hidden in the trompe-l'oeil of an Italianate garden, which led into the kitchen quarters.

On the centre table in the large, well-lit kitchen stood his tray of cup and saucer in finest bone china with a silver coffee pot and milk jug, all covered with a large damask napkin embroidered with his initials, which his manservant had prepared in readiness the night before. He opened both doors of the large Westinghouse refrigerator knowing he would find his grapefruit sliced and de-pipped and a clingfilm-wrapped plate of Ryvita and cottage cheese. First he inspected the racks of pots and cartons. On each was a neat, handwritten label giving both the calorie and cholesterol content of each portion, from the low count of cottage cheese to the stratospheric count of a rich chocolate gateau. This arrangement was Guthrie's concession to his worried doctor who had serviced him, as Guthrie liked to describe it, since they had met in their twenties.

'Guthrie, you must lose weight. Think of your heart!'

'But I do, Daniel, all the time. It pumps away, though, bless it. It's *used* to me, you see, Daniel. It knows what it's got to do, it's always known.'

'All the same . . . after all these years . . . the strain.' Daniel sounded as anguished as he looked.

'But my dear, don't you understand, I was born with a different heart to you – one designed to deal with bulk. I was a thirteen-pound baby and nearly killed my poor mother – she couldn't face childbirth again, it's why I'm an only child, thank God. I'd have hated to share anything with anyone.' He shuddered and the tremble undulated through his body, making his flesh ripple beneath his kaftan, like waves lapping idly at the shore. 'A saint, my mother. I'd have hated me if I'd been her but what did she do? – doted on me, no doubt ruined me with all her spoiling. So there it is. My old ticker's been pushing the blood around an overlarge body since day one. It must have got the hang of it by now, don't you think?'

'But you're getting on, Guthrie. Please, try to cut back a bit on the fats if nothing else. Watch the cholesterol for a bit – for your friends' sake if not for your own. We all love you, Guthrie, you know.' And Daniel Rosenblum, medical practitioner for the rich and famous, sleek Harley Street operator that he was, had tears in his eyes as he spoke.

'Dear Daniel, always such a concerned sweetie.' Guthrie patted his hand. 'For you I'll give it a whirl – for a bit, anyway. Steamed fish and prunes from now on, I promise.' He patted his large stomach, which was a mistake, for he then had to hold on to it with both hands to stop the movement. 'Maybe you're right.' He laughed good-naturedly. 'I seem to have a lot more of me to wobble these days.'

'I'm glad,' said Daniel, not believing for one moment that Guthrie, famed for his love of food and fine wines, had any intention of keeping his promise.

Daniel was not totally right. Guthrie did try. By dint of having his chef weigh every ounce of food and watching the cream and butter, Guthrie had lost six pounds in six weeks. Given his bulk, this loss of weight was not notice-able to anyone but Guthrie and his Salter scales – it *was* depressing.

This morning, however, everything had hit an all-time low. When he had weighed himself his measly six-pound loss had shrunk, or expanded, he wasn't sure which, to an even more measly four pounds.

For once it wasn't his fault either. It was Walt who had ordered the meal for all of them. It would have been discourteous of Guthrie to have refused his host's choice. He would have been quite content with a light consommé rather than the large platters of hors d'œuvre that Walt offered. And he would have settled for a grilled sole rather than the admittedly very delicious lobster in pastry shells flavoured with truffles. And after something so rich he would never have dreamed of ordering the châteaubriand with cognac and foie gras, but Walt had, and naturally Guthrie could hardly demur and had eaten the lot. He preferred not to think of the cheese followed by the pudding which, admittedly, was his to choose and choose he did – a wonderful mousse au chocolat. But then it really wasn't his fault that everything he had eaten before had seemed to whet his deprived appetite for more.

A small voice inside him told him he could make amends today, but another, louder one said rubbish. Guthrie listened to his voice for a split second only and, like a swimmer plunging into the deep end of the pool, he dived into his refrigerator sweeping his grapefruit and cottage cheese to one side, and emerged with his arms full of pots and cartons of food.

On his tray he placed butter, croissant, jam, slices of ham, salami, smoked salmon, potato salad and, as a last gesture, a whole quarter of Chaumes cheese – Guthrie's smelliest favourite. He filtered his coffee, added cream and sugar to the now seriously laden tray and padded back the way he had come to the dining-room where a place was set for him at the long glass and marble table. Happily humming to himself, he spread out his haul in front of him. He paused to survey it and clapped his hands gleefully, as any child faced with a treat will do, and tucked in.

As soon as he had finished eating, the happy mood disappeared. Like all dieters before him who have slipped from the virtuous path, he rapidly descended into a mood of self-disgust and hatred. He sighed mournfully as he looked at the remnants of his meal. Why had he done such a stupid thing? He was a disgusting, ugly pig, he told himself. This self-lecture, however, only reduced him to a deeper degree of self-loathing. Almost defiantly he pulled his plate towards him and piled it high with food again. Quickly he gobbled the lot as if he was afraid that if he didn't, it might escape.

Finally satiated, he pushed his chair back and stood up. He moved towards his study with a surprisingly light step, given his weight, on his equally surprisingly small feet.

Guthrie had an upright posture, a smooth, graceful walk, and he carried himself with a natural dignity. His bearing was so majestic that no one could ever remember anyone being insulting about his size. His presence was so imposing that everyone forgot just how fat he was – except for Daniel Rosenblum.

His desk was a large slab of white Carrara marble set on solid matching legs. On it stood a telephone console on which, as well as making outside calls, he could contact every room in the house. He had a large white bowl filled with white-cased pens. There was a side-table, also white like everything in the room except for the magnificent collection of paintings on the unrelieved white walls – there was a Picasso abstract in blues and black and beige, a fine Rouault, mainly black, and a sensitive Gris still-life of a pear in muted greys and greens highlighted with scarlet. It was a lovely, restful room, the abode of an aesthete.

From the side-table Guthrie took a white ring-folder which he opened and began intently to study the notes inside. Some were his own scribblings, there were faxes and there were official typed reports and photocopies of other documents. It was a dossier. The subject? Walt Fielding and Dieter von Weiher.

He pulled a large pad of paper towards him and selecting a pen began to write copious notes under several headings. He worked like this for several hours until the house began to awaken around him and his formidable concentration was broken.

En route for Spain – autumn 1992

The disembodied voice of his on-board computer informed Dieter that he had enough petrol for only twenty more miles. He registered the fact with surprise. He'd been miles away thinking about the past – so deeply that he had not even taken in the previous two warnings the voice would have given him ... or else there was something wrong with the machine, but that was unlikely. It was also unlike Dieter not to have filled up the tank to capacity before leaving Cannes. But he'd been in such a hurry to leave, given the break in the bad weather, that he had pushed on, meaning to fill up sooner than this.

Now he had the anxiety of wondering how much further the next filling station was, or had he just passed one? He shook his head and wound down the window for fresh air, not strictly necessary in his air-conditioned cocoon. What was wrong with him? He prided himself on being a fast, competent driver, virtually as good as any professional. Such sloppy driving habits were unlike him.

A sign loomed. He felt as much relief as a novice driver to see that a petrol station was only fifteen miles further on. It would have been mortifying to have run out and have to use the emergency phone for help – hadn't he frequently belittled stranded drivers for their inefficiency?

If he allowed himself to think, he knew why he was so preoccupied, why he'd been thinking about the past – he'd been trying, no doubt, to escape the present.

He was mortified with himself. What on earth had induced him to lose control and hit Magda, his wife, when he was about to set out on this trip? Dieter did not like to lose control. He'd beaten Gretel, his mistress, too often for comfort – it wasn't something he was proud of, he certainly didn't do it from choice or for some perverted pleasure. It was frustration, pure and simple. Frustration that with her, whom he did not love, he could make love as often and whenever he wanted. Whereas with Magda, the woman he loved, such a joy was impossible.

Poor Gretel. It wasn't fair on her. She deserved better when all she gave him was love and devotion. And yet she forgave him, seemed almost to understand. Sometimes, he thought, she understood him better than he understood himself. He'd make it up to her somehow – take her to Fossbaden's, she loved eating there. Maybe he would buy her a pretty jewel. It would be easy, too easy, he realized, for him to make amends.

But Magda, that was different. What must she be thinking, what hurt must he have caused her? – he who rarely raised his voice in anger to her, having no need, for she was the perfect wife, even if he wasn't the perfect husband. He banged the steering-wheel with fury at the thought, that terrible thought which consumed him night and day, and which ate at his very soul, touching and marring every aspect of his life.

Dieter von Weiher – impotent!

The large service station appeared. He signalled and turned off. The car was quickly filled, the windscreen wiped. He parked outside the restaurant and shop complex and switched on his car phone – he always switched it off when driving, he did not like the distraction of it ringing.

'Magda. My darling . . .'

'Dieter, dearest. Are you safe? Are you well?'

'I'm sorry, Magda. I don't know what got into me.'

'I know, my sweet. Don't give it another thought . . .'

They talked of inconsequentials. His call disconnected, he locked the car and entered the building. With a look of distaste he rejected the hurly-burly of self-service, choosing the restaurant where he paid for a full breakfast just to get a cup of coffee. He would normally have complained and made a fuss but this morning he could not be bothered.

His coffee and his apology had not made him feel better. He felt depressed, deeply so, as he re-entered his car and started the powerful engine. He eased himself back into the motorway traffic.

Why? There had to be something in his past that made him how he was in his present. The large car began to devour the miles but Dieter drove like a robot. Already his mind had slipped back into the past . . .

Berlin – late summer 1945

In those first few weeks in the city Dieter and his mother could almost look back upon their journey with nostalgia. Survival had been easier with berries in the hedgerows, the occasional rabbit to snare, fish to catch, farmers' wives happy to barter their produce, and clear streams to drink from. Survival in the city, in contrast, was an unending chore.

Both of them were kept busy in the constant search for food. Fresh bread was an unbelievable luxury and meat but a dream. At the merest whisper of a source of new supplies they would race across town and join the seemingly endless queue. The worst was when they got to the head of the queue to find that whatever had brought them here – fresh vegetables, eggs – was sold out. They lived on a diet of dried beans and sausages, the contents of which they had made it a point not to discuss.

The city had been divided into four zones – one each for the powers that had 'liberated' them, American, British, French and Russian. They knew they were lucky to be in the British zone rather than the Russian, where they heard life was even harder, although they often debated whether they might not be more fortunate in the American one, with that nation's famous largesse.

Dieter had registered with the authorities and had been issued with all the correct papers and a ration card which did them little good when supplies were inadequate or did not come at all. There was a black market which flourished despite the exorbitant prices asked and which, of necessity, they frequented.

His mother had no papers.

'Why won't you register too? You've a right to, as my father's widow.'

'I don't want to,' she replied shortly.

'But it's silly not to.'

'Not to me. I've made sure you are all right. I don't think your father would like me to,' she said firmly. As always, for Dieter, such reasoning was sufficient and he never bothered to ask her again.

Although crossing from one zone to another was not easy, it was possible, and Dieter could not understand why his mother, French by birth, should not attempt to cross to them – at least they would be able to communicate more easily with those in control and even, Dieter suggested, be repatriated quickly to France.

'No, it's better we stay here, we've a roof over our heads, it might be worse there,' Sophie countered.

'But if we were sent to France, Mama . . .'

'We're not going, Dieter, and that's that,' she said

firmly, and Dieter didn't mention it again, for talking about it seemed to make her sad. And in a way he was pleased. He was not sure how he would have felt at leaving his beloved homeland. He thought he would prefer to stay, that it was his duty to remain and help rebuild it.

Sophie became obsessed with the thought of winter and the cold it would bring. They scoured the ruin above them and those along the street for any wood which might have been left behind by previous scavengers who had stripped the buildings bare. What little they found they stored in their basement in what had once been a pantry full of sausages, hams and game from his father's country estate. One of Dieter's pleasures was to sit quietly in the room sniffing at the smell of food which still lingered and day-dream of the succulent meals that must once have been served in the dining-room above him.

He had never visited Berlin and so had never seen his father's home in all its splendour. He pestered his mother to tell him about it but her description was disappointingly sketchy.

'There was a large crystal chandelier, I remember – that must be all the glass we crunch over . . . and yes, the hall floor was pretty marble – so many colours . . .' she added dreamily.

'And the dining-room, what was that like?'

'I never went in there.'

'Never went in the dining-room? How strange.'

'Is it? I don't think so,' she said quite sharply, and Dieter registered that this was another subject she pre-ferred not to talk about. But he could dream of what it must have been like and he could plan how, one day when he was a great and rich man, he would rebuild it.

In what spare time he had left, Dieter helped the hastily organized teams of women who with toiling efficiency were clearing the roads and bombed sites of rubble by hand. Long, patient lines of citizens handing the stones from one to the other, setting any bricks aside to be scraped clean and re-used in the building of the new Berlin which they all dreamed of.

Sophie had finally used the last gold coin and piece of jewellery to barter for food. It was a miracle it had lasted as long as it had and was a measure of her husband's generosity to her. All she was left with now was a pile of paper money — completely devalued and of no use to anyone.

For nearly a week they had been without food. They had eaten their last pan of boiled dried beans which, without salt or any other seasoning, had been unpalatable. One evening before the curfew, Dieter returned empty-handed from his foraging to find his mother in a newly washed dress, which she had 'ironed' by sleeping with it under the mattress he had found for her on one of his treasure hunts – he himself slept on a pile of old sacks.

Sophie was sitting at her make-up case, carefully applying her make-up, peering at the cracked mirror in the lid.

'This broken mirror makes me look as if I've had a stroke,' she said, smiling up at him. He sat watching her at her task, fascinated as he had been when smaller, when he would watch her prepare for the evening.

'That's the first time I've seen you do that for a long time,' he said.

'I couldn't waste my make-up,' she replied. He saw there was a slight tremor in her hand which made her smudge her lipstick. 'Look what you've made me do.' She laughed but he noticed it wasn't a real laugh, more like one he'd noticed adults use when they were being polite with each other.

'Are you going out?' he asked finally, curious at all these unusual preparations.

'Yes. To a party,' she replied brightly. 'Aren't I lucky?'

'A party?' he repeated, amazed at the very idea. 'Where? When? Can I come?'

'Sorry, my precious, but no. It's for grown-ups only – you'd be terribly bored.'

'Oh, I see.' He turned away, disappointed. They had not spent one evening apart since they had left the castle.

'But what about the curfew, Mama? What if you are arrested?' he said, his face creased with concern.

'Oh, la! How fortunate I am to have a son who worries so about me.' She laughed. 'Dieter, I've been thinking.' She swung round to face him. 'You're a big boy now to be sleeping in the same room as your mama. I've turned out the small room at the back – just for you. Think, a room of your own again. And dear Frau Schramm – you know, the lady in the house four doors down – she gave me a mattress for you.' Her eyes shone at the thought of such kindness amidst such degradation.

At this news Dieter perked up considerably. He had not minded sharing a room with his mother, but to have somewhere of his own again was a nice thought. He could hide his treasures away, maybe he could loosen a brick to make a safe, just like Papa had, instead of having to carry his rucksack with him, always afraid he might be robbed. When he left it in the basement he was always scared when he returned that it might have been broken into and stolen.

His mother could not have been gone ten minutes before he had his rucksack open and everything laid out on his new mattress to admire. He liked playing with the daggers, making wild, brave thrusts in the air, but what fascinated him most was the small tin of pieces of shiny glass. These he could play with for hours, lining them up like soldiers, running them through his hands so they glinted like water.

He supposed, now that his mother's jewellery had all gone, he was going to have to tell her he had these things – maybe someone would barter for a dagger or an Iron Cross. Still, it would not be honourable to keep them a secret from her any longer. No one would want the pieces of glass, he could keep them.

He was tired and soon asleep and did not hear his mother return a couple of hours later with a man. Nor was he woken when she left and came back a short time later with another.

When he rose in the morning to the sound of his mother singing and the smell of real coffee and he saw the fresh bread and, unbelievably, a slab of golden butter on the table, he could hardly believe his eyes.

'Where did all that come from?' he asked.

'A kind friend at the party gave them to me.' She fussed about him, kissing the top of his head. 'Now, eat, eat until you're full and can't get another morsel in,' she laughed at him.

He didn't tell her about the daggers and medals, he did not need to. His mother went to parties nearly every night now and food was never a problem. But Dieter never awoke to hear or see the parade of men who visited their apartment for a short time.

In the unstable world he lived in, one thing was clear to Dieter: he loved, admired and respected his mother. There was nothing he would not do for her, he would even die for her, he was sure. She was his queen and he was her knight. Had he not killed to defend her? He had forgotten that there had been a time when he had thought her silly and unimportant compared to his father. Their journey, their fight to survive here in the city, had changed all that. Nothing, he was certain, could change it back. He was wrong.

4

Berlin – winter 1946

'Dieter, my darling, I want you to meet a friend of mine,' his mother called.

He left his room eagerly – they knew only their immediate neighbours; a new friend was an excitement, or maybe, and even better, it was someone who had known his father. He made for the sitting-room – they could call it that now for his mother had appeared one day with a van full of furniture and they had a table and chairs, a sofa, a coffee table and a wind-up gramophone. His mother had converted another of the basement rooms and had created a boudoir for herself with a grand bed with an ornate gilded headboard, sheets, an elaborate lamp and a pretty mirror. Another day she had returned with heavy brocade curtains. In six months his mother had contrived a veritable palace for them compared with how it had been.

He entered the sitting-room lit by candles – they had electricity now but his mother always preferred the prettier light from the wax candles.

'Darling, this is Captain Peter Russell.'

Dieter stood rigid in the middle of the room as the handsome man in the uniform of the enemy stepped forward, his hand outstretched in welcome.

'Good evening, young man,' he said in excellent German.

Dieter held his hands behind his back.

'Say good evening to the captain, Dieter.' His mother smiled at the soldier as she handed him a drink. It was a beautiful smile but it was the smile she had once only used towards his father. 'Dieter, did you not hear me?' She frowned now, almost imperceptibly.

'Heil Hitler.' Dieter's right arm flashed up in a salute.

He saw his mother clutch her hand to her mouth to suppress a gasp. The captain rocked back on his heels and roared with laughter. Dieter, his arm still held out straight, felt angry and mortified – how dare this man laugh at him for saluting, for showing his pride in his fatherland, how dare his mother bring him here?

'Dieter! Your manners!' his mother said sharply.

'*How could you entertain him here, Mama? He is our enemy.*' He spoke rapidly in French.

'*But we are all friends, young man. And in any case you too are French,*' the officer replied in heavily accented French.

'I am not! I am a German and proud to be,' Dieter corrected him, standing firm but lowering his arm for he had begun to feel ridiculous standing at the salute when this man still smiled at him as if he found him a subject of great amusement.

'I understand how you must feel,' the captain said kindly.

'I don't think you do,' Dieter said, and quickly turned and left the room, but not before he had had the satisfaction of slamming the door, even though a shower of plaster fell from the ceiling in a fine dust. He went to his room and barricaded the door with the box he used as a bedside table. He sat and listened to the laughter from the other room, feeling the anger boiling up inside him. He did not emerge until he had heard them leave and the front door slam.

He did not go to sleep that night; he tried but he could not. He lay in the dark wide-eyed. When his mother returned he would speak to her, tell her she should not have such friends, that his father would not like it, that she was being a traitor.

He sat bolt upright when, hours later, in the early morning he was sure, he heard the front door being pushed open. And then he heard voices and his mother's trilling laugh and then a man laughing in reply. She'd brought him back with her! He thumped his mattress with frustration and sat huddled on the bed waiting for the soldier to leave. A few minutes passed and he heard them in the corridor and the sound of his mother's bedroom door opening. Then they were whispering and giggling and Dieter sat on his bed and raised his hands to his chest for he felt a hard lump there, a lump of anger.

He did not know what to do, he felt excluded, too young, a baby once more. Suddenly he heard his mother cry out. He leaped from the bed and crossed the room, and in the dark scrabbled at the wall, removing the bricks he had laboriously eased out months before. From the hiding-place he grabbed one of his guns and with shaking fingers loaded it as great groans from his mother filtered through the walls. And then she screamed, her cries heightened by the silence of the night, and Dieter was out of the door at speed and running along to her room, when suddenly Sophie laughed, a happy, gurgling sound.

'Oh, Peter, that was wonderful,' she sighed.

Dieter stood in the dark corridor outside his mother's room, the gun in one hand, the other on the knob of the door. He was confused, he was sure he had not imagined his mother crying in pain. Both hands dropped to his sides and despondently he returned to his own room.

He did not mean to fall asleep but eventually he collapsed in a heap. When morning came he felt he did not want to see her, felt she had betrayed him and the memory of his father. He slipped into the kitchen to get some bread, intending to be out of the basement before she awoke.

'Dieter, I want to talk to you.' His mother was standing in the doorway barring his exit.

'I don't want to talk to you,' he said petulantly.

'We need to. There are things you don't understand.'

'I do! You make friends with the enemy. You took him

to your room. He slept in your bed – only my papa slept in your bed.'

'I know, it's hard. But Dieter, we can't afford to have enemies any more. I need Peter and people like him to help us – how else do we survive?'

'You have me,' he said proudly.

'Of course I do, I'm grateful for everything you do for me. But as hard as we try there is no way we can continue. Do you know how many people are dying out there in this bitter cold? Do you know how lucky we are to have food to eat and coal to burn?'

'Peter gave you our food and fuel?'

'Yes, he and some of his friends.'

'Then I'd rather starve and freeze to death than take from *them*.'

'Dieter, Dieter, my sweet.' She put her hand out to touch him but he shied away from her touch. 'This is silly talk. They are good to us and they risk a lot. They are forbidden to have contact with us, you know.'

'Then he is a bad soldier, he should obey orders. My father would never have disobeyed.'

'Not if he saw we would die if he did not help us?'

Dieter frowned, imagining the scene, trying to think what his father would have done.

'He would have allowed us to die rather than disobey and betray the Fatherland,' he finally announced.

'Oh, my darling, you're so wrong ... Listen to me. Your father had long been disillusioned with the Nazis. He longed for the war – a wrong war, he said – to end, even if it meant that Germany was defeated—'

'No! No!' Dieter cried.

'You are confusing love for your country with loyalty to a wicked man – Hitler.'

'If he was so wicked why did my father serve him?'

'Because he had no choice. Because by the time everyone realized what Hitler meant it was too late.'

'I don't believe you,' Dieter said, feeling confused. How could his father have said one thing and meant another? To his father honour was the most important attribute of an officer and a gentleman. How could he have served and yet thought differently? Dieter shook his head. 'I don't believe . . .' he said, but with less conviction.

'Then why was he shot? Why was he left in that cellar like a dog? Because he hated what was happening to Germany . . .'

'No. That's not true. My father was always loyal. It must have been an accident . . .'

'But Dieter . . .'

'I'm going out. I want to get away from here.' He turned abruptly and ran from the room. But before he left he went to his precious hoard and took two of the daggers, one with a plain hilt and one decorated in shiny glass, and he tied them in the band of his trousers and covered them with his jumper.

He had learnt much in the eight months they had been living here – most importantly that everything had a value to someone; followed by the almost equally important discovery that, whatever it was, the Americans, rasher and freer with their money than the other Allies, were the most likely to buy. Although it was necessary officially to pass through the checkpoints, it was easy enough for a child to get to the American zone, if he knew the city as Dieter now did.

He made a third important discovery that morning – that the dagger with the shiny pieces in the hilt was preferred to the plain one, and so was more valuable. Within an hour he had a sack of coffee, a carton of tins of corned beef, another of sliced peaches, sugar, a tinned ham and several tins of milk – a cornucopia. His dagger was worth so much that the next problem was how to transport it all home.

'You got any more of these?' the burly sergeant asked

him with a combination of pointing, exaggerated hand gestures and shouting – as if by shouting at him he would understand better.

Dieter nodded that he had.

'Then you come with me, buddy.'

Dieter arrived home triumphantly, clinging on to the side of an army jeep.

'There you are, Mama,' he said as the last of the cartons was unloaded and stood in the middle of the sitting-room floor.

'Dieter, how did you get all this?' She looked up anxiously at the sergeant who was standing grinning at them both.

'It's a swap, ma'am,' the American said, sensing what her question had been. 'Your son had a couple of fine daggers he wanted to exchange.'

'How kind of you.' Sophie smiled at him. Dieter didn't like the smile, he felt excluded by it.

'He says he's got more.'

Sophie translated for Dieter. He left them alone reluctantly for his mother was behaving stupidly, smiling too much, laughing too loudly. He removed the brick from his 'safe' and studied his cache. He had two other pretty daggers, three plain ones left. He sorted through his cap badges and he shook the tin of glass beads. Were they the same as the shiny pieces in the dagger? If so, maybe they were valuable too, maybe the sergeant would like them? But then he changed his mind. He liked playing with the glass beads too much to let them go. He replaced his personal possessions – the book and the tray – and took three of the cap badges instead, not the Iron Crosses, he was too proud of them to let the enemy have them, which he felt would debase them.

He stood silent as this time his mother bargained. He was impressed; he had realized she knew some English but she had learnt a lot more, judging by the speed with which she spoke – the captain had taught her, he thought miserably.

Eventually the American left.

'You wonderful boy. Do you know what he's bringing back? The same again.'

'Just for the cap badges!'

She patted her hair and giggled nervously. 'Yes, just for those.' But he wondered why she suddenly went pink. 'Have you any more?'

He ran from the room and returned with the rest of his badges and the daggers. His mother was better at this bartering than him, he thought, as he handed them over.

'Dieter, this is wonderful. And that's all you have?'

'Yes, Mama,' he lied, and hoped she did not notice he was blushing this time. But his mother was too busy sorting out the badges with squeals of delight. 'We won't starve now, will we?' she said excitedly.

'No, and we don't need help from the English any more, do we, Mama? You see, I told you, you have me to care for you.'

5

Berlin – 1946–1947

Sophie continued her friendships with the enemy – American soldiers as well as English – and now Dieter felt bitterly betrayed by her.

He was also dejected and angry over the fate of his haul of treasures, for Sophie had soon exchanged them, despite his pleas that they should keep them in reserve – like the money Papa had kept in the bank. And it was what she acquired that annoyed him still more – a silk bed-cover, more furniture, a sable coat to add to her mink one – no food, no oil, no coal. When he remonstrated with his mother she became angry with him and dismissive, as if it was none of his business. But it was his business, they were his possessions.

He began to avoid her, spending less and less time in the basement flat – it was easier to do so now, with spring in the air. And also he had begun to go to school. A teacher in the same street had started a makeshift school in the ruins of his old one. There were no desks – they sat on planks of wood supported by piles of bricks. They had few books and had to share what there were. Paper and pencils were at a premium so they scraped with lumps of chalk on roof slates. They did not realize that, because of the lack of equipment and their need to listen carefully to the teacher and to remember what he said, they were forging phenomenal memories to use in the future.

Dieter was nine now and eager to learn, but though his mind was stretching his body wasn't – he was short and hated it. He measured himself every week in the hope that he had grown. He wanted to be as tall as his father instead of short like his mother – her shortness was now something else he resented. In the same way he blamed her for his own dark hair; he wanted to be blond like his father, a true Aryan. He had the right-coloured eyes, so it seemed a shame he did not have the right hair to go with them.

Herr Schramm, the teacher, aware of Dieter's hunger to learn, began to take an interest in the boy. Jürgen Schramm and his wife, Lottie, had been luckier than most in that half their house stood and Jürgen had years ago, before the raids had even started, moved his precious library of books into his cellar. It was these books which kept the little school going. But noting Dieter's brightness and eagerness he began to lend him books to take home to read – the only child he trusted with them. So, of an evening, when his mother was out, Dieter was quite content to stay at home to read and learn.

Jürgen was a good teacher and with a teacher's antennae

realized that here he had an unusual child and one worth teaching. He contrived a reading list for the boy; finding that Dieter's French was better than his own, he began to teach him Latin; and discovering that the child had a grasp of mathematics which soon exhausted his own knowledge for he was an arts graduate, he enlisted the help of a professor of mathematics. Both teachers agreed that young Dieter was so gifted that he would be capable of doing anything in the new Germany which would one day arise.

Dieter loved visiting the Schramms and soon began to spend more time with them than at home, slipping like a wraith between the houses, for the curfew had not been lifted.

'Doesn't your mother mind you being here?' Lottie asked him one evening as she helped him to a plate of sausage and potatoes.

'She doesn't care, she's always out – at parties.'

Lottie looked over Dieter's head at her husband and a look of knowing sympathy passed between them.

'Still, she's very young, she needs some fun,' Lottie, middle-aged and comfortable with it, said kindly.

'With the enemy?' Dieter looked up. 'I can't forgive her that.'

'We have to begin to learn to think differently, Dieter, if a new world, a new Germany is to emerge. We cannot keep this hatred in our hearts for ever.'

'I can,' the child said stolidly.

'But have you not thought, Dieter, that perhaps we were misled? That those who had control of us were in fact the real enemy?' Jürgen said in his quiet and modulated voice.

'No, I can't believe that. Never.'

'But they shot your own dear father,' Lottie said softly.

'I'm sure it was an accident. My father was a loyal soldier to the Fatherland,' Dieter said heatedly.

'I'm sure he was and maybe because he was not like the others . . .'

'Herr Schramm, my father was an officer and a gentleman. Honour meant more to him than life. I am the same.' Dieter sat upright in his chair as if sitting at attention.

'Quite,' Jürgen said non-committally, taking his pipe from the mantelshelf and patiently packing it with a little of his precious store of tobacco.

'More sausage, Dieter?' Lottie fussed over the child. She had grown fond of him and knew she was beginning to regard him as the grandchild she would never have; her only son had been slaughtered at Stalingrad.

'And then shall we tackle that next passage in the *De Bello Gallico*, Dieter?'

'Oh, yes please,' Dieter replied, unlike any other child Jürgen had ever dealt with.

He could never pinpoint the time he learned his mother was a prostitute. It was a fact that seeped into his mind as he, a child, became more worldly-wise than a boy of his age should have been.

Now he had books to read in the evening he often lay long into the night reading. So it was that he heard his mother, some evenings, returning to the flat several times. He would listen and hear the voices of men. He would listen and hear his mother sighing and moaning. But now he knew what that meant. One evening, walking back from the Schramms, he had come across a couple in the park, across the way, half-naked, lying on the grass. He was curious and dawdled, hoping he would see the woman's breasts and, if he was very lucky, her 'thing'. The boys at school spent a lot of time discussing the anatomy of women and where babies came from – there were a lot of theories. He hid in a bush and watched as the man had pushed his 'thing' into the woman's who was lying with her legs wide apart and laughing. She had then moaned and screamed and the man had slapped her across the face and she had screamed louder and he had slapped her harder. And Dieter was wondering what he should do about it when the woman laughed, curled her legs around the man's back and pulled him down on her. He was pretty certain that was what his mother did. He could have seen easily enough if he'd wanted – there was a gap in the wall between their rooms where a crack was widening ominously. But he didn't. He could not bring himself to – the sounds were bad enough.

Then at school he'd heard talk of women who did *it* for money; that there were special houses full of them and there were others who walked up and down the street asking for *it*.

He found himself eyeing all women he met on the streets with suspicion – all except Lottie; Lottie, he was sure, would never do any such thing.

Then one day the mother of one of his friends had wondered aloud, while he was in the room, why Dieter and his mother never queued for food, always had plenty, why, enough to give away. She indicated the tin of Spam he had brought as a present and now wished he hadn't.

He asked his mother one evening at the onset of a winter colder than any other they had ever experienced, 'Mama, do you sleep with men for money?'

'Good gracious, what a strange question.' She laughed as she ironed a dress, ready to go out.

'I think you do.'

'Why should you think that?'

'We have more than other people. You're never in. You bring men here. And I hear you moaning and groaning.'

'Oh, Dieter . . . I don't know . . .' Her eyes filled with tears. He had not seen that for years; he began to feel sorry and then stopped himself – no, she had often done that in the past; she could live without crying – he'd seen it for over two years now.

'How could you?'

'We need to eat.'

'We don't need silk scarves and pretty lamps.'

'I need them.'

'I'm ashamed.'

'What can you possibly know about it? You're a child.'

'I know it's wrong.'

'And what is right?'

'Others manage.'

'I didn't know what else to do.'

'My father would be so angry.'

'Your father was the last person to have had the right to stand in judgment.' A bitterness he did not understand was in her voice.

'My father would never forgive you – would never understand – letting the enemy into your bed.'

Sophie shrieked with laughter, a shrill, ugly noise. 'I don't believe you.' She stood, the iron in one hand, the slip of a silk dress in the other. 'So it's all right with a German but not with the Allies?' She shrieked again and wiped a tear from her cheek but it was a tear of laughter. 'Oh, Dieter, you are priceless.' She moved towards him.

He stepped back from her. 'Don't touch me,' he shouted.

She replaced the iron on the stone she had perched on the end of the plank of wood she had put between two chairs as an ironing board. 'Dieter, please, listen to me. I shouldn't have laughed. We have to talk.' She sat on one chair and patted the other; reluctantly he slid on to it. 'Dieter, I was at my wits' end. We needed food. I'm not capable like some of the women – you know how we lived, how spoilt I was – I could not think what else to do. I did it for you . . .'

'Oh, no, you didn't. I gave you my daggers and my badges – you wasted them. We could have lived for over a year off them. There was no need.'

'I needed friends.' She began to sob.

'Why not German friends?'

'They had no money, no food. Be practical,' she said sharply. The sobbing stopped as abruptly as it had begun.

'People are talking.'

'I don't give a damn if they are.' She tossed her pretty hair. 'These aren't normal times.'

'I don't want to stay here.'

'Where else could we go?'

'France – you're French, we could go there.'

Sophie looked down at her hands which she was twisting and turning one inside the other. She looked at them as if they did not belong to her, as if they were a curiosity. 'We can't.'

'Why not?' he persisted.

'Because of your father.'

'I don't understand.'

'He was not welcomed by my family.'

'But you knew him before the war. You were married before then. I was born two years before the war started. You couldn't have known what was to happen.'

'I know, but even then they did not approve. The memories of the first war were too strong in them. And then I followed Heinie . . . and my father said I was dead in his eyes and I was never to return.'

'That's silly. The war's over, Papa's dead.'

'No, you see, for some people the war is never over.' Dieter nodded at this; that he could understand. 'And I've heard stories of terrible things done to women who had anything to do with the Germans. They cut their hair off . . .' She touched her own nervously. 'Tar them.' She shuddered. 'I can never go back.' She looked through him, beyond him as if she was looking into a past long gone, and a past which filled her with sadness.

Dieter felt such sorrow for her. He touched her hand. 'We'll manage, Mama. I'm sorry.'

'That's all right.' Sophie looked at her watch. 'Good heavens, look at the time. I shall be late . . .'

Dieter frowned, that was not what he wanted.

The parade of men, the lustful sounds continued, and Dieter felt impotent rage at what his mother was doing. She had been perfection, his shining star, but now the star was rapidly tarnished. He could not understand how she could lie with strangers, how she could allow their naked bodies to touch hers. With each sexual act he heard, a little more of his love for her died. It slipped from his grasp and he did not know how to retrieve it and a day dawned when he wondered if he wanted to.

Dieter was alone in the apartment when, four months later, he opened the door to an impatient knock. A man stood on the step in the dark area which was lightened this night by a drift of snow. The man stamped his feet from the cold.

'May I come in?' He stepped into the hall.

'Papa!' Dieter exclaimed in excitement. 'Papa?' he asked in wonderment. The man was tall, blond, in a suit – thinner than his father had been but in every other way he was the same – even the way he laughed, as he did now at Dieter's excitement.

'Sorry, young fellow. I'm Heinrich's younger brother.'

'Oh, of course. This way . . .' Feeling rather foolish for the mistake he had made, but bubbling with excitement that he had a relative of his father's here with him, Dieter led the way into the sitting-room.

'You've made yourselves comfortable.' The man looked about him with an arrogant expression. Dieter did not much like the way he looked at everything, almost dismissively.

'My mother is very clever with her hands,' he said defensively.

'So I've heard.' He laughed again and now, in the better light, Dieter could see this man was not like his father at all. He had a cold expression and when he smiled it was only with his mouth, not his eyes.

'Is your mother in?'

'No.'

'Are you expecting her back?'

'Perhaps.'

'Then I shall wait.' He sat on a chair that Sophie had carefully covered in a length of pretty cloth and which was meant more to be looked at than sat upon as the cloth crumpled up under his weight revealing the worn upholstery beneath it.

'Do you remember my father well?' Dieter asked with an eager expression.

'Of course.'

'He was very brave.'

'Of course.'

'And honourable.'

'Of course.'

'Would you like a drink?' Dieter waited to see if he would say 'Of course' again.

'Whisky,' the man ordered curtly. Dieter slipped into the small kitchen to pour the drink proudly from the supply of bottles his mother had accumulated – doing so made him feel a grown-up. He felt afraid of the man but he was a relation – noble too – a blood relation! No doubt he had come to rescue them, to take them away from this basement and this life. He would have liked to fling himself into his uncle's arms as he had into his father's, but instinct told him this would not be a good idea, that this man would not appreciate him doing so. He wondered if he should confide in him about his bag of diamonds. He knew what they were now and though he did not know their value he was aware it must be considerable. He broke out in a cold sweat when he thought how easily he could have got rid of them. He had begun to realize that with them he could change their life dramatically – they could move into the country, buy a farm. But now this relation was here, he would be sorting everything out for them. He would not tell him, he'd keep it a secret a little bit longer, he would make sure he could trust him first. This life had taught Dieter one thing, that there were not many he could trust. He returned with the glass of whisky.

It was an uncomfortable hour as they sat opposite each other. Dieter had quickly run out of ideas to talk about for all he received was virtually monosyllabic answers. And he was smarting . . .

'How old are you?' his uncle had asked.

'Nine, nearly ten.'

'You're short, aren't you?'

Dieter had given up after that and sat silent and hurt. His father would never have been so tactless.

There was a clattering in the area as they both heard his mother returning. Dieter hoped she was alone – the war might have been over for two years now but he did not want his uncle to see her with one of *them*.

'Darling, it's so cold . . . get your poor mother a tisane . . .' Sophie entered the room, her face glowing from the cold, snowflakes still scattered like his diamonds in her hair. She was so beautiful.

'Johannes!' she exclaimed, but not with a pleased expression. She crossed the room to Dieter and immediately put her arm around his shoulders. 'How long have you been here?'

'Not long.'

'When did you get home?'

'Five weeks ago – the Russians were loath to let me go but I had some important Americans intercede for me, I was one of the lucky ones. The hell was over.'

'I'm sorry.'

'Were you taken prisoner?' Dieter asked with great interest.

'You have to leave here, Sophie. You are aware of that,' Johannes said, ignoring the child.

'Johannes, please, no. Where would we go?'

'That is of little interest to me.'

'But the child . . .'

'A trespasser, just as you are,' he said coldly.

'I'm not. This was my father's house so now it is mine,' Dieter interrupted forcefully.

'Tut, tut, have you not explained things to the child? That was a little stupid of you, Sophie.' He turned quite slowly to face Dieter who stood, his small heart pounding, feeling that something horrible was about to happen. 'This is my house, I am your father's heir. You are illegitimate.'

Dieter looked up at his mother and with irritation saw she was crying. How could she shame him? 'I don't understand . . . I don't know what that word means . . .'

'Illegitimate?' Johannes asked, smiling sardonically. 'It means you have no rights. It means your mother and father were not married. It means your mother was my brother's mistress only. It means you have to get out of here.' He held out his glass as if asking for another drink. Moving like an automaton, Sophie refilled it when Dieter would have liked to smash it into his face.

'No! I don't believe you,' he shouted.

'Johannes, please. You know Heinrich loved me. You know he intended to marry me, he told you.' Sophie was begging.

'I know no such thing. How long were you together? Six, seven years? He was taking a long time to decide, wouldn't you say?' He leaned forward so that his face was only inches from Sophie's. 'You were a convenience to him. Nothing more.'

'But he moved us to the schloss.'

'For expedience only. He was to marry Frieda von Zollen after the war – they were engaged. Didn't he tell you? He must have forgotten.' And then he laughed, a cold, mirthless sound.

'I don't believe you, I can't,' Sophie wailed.

'I think, sir, it's better if you leave.' Dieter stepped forward; as yet he had not assimilated this conversation.

'Oh, no, young sir. It's you who are leaving. I'll be reasonable, I'll give you until the end of the week. Then I shall be moving in myself.'

'Johannes, I'll do anything . . .' Sophie flung herself at him but he removed her hands from his coat as if removing an unpleasant insect.

'No, Sophie. It's too late for that. You had your chance – you made the wrong choice though, didn't you? You went for the rich one, but now Heinrich's dead – a lot of good he was to you. You chose the wrong brother after all as it's turned out!'

'I'll go to the authorities.' Dieter spoke up, not afraid, aware that he must take control, that his mother was going to be useless.

'Oh, yes? I'm sure your mother wants you to do that. What will you use for papers?' He glanced up quickly at Sophie, grinning. 'That must have been quite a problem for you – no papers.'

'Of course we have papers. I'm a German citizen, I've my papers, she's my mother – they wouldn't separate us.'

'You? A German citizen? Oh, dear, dear. Hasn't your mother told you? You're not German. You're French, you were born in France – and they don't much like bastards there either.'

'No! You lie!' Dieter roared as loud as his lungs would allow and he flew across the room and began to pummel and kick the man. 'I'm a German, don't you dare say otherwise,' he screamed before the man hit him hard across the head and he lost consciousness.

When he awoke he was lying in bed. His mother was sitting holding his hand, calling his name softly.

'Oh, Dieter, I thought he had killed you.' She hugged him to her. Irritably he extricated himself from her embrace.

'Tell me it's not true, Mama. Please.'

'I'm sorry, my darling. Perhaps I should have told you . . . I suppose I hoped Johannes would die like the rest of them . . . I hoped . . .'

'Then it's true.'

Sophie stared intently at her hands.

'I think you had better tell me,' he said calmly.

The story was worse than he might have imagined. His maternal grandparents, rather than living in the grand château he had imagined, were in fact the owners of a bar in a small northern industrial town; their parents had scratched a living from the land. By comparison Sophie's father had done well, she was at pains to tell him.

'They were peasants, you mean?' he said coldly.

'Yes. But good people, kind. When your father came into the bar they welcomed him . . .'

'You met my father in a bar?'

'Yes.'

'Why did you lie to me? Why did you tell me your parents were rich? That you met my father at a ball in Paris? That you were on holiday from your finishing school?'

'I don't know . . .' She cried, but her tears made his anger deepen, made him feel as if a shard of ice had replaced his heart.

It was a sorry tale. How she became pregnant, and her parents threw her out when they discovered this. His father had set her up in a small flat in Paris where Dieter was born. She recounted how when the war began it was no longer safe for a young woman to have a German protector and so he had moved her to Germany, to his schloss where none of his family knew of her and Dieter's existence except his younger brother, Johannes.

'But he loved us,' Dieter frowned, puzzled.

'Yes, he did. That you must always remember.'

'Would he have married you when the war was over?'

'Of course.' She tossed her head and laughed.

'The truth, Mama.'

She looked at him, her large dark eyes full of sadness. 'I don't know, Dieter.'

He sat with his knees hunched up, his arms about them. 'So that's why you couldn't register?'

'Yes, it was easy enough for you to do so with so many orphans with lost papers – no one asked questions.'

'I think I'd like to sleep now, Mama.' Dieter turned wearily away from her.

When she had kissed and fussed over him and had left him, Dieter sat up again. He sat in the dark, his fists clenched, and he was muttering to himself.

'I am a German. I am. German! German! German!'

6

Berlin – 1947–1949

Sophie, faced with eviction, solved the problem. She chose to marry.

Dieter disliked his stepfather on sight. He was old, he was fat, he was uncouth and he was English.

It took time for the marriage to be arranged. Fraternization was still frowned upon. Sophie might be French – marrying a German woman would take for ever, her future husband joked – but she had no papers. In her rush to leave the schloss she had packed what she saw as necessities, quite forgetting the most important of all. But the

French, sympathetic to the plight of lovers, did everything at great speed to supply her with the essentials.

The British authorities were not happy. Sophie was questioned long and hard about her relationship with Heinrich and why she should have spent the war years in Germany. The feeling was she had to be a spy, but for whom? Common sense finally prevailed – her intended, Sergeant Bob Clarkson, was part of the catering corps and hardly likely to have access to any military secrets.

Sophie would have preferred to marry one of the dashing young officers who had befriended her. But Sophie was not naïve. Her activities in the past two years were well known. They might enthusiastically wine, dine and sleep with her, but marriage? Never, she realized.

Bob Clarkson, on the other hand, was only too happy to oblige. A forty-four-year-old widower, he could not believe his luck when this vivacious, elegant and pretty young Frenchwoman showed such an interest in him. He was even more amazed when she said she wanted nothing from him, unlike the other Fräuleins he'd met who wanted not only money but food, cigarettes, nylons, anything he could lay his hands on. Sophie, his Sophie, was different: it was him she wanted, his company, his friendship and his love.

It was all a dream and one he was afraid would disappear when, after knowing her for only five days, he proposed. When she accepted he could hardly believe his luck.

She had told him about the problem of her little flat and how her dead husband's brother was throwing her and the kid out into the snow – she realized that the truth would not have sounded nearly as heartrendingly dramatic. All it needed was a word with the officer in charge of the lists of accommodation for the homeless. Sophie could stay in her apartment.

Bob sometimes felt he wanted to cry when he saw her and her son in their basement. To him it was dark and shabbily, if bravely, furnished. He would have liked to find them somewhere really nice to live where the sun shone through the windows. But Sophie clung to the flat with such a sweet passion, he relented. It would mean problems when they married – he'd be a long way from the barracks and the authorities didn't like their soldiery scattered about the city – it was too dangerous, for resentment still smouldered. Even now there were parts of the city which were out of bounds. But he was a popular sergeant with officers and men; a word in the right ear and a case or two of whisky from his official catering supplies, and he'd get his way.

If there was a problem it was with the boy. Bob was normally good with children but he could not seem to get through to this one. He wouldn't go so far as to say the kid hated him but sometimes when he saw Dieter looking at him, it was pretty close to hatred.

'I'm sorry, Bob. You're so kind to him and he's so rude,' Sophie fussed one day, as they both surveyed the wonderful toy train set which he had bought from a soldier who had 'found' it and which Dieter refused to play with.

'We've got to give him time, Sophie, my love. Don't forget his dad's dead, he's been the man of the family up until now – he resents me, he'll come round.'

But Dieter didn't. What neither of them realized was that he no longer cared what his mother did, it was who she was doing it with that upset him.

Dieter spent most evenings at the Schramm household learning with an almost desperate hunger. At home he preferred his own company, looking at his books, counting his diamonds – which he did every day now, not trusting Bob. He now knew their true worth. And Dieter had begun to deal in earnest. He found it easy enough for in his home there was always much that others wanted – whisky, cigarettes, canned food. He did not deal for money, he dealt for relics of the war — parts of uniforms, badges, handguns. Mr Schramm had a collection of artefacts from both the Franco-Prussian War and the Great War and often boasted of their value. Logically, Dieter decided, if one collected things from this war then one day they would be valuable too. He used one of the store-rooms in the large basement and hid everything there. He kept a neat book listing everything he owned and what commodity he had paid for it.

Dieter had three great ambitions. To ruin his father's brother; to become rich; to buy his father's schloss. He did not know how he was to do it, only that he would.

Just before his eleventh birthday Dieter began to attend a real school. Equipment was sparse but an organization of sorts was being evolved. Many of the children, after years of running wild in the city, resented the restrictions of school routine, but not Dieter. He was a conscientious pupil and a grateful one.

His stepfather had ceased trying to get through to the child and there was now a cold but polite armistice between them. They said 'Good morning' and 'Good night'. The rest of the day they were either at work or at school and at weekends they ignored each other.

To Dieter's surprise Sophie seemed happy with her husband, though how this could be mystified him; the man had little conversation other than news of his work in the army storehouse. He made a disgusting noise when he ate. He belched and farted with abandon and without apology, and he drank to get drunk. The only advantage that Dieter could think of was that he now spoke English fluently.

But Sophie blossomed. She put on weight which, although it distressed her, suited her. The sad look had gone from her eyes. She had all the smart clothes and make-up she wanted which Bob somehow acquired for her from his ever-widening group of contacts. She was becoming as she was before.

For two years life settled into a routine until one evening Bob returned with the news that he was being posted back to England. Dieter sat silent as he watched his mother's excitement with amazement.

'How wonderful! Bond Street, Harrods, I can't wait to see them – to shop there.'

'Hang on, old girl, we've got strict rationing, you know. You can't just swan into a shop and buy whatever you want.' Bob smiled at her indulgently.

'You'll get me what I want, though, won't you? You always do, you're so clever.' She stroked the back of his neck and giggled and Dieter turned away in disgust.

'And what do you think, Dieter? Fancy going to an English school – a proper school?'

'No, thank you.'

'Oh, Dieter, don't be silly.'

'I'm not being silly, Mama. I don't wish to go to England, I wish to remain here.'

'How can you, a little boy, not yet twelve, manage all on his own in the city? You're English now since Bob adopted you and you can grow up in England as a proper gentleman. And you'll meet Bob's son Robbie. He'll be a friend for you.'

'Yes, Mama,' he said automatically.

'There. I knew you'd come round to the idea,' Sophie said gaily.

Dieter excused himself and went to his room.

'He doesn't seem too happy,' Bob said gloomily.

'He will be . . . he's got this silly idea he wants to be a German. Once we're in England he'll forget all about it.' And Sophie spent a happy evening planning their new future, even going so far as to hint this might be a good time to have a baby — 'Bob's baby,' he said, dewy-eyed.

Dieter did not go to school the next day. He said he felt unwell. He endured his mother's fussing and then waited until Bob went to work accompanied by Sophie; she had a small part-time job now, helping with translation at the barracks.

He leaped out of bed, collected a box and two large cases and carefully packed his store-room of war relics. He raided the store-cupboard and took all the tinned food and a tin-opener. He rolled up his mattress and bedding. From his mother's room he took from a drawer all the papers he would need, including his hated adoption papers and British passport — he might hate them but was aware that in this city they would make all the difference in the world to his safety. Lastly he returned to his own room and from the wall safe took his tin of diamonds, his guns, his father's precious book and mess tray.

In the area he had an old trolley he had found on a building site. He had never used it but with his instincts for hoarding anything that might be useful he had wheeled it home and hidden it under some sacking. He manhandled it into the street. But before he left the flat he returned to the sitting-room and took the large photo of his father which stood beside the radiogram Bob had bought.

He knew where he was going. He supposed he had always known this might happen one day. Years ago in his explorations in a wood, where some trees had miraculously escaped the bombing, he had found a small shed — no doubt once used by woodmen. It was in a copse, almost covered by creepers and bracken — so hidden he had almost missed it himself. He had never used it, but had left it, making sure with leaves and branches that it was

even more hidden from others. He had kept its whereabouts in the back of his mind, just in case he might need
it one day.

That day had now come. The shed would be his home
from now on. He might only be twelve next birthday but
to be that age in Berlin was to be almost an adult. He
could manage.

Pushing and pulling, it took him several hours to reach
the place. He unloaded his possessions, hid his trolley
further away in the wood and returned to his new home.
The first thing he unpacked was the photograph of his
father. He searched the wooden walls for a nail to hang it
up safe.

'I couldn't go, Papa. I need to stay,' he said to the
smiling image.

Spain – present day

Dieter glanced at the digital clock on the many-dialled
fascia of his car . . . how time had flown. It had been an
easy drive, thanks no doubt to the monumental storm
which had kept less intrepid travellers at home. It was odd,
he thought, that for most of the way he had been thinking
of his childhood.

'Childhood!' he snorted out loud. 'Some childhood!' He
smiled to himself; as he was always pointing out to his
wife, it was probably such a hard beginning that had made
him the success he was – that, and the artefacts he'd
hoarded. But the small arsenal of firearms he had eventually collected had been important. He had discovered there
were always willing buyers for such things – nothing had
changed.

He shuddered now to think of the risks that small boy
had taken. In the early days, possession of a gun could
mean death or imprisonment. But he had nipped about

Berlin, armed to the teeth. No one had thought to stop a child – funny, really. Without taking his eyes off the road, he picked out a CD at random, slotted it into the state-of-the-art player in the dashboard and belted down the motorway to Wagner – fitting, he thought.

He arrived at his destination in the Spanish coastal resort as he had intended, by late evening. He booked into the hotel. In his room he washed quickly, changed his shirt and tie, checked that his cases were locked and he had the keys to his room in his pocket, and left. He ignored the elevator and ran down the stairs – not the main staircase but the service one. He knew this hotel of old – the lifts, all together with the main staircase to one side, were very easy to keep an eye on. The service stairs, on the other hand, exited at a small door close to the reception desk where there was always a crowd milling even at this time of night. It was then the easiest thing to slip out into the street.

He walked quickly along the still bustling main street. When he had booked in he hadn't liked the look of the two men sitting on the banquette opposite the lifts. They might be innocent travellers but best to take no chances, he'd decided. To make sure he wasn't being followed he adopted the usual ploys: abruptly turning round and walking in the opposite direction; pausing to look in shop windows; bending to tie his shoelace – but he was confident there was no tail.

He stopped on the corner of the main street and a side road, a chemist on one side and a mini-market on the other. From his briefcase he took a copy of *Le Figaro* and stood reading it. He had only to read it for a minute before a cab pulled up.

'You booked Juan, sir?' the cab driver said, leaning out of the window.

'Wednesday afternoon,' he replied in faltering Spanish – this was not one of his languages.

'A nice day, Wednesday.' The driver grinned, turned in his seat and opened the door for Dieter.

Dieter settled on to the back seat. He rarely travelled on public transport, he had no need. He wrinkled his nose at the unpleasant smell of stale tobacco, lingering garlic and human sweat. He moved uncomfortably on the seat and wished he'd put his newspaper on it to shield his clothes. The cab driver swung the car into the flow of traffic without apparently glancing in the wing-mirror, presumably depending on the small, gaudy, plastic Virgin Mary and rosary which dangled from the rear-view mirror, to keep them safe.

The driver spoke, Dieter ignored him. He had no time for pointless chit-chat with taxi drivers whose Spanish, in any case, he barely understood. Pointedly he opened his briefcase and took out a sheaf of papers. The Spaniard shrugged his shoulders, lapsed into silence and concentrated on his execrable driving.

Dieter was not reading the papers, he had no need, he knew the figures they contained by heart. He glanced idly out of the window as the taxi careered through the labyrinth of back streets. If they were being followed it was unlikely anyone could keep up. He had no idea where he was or where he was going. Such ignorance, given the reputation of His Excellency, was advisable.

He wasn't even sure why he was here – old times' sake, he supposed. Once most of his interests had been tied up in the illegal arms trade – small stuff then – gun-running to Palestine, Ireland, any number of African states, wherever there was a 'little problem' as he lightheartedly put it. They were fun days too, chugging the seas in a clapped-out old motor torpedo boat, giving the authorities the slip; the heart-stopping times they were boarded by customs and nothing found. Then at dead of night rendezvousing and unloading in some isolated bay, best on a moonless night. Yes, exciting times, almost orgasmically so.

He shifted in his seat, uncomfortable again at the use of *that* word in his thoughts.

He'd done nothing like that for years now. He never touched a weapon, never saw them even, nothing in writing; carefully coded phone calls, that was all, and with only a selected few – the big spenders like His Excellency. Others took the risk, did the transporting, the handing over, not him. He sat in the middle, anonymous, unidentifiable should the crunch come. And all the time his numbered account at his bank in Geneva growing larger from the interest it earned.

He did not need to do it either. His legitimate affairs thrived. He had enough money now to last him out and no children to worry about. Business was booming. As sanctions were applied to nations by other nations, they were broken with incredible ease by the likes of Dieter, who grew richer on the rest of the world's conscience. Whenever he decided that was the last time he could almost guarantee that a call would come, always one he couldn't resist. He was greedy, he supposed, always wanting more, just in case – squirrelling it away, just as he had as a child when he counted his pfennigs into marks and hid them in an old sock. Now he dealt in Swiss francs only – US dollars were out. And he had to admit he still got as much of a kick counting his millions as had the child counting his hundred marks.

The cab screeched to a halt. A large black limousine purred out of an archway. Nothing was said, he simply got out of the taxi and transferred to the luxury of the sleek car. He felt more at home in its black calf and air-conditioned interior.

His Excellency wasn't a friend – Dieter had never made that mistake. He had no feelings one way or the other about the man, just as he had no feelings about his activities or how many innocents he would be likely to kill with this shipload. It had nothing to do with him, it was something he never thought about — he would never have lasted in the 'toy' business if he had.

The limousine had left the city and was heading into the hills; there was nothing to see in the darkness. If he turned and looked out the back through the tinted glass he could see the lights of the town shimmering on the sea like fluorescent pearls.

Half an hour later they passed through remote-controlled gates along a long cypress-lined driveway and stopped in front of the large, ornate white building which was certainly not his Excellency's but borrowed by him for the occasion.

'My dear Toto,' Dieter said, alighting from the car, hands held out in greeting to the white-robed figure standing on the steps waiting for him.

'What a joy to see you again!'

2 Walt

1

On flight to India – autumn 1992

Walt climbed off the supine body of the beautiful young woman, stretched his arms above his head and yawned as if his lack-lustre performance was of no interest to him. She looked up at him and smiled, almost shyly. What a way to make a living, poor bitch, he thought as he automatically smiled back. She moved into a kneeling position and bent down over his flaccid penis. She looked at him questioningly. He shook his head, he felt tired.

'That's a fine member you have there, Mr Fielding.' She fluttered her eyelashes and chuckled softly, gently stroking him, trying to interest him. He liked that. He liked his women to be feminine and flirty and he'd never approved of women, even whores, who talked dirty. He appreciated her formality, the respect it showed.

'Them Texans like to think that only they have the biggest and best, but I can tell you, ma'am, there's a lot grander come out of Oregon,' he said with an exaggerated accent but almost automatically as if the banter was expected of him.

He got off the bed and, naked, padded to the shower-room. At the door he turned.

'Get dressed and go into the main salon. See my male secretary – you'll find him there. He'll arrange a present for you and how you're to get back to Nice, when we land.'

She looked alarmed. 'I'm sorry, Mr Fielding.'

'Nothing to be sorry about, ma'am. Not your fault,' he said gruffly.

'Don't you want me to stay?' She slid her fine tanned body seductively on the white linen sheets – a pretty picture with her long, straight, shiny blonde hair. An appealing picture with her disappointed expression and one that would once have given him an immediate hard-on – not today, not recently, if he was honest.

'Nope,' he replied abruptly, and shut the door to the shower-room sharply.

He never let them stay, it could easily lead to complications he did not like or need. Women liked him and what he could do for them in the sack and out of it. From past experience he knew how easily they could fall in love – not with him but with the luxury he could give them. And he knew how difficult it could sometimes be to rid himself of them.

He had strict rules about these encounters. They were always set up by his male secretary – never by Beth, he would not have regarded that as proper, his belief that she did not realize they were professional women was real. Carlos, the secretary, was instructed only to supply women in their mid-twenties – he didn't want them inexperienced, nor did he want them on his conscience, which could become the case if they were too young. He didn't want them older than that for he had found such women had begun to become frightened of what their future might hold and he wanted none of their problems.

He preferred blondes. They had to be well covered, with generous tits, he did not like screwing skeletons. They were instructed never to talk about themselves unless he asked. Time had been when he was often curious but no longer; he did not care to know anything about them – their pasts, their hopes. Such talk was involvement and Walt was seriously against involvement on any level.

Most important of all, they had to have a valid certificate that they were HIV negative – you could not be too careful these days. Not that he needed to have bothered with other women. For years he had always maintained an obliging mistress. The present incumbent, Valerie, was sweet-tempered, acquiescent in the sack, she did not love him, nor did she expect his love in return. The size of her allowance and the luxury apartment in which he had set her up in New York ensured she was faithful.

Just recently he'd begun to wonder why he went to the expense of keeping her – old times' sake, he supposed, that and the fact that, despite what his competitors in business said, he was not a cruel man. He'd once visited her on a regular basis – less often recently. And now he was faced with the humiliation of not knowing if he was going to be able to perform or not. He had the doctor check him out and there was nothing wrong with him physically, just that he seemed to be losing the inclination.

Apart from keeping a mistress, he had always enjoyed a varied sex life with a constant supply of temporary partners like the poor girl he'd just sent packing. Now the same thing was beginning to happen with them.

Once he'd enjoyed sex, couldn't live without it. But now, he hated to admit it even to himself, there were times when it all seemed a bit of a chore and certainly the enjoyment was not as intense as it had once been. He still needed sex, yes, but it had become more of a physical relief – the joy had gone from it. Too often he was aware he resorted to the bed to shut out the loneliness which haunted him.

He soaped his body with his Atkinson lavender soap. He always used it because it reminded him of long ago and the only woman he had ever loved and respected. He did not respect any of the others, he didn't even like women. That was the crux of it, no love, no respect. That was until one woman entered his life – he respected her, he'd have liked to love her too but he'd never tried. Winter Sullivan. Now there was someone different. He turned the shower on full. Truth was he tried not to think about her too often, it made him feel uncomfortable with himself because he didn't understand what it was about her that made him feel like a tongue-tied youth in her company. The one woman he'd never tried to screw. That damned respect he had for her stopped him, he supposed. He knew why he did not respect most of them – Charity. He snorted with laughter as he thought of her. If anyone had been misnamed it was her. Walt was a large man in body and spirit and only one person in the world frightened him – Charity.

He flopped into the bed still wrapped in his towel. Charity – the biggest mistake in his life . . .

Oregon – 1956

The child cowered in the dark cellar. He put his hands over his ears to shut out the sounds that came through the board floor above him. He had brought his knees up, pressing them against his chest, his head was bowed. He urinated from fear, his soaked trousers clung coldly to his thighs – he did not even notice. The noise increased, he heard furniture overturned, glass shattering, the unmistakable sound of flesh striking flesh. He heard his mother scream, begging for pity.

'No!' He leaped to his feet, scrabbling in the dark, tripping over an unseen box, sprawling on the damp, cold floor. 'No, please. Stop it!' he screamed, banging his hands on the floor with frustration. 'Stop it,' he sobbed. He was full of hatred. Hatred for his father who might be killing his mother and hatred for himself that he was too young to defend her, too weak to strike back.

He lost track of the time as he lay in the dark, fearful for her, for himself. But finally there was silence, a dense, penetrating silence which, as he lifted his head to listen, was more ominous than the dreadful noise of before.

The door at the top of the cellar steps opened abruptly, bright light shafted into the gloom, the child shielded his eyes from its hurtful glare.

'Come here, you little shitface,' his father roared.

He began to get to his feet but not quickly enough for the man, who hurtled drunkenly down the rickety wooden stairs, grabbed the boy by the arm and pulled him behind him back up the stairs and into the brightly lit kitchen.

'Look at you, you snivelling rat.' His father pushed him with a disgusted gesture and held him at arm's length.

In the corner of the once immaculate room he saw his mother slumped on her face on the floor. The ingredients of the meal she had been cooking were strewn all around her. She lay still. She was dead, he thought.

'Mom! Speak to me!' he yelled, wrenched himself free of his father's hand and rushed to her side. 'Mom!' he cried, trying to turn her, trying to see if she was breathing.

'You've pissed yourself, you filthy bastard,' his father shouted, and stamped across the room towards him, unbuckling his belt as he came. It was his turn.

He rolled quickly across the floor to deflect any blows from his mother's already battered body and curled himself into a foetal ball. He covered his head with his arms, drawing his legs up to protect his belly, and biting his lip hard to stop himself from crying out, from screaming. He would not give his father the added pleasure of hearing him plead.

He was belted, punched, kicked, and as quickly as the attack began it ceased. His father, cursing his wife, his son, life in general and God too, blundered out of the room.

The boy lay quiet. Listening. He heard his father's heavy tread on the wooden porch; the slam of the door; the clattering of nailed boots on the yard; the roar of a too-quickly revved engine; the crash of gears; the coughing, spluttering of the badly maintained vehicle as the truck was driven down the steep track.

The boy unwound himself and crawled across to his mother who made no sound. Painfully he pulled himself up and limped across to the sink. He found a cloth and wrung it out in cold water. Ignoring his own injuries, he returned to the woman and gently lifted her head and began to bathe her swollen face.

A long, deep sigh escaped her bruised and split lips.

Then he cried, a soft, sibilant cry, an almost inaudible sound. He cried not for his pain, which was great, but because she whom he loved far more than he could ever find words to describe, was alive.

'My poor baby, what's he done to you?' She was struggling to sit up.

'Lie still, Mom. I'll get Mrs Martin,' he said, referring to their neighbour a half-mile away.

'No, Walt. No. I don't want anyone to see me like this . . . it would upset your father. Let me wash up a little, then I'll be fine.' She tried to smile but the pain in her lips made tears spurt into her eyes. She turned her head away from him; he knew it was so that he wouldn't see her distress, but he had.

He helped her to her feet, feeling her sway as he did so. He was tall for his age and she was small and he held her carefully so as not to hurt her more for she must be covered in bruises beneath the simple cotton frock she wore. His heart felt huge inside him, swollen with his great love for her – he could feel it, real, hard – but he couldn't quite bring himself to say it in words – he had to be strong for her, not a sissy.

'You'd best clean yourself up,' she said kindly from the kitchen sink.

'I didn't pee my pants, Mom. It's the cellar floor, it's damp,' he said defensively.

'Of course you didn't – a man like you.' And she turned

back to the small pump which brought water to her kitchen sink. Walt could have kissed her with gratitude, if kissing had been allowed.

He walked tall and straight out of the room and only when he was outside did he allow his body to sag from the pain and allow one leg, which his father had kicked particularly hard, to drag. He went into the lean-to shed which covered their well and where his father had contrived a shower of sorts. He stripped naked. He filled a bucket of ice-cold water from the well and, standing on a box, poured it into the small tank attached to the wall. He stood underneath and pulled a rope to one side which slid a metal sheet out of the tank and the water cascaded down on him in a heart-stopping rush. There wasn't soap, either the force of the water cleaned you or it didn't. He shook himself, grabbed his clothes and streaked across the yard, back into the house and up to his room beneath the eaves of the wooden house.

At least the cold water had numbed the pain, he thought, as he twisted first one way and then the other, trying to inspect himself, to count the bruises. There was no need to find a towel to dry himself, for the room in this hot spell was like an oven and he was soon able to dress himself again.

He loved this room. He felt the eaves of the house were his private place since there were only two rooms up there and the other was used as a store-room. He was aware that the other room should have had another child sleeping there but it was not to be. He'd had a sister once but she had died of polio and his father had torn down the pink curtains in angry grief and had bundled the bed with its pink covers and all the clothes in the chest of drawers on to a bonfire and, with tears pouring down his cheeks, had burnt the lot.

Alicia, she had been called, but Walt could not remember her for he had been only two when she died. All they had were a few black-and-white snapshots in an album which his mother hid from his father because the sight of them grieved him so.

If he thought about his dead sister it was with feelings of jealousy for it was apparent that his father had loved her. So he was capable of love; so, therefore, why did he hate Walt?

Then the room had been redecorated in pale yellow, a crib was bought and his mother spent a lot of time in the room folding baby linen and humming to herself. But one day she went to bed in the middle of the day, something she never did, and no baby ever came to the painted room.

Twice more the room was prepared for a small occupant and twice his mother lost the baby. He was older by then and understood more of what was happening. After the last one it was as if his mother had given up on the idea for soon the room became cluttered with a multitude of things she did not want any more but which Walt, at intervals, inspected in case there was something there he might want himself.

Walt loved the house and, if it had not been for his father, would have been happy there. It was two miles distant from the nearest small town, which suited Walt for when he started school his father had had to buy him a bicycle – the roads were unmade through the forest that surrounded them so the big yellow school bus which serviced the other hamlets could never get through for him. So he cycled a mile to his friend Gubbie's house and caught the bus there.

The house was built of wood – stone and bricks would have been wrong in this setting. From his bedroom window Walt could see the great redwoods and cedars which seemed to guard the house. If he walked into the forest and climbed one of them he could see the sea and often huge schools of whales as they travelled on their migrating routes. He could easily cycle to the deserted shores with dramatic rock formations which were one of his playgrounds. He fished in the rivers that drained down from the mountains. And it was no distance at all to a large lake, whose water was cobalt-blue – bluer even than the sky in high summer. Its sides were precipitous, its waters difficult to reach, which suited Walt for it meant few people ever ventured there.

The surrounding forest teemed with wildlife – bears the most feared – eagles soared in the crystal air and spotted owls lulled him to sleep at night. He was never lonely, not when he had the forest to play in.

They were not rich, but then neither were they dirt-poor. His father, Steve, was a woodsman, employed by the state to tend the forest. He was a giant of a man from Scandinavian stock – blond, blue-eyed, muscular, with legs like the trees he looked after. He was handsome and noisy. From him Walt inherited his build and his looks.

From his mother – short and dark, soft-spoken and musical – he seemed not to have inherited anything. She was English by birth, a Celt, and had arrived here almost by accident. Her father, Denzil, was a Cornish tin miner who, at the turn of the century, because of the shortage of jobs at home, had, like so many others, travelled to America in search of work. He had settled in California and worked successfully for the Bourn family in the Empire gold mine, one of the deepest mines in the world. He had not been a roustabout but had worked diligently and saved. When, at thirty, he felt it was time he married, he had returned to West Penwith and married his Rose, just as he had promised when they were both children.

Rose had become pregnant on their wedding night and he had returned to America alone; his wife and child would follow him when Rose felt strong enough to travel. So it was that Walt's mother, Rosamund, had been born English. She had no memories of St Just, where she had been born, for she was only two when Rose finally screwed up the courage to take a tearful leave of her parents and make the great journey across the ocean and continent.

Rosamund had only happy memories of her childhood in California until three catastrophes occurred all at the same time.

William Bourn, who owned the Empire mine, distraught with grief at the death of his only daughter Maud, and losing all interest in his affairs, closed the mine. On his last working day, Denzil fell and slipped a disc – his mining days were over. A week later his beloved Rose died in childbirth, and with her the son he had longed for.

With a damaged spine, and crazed with grief, Denzil wanted to get away from California and his memories. He loaded as many possessions as he could manage into an old car he had bought and, with an excited Rosamund beside him, had travelled north to Oregon.

They had both fallen in love with the beauty of this wild state. Crystal-clear rivers, teeming with fish, cascaded from the mountains. Deep lakes, protected by towering cliffs, glinted an improbable blue. Dense forests of red-woods and cedars, so tall they seemed to brush the heavens, were sanctuary to an abundant wildlife, and flowers bloomed with profligacy. They thought they had found paradise and decided to settle. Denzil, always careful with money, had adequate savings to buy a small house with enough land for vegetables to meet their needs and a pig and cow – sufficient for him to manage alone with his weak back.

Among his possessions he had a book of receipts which had belonged to his own grandmother who had been famed in West Penwith as a white witch. They were not receipts for cooking but for medicines and unguents. More to amuse himself than from any commercial motive, he had begun to experiment. What had started as a harmless hobby soon became an obsession. He would take Rosamund into the forest with him, searching for plants and mosses for his various medicines. As he worked he taught Rosamund. News of his activities soon travelled among the sturdy local people who had greater faith in nature's healing than anything a city-trained doctor could give them, and they were soon beating a path to his door. Inadvertently Denzil had found a new career, and one which suited his back far better.

Walt knew that while he showered and changed his mother would be making up a potion that would take away the bruises and soothe him and herself faster than anything the doctor could prescribe.

Even as he thought this he heard his mother slowly climb the steep stairs. She entered his room. He was lying on the bed waiting.

'I knew you'd come with something.' He smiled at her as he lifted his shirt and she gently bathed his bruises and welts. 'What is it?'

'An infusion of the bark of the hamamelis,' she told him.

'I hate him, Mom.'

'Shush . . .' She put a finger to her lips. 'Don't say such things.'

'I mean it. Why does he treat us so bad?'

'He doesn't mean it. It's only when he's drunk – he's always sorry after.'

'Then why does he drink?' he asked with a child's logic.

'Because he is sad. He still mourns for Alicia.'

'You are still sad for my sister, but you don't drink.'

'No, but then I'm not a man. I can cry – he feels he can't. His anger and frustration come in a different form. Try to understand him, try to forgive him,' she said quietly.

'I still hate him, Mom. I can't help it.'

'But he hates himself more, you know,' she replied, folding up the linen she had bathed him with, recorking the bottle. The skin had broken in two places on his back; gently, she rubbed a cream into the area, so tenderly that he did not even wince.

'What's that?' He did not ask because he was alarmed but because he was curious.

'A moss your grandfather swears by, in lanolin.'

'Ah,' he said, contentedly enjoying the touch of his mother's hand, the smell of lavender which she always wore.

'There, that should ease the pain, and no infection.' She stood up to go. He would have liked then to tell her how much he loved her, but he could never quite bring himself to say so.

She was right, he did feel easier. But then, he wondered, who was there to bathe her bruises? Maybe he should offer, but he'd never seen his mother without her clothes on, it wouldn't be proper.

She was right about his father too. He returned the following day, his eyes bloodshot, his face red and puffy and his hands trembling, and he begged Rosamund to forgive him. Walt watched as she put up her arms to him, smiling, and had to look away as they embraced and his father gave her a gaily wrapped box. She squealed with delight as she opened it to see a bottle of her favourite cologne, 'Old English Lavender'.

For Walt there was a new baseball glove. He accepted it, said thank you, even, but it didn't change anything. He still hated his father and wished he did not exist.

2

Oregon – 1958–1960

Walt was twelve when he was sent away to school. At the time he felt betrayed. There had been no warning it was to happen. His mother had had a long talk on the telephone with her father, which was not unusual, he called her every week. What was different about this call was that when she replaced the receiver she looked very serious, and asked him to go outside to play while she talked to her husband.

He had gone obediently enough but resentfully. He hated it when his mother excluded him like this; it made him feel jealous of his father, fuelled the loathing for him which was always close to the surface.

When, half an hour later, he was summoned, he saw his mother had been crying. He looked sharply at his father but his handsome face looked impassive – for once he was not the cause. Walt was.

'That was your grandfather, Walt,' she said unnecessarily.

'I know,' he replied sulkily, still smarting from his exclusion.

'He's made us a wonderful offer.' She paused and looked thoughtful as if searching for the right words. 'A truly great offer.' Walt stood patiently waiting for her to continue. 'He's offered to send you away to school – to get a fine education.' She said this in a rush as if afraid that unless she said it quickly she wouldn't say it at all.

'But I don't want to go,' he blurted out, and felt dangerously close to tears. He knew he would never recover from the shame if he cried in front of his father. 'I won't go!'

'You'll do as you're told, boy, make no mistake.' His father spoke.

'I know it's a shock, Walt. But when you think about it I'm sure you'll come round to the idea.'

'I can't leave you, Mom.' His bottom lip trembled.

'Oh, my poor darling,' she said, and at the loving tone of her voice, he couldn't stop a sob escaping.

'That alone is enough to show me you should go.

You're turning into a namby-pamby – a mommy's boy,'
his father goaded him.

'I'm not.' Walt sniffed and stood up straight. 'I can't go,
who'll look after her? Who'll be here when you attack her
again?'

'Why, you little . . .' Steve stepped forward, his arm
raised. Walt flinched.

'Steve, no . . . please . . . let me talk to him. Please leave
us alone.'

To Walt's surprise his father heeded her words and
made for the door, but as he got there he turned and
pointed a finger at his son. 'But you're going, boy. And
that's a promise.'

With his father out of the room Walt could finally let
go of his emotions and cry unashamedly. His mother
fussed about him, making soothing sounds which
reminded him of a pigeon.

'You're too clever to stay, Walt. Don't you see? The
school here has been fine up until now but you can't get
the education you should. Why, you can do anything you
want with that brain of yours. You could be President one
day, if you set your heart on it.'

He knew what she was saying was true. Already he ran
rings around the other pupils; already he knew the teacher
was at her wits' end to keep him amused. The junior high
school and then the high school here were adequate if all
one wanted from life was to become a woodsman, or a
fisherman, or drive a truck or a train. He'd heard of pupils
going on to a college education after they graduated from
the High but he knew they were few. He longed for a good
education and knew that it would be the only way to fulfil
his dream. It was a dream he had told only one person –
Gubbie Hornbeam, the local marshal's son. To him he had
confided his longing to be rich. It was a desire not for
himself, but so that he could one day run away with his
mother, set her up in a fine house with servants and silks

and satins and never see her sad and bruised again. And here was the chance and yet, if he went, he would leave her vulnerable and alone.

'I can't leave you with him, Mom. I'd be scared silly every day we were apart.'

'I'll be fine, son. You're not to worry about me. He's much better these days, you know he is.'

This was true – if one could count a monthly beating as being better than every week. Walt looked at his feet and felt trapped: if he went he was deserting her, if he didn't he'd be letting her down.

'Walt, my darling. Please do this – for me. I want to see you rich and famous – you won't be if you stay here.'

So he had gone, and the morning he had left he had wept as he said goodbye to his mother. He sat hunched and miserable in the truck as his father drove him to the station.

'You needn't wait for the train, Dad. I won't run away, I'll get on it,' he said, hating to have to stand and wait with the man, wishing his mother had come with them.

'No, I'll stay, it's the least I can do.' Steve's voice sounded strangely muffled. Walt looked up and to his astonishment saw his father wipe a tear away. 'Here, take this – it might come in handy.' And his father pressed a small wad of dollar bills into his hand. 'And write regular, won't you?' He turned his huge head to one side but not before Walt saw the tears running down his cheeks. He felt no need to cry in response.

When the train had finally pulled away, Walt counted the dollar bills – there were twenty! And his father had been upset and had cried. Now, that was truly odd.

He had not expected to be happy but he soon forgot how surprised he had been when he found he was. He enjoyed the masculine environment of a boys' school. He was a big, noisy boy and the rough and tumble suited him. He had led a very isolated life until now – his contact with other children had been limited to school since he lived so far out. It was only recently that his mother had allowed him to sleep over at Gubbie Hornbeam's. He had never minded the solitude since he had known nothing else, but now he was constantly surrounded by others he found he wallowed in companionship. Shy at first, he had quickly discovered that his size and ability on the football pitch, coupled with an ability to fart at will, soon made him popular.

His mother wrote every week as he did, at the beginning, but as the school began to absorb him, his letters became more sporadic. He realized one night when he lay in the dorm in the dark and, oddly for him, could not get to sleep, that he was happier than he had ever been, that not knowing what was going on at home was like a ton weight of responsibility lifted from him.

Such thoughts were also helped by his mother's letters, for she sounded happy in them. He might have thought she wrote that way because she had to, since Steve would no doubt read the letters too, but reassuringly there was always a postscript added which told him she was all right and his father was behaving. That puzzled him too and he wondered if in some mysterious way he had been the cause of his father's brutality – not that he could think of a sane reason why. Final proof, if proof was needed, that Steve was reformed was the excited news that they were having a real bathroom with shower installed and a smart fitted kitchen was planned for the following year. Odder and odder, thought Walt.

He still got beaten – he was too boisterous and naughty to escape the odd punishment by staff. His stoicism when enduring this added to his popularity with the other boys. They were not to know that, compared to what he had endured before, school beatings were nothing.

That first term he became depressed only once, when he realized he was too far away to get back home for Thanksgiving. But there was always Christmas.

It was to be one of the happiest Christmases of his childhood. His father was a changed man. He looked fitter, he laughed and sang, he was kind to Walt. And Walt would have had to be blind not to see how happy and radiant his mother looked. While, on the one hand, he was relieved to see her like this and to know she was no longer being beaten, he also felt a deep sense of loss. Before, it had been the two of them against Steve. They were linked because they were his victims. It was, he had thought, an unbreakable bond. But now he felt he was the outsider; he felt almost as if she had betrayed him again.

'What happened to Dad?' he asked his mother one day as he sat at the kitchen table and watched her making pastry, something he had always liked to do.

'What *do* you mean?'

'He's different. He's really happy.'

'He is, isn't he?' she said, looking up from the pastry board with an almost dreamy expression which he did not understand.

'He's not drinking,' Walt stated. 'Why? Why did he stop?'

Rosamund looked over her shoulder, checking they were alone.

'He had a funny turn . . . dizzy, you know.' She touched her head. 'He went to the doctor – he was really frightened – I'd never known him to go to the doc before. The doctor said if he didn't stop the hooch then he could go at any time. So he stopped.'

'Thank God for that!' Walt said with feeling. 'So he doesn't beat you up any more?'

'Beat me up! Oh, don't exaggerate, Walt. I admit your father occasionally hit me, but then, what man doesn't hit his wife? I probably asked for it.'

Walt's mouth dropped open with stunned amazement. He could not believe what he was hearing. 'But . . . but . . .' he spluttered. 'What about me? I'd call that beating.'

'Well, you were a naughty boy, sometimes.' His mother smiled fondly at him and Walt thought that either she'd gone soft in the head or this was the greatest betrayal of all.

Initially Walt regarded this change in his father with suspicion, sure it would not last. But at each break in his school year he returned to a happy home and a contented mother. The kitchen followed the shower-room, as promised. The only disappointment for them – not for Walt – was following a letter bursting with joy at the news she was pregnant; a second letter a couple of months later, tear-stained, told him his mother had lost another child. Not interested in babies and quite content to be the only one, he was not unduly put out by the news.

Now that the bad times were over, he saw how like his father he was. He looked like him and at nearly fourteen was so tall that it was obvious he would be a giant of a man like Steve. He shared his father's love of the outdoors and they began to go hunting and fishing together. There was a raucous side to his father with which he identified – a broad sense of humour and the noisiness his teachers so often complained of. And he saw now that his keen intelligence, lacking in his father, came from Rosamund and his grandfather. He was a mixture of the two after all.

There had been a time when the very idea that he was like Steve would have filled him with horror. Not any more. To his surprise he found he was proud to be known as this big, popular man's son.

3

Oregon 1961–1962

On his trips home Gubbie Hornbeam was still Walt's only friend. This was from choice, not necessity, for Walt was popular wherever he went. He was not handsome in the conventional sense but there was a ruggedness to his strong, square face which the girls seemed to find more attractive. His eyes were his best feature, large, honest-looking and clear grey which seemed to change with what he wore, so that some swore he had blue eyes, others green and yet others the truth, grey. He had a marked following of teenage girls, not that he felt the same interest in them, in fact he was more embarrassed by their intentions. The other boys might be a little jealous of his success with girls and his brains but they respected his prowess in the school football team – written about in the local paper – and were in awe of him because he could combine that with good grades. Most of all they were in awe of his size.

By fifteen he and Gubbie had dated girls occasionally but both had decided it was a waste of time and money – most importantly money. They both thought girls were rather silly and neither of them found it easy to make conversation with the creatures. And Walt compared all of them unfavourably with his mother, convinced he would never find any female to measure up to her.

Gubbie was his friend because over the years he had discovered Gubbie was beaten by his father too. And Gubbie, he learned, loved his mother as much as Walt loved his and didn't think it sissy to do so. Early on in their relationship, Gubbie had confessed about his father to Walt who, relieved to find he was not alone in the world, had poured out his heart to Gubbie. In some ways Gubbie was in a worse position than Walt. Walt had decided if things got bad again, this time he would tell, he would go to the authorities and ask for help. And who was that? The marshal. But who could Gubbie tell and who would believe him? Gubbie stayed at home for one reason only – his mother; although his father did not beat her, as far as Gubbie knew, he was always afraid that if he wasn't there to take it his father might start on his mother and sister. At fifteen, Gubbie was thin and asthmatic, pale-skinned and red-headed. He was still being beaten and could only envy Walt his good fortune that his torment appeared to be over.

So, while the other boys in the locality bragged and behaved like rutting stags, Gubbie and Walt preferred to spend their time walking for miles together, or closeted in each other's rooms talking. They talked of politics, of sport, of music. They talked about money and of how they were going to make it. And they spent hours planning the best way for Gubbie to murder his father.

The only disadvantage of having Gubbie as a friend was his sister, Charity. At thirteen she was too tall, too thin and too gauche. She had a long face with a strong jaw; her sharp nose reminded everyone of a bird's beak; the braces on her teeth did not help her; her mousy hair was lank and permanently greasy. She was too plain for even her doting mother to hope she might one day be beautiful. Her one good feature – her hazel eyes – could not compensate for everything else that was wrong about her. But she did not have that strong jaw for nothing: she was a determined and stubborn child.

Charity had loved Walt ever since she was eight and had long ago confided to her diary that she intended to marry him. His going away to school had broken her heart and she still wrote to him even though he never bothered to reply. She was beside herself with happiness when the school terms ended and he was back home again. She had no friends, she could not waste the time on them when she needed to be always hanging around watching for Walt to

visit her brother, or to follow Gubbie — at a safe distance
— when he went to Walt's. Sometimes she asked to go with
them when they went to the milk bar, the cinema, out in a
boat or on walks and bike rides.

'Buzz off, pest,' they would hiss at her in unison, and
Gubbie would apologize for his sister yet again.

'Doesn't bother me,' Walt would lie gamely; secretly he
would have liked to throttle her. The boys wasted many
hours working out elaborate plans to avoid her.

Every summer Charity had to do without Walt for
nearly two weeks. That was when Rosamund would load
the refrigerator with food, pack the small car Steve had
bought her and take Walt to visit her father Grandpa
Tregidga. This was a new routine; in the past Steve
would never have let her go, and she would not have
dared to leave him. They could not go as a family since,
unknown to Walt, his grandfather had banned Steve from
his house.

His grandpa lived a two-hour drive away across the
state. Like them, he lived in a wooden house close to a
forest. The cow and pig had long gone to be replaced by a
luxuriant garden of flowers and herbs. If Walt's mother's
knowledge of herbal remedies was good, her father's was
encyclopaedic. Over the years his fame as a healer had
spread, folk now came from miles around, even from the
towns these days, to seek his help.

He would assess his clients with a canny Cornish eye,
registering the car they drove up in, the clothes they wore,
their jewellery, and most especially the quality of their
shoes — 'You can always tell the state of a man's bank
balance and his character from the state of his shoes,' he
was fond of saying. Then he would judge what to charge
them. For those he decided were rich it was an expensive
consultation, for those he deemed poor there was no
charge at all — even so he was not above accepting the
odd gift of gratitude, eggs, chickens, bread, vegetables, a

crocheted antimacassar, home-made wine, moonshine. His thanks were effusive, whether payment was in money or in kind.

He lived comfortably in the sprawling house which had grown over the years. He could afford malt whisky, to which he was very partial, and his second-hand Cadillac which was his pride and joy; and he could also afford a housekeeper, Dolly, fifty, buxom and jolly. With his awakening interest in matters sexual Walt wondered if she did more for his grandfather than housework and cooking, but he was not sure for it was a matter which was never discussed. Certainly not with his mother, it wouldn't have been right. But most importantly for Walt, his grandfather could afford to pay for the excellent education he was getting.

Walt liked to listen to his mother and her father talking about their remedies, and often she would consult him about a friend who needed help and whose treatment was beyond her. He loved walking about the garden with them, listening and learning as his grandfather talked about his plants, their cultivation, their properties. It was on the visit in his sixteenth year that he produced a notebook and began to take notes as they talked.

'Looks as if we're going to be carrying this on into the next generation, Rosamund,' his grandfather laughed, nodding at Walt who was following them along a garden path frantically scribbling in his book.

'I do hope so, Dad.'

'I think this is a great thing,' Walt said, grinning at them, gesturing to encompass the garden. 'I reckon we could make a lot of money out of this.'

'I don't do so badly,' the old man said, leaning on his stick.

'Yes, Grandpa, but in a small way. If we could market all this . . . I think in the future cures and medicines like yours are going to be very popular. Why, I was only reading the other day that in California those hippies are all doing it.'

'And my make-up and face creams too. I think people will become tired of the new and want the old,' his mother added.

'And so they should. When I think what some women are putting on their faces – it's disgusting. Placentas, foetuses, beetles' blood.' Grandfather Tregidga shuddered. 'The old ways are the best ways.'

Walt wrote quickly. 'There's your marketing slogan – I can see it: *The old ways are the best ways.* Grandpa, you're a genius.'

'Hold on there, Walt. Don't get too carried away. Remember, this is a service for people who need help, not a way to make money,' his mother admonished.

'Sure, that too,' Walt added hurriedly.

It was later on during that visit that Dolly came to tell him his grandfather wanted to see him in his greenhouse. The large greenhouse was at the far end of the garden, south-facing and protected from the winds by a high hedge. It was where the plants were propagated and where his grandfather experimented with plants sent to him by fellow horticulturists all over the world – always under-cover and undeclared, for it was illegal.

'Walt, come in. Would you care for a malt with me?'

Proudly Walt accepted and his grandfather settled them both in a pair of old cane chairs among the flowerpots and under a particularly beautiful and luxuriant passion-flower plant.

'Walt, I've been thinking about what you said the other day about making real money. Were you serious?'

'Never more so.'

'Have you decided what you want to study at college?'

'Mom doesn't like it when I say it, Grandpa, but I want to be rich – you're important if you are, people notice you.' Walt leaned forward, his face eager as he talked.

'Does it matter if people notice you or not?'

'Yes, I think it does – you can get things done.'

'Such as?'

Walt thought rapidly . . . he could hardly tell his grandfather that one of the reasons he wanted wealth was to take his mother away from his father – his grandfather might not approve. Nor the other, that he longed to be famous and by being so know the famous – that sounded too fatuous. 'To help people,' he said vaguely instead. 'I think law is the surefire way to being wealthy. Have you ever met a poor lawyer?' He grinned.

His grandfather looked serious and Walt wondered if he had made a mistake in even mentioning it.

'Rosamund is a romantic – that's always been her problem. I'd agree with you – I don't know if being thought important is that important, but I'll tell you what is. No worry about the damn bills and a measure of comfort. When I think how hard I had to work in the mines just to keep body and soul together . . .' The old man shook his head despondently at the memory. 'I don't want such a life for you.'

Walt beamed his agreement and waited as his grandfather looked into his whisky tumbler, obviously thinking.

'How's your chemistry?' he finally asked.

'Not bad. I get straight As in everything,' Walt boasted. 'Thanks to your generosity,' he added quickly.

The old man waved his hand as if dismissing the thanks as of little importance. 'Then I think you should forget all about law. I think you should study chemistry proper. You're right – I've creams and potions which could make a fortune but the Federal Drug Administration would never let them through. They've got to be properly prepared, pure and correctly tested – all legit to satisfy that there FDA. Now, with my knowledge and you as a trained chemist we could do that. I'd never trust my secrets to anyone outside the family, that's for sure.'

'You want to be rich too, Grandpa?' Walt smiled.

'I want to go home, boy. I want to buy a nice cottage on the cliffs near St Just where I was born. I want to end my days there, you see. I've never really belonged here in this country – you have to be born here to be a true American, I've decided.'

'Couldn't you go now?'

'I could, but you're my only grandchild – I want to see you straight. And also . . .' he paused, as if making up his mind whether to continue. 'I want to make sure that my Rosamund's all right for the rest of her life. I want to give her real independence – just to be on the safe side.'

Walt looked closely at his grandfather, unsure if he was interpreting him correctly. He was so used to Steve's abuse of them being a secret, he did not expect even his grandfather to know about it.

'You knew, Grandpa, didn't you?'

'Knew what?' He looked at Walt shrewdly.

'That he used to beat her?'

'Yes, I knew,' he said sadly.

'Couldn't you have stopped him? Taken us away from it?' Walt asked, feeling angry with his grandfather for the first time ever.

'Walt, you must believe me, I suffered agonies knowing what was going on. I begged Rosamund to get help, go to the church, the police, your doctor. She wouldn't listen. Each time she believed him when he said it was the last time, that he was reformed, that he would not do it again. I used to sweat before I picked up the phone sometimes, scared at who might be on the other end and what they might be telling me.'

'But why didn't you do something, then?'

'And lose my daughter for ever? If there's one lesson you have to learn in life, Walt, when you have children of your own, it's that there's nothing you can do. You have to sit back and watch them wreck their lives, they won't listen to you. All you can do is to be there to pick up the pieces for them.'

'I'm sorry, Grandpa. It must have been bad for you too. Still, it's over now.'

'Is it?'

'Grandpa, you don't think . . .'

'Oh, it's fine now and I pray I'm wrong, but I've never heard of a leopard changing its spots, have you?'

4

Oregon – summer 1964

Since his grades were so good Walt had had no trouble changing the subjects he wanted to major in at college. When he graduated from high school it was as a straight A student in sciences, Valedictorian, and just short of his eighteenth birthday he had a place at the pharmacy school of the University of California where he would major in chemistry and minor in business studies. It would be expensive since he lived out of state and did not have the residency qualifications for any financial aid from the authorities, but his grandfather waved his doubts away. Walt was euphoric – he had a place at one of only three pharmacy schools in California and he knew he was going to the best even if it meant being even further from home.

He returned home having left school for the summer holiday, aware that it might be his last one there of any length. He had only been in the house five minutes when he sensed something was wrong. The old sadness was in his mother's eyes, she seemed distracted and less interested in his news than she normally was.

'Are you all right, Mom?' he asked, as he settled down to a wedge of her angel-food cake and a mug of coffee at the kitchen table.

'Me? Never felt better,' she replied gaily from her position at the stove where she was creating a special meal for supper with apple pie to follow, to welcome him home. But she did not turn round to look at him, he noticed.

'You sure?'

'What on earth makes you ask?' She was standing, a wooden spoon in her hand lifted from the pot she had been stirring, her whole body tense, her head held slightly back, her posture that of one waiting intently for an answer.

'You look sad again. Has Dad . . .'

'What a silly boy you are. I'm fine – never happier.' She laughed, but Walt did not like the laugh, it sounded false to him.

'You would tell me, you know, if . . .?' He spoke abruptly, in short bursts, unable actually to say what he wanted.

'I would – though it won't be happening, so it's a silly promise to make.' And she returned to attending to the chowder which was his favourite, as she knew, and which she was making with love. He pretended to concentrate on his coffee while he tried to control the anger which had begun to build up in him as the certainty grew that he was right. Why else would she not look at him?

'Where is Dad?' He tried to sound as nonchalant as possible.

'I doubt if he'll be back until late . . . He had to go and see someone about a new truck he's thinking of buying.'

'Didn't he know I was coming?'

'Yes, of course . . . but this truck came up – it's a Dodge – it's just what he's been looking for, right model, the mileage is good and he didn't want to lose it.' She spoke quickly as if she had rehearsed.

'I see.' He sat frowning, it did not matter for she still had her back turned to him.

'I think I'll go and see Gubbie.'

'Yes, why don't you, that'll be nice for you. And give his mother my regards.'

He was pretty sure she was crying, her voice sounded too controlled. He would have liked to go to her, put his arms about her, tell her it was all right now he was home. But he didn't. He respected her pride. He would not let her know how much he realized from her actions, and in any case they weren't a kissing family.

From the back porch he walked straight to the garage, which was detached from the house. Amongst the clutter he found his old bicycle. He pressed the tyres, which were flat. He pumped them up, hoping they had no punctures. He pumped hard, venting some of his anger.

He cycled furiously through the forest, not taking notice of anything as his athlete's legs pounded at the pedals. He did not stop at Gubbie's house but rode past and into town. He rode quickly along the main street, oblivious of the waves and greetings of people glad to see him back. He rode as if blinkered, seeing only his goal ahead of him – Hicky's, the local bar. He braked, kicking up a swirl of dust as he did so. He didn't go into the bar, he didn't need to, he could hear his father's loud laugh from the sidewalk. He felt bleakly angry. He turned his bicycle round and, more slowly this time, rode back to Gubbie's.

Mrs Hornbeam answered his knock and smiled warmly in greeting. Sometimes, when he saw Mrs Hornbeam always smiling and jolly, he puzzled about why, big as she was – not small like Rosamund – she allowed her husband to beat her son. Why didn't she stop it? Why didn't she tell? Why did she stay? He reckoned women were strange and he'd never understand them.

'Why, Walt, now here's a pleasant surprise. Home for the holidays? Come on in, I've just made some cookies . . .' The large, pleasant-faced woman opened the storm door wide for him and ushered him into her spotless kitchen.

'Is Gubbie in, Mrs Hornbeam?'

'He's just gone down the store for me, he'll be back soon, I expect, unless he meets up with that flighty Mary-Lou.' She laughed as she made him sit and, despite his protestations, insisted he eat her still warm cookies and poured him a glass of milk.

'Gubbie? And Mary-Lou?' said Walt, hardly believing what he was hearing.

'My, yes, they've been dating for a couple of months, didn't he write and tell you?'

'Nope – only that he'd got a car.'

'Oh, that car! I tell you, Walt, he loves that car. If he could take it to bed with him he would. Another cookie, Walt?'

'No, really, Mrs Hornbeam. I'm full. I've just had a slice of Mom's cake.'

'No one bakes an angel-food cake quite like your mom's, do they? But you're such a big boy, you'll be needing fattening up after that school food – have another cookie?'

He grinned defeat and took another, not wanting to hurt her feelings.

'And how is your mom? I haven't seen her in a long time.'

'You haven't?' he asked anxiously.

'Well, no. In fact I haven't seen much of her all year – no one has. Only at Easter when you were last home. Then when you left she went into herself, so to speak. Oh, I called her several times but she was always so busy . . . she said.' Mrs Hornbeam busied herself about her already clean kitchen and Walt wondered if he was being questioned or warned.

He sat wondering if he should confide in her. Tell her of his fears about his mother. Who better? She knew about domestic violence, she would understand more than most; maybe she'd have some ideas what to do, who he could ask for advice.

'Mrs Hornbeam . . .'

She turned to talk to him as the kitchen door opened and Charity walked in.

'Why, Walt. How nice . . .' she gushed.

'Hello, Charity,' he mumbled, and looked long and hard at the cookies on the plate instead of at her.

'You home for long?' She sat down opposite him at the plastic-topped table.

He bit into another cookie so as not to have to answer.

'There's a dance on tonight, you wanna come?'

'Sorry,' he said, his mouth full.

'It's the prom,' Mrs Hornbeam explained. 'Charity here hasn't got a date.'

'I'm sorry,' he said again, not sure what else to say.

'Would you take me?' Charity, always forthright, asked.

'I've no tux.'

'You're as big as my pa, you can borrow his, can't he, Mom?'

'I'm sorry.' He looked down at his large hands which seemed to grow in size as he did so, and wished he could think of something else to say.

'Of course you can – the marshal would be pleased to oblige.' Mrs Hornbeam was looking at him anxiously in the way of a mother with a daughter she feared might be unmarriageable.

'I'm sorry, Charity, I can't. My mom's planned a special evening for my homecoming. I couldn't let her down now, could I?' he said, slumping with relief at this inspired answer.

'I could call her, ask her if she minds,' Charity persisted.

'No, Charity. You can't do that. Walt's right, he must not disappoint his mother. You're a caring son, Walt.' Mrs Hornbeam bestowed an approving smile on him. 'Ah, is that the love of Gubbie's life I hear?' She laughed as they all heard the unmistakable rattle and spluttering of an old jalopy.

'Walt!'

'Gubbie!' Walt leaped to his feet as his friend came in, his arms full of brown bags stuffed with groceries. As soon as he had placed them on the table both boys raised their hands and slapped each other's palms and made a whooping sound in ritual greeting.

'Come and see . . .'

'What?' Walt grinned.

'My car, of course.'

Walt admired the 1950 rag-top Cadillac in powder-blue with white leather interior – it was not difficult, it was a pretty car. He admired the exterior, the interior, the trunk, the engine.

'She's beautiful,' he said genuinely.

'Goes like a rocket,' the proud owner explained. 'Care for a spin?'

'And why not, my dear fellow?' Walt slipped into a fair approximation of an upper-class East Coast accent as he leaped into the passenger seat without opening the door.

Gubbie started the engine and they roared down the street far too quickly.

'Doesn't it sound a bit rough?' Walt asked with concern at the alarming noises coming from the engine. He did not know much about cars since he did not own one, and wouldn't, he'd decided, until he could pay for it himself, but even he could hear the piston slap.

'When I've finished with her she'll be right as rain. That noise is why I got her dirt-cheap.'

He drove expertly through the traffic, not that there was ever much in this small town, and headed for the coast. Walt lay back against the soft leather, the wind ruffling his hair, the sun on his face, and enjoyed himself for a moment as he forgot about his mother.

'Got any music?'

'It's busted . . . but I'll fix it . . .' Gubbie grinned. 'You should get wheels, you know, does wonders for your love life.'

'So I hear. Mary-Lou, no less.' Walt referred to the pretty girl who was now his friend's date. Gubbie coloured.

'She seems to like me.'

'Sure it's not the car?' Walt laughed. Gubbie hit him playfully and the car slowed as they reached the end of a side road Gubbie had taken. They sat smoking, looking out to sea.

'I don't know when I've been so happy, Walt. She's all I ever wanted,' Gubbie said seriously. 'It's goddamn wonderful.'

Walt swung round in his seat. 'You mean . . . you've done *it*?' he asked, excited. Gubbie's colour deepened even further until his skin almost matched the red of his hair. 'Tell me, what's it like?'

'It's like nothing else. It's like you're climbing this mountain and you get to the top and it's all there and you're supreme, you can do anything. And then there's this explosion in your body and your head and you're tumbling down the other side and it's almost like falling into nothing, as if you're dying.'

'Every time?'

'Yep.'

'And Mary-Lou, was it difficult, you know?' He wasn't sure why he had asked such a question.

'No, no problem. Best thing is she loves doing it.'

Walt said nothing. He did not know Mary-Lou well but he'd heard enough about her to be concerned for his friend. Then he knew why he'd asked about how it had been for her. It confirmed his concern. He knew Gubbie was a virgin, it was pretty obvious she wasn't.

'We're getting married,' Gubbie said, almost offhand.

'No! When?'

'Oh, next month – you'll still be here?'

'Yes, but . . . I mean . . . isn't that a bit sudden? Your mom said nothing.'

'She doesn't know. No one does, only you. You see, the point is . . . well . . . Mary-Lou's . . . pregnant.' He coloured up again.

'By you?' The words were out before he could stop them.

'Who else, for Chrissake?' Gubbie rose up in his seat.

'Sorry – dumb thing to say.'

'You can say that again.' Gubbie subsided and offered Walt another cigarette.

'But what about college?'

'I'm not going.'

'But your plans to be a lawyer?'

'Oh, I think I just used to say that. I've got a job – Mackinnon's taken me on.'

'Doing what?'

'Trainee mechanic.'

'You? But that's madness, Gubbie. You'll hate it, you'll be bored to tears.'

'I love cars.'

'Yes, but not as a career. You'll be stuck here for ever. I thought we were going to go to New York together, take the world by storm.'

'Kids' stuff, Walt. Just dreams. I'll be happy here. I guess I never wanted to go anyway.'

'I don't believe that. I just don't.'

'It's true. Why would I want to go any other place when I've Mary-Lou and a baby on the way? Jeez, me a dad – crazy, isn't it?'

'Where will you live?'

'There's a new trailer park out by Mason's. There. We move in first of the month.'

'And your parents know nothing?'

'No.' Gubbie laughed nervously.

'What will your father say?'

'Oh, he won't give a damn – he'll be happy to get me out of the way, one responsibility less. Mom'll be upset, I expect, but I'll get round her and when she knows she's going to be a grandma . . . she loves babies, you know.'

'Oh, Gubbie. I do hope you're doing the right thing.'

'Never been surer of anything in my whole life, Walt.'

They sat in silence, Gubbie dreaming of his happy future in the trailer park and Walt full of concern for his friend. Gubbie was too intelligent for this – the job, Mary-Lou, hometown life for ever. He was lying, Walt was sure, putting a brave face on a disastrous situation. It wouldn't happen to him, he was sure, he'd make certain it didn't. He'd lived this long without sex, he could always masturbate – he'd rather do that than risk his whole future on a chick. Madness!

'Gubbie, tell me. Has my dad been drinking again?'

Gubbie's thin, sensitive face creased in a worried frown.

'Yes.'

'How long?'

'Most of this year.'

'He didn't when I was back at Easter.'

'No, he told my dad he'd laid off it, some promise to your mother.'

Walt suddenly realized his hands were clenched into tight balls.

'My mom's worried about yours. You know, in case.'

'I thought she was. I thought she was trying to tell me something.'

'Still, you're back now.'

'Yes, I'm back.' Walt looked far out to sea – but what would happen when he left for California? Could he even leave with his mother's safety on his conscience?

5

Walt's father was not drunk when he returned home in time for supper. He appeared genuinely pleased to see his son and punched him playfully in the best fatherly tradition. He was in an amusing mood. Walt wondered if he had over-reacted at his being in the bar and if Gubbie had got it all wrong and presumed his father's good humour was drink-induced.

'How was the Dodge?' Walt asked over the bottle of Coke he was sipping from.

'The what?' His father looked puzzled and glanced quickly at his wife who was looking trapped.

'Mom said you'd gone to look at one – thinking of trading in the old one,' Walt said affably. He'd decided it would not be right to say he knew he had been in the bar. However, he could not resist putting his father on the spot.

'No damn good – carburettor's spent.' His father recovered quickly, he noted.

That evening his father was in fine form, joking and teasing. Walt found he could hold his own now where story-telling and jokes were concerned. It seemed to him that he grew to be more like his father with every passing year. It was a thought which had begun to please him. But now? Those memories, stark, brutal memories, were filtering back into his mind. And although he thought he loved his father these days, deep inside him was a voice, perhaps the voice of the little boy he once had been, so full of hate, and that voice said, 'Oh, yeah?' in a cynical way.

'Another beer, son?' His father held out a bottle to him. It was a hot night and in the lamplight the bottle glistened invitingly, its sides frosted with cool moisture from the refrigerator that purred in the corner of his mother's smart, butter-yellow, Formica-covered kitchen.

'No, thanks, Dad. I've had my limit.' He shook his head and walked over to the fridge to get himself a Coke.

'Your limit? What's that? I've never heard of a *man* who had a *limit*.' His father spoke disdainfully.

'I like to keep fit, I want to get on the team,' Walt explained. It was half the truth, the other half was his fear that, if he was becoming so like his father, if he drank too much then the metamorphosis might be complete. He refused to get drunk and never had been, he was scared of what he would find out about himself if he ever was.

'I'm fit. I've drunk my share.' His father flexed his biceps. 'Feel that, solid. Bigger, harder, than yours, I bet.'

'Sure,' Walt agreed, not wishing to get into a competition.

'Let's see, then.'

'I thought you weren't supposed to drink.' Walt opened his Coke and drank straight from the bottle.

'Ah, bullshit! Crap doctors don't know what they're talking about. You know what, son? That damn doc who told me to lay off the hooch, know where he is?'

'No.'

Steve pointed downwards with his thumb. 'Six foot under.' He laughed, throwing back his head, showing the rotten teeth at the back for, big as he was, Walt knew his father was too terrified to go to the dentist. 'And he was younger than me. So, so much for his advice.' He snorted and grinned with satisfaction. 'You still haven't shown me.' He banged the table with his fist and the plates still there jumped and rattled. His mother hastily began to clear the remains of their meal. 'Ashamed, are you?' his father laughed again.

'Of what?' Walt knew very well what his father meant. He was in no hurry to comply for there was a note of challenge entering his father's voice. He saw his mother looked nervous. He sensed a change in the atmosphere in the room.

'Your biceps. Ashamed you're not as strong as your old man, aren't you?' His father opened another bottle of beer, using his hands to pry off the metal top, and looked Walt straight in the eye as he did so, flicking the top across the room where it rolled on the floor. Rosamund scampered after it. 'Get the bourbon, honey,' he ordered.

'Steve, should you?' she asked anxiously.

'Too goddamn right I should. I want a drink with my son here. *Reached his limit*, I've never heard such bullshit. Are you my son or not?' His voice boomed.

Walt leaned against the fridge watching his father, aware of his mother folding and refolding a tea-towel by the sink. He pushed himself away from the refrigerator.

'Yes, I'm your son,' he said, advancing from the shadows towards the brightly lit table.

'Then you'll drink with me?'

'If I must.'

Another bottle of beer was flicked open, a large slug of bourbon was poured. Walt picked up the glass and drained it clean, then he picked up the bottle and drank deeply of the beer. Already his father had recharged their glasses but this time to the brim.

'All right, then, let's see those muscles,' he ordered his son.

Slowly Walt removed his checked shirt and sat, his chest bare, the light from the lamp playing on the profusion of blond hair on his front. He flexed his right arm, drew his hand back, his bicep bulged.

'Not bad. But not quite good enough, wouldn't you say?' His father pumped up his own muscle. To Walt it looked smaller but he said nothing, what was the point? 'What do you say, Rosie?'

'You're both fine figures of men,' she said diplomatically. She had stopped folding the tea-towel and was now concentrating on drying a glass. Round and round she turned it in her hand, held it to the light and, dissatisfied with it, began the polishing process all over again.

'Drink up, son.' Steve indicated with the bottle to Walt's

untouched glass. Walt obediently drank from it, following with the beer chaser. No sooner was it done than his glass was refilled, and another bottle of beer appeared.

His father suggested they arm-wrestle. Space on the table was cleared. Elbows were placed, hands clenched, concentration began. Within seconds Walt realized he was the stronger by far. He allowed his father to lower his arm, pretending to struggle. His hand was slapped on to the table.

'Ah! See!' his father roared excitedly. 'You might be big but you ain't big enough yet.' And he went through the ritual of filling the glasses again.

Walt let him win four times and then something happened. He was bored with this game and he had drunk more than he usually allowed himself, even if it did not yet show. He wanted it over. He wanted to get to bed. This time he quickly forced his father's arm down without even sweating.

'You caught me off guard, I wasn't ready,' Steve blustered.

Walt shrugged his shoulders and proffered his arm again. Their huge hands clenched, he again knocked his father's arm back.

Steve shook his head as if trying to clear it.

'You cheated!' he ranted. From the corner of his eye Walt noticed his mother avert her eyes as if she did not want to see more. She shook her head at him as if telling him to stop.

'I did no such thing,' he said, annoyed.

'You can't beat me.'

'I just have, Dad.'

'Don't you badmouth me.' He glowered at his son. 'Have a drink?' he offered amicably, then 'Think you can beat me, do ya?' he said angrily again. Rosamund, her arms clasped about her as if shielding herself from the cold, left the room.

Steve insisted they had two glasses in quick succession. Then they went back to the wrestling. Walt won again, and then with his left hand, twice.

He stood up.

'That's it, Dad. I'm off to bed.'

'No, you ain't. Not till we've finished this.' The big man stood up, waving the depleted bottle of bourbon, trying to focus on his son, his eyes rolling in his head.

'Don't you think you've had enough, Dad?'

'You smart ass . . .' But Steve did not finish. It was as if this last remark of Walt's was the last straw — tears began to roll down his leathery brown cheeks. 'Think you can fucking well come home and make a fool of me,' he shouted, took a step forward, swung a right hook at Walt, missed, and collapsed in a heap on the kitchen floor, clutching his bottle between his hands like a baby's milk bottle.

Walt stepped across and looked down. He prodded his father's inert body with his toe. He did not move. He turned Steve's head to the side in case he was sick. He took a coat of his mother's off the door peg and covered him. Then he turned out the lights, wearily climbed the stairs to his bedroom, and flopped down on the bed fully dressed.

He was quickly in a deep sleep. He woke once in the night, startled by a piercing shriek. He sat up and listened, it did not recur. An animal in the forest, he told himself, as he flopped back on to the pillows and was quickly asleep again — a deep, alcohol-induced sleep.

He had overslept. He couldn't believe it when he awoke to find the sun high and himself still in his clothes. He ran quickly and quietly down the stairs in stockinged feet. He heard a quiet sobbing. Silently he pushed open the kitchen door. Rosamund was standing at the kitchen sink, leaning against it, her shoulders shaking.

'Mom?' he asked from the doorway.

'Oh, you've woken. I thought best to let you sleep. You'll be wanting breakfast.' She spoke without turning.

'Mom, look at me,' he said gently.

'Bacon? How d'you want your eggs?' He noticed that she seemed to be hanging on to the sink, as though, if she let go, she would collapse.

'Mom . . .' He crossed the kitchen and made her turn to face him. She had a livid bruise on one eye which promised to darken further. The other eye was bloodshot. Her mouth was swollen and although she had tied a scarf around her neck he could still see red weals on her flesh. 'Christ!'

'I'm all right, Walt.'

'You're not, Mom. Just look at you. Let me get the doctor.' His anger was deep inside him like a heavy stone in his gut. It filled him, made him feel he would suffocate. Made him want to vomit.

'No, don't do that, Walt, please. The shame.' She grabbed hold of his arm, her thin fingers cutting into his flesh.

'Jeez, Mom. Who'd know? Just you, me and the doctor. Please let me.'

'No, Walt. I forbid you.' She stood straight. 'It looks worse than it is.'

'Christ, if I hadn't had so much to drink I'd have heard you. I *did* hear you.' He banged his forehead impotently with his fist. 'I thought it was an animal in the forest.'

'It would have been an animal. I didn't cry out – I didn't want you to hear. I didn't want you to know.'

'Look at you. What am I supposed to think? That you walked into a door? For Chrissake, Mom. He's going to kill you.'

'Oh, no, he won't do that. It's not usually this bad . . . and never normally my face. Last night he was different . . .'

'*Usually*? He's been doing this again, hasn't he?' She

nodded. 'All this year?' She nodded silently again. 'Different, you say? Oh, my God. No!' He turned from her and went towards the door.

'Where are you going? Don't go, Walt. Don't say anything to him, please!'

'I need to be alone, Mom. I've got to think. I won't go looking for him. I couldn't. If I found him I'd kill him!'

6

Oregon – summer 1964

Walt must have run three miles from home and around the perimeter of the great lake before slithering down one of the steep cliffs and collapsing on to a small stretch of sand, gasping for breath. He sat up looking out across the water but he did not notice how calm the blue water was. Birds were wheeling about the rocks. He did not see the beauty of the sun playing with its reflection on the rippling water. He sat up, hunched, and he was sobbing. His large shoulders shuddered. He was no longer a giant of nearly eighteen with all the world before him. He was that small, terrified boy again and all the fear and the dark emotions, the feelings of impotence came flooding back.

This time he was more confused. As a child, he had hated his father. Now, as a man, he loved him – he had allowed this to happen. He never should have permitted such feelings. He should have listened to his grandfather's warning that no man ever changed that much.

This time it was worse, for this time it was his fault. He should never have allowed his father to drink so much, he'd have probably behaved. He had wanted to keep the pretence up until Walt was safely out of the way again before he began to torture the poor wretch he was married to.

But doubly worse, it was his fault because he, Walt, had goaded him, shamed him. What would it have cost him to lose the arm-wrestling contest? Nothing. What had it cost his father? His pride. Walt had allowed irritation and his own grotesque male pride to get in the way of reason, had allowed himself to ignore all the warnings. He was as much to blame as his father in one way.

He finally stood up to begin the long walk home. He started the steep climb up the cliff when he heard someone calling his name from the lake. He shaded his eyes against the water's glare. It was his father, in his fishing boat, hailing him. His first instinct was to walk on, ignore him. But he paused. His father began to row to the shore.

'Walt, I want to talk to you,' he shouted back.

He waded into the cold water and waited until the boat drew alongside. He clambered into the small craft and stepped over the dozen or so dead fish in the well of the boat. Walt sat on the seat opposite his father and looked at him with loathing. Without speaking, his father pulled on the oars and the boat slid away from the shore. There was silence – only the rhythmic sound of the oars slapping into the water, the rowlocks rattling at each stroke. Finally his father stopped rowing.

'Have you seen your mother?'

'Goddamn right I have.'

'Walt, I don't know what to say. Sorry isn't much use, is it?'

'None at all.'

'I don't know what got into me.'

'Drink?'

'Yes, probably. But . . .' And then to Walt's disgust his father began to cry.

'Oh, for Chrissakes, Dad.' He turned his head away so as not to see.

'We were so happy, boy. And then . . . I couldn't keep out of the bar . . . you know how it is, you want to see the boys and that's where they are. And I began to drink again – not much at first, you gotta believe me. But then when I do, I change. It's not me who does it, Walt. It's something inside me, something else, something so evil I sometimes feel like ending it all.'

'Look, I don't know what to say.' Walt felt embarrassed and disgusted by this great giant of a man who was crying like a baby at the other end of the boat.

'I love her, you know. I've never been with another woman – never. I worship her and yet . . .'

'*And yet* – exactly, Dad. It's got to stop, it can't go on like this.'

'I know, you're right. It will stop, I promise. I won't do it again.'

Walt turned his head away, how many times had his mother heard that refrain in the past? The boat began to rock, he looked up. His father was standing, moving towards him.

'Walt, you'll help me, won't you? Stay, don't go away, if you're there . . .' He touched his head, a puzzled expression on his face. 'Shit . . . the pain . . .' He swayed, took another step towards Walt and toppled into the lake.

Walt was on his feet, calling his father's name, peering over the side of the boat. There was no sign of him. Should he dive in, search for him? He slumped back into the boat. He felt a great wave of relief flood through him. It was over, his mother was safe . . .

'Walt . . . help . . . me . . .'

Walt swung round. His father had surfaced, his face a strange blue colour, his fingers clinging to the side of the boat as he desperately tried to haul himself back in. 'Help . . . me . . . son . . .' he spluttered.

Walt's emotions of relief swept away from him, panic and fear took their place. He scrabbled in the bottom of the boat for one of the oars.

'I can't, Dad, I can't help you no more,' he yelled,

swung the oar high above his head and brought it down, with all the force in his body, on to his father's head. Steve looked at him with an expression of total surprise and slipped almost gently under the rippling blue water.

The cobalt-blue water was still, the birds wheeled and displayed, a gentle breeze touched Walt's skin as he crouched, holding the oar, waiting for his father to rise again. But nothing disturbed the gentle rippling waves.

Walt had no time to think, no time for regrets, self-preservation came to the fore. He stood with legs apart, and moving his body from side to side rocked the boat back and forth, back and forth, higher into the air, deeper into the lake. Until, with one final lunge, the boat's gunwale hit the water. It flipped on to its side, as the water raced in, and sank as Walt struck out and swam strongly to the shore.

He pulled himself out of the water, lay for a moment on the wet sand, then dragged himself up and began the strenuous haul up the cliff face. At the top he began a slow jog along the ridge towards his home.

He had only run a mile when he saw a figure racing towards him. The figure drew level.

'Well, there, Walt. That was not a nice thing to do to your daddy.'

'I don't know what you mean.' He stopped jogging and looked down, his heart racing now and not from exertion.

'Yes, you do, Walt. You just killed your daddy back there. You knocked him on the head with an oar and then capsized the boat. I was up on the cliff. I saw it all.'

Walt slumped down on to the grass and rested his head on his knees. So much for all his dreams now, was his uppermost thought.

'Not that I blame you, Walt. I like your mom, a nice lady. I just wish someone would do the same to my daddy.'

'What are you going to do, Charity?'

'Well, that depends on you, Walt. But I've got a proposition to put to you.'

No one in the vicinity could ever remember seeing such grief as Rosamund suffered at the news that her husband was dead. The fact that her face was bruised did not go without comment and it was difficult to find anyone who believed her story of tripping on a rug and smashing her face into the side of the wardrobe. That apart, she had everyone's sympathy, and the community, in the way of small, isolated groups, turned in on itself and offered her all the help she could have wished for.

A search was immediately set up, led by Marshal Hornbeam, but the locals, knowing the treacherous currents in the lake, doubted if Steve's body would be washed up inside the week. 'Sinks mighty deep first, then them there gases push it back up,' the old-stagers counselled. However, they could helpfully pinpoint where, given the place it had sunk, the body would appear.

Everyone agreed how fortunate it was that Walt just happened to be home, and what a comfort he would be to his mother, and the doctor and the pastor both saw it as their duty to counsel the boy in this moment of great loss.

Rosamund's father arrived with Dolly who immediately took over all the domestic chores from Rosamund so that all she had to occupy her was her grief. They were still there when the body was recovered. It was not a pretty sight. The fish had dined enthusiastically and a sudden squall had smashed what remained against the jagged rocks of the cliffs which were such a feature of the lake.

Grandfather Tregidga accompanied Walt to identify the body and it was he who helped him through the trauma. His grandfather was also close by when Walt gave his evidence at the crowded inquest. It was a crowded hearing because there was not much excitement in these parts and Steve's sudden death came into that category.

The doctor gave his evidence that his predecessor had advised Steve against drinking, that he had very high blood pressure for which he had refused all medication. And, the doctor added, he had himself seen Steve drink recently on a couple of occasions. And from what Walt had told him it seemed in all probability that Steve had suffered a stroke.

If there had been any doubt at all of what the findings would be they were totally quashed by the evidence of young Charity Hornbeam who had been on the cliff, bird-watching, and had seen the whole thing happen. How Mr Fielding had stood up in the boat, had held his head, had stumbled and fallen into the water, capsizing the boat. And how Walt dived time and again in search of his father until, exhausted, he had had to swim to the shore to save himself.

Walt was the hero of the hour.

The funeral was over. Walt and his grandfather were walking in the forest – Walt avoided the lake now. The sun was setting and there was a chill in the air but both men were, without consultation, avoiding returning to the hysteria in the house; both felt Dolly was better able to deal with it.

'I hope this won't stop you going ahead with your plans, Walt.'

'It's difficult, what with Mom . . .'

The old man stopped walking. 'Look, Walt, it's difficult to believe this now but she will get over this. I've offered her to come and live with me and Dolly thinks she'll come round to the idea. It's best to get her away from all the memories here. And that goes for you too, boy.'

'Grandpa, there's something . . .' He looked long and hard into the distance at the great trunks of the trees he loved, as if they might tell him what to say. His grandfather stood waiting patiently.

'Yes, what?' he eventually asked, when the long silence made him wonder if Walt was going to continue.

'I killed him, Grandpa,' he said baldly, for what else could he say?

'Ah. I see.' His grandfather lowered himself down on to the forest floor and leaned his back against a great cedar. 'He'd started beating her again, hadn't he?'

'Yes. I saw her . . . her face . . . it was dreadful. All the hate came back and yet . . . I loved him . . . I felt sorry for him but still . . . I did it.'

'I don't see what else you could have done.'

'You what?' Walt turned round with surprise.

'Oh, your father *could* be caring, *could* be kind, *could* be, but for how long each time? He was an evil bastard as far as I'm concerned, and the world's a better place without him. Don't think on it, boy.'

His grandfather thought awhile. 'Look, Walt, you told me and you shouldn't have . . . it's always best never to tell anyone, these things get out. And whatever you do, never tell your mom.'

'Won't she be happier now without him?'

'Rosamund, never. She was besotted with him, loved him something crazy – you know that. No, she'll never forget him and she could never forgive you.'

'But you see, Grandpa, someone else does know . . .'

'Charity?'

'How did you know?'

'I thought her evidence was too pat. And I saw how she looked at you. I'm surprised no one else put two and two together either. But they didn't, thanks be.'

'Charity says she'll stick by her story provided . . .' He bent down and picked up a handful of soil and let it run through his fingers. 'Provided I marry her in two years' time, otherwise she's going to tell her father.'

'You ain't got much choice, then, boy, you'd best marry her. You can always make love in the dark.' The old man chuckled.

On flight to India – autumn 1992

Walt did not know how long he had lain thinking about the past, or why. It never did any good thinking about what was done and could never be undone. Look what his action had cost him. Charity for a wife. Still, twenty-nine years later, she held it over him.

'Do this or I go to the police.'

'Do that or I tell.'

'I want, or I'm telling my daddy.'

Such had been the refrain of his married life.

He began to dress. He liked remembering his grandfather, though. He often did, and rightly so, for everything he was, and had become, was because of him and his wisdom in the old ways.

He began to knot his tie. He wondered what his grandfather would have thought of the notion of an Elixir of Life?

'*Go for it, boy,*' he would probably have said. '*You never know what's out there and what it can do for mankind.*'

He'd strayed a long way from the philosophy of his grandfather, that was sure. Had he ever truly aspired to it? He'd always wanted money and the freedom it gave one; helping mankind had come a long way behind. Some freedom he'd acquired! Trapped by Charity but also by the enormous demands that his huge business made upon his time as well as his energy. He patted the knot straight. So what was the difference in what he normally did and this possible goose-chase of Guthrie's? After all, how many cures for baldness had he chased around the world? How

many aphrodisiacs had he wasted money on? And what
was a million and a half dollars? Chicken feed, and it
might be fun — it might help him forget for a short while
the nagging worry that his body might be ageing too fast
for comfort. He'd cable old Guthrie, let him know he was
on.

3 Jamie

1

Cannes – autumn 1992

Despite the amount of wine and brandy he had consumed
the previous night, Jamie awoke feeling very bouncy. A
wallet full of money poking out of his back trouser pocket
was the prime reason for his good spirits. After Dieter and
Walt had gone to bed he and Guthrie had found a
backgammon game in progress. Jamie liked this particular
game and as dawn broke had wiped the floor with the
other players; Guthrie, too, having laid some substantial
side bets on Jamie and the outcome, had sauntered off
home equally content.

Jamie had one great attribute for someone whose
income, these days, came primarily from gambling – a
wide-eyed, innocent expression which frequently fooled
those who did not know him into thinking he was stupid,
and ripe for the picking – a judgement they invariably
regretted when he had cleaned them out.

He lay on his back, his hands behind his head, studying
the ceiling. Old Guthrie was a strange cove, he thought.
All that money he possessed and yet last night he'd been
as excited as Jamie, if not more so, at his winnings. In
Guthrie's terms they had to be peanuts. And this treasure
hunt? Now, there was an odd thing. The *Elixir of Life*.
Cobblers! No such thing could possibly exist except in the
mind of a con-man and Guthrie wasn't one of those, he
had no need to be.

Jamie felt for his packet of cigarettes on the bedside table, not bothering to turn his head but fumbling for them with his fingers. He placed one in his mouth and lit it with his gold Dunhill lighter, the only one of his possessions which had never seen the inside of a pawnshop. He inhaled deeply, enjoying the feeling of dizziness which the first cigarette of the day gave him. So what was Guthrie's game?

Money? Unlikely, Guthrie oozed with the stuff.

To make fools of them? Equally unlikely, Guthrie was not a malicious type.

A game? Jamie pondered this idea. More likely, he decided. But then, was it? Neither Dieter nor Walt was the type of character Jamie would have liked to play games with – not if they lost. Not if they felt they'd been taken for a ride. Hell, Walt was famous the world over for his ruthlessness in business. And there was a chilling side to Dieter; Jamie thought he could turn quite nasty if goaded too far. Both of them loved the money they had amassed with a quite vulgar passion – if cheated of any of it, their reaction might make life a trifle uncomfortable for the perpetrator.

Maybe he was just trying to work out a plot for a novel – he wouldn't put that past Guthrie. He'd once asked him where he got his ideas for his books from.

'Frigging life, my old darling,' Guthrie had replied.

That was probably it. Jamie stubbed out his cigarette and wondered, as he often did, if perhaps he shouldn't give it up – it was reaching the point where so few of his friends smoked it was becoming more of a hassle than it was worth.

Still . . . he puffed up a pillow and propped himself up so that he could see the rain lashing the beach out of the window. Still . . . whatever Guthrie's motives, they were all academic to Jamie. He didn't have a hope in hell of raising the ante, let alone taking part in the treasure hunt.

A shame, really, he'd have enjoyed it, something different to do.

Even if Guthrie bought his Romney he had other things to do with that money. Pay off the Elysium Club for a start – it was a bit of a bore, when in London, not to be able to go to his favourite watering-hole where all his friends hung out. He supposed not going there had its advantages, though; he was not led astray quite so often. He knew his rich friends thought him a fool to gamble but he liked it, loved the excitement. He didn't feel so empty when he played the tables.

Empty, that was a good way to describe how he felt most of the time. When he was happy he didn't have the same need – nothing like.

Guthrie's study, immaculate at five a.m., had by nine deteriorated into chaos, but organized chaos, since Guthrie knew where to lay his hands on whatever he wanted. The desk had disappeared beneath a snow-storm of notes and memos. The coffee table, occasional tables and the cushions on the long sofa were covered in reference books with yellow 'post-its' protruding out of their pages as markers. The fine parquet floor was now carpeted in maps, both modern and ancient, and the large globe of the world was still spinning from when Guthrie had last checked the position of somewhere on it.

The books' subjects encompassed many places – Egypt, Greece, Rome, Scotland, North and South America – and many subjects – architecture, poetry, biography, history. Guthrie spun about amongst the clutter with a light step and a gleeful expression as he checked one source book with another and counter-checked against a map, then consulted airline and train time-tables and added more copious notes to the piles on the table. He appeared to be in his element. He hummed a rather pretty melody to himself and then, as if suddenly aware of it, opened a drawer, took out some manuscript paper and immediately notated the tune before he forgot it.

'Such a good day's work already,' he said to himself as he began to replace the books he no longer needed in the bookcases and piled the others up for possible future reference.

Seated at his desk, he sifted through the notes. Some he tore up and threw into his wastepaper basket, others he filed away alphabetically in bright-coloured folders. The remainder he moved about the desk-top as if shuffling cards in a complicated game of patience.

He was left with ten possible clues for his treasure hunt. Clues which would take them all over the world. He frowned. It was too many, his victims were busy men, they would baulk at the time the hunt was taking and might drop out too soon and spoil the fun. He re-read his clues, smiling at his own cleverness. Reluctantly, he threw out the rather clever reference to the minotaur and the even smarter one to Rasputin. Pity . . . he pursed his lips as he tore them up. Ideally he needed five or six. That decision made, he stacked his notes neatly, placed them in a paper folder, opened the safe in the wall behind him and locked the clues inside.

'Victims . . .' He said the word out loud, but softly, as if lingering over the sound of it. An odd word to choose for Walt and Dieter, or was it?

He thought back on the clues and realized that as a European Dieter would have a much greater advantage over Walt the American who no doubt knew no European history of note and might even have a strange idea of the geography of the rest of the world. He needed someone to help out and someone who could keep an eye on them. Dieter in particular, he felt, was quite capable of cheating to win. Guthrie had always doubted Dieter's claim to his title. His recent research into the man had shown this to be justified and had also let him in on the secret of Dieter's precarious start in life in the ruins of Berlin. Guthrie had known others who had managed to raise themselves from the gutter. They clung to their wealth with tenacity, and no matter how large their fortune was, deep inside them lurked that self-same hunger to acquire more by any means, legal or otherwise.

He needed a referee, someone who'd make sure things didn't get out of hand. Despite what he'd learnt he liked Walt and did not wish him harmed.

Jamie! He sat bolt upright at the thought. Of course, Jamie was the very person. He pulled the phone across the desk and called the Carlton.

'Jamie, my dear chap. How's the old *tête*?' Guthrie said as soon as the call was connected.

'Magnificent, Guthrie, couldn't be better. Good night, wasn't it?'

'Hope this isn't too early to call you . . . I get up with the birds.'

'We went to bed with them last night.'

'Oh, a couple of hours' sleep does me . . .'

'I've been up ages,' Jamie lied, and wondered why he invariably did so when caught in bed past nine in the morning.

'Are you flying back today?' Guthrie asked.

'Maybe . . .' Jamie answered. He had long ago learnt that, when asked a direct question which might, just might, turn into an invitation, it was best to prevaricate a little.

'Ah, well, if you've not made any definite plans I wondered if you'd care to join me for a few days' stay. There are one or two things I'd like to mull over with you, sweetness.'

'Be a pleasure, old sport.'

'Shall I send a car?'

'How kind.'

No doubt about it, thought Jamie as he swung his legs

over the side of the bed and stood up, the day was shaping up better than he'd dared hope. Maybe he could make it even better.

He dialled for an outside line and then punched in his home number. He listened, feeling his euphoria sliding away from him as the telephone rang unanswered in his London flat.

Where was she?

He'd let it ring another six times.

. . . four, five, six. Well, maybe another five . . . There was no reply. Frustrated, he slammed the receiver back on its cradle as if it was the telephone's fault that his wife was not at home.

He fingered his lighter. 'Jamie, my undying love, Mica,' he read, as he often read the engraving in tiny letters on the side. He'd believed her, he still tried to cling to that belief but it was becoming harder.

Beautiful, spoilt, haughty Mica, the love of his life and his tragedy – for what was worse than unrequited love? He should know . . . Wasn't she the second woman in his life he had worshipped and who had not cared for him . . .?

England – 1955

'Why the hell you don't send the brat away to boarding-school, I don't know. You know he gets in your way.'

'Oh, hardly, Hugo. Don't be silly – Esmond's a baby still and you're scarcely aware that Jamie's around.'

'I'm always aware, Poppy. It makes me uncomfortable knowing Jamie's in the flat . . .'

'What a sensitive old Hugie baby you are.' Poppy laughed, a wonderful bubbling laugh, almost musical.

'It just doesn't seem right. What about their father? Can't he spend more time with them?'

'He loathes small children – he won't have them, not if I'm not around.'

'Then why did he have them?'

'Heir and a spare . . . you know. Don't be so silly, Hugie. He had to have them, it was expected.'

'And you?'

'God, this conversation is getting so boring.' Poppy sighed deeply.

'And you?' Hugo persisted.

'I knew what was expected of me too. And I've done it – two sons, not a blemish to my name. But now I'm free.'

'I don't understand you, Poppy. You don't talk like a mother at all. And you usually don't behave like one.'

'Oh, for God's sake, Hugo. Do stop moralizing. Are you complaining about the way my life is arranged? No? Then shut up . . . and stop sounding so wretchedly middle-class – it's so boring . . .'

Jamie, from his position in the sitting-room next door, listening through the door which had inadvertently been left open a crack, could just imagine his mother's face. She'd be pouting now, her full lips, bright with lipstick, pushed forward like they were when she bent to kiss him. He quietly picked up his toy car which he had been silently pushing back and forth across the thick pile carpet. He left the room as quietly as he had come into it.

He wasn't listening at doors on purpose, he could not help but overhear. If his mother had been alone he'd have crept in and watched her dressing, or putting on her make-up – he liked that best of all. He did it less often these days for ever since his brother had been born nine months ago, he saw less of her. Either she was out or she had friends in. Of them all – and there seemed to be a lot – he liked Hugo the best, he gave him toys, pennies, talked to him, not like some who chose to ignore him. But this was something new, this talk of schools and being in the way. That wasn't like Hugo, he'd sounded quite grumpy.

Jamie sidled into the nursery. Nanny Bottrell was sitting at the table, her back to him, shuffling her cards.

'Nanny . . .'

'Good heavens, Jamie – can't you make more noise? You'll scare a body to death one of these days, creeping round like a mouse.'

'Sorry.' He grinned in apology. 'What are you doing?'

'Clock patience. Want to learn?'

'Please.' He climbed on to the chair and watched as Nanny Bottrell's soft fingers shuffled the cards and then laid them out in a circle, explaining the game simply so that he could understand. 'See. It's them grumpy old kings you've got to watch out for, otherwise it's easy.'

'To win?'

'No, to play. It rarely comes out . . .'

'Bet you can do it.'

'Couldn't take your money, Jamie – it would be like taking sweeties from a baby.'

'Go on . . .'

'Very well, then. You try. Bet you a penny you don't do it.'

'Done.' Jamie slapped the palm of her plump hand with his small one. Concentrating hard, he began to turn the cards up, placing them in a circle with mounting excitement as no kings appeared. And then the tumbling disappointment when, in two turns, two kings appeared.

'Ah, see, I warned you,' Nanny Bottrell called. 'Bet the other two old buggers turn up now.'

'Next turn?' Jamie asked.

'You're on. Halfpenny.'

'Done.'

His heart was thumping as he turned the card. A two!

'Aha!' he squealed with an excitement which was short-lived as his next card revealed the loathed king of spades, followed shortly by the king of hearts.

'Still, I lost a halfpenny so you only owe me a half in

return,' said Nanny Bottrell, taking a small notebook and pen from the drawer in the nursery table. 'There.' She scribbled down a figure and then, using her fingers, did some adding up. 'You now owe me one and fourpence. You mustn't let it go much higher, Jamie. You must always pay on the nose, you know.'

'I do know, Nanny. But I so longed for that new signal for my train set.'

Nanny Bottrell smiled benignly at her charge. She'd been with him since his birth. Then, at barely sixteen, she had been the nursery maid until Nanny Smithers had had a horrendous row with Lady Grantley which had ended in Nanny resigning her post, beating dismissal by a whisker, and Lou Bottrell's elevation to the lofty role of Nanny. Much to her annoyance, no new nursery maid had ever been appointed. It hadn't mattered too much until young Esmond had been born nine months ago when her workload had increased dramatically. She was now in the throes of delicate negotiations with her boss, whom she loathed and despised, to get extra help.

Lou Bottrell was plump, with a pleasing curved figure, and Jamie was not alone in liking her large, soft breasts. She had a perfect creamy complexion, pretty blue eyes and a sweet, constantly smiling mouth which always made Jamie think of ripe cherries.

She had been born in the village of Grantley; her father, grandfather and great-grandfather had been gamekeepers to Jamie's family and the different generations had lived in the same cottage set in a small wood on the Grantley estate. Lou was happiest when at Grantley. She neither liked nor approved of London.

'Nasty, smelly place,' she had told her mother. She felt the other nannies she met on her walks in the park were stuck-up and looked down their noses at her and her soft West Country accent. But most of all she neither liked nor approved of her mistress.

To Lou, Poppy Grantley was a rich, spoilt, bad-tempered bitch, who didn't deserve her good fortune in life and certainly not the gentle, kind, handsome husband she had managed to ensnare. Nor did Lou find Poppy's razor-thin elegance beautiful. She could never understand how any man would want to kiss her gaunt face larded with all that sticky make-up.

She could have got another job easily enough, even one abroad if she'd wanted to travel, which she didn't. She stayed because she loved Jamie and Grantley.

If asked whom he loved the most, Jamie, without a moment's hesitation, would have said Nanny Bottrell. To him she was warmth and security and love.

If asked whom he adored, he would without a pause have said his mother. To him she was the most beautiful woman in the world. He admired her elegance, longed, in the darkness of night, for her smell. Wished fervently that she would love him. She never did, never said, but was always the distant, cool shining star who each evening came and kissed him goodnight. But the kiss was never accompanied by a hug and was of such a light touch and of such quick duration that there were times he wondered if she'd kissed him at all.

Jamie, like his nanny, preferred Grantley to London. He disliked the formality of life in the city. He loathed going to the parties of other *suitable* children. He dreaded the school at which he was a day pupil and where he never seemed to catch up with the other children. But most of all he hated the clothes his mother made him wear when they were in town – velvet suits, frilled shirts and buckled shoes.

At Grantley he could run wild. It did not matter if his clothes had holes in them, or his knees were dirty. He had a dog and a pony there, and the village children to play with in the acres of parkland.

There was only one thing wrong at Grantley and that

was the fact that his father preferred it too. Jamie was afraid of him and did not understand his cool remoteness, being too young to understand it was a form of shyness in an emotionally inhibited man.

'Nanny . . .' he said later that evening as he studiedly dipped his bread-and-butter soldiers into his soft-boiled egg.

'Yes, my pet?'

'Mummy and her friend Hugo were talking about me going to boarding-school.'

'They what?' Nanny dropped the mending she was doing on to her lap.

'Hugo said I got in Mummy's way, that it would be better.' His eyes filled with tears, he'd hate it, he knew he would.

'We'll see about that, my precious, don't you fret.' And Nanny Bottrell's pretty mouth set in a most determined way.

2

England – 1955

'Honestly, I was really shocked. It just doesn't seem right to me – a little scrap like that. Why, just the thought of him away at school gives me the shivers!' And Lou shivered dramatically to emphasize her point. She levered herself up on her elbow the better to see her companion who was snuggled down under the large feather eiderdown.

'He's got to go away to school one day.'

'Yes, but not yet. Not when he's only six.'

'It *is* young.'

'Too young. And what for? So that Madam's social life isn't too inconvenienced.'

'Now, come on, Lou, that's not nice. You know you promised . . .'

'I know what I promised, Harry, but this has made me hopping mad.'

'I was sent away to school when I was eight.'

'You never were?' Lou sat bolt upright and as she looked down at the man beside her, her blue eyes filled with tears. 'That's blooming awful.'

'It's normal. Prep school at eight, then public school at thirteen.'

'And your mum, didn't it break her heart?' Lou wiped a tear away with the back of her hand.

'My mother?' The man snorted with laughter. 'I shouldn't think she noticed I had gone.'

'I can't bear it, my poor love . . .' And she scooped him into her strong arms and held him tight against her ample breasts.

'That's nice,' he said, nuzzling into her softness. 'Most satisfactory. Almost worth all the misery of my schooldays.'

'And you want the same for *your* son. I don't understand you lot at all.'

'Who does?' he laughed again. 'But I promise, I'll talk to my wife about the boy,' said Jamie's father.

Jamie's father visited his mother in the flat in London, in itself a rare occurrence. Jamie was summoned but had to wait while Nanny powdered her nose and sprayed some perfume behind her ears. He watched, fascinated – he'd never seen her do that before and wondered why she did.

'Got to smell nice for His Lordship, now, haven't I?' she said, as if reading his thoughts, and she giggled and fluttered about the nursery as if she was nervous too.

Jamie waited awkwardly in the doorway, looking shyly

at the father who was almost a stranger to him. He felt uncomfortable and hot in one of the hated velvet suits his mother insisted he wore which, with his knee-length white socks and patent leather silver-buckled shoes, made the other boys in the park poke fun at him.

His mother stood on one side of the fireplace, beautiful and elegant in beige slubbed silk. He thought her the loveliest creature in the world and longed to race across the room and fling himself into her arms and to have her kiss him and tell him she loved him. He didn't, for she would not have been amused and would no doubt tell him off for messing her hair and clothes. His father stood on the other side, tall, slim, elegant and with a distant look in his cold blue eyes.

'Come here, Jamie,' his mother ordered. 'Come and say good afternoon to your father.'

Reluctantly Jamie let go of the comforting hand of his nanny who waited beside him.

'That will be all, Nanny,' Poppy said, rather haughtily, Jamie thought.

'Good afternoon,' he said, holding out his small hand in welcome.

'James.' His father nodded his head in a form of a bow and shook hands formally. 'And don't you remember? You call me sir.'

'Have you been listening at doors, Jamie?' Poppy looked at him sternly.

'I'm sorry?'

'You heard. I know you snoop, Jamie, so don't lie to me. Have you?' Poppy lit a cigarette and Jamie noticed that her hands were shaking slightly.

'No.' He stood firmly on his sturdy legs, his feet apart as if balancing himself.

'Don't lie . . .' His mother's voice rose in a screech.

'I'm not.' He stuck his hands in his pockets and felt afraid.

'A gentleman doesn't put his hands in his pockets, James,' his father admonished.

'I'm sorry.' He withdrew them quickly. 'I don't know what Mummy is talking about . . . sir,' he remembered to add. He looked up and up at his father's face, hoping to see some sympathy there, but there was none that he could discern.

'Your mother is under the impression that you have been listening at doors, like a spy, to her *private* conversations and, not unreasonably, she doesn't like it.'

'But I haven't . . . sir,' the child said stolidly. He was confused, he really had no idea what they were talking about.

'Are you sure?'

'I sometimes hear Mummy talking to other people if I'm in one room and she's in another but I've never listened at her door. *Never*,' he added vehemently for good measure while trying to control himself, for he was close to tears. He loved his mother, he did not want her to be cross with him about anything.

'Then how else could the little bitch have found out unless *she's* listening at doors?' Poppy said angrily, sucking deeply on her cigarette.

'That will be all, James.' His father held his hand out again. Solemnly Jamie shook it, turned on his heel and quickly left the room, closing the door quietly behind him as he had been taught to do.

Nanny was waiting in the hall, pink-cheeked, her eyes flashing with anger.

'Who's calling the kettle black!' she huffed and, putting her finger to her lips, bent down and put her ear to the door.

'No, Nanny, you mustn't. It's wrong.' He began to pull at her sleeve. 'Please, they'll be cross with us,' he begged.

'Shush . . .'

From inside the drawing-room the voices which had

been conversational began to rise in volume and, like a train picking up speed, the words began to tumble out faster. Soon he heard his father bellowing and his mother screeching.

'Don't, Nanny . . .' Jamie tugged at her again. Nanny Lou looked up at him, her face had changed, it was still pink but she was smiling and now her eyes were sparkling with excitement.

'That's my Harry!' she said suddenly and standing up straight took Jamie's hand. 'Come on, young whippersnapper, let's go and toast some crumpets.'

'Yes, please.'

'And get you out of them stupid togs.'

'Oh, yes, please!'

Crumpets and tea in front of the nursery fire with his nanny was one of the joys of Jamie's life, he always felt safe when with her. It was a shame it was an electric fire, as Nanny always said when holding the crumpet pronged on to a toasting-fork which had a Cornish pixie in brass at the top of its handle. A pixie with a wicked, distorted face who Jamie had long ago convinced himself was the devil in disguise.

'We've got five crumpets, Jamie. Now, how can we share them out?'

'I'll have two and you can have three.'

'You'll make me fat.' She laughed.

'No, you're not fat, you're nice.' He grinned.

'You calling me plump, then?' she said quickly.

'No, just perfect. All soft like a cushion.'

'Well, I never, the things you say.' She slid one toasted crumpet on to the plate and pierced another. 'Tell you what. If the next vehicle into the square is a taxi I get the extra crumpet. If it's a car it's yours.'

'What if it's a van or a lorry?' he queried.

'Don't count. First taxi or car.'

'You're on.' They shook hands on the bet and they both raced to the window and waited expectantly. A green Harrods van drove round the corner. Then the road sweeper with his cart. They both held their breath in expectation.

'Damn, you win,' said Nanny as a car turned slowly into the square. They returned to their task. Nanny Lou was just buttering the crumpets when the maid tapped on the door.

'Her Ladyship wants to see you, Nanny.'

'What, this minute? Drat.' She finished coating the last crumpet with butter. 'You get on with yours, Jamie, while they're still hot. Megan, you pour him his tea, lots of milk, no sugar.'

'No sugar? Ugh.' Megan shuddered.

'It's bad for his teeth,' said Nanny Lou as she bustled out, her starched apron making a creaking noise like the sound the sails of an old boat would have made, Jamie imagined.

'Do you really like your tea with no sugar?'

'No, I hate it, but last week Nanny decided.'

'Well, if you don't tell her I won't.'

Jamie promised on his life he would not breathe a word and settled down to eating his crumpets while reading a large picture-book on dinosaurs, his most recent passion.

Ten minutes later the door burst open and Lou, her face red with anger and tears cascading down her cheeks, rushed into the room.

'Good grief, Nanny! What's happened?' Megan jumped to her feet with concern.

'I've got the bloody sack, that's what! Me! After all I've done for this family.'

'Oh, she never has. On what grounds?'

'She accused me of snooping; listening at doors, cheeky cow.'

'What will you do?'

'What else can I do? *She* won't give me a reference, or at least not one that'll count. I'll have to go back home.'

'To Grantley? But won't that be difficult . . . you know, when the family's there and everything? I mean, what if you should bump into Her Nibs?'

'Sod her if I do.' Lou flounced.

Jamie sat on the hearth-rug, not sure what was going on, not knowing what 'the sack' meant, but concerned to see the tears which were still pouring down Lou's cheeks.

'Here you are, Nanny. You have the third crumpet, I don't want it.'

He was horrified by the effect his offer had. Until now the tears had tumbled almost silently, only punctuated by the occasional sniff. But suddenly Nanny Lou let out a great wail.

'Oh no! I can't stand it. Oh, Jamie, how can I live without you?' And she was on the carpet beside him, hugging him which he liked, but too tightly which he didn't.

That night when he went to bed he cried himself to sleep. And when after a few hours he awoke he began to cry again. By the light of his night-light he crossed the room and climbed into bed beside Nanny.

'Jamie,' she sighed. 'I love you.'

'I love you too, Nanny. I'll die without you.' He sobbed into her soft, sweet-smelling breasts.

3

England – 1955–1963

Nothing was ever explained to Jamie. This was not new, it would never have crossed his parents' minds to ask him what he wanted to do, where he wanted to be, who he preferred to be with. It was their decision, everything about him and his life was theirs. In the hierarchy of the Grantley household Jamie was as yet a lowly creature. In the pecking order of importance, he was above the maids and footmen but below the housekeeper, cook and butler and far beneath the horses.

During the sad week after his nanny had left, when he was sure he would never stop crying, there had been many rows between his parents. He knew because he could not help hearing them, everyone in the large flat heard, others in the apartment block and even those walking the streets three floors below must have been aware. They were colossal arguments – his father roaring, his mother screaming, ornaments broken.

He was greatly relieved when his father woke him one morning and told him to get washed and dressed quickly, that he was accompanying him to Grantley.

Megan packed for him and was to travel with him. She had been looking after him since Lou had left. In a way Jamie felt sorry for her for she was a pleasant, kind girl, but she wasn't his nanny and so he had behaved nastily towards her, sulking, not doing as she ordered, even going so far as to poke his tongue out at her. His guilt had not been eased by the patient way the young girl accepted his tantrums.

'Poor scrap, he's missing Lou, I can't be cross with him . . .' He had overheard her saying this to the cleaning woman who came to help each morning. Her understanding made him feel ashamed, so he had apologized.

'Right little gent, aren't you?' She had smiled as she accepted his apology and went on with his packing.

'Is Esmond coming too?' he asked, from idle curiosity only since his baby brother was of no interest to him whatsoever. Quite the contrary, he had resented his arrival and having to share Lou with him.

'No, he's staying with your mum, here in London.'

Jamie frowned. 'My mother isn't coming with us?' He felt he was going to cry and he didn't want to – it was sissy and he'd cried too much recently.

'No.' Megan looked away quickly and found it necessary to delve into the back of a cupboard she had already cleared out.

'It's all very odd,' he said sagely.

'I expect it is, dear. But divorce is odd.'

'What's divorce?'

'You'd best ask your father, dear,' said Megan, slapping a hand across her mouth like Jamie did when he wanted to stop any more words coming out.

'He won't tell me. He doesn't talk to me much. I don't think I'd like to ask him anything.' He watched and noted Megan was piling all his velvet suits on to a bed and not into the case. 'Why are you doing that?'

'His Lordship's orders – I'm to leave out all your pretty velvet suits – such a shame.'

'Good! I hate them,' he said with satisfaction – perhaps things were looking up. At first he had been appalled at the thought of leaving his mother – she might be distant but he loved her and she'd always been there. But, given a choice between no velvet suits or his mother, he would quickly choose the former. 'Will Lou be there?'

'I haven't heard she's got a new position. I expect so, her parents live there, don't they?'

'That's wonderful . . .' And he began to help with the packing, anything to hurry the process.

Now, here he was, six months later at Grantley, convinced he had died and gone to heaven. The flat in London, the velvet suits and the boring walks in the park were all distant memories. Esmond had disappeared from his mind completely, and only sometimes, when it was bedtime and his mother would have come to tuck him in and give him a kiss before wafting off in her pretty dresses to a party or dinner, did he miss her.

There was no time otherwise to pine for anything or anybody. He had a governess, Miss Timpson, a good teacher who he wished was a bit younger and not so sour-looking. He had a pony, Tom, to groom and ride. He had several thousand acres of parkland, woods and farmland to explore. He had Jim, the stable boy, as a wise and shrewd companion. But best of all, across the park, in the gamekeeper's cottage, he had Lou.

If anything, Lou was even prettier here than she had been in London, he had decided. Her skin, so smooth and creamy that he loved to touch it, glowed with health. The blue eyes sparkled, her blonde curly hair shone. In London she had always been bright and cheerful – here she never seemed to stop laughing.

In the afternoons when he had no lessons he would search her out. They would often go for a long walk, returning to scones and jam with clotted cream and seed cake which he adored, all baked by Mrs Bottrell, Lou's fat and pleasant mother. If it was too cold or raining they would play cards or spillikins and chat in front of the fire which Mrs Bottrell always lit in the parlour especially for him, he was told.

'Why don't you come and live in the big house with us?' he asked one day as he prepared to return across the park.

'What does a big lump like you need a nanny for?' Lou ruffled his hair. 'You've got Miss Timpson now. Your nursery days are over.'

'But she doesn't look after my clothes and things. You

could do that, Lou,' he countered, using her name – he had stopped calling her Nanny.

'You've got Megan . . . there wouldn't be enough for the two of us to do. 'Sides, I like this life of leisure.' She laughed at that, a long, deep-throated chuckle, and then looked at him sideways as if weighing up whether to tell him something. 'I'm moving soon.'

'Oh, no, Lou, where?' He looked dejected and, when she laughed again, hurt.

'Over to Simon's Copse, to the cottage there.'

He banged his chest in relief. 'Wow, you frightened me then, I thought you were going away.'

'Me? Leave Grantley? I did that once, not again. No, your father's said I can stay in that pretty cottage over there for as long as I like.' At this, Mrs Bottrell made a strange snorting noise and walked out of the small parlour and slammed the door shut.

'Doesn't your mother want you to go?'

'No.'

'I expect she'll miss you.'

'Yes, something like that.' And Lou dissolved into gales of laughter which only made Jamie think how odd grown-ups sometimes were, even his beloved Lou.

In his first year away from his mother he never saw her. He now knew what divorce meant and, from conversations he managed to overhear before those speaking were aware of his presence, he had learnt that his parents' divorce was an acrimonious one. He gathered his mother was being difficult and his father intransigent.

Matters were finally settled and Jamie was driven to London by a silent father to visit his mother. She no longer lived in the flat – his father stayed there when in town – but instead had a pretty and elegant house in a square behind Knightsbridge.

After her initial welcome when she had covered him in kisses, fussed over him, taken him to Harrods' toy department and allowed him to buy whatever he wanted, to the cinema and out to tea, she seemed to lose interest in him. He had a room at the top of the house which she was at pains to tell him was his, where he spent most of his time. Next door was his brother's nursery but he was only two and no company for a young man of nearly eight.

Jamie quickly realized he did not like it here. Despite the excess of toys he was bored and longed to be back in the country. He was tired, too, for he found it difficult to sleep, there always seemed to be a party going on two floors below him. He was glad that there were only three of these visits and then he did not go any more.

At first he had been afraid of living so close to his father. He need not have bothered. He rarely saw the man. He had his suite of rooms and Jamie had his. They occasionally met on the stairs and would greet each other formally, and a few times Jamie had been summoned to the drawing-room when his father had guests. He would be introduced and for half an hour he would hand round nuts and olives while the guests drank, but he didn't mind that, not when there were other people around. It was being alone with his father that frightened him, for the few times this had happened he did not know what to say to him. The long silences embarrassed him and, he was quickly aware, embarrassed his father too.

His love for his mother faded, his love for Lou grew stronger. And there came to be another love in his life – Grantley, the house.

This happened slowly and it was some time before he was aware of it, for he had not known it was possible to love a thing. He realized it one evening in summer when he walked back from tea with Lou in her pretty cottage. The evening sun was still warm and the old house was bathed in it; the stones were no longer cold and grey but warm and golden. He had paused on the small rise and looked down at the great sprawling mansion, nestled at the foot of steep hills which in spring were crimson with flowering rhododendrons. The long casement windows in their stone mullions seemed to wink at him with a myriad flashes of colours. Thin wisps of smoke spiralled from the chimneys as the fires were lit against the evening chill. The large oak front door stood open in welcome. The young boy stared at the scene as if for the first time and felt a great swell of pride in his chest as if it would burst. He knew he never wanted to live anywhere else in the world, that this was home and wherever he went it would always be with him. He suddenly knew how important something he had only been vaguely aware of before was – that one day all this would be his. And he knew in that moment that he loved it and always would.

He was torn away from this child's paradise when he was eight. Since he so rarely spoke to his father there had been no warning. He had been summoned one morning to his father's study and told they were to go to London the following day when his uniform for his prep school would be purchased, and that the following week he was to be put on the train for Lincolnshire and the unknown.

He had raced to Lou to say goodbye. He did not cry, even though he wanted to, he just knew that boys of eight didn't.

Lou did. Her tears made his cheeks damp, his hair wet. And her crying made it harder for him not to.

'Still, little scrap, I saved you two years of purgatory.'

'You did?'

'Yes, didn't you realize? It was me who persuaded your father not to let your mother pack you off at six. Shan't be able to do the same for that little blighter Esmond.'

'I'll never forget you did that, Lou.'

''Twas nothing. Bet you don't write.'

'Bet you I do.'

'How much?'
'Half a crown says I'll write you every week.'
'Done!'
They shook hands on it.

The next five years were years of fear, loneliness and, at times, sheer terror. The school in Lincolnshire was isolated, as if the headmaster was afraid to let the world too close. Of the old school, he was sadistic and allowed the older boys to learn sadism in their turn.

Jamie worked hard, kept his head down, and longed for the holidays and the safety of Grantley.

When he was thirteen Jamie was sent to public school – one of the oldest and most prestigious establishments in the country. As he entered through the ancient gate-house and into the main quad and saw the crowds of sauntering, confident older pupils he felt physically sick. He knew enough not to walk on the turf in the middle which was reserved for the 'Men', as the school prefects were called. He was not the only boy who stood and watched in awe as these lordly creatures strutted across the grass; they wore gaily coloured waistcoats under their jackets and glistening white spats on their feet – both commensurate with their seniority.

He watched them with fear, too, for he knew that he would be used to fetch and carry for one of them, like a personal servant. The stories he'd heard at his prep school of the savagery endured by fags at the hands of the older pupils were enough to make the stoutest heart quail. Which one would he be assigned to? he wondered.

'Fag!' a voice yelled from the landing above.

'That's for you, Grantley.' Another of the junior boys prodded him as they sat, miserable and nervous, in the fags' room awaiting their summons. 'Remember you've got one minute to get there or you get a beating.'

Jamie hurled himself up the stairs and along the landing where the sixth-form studies were positioned. He'd been told that all the doors would be shut bar the one where for the rest of the year he would be expected to act as unpaid servant, mistress if required, and where no doubt at some point he'd be punished.

He knocked three times as he'd been told to do. 'Permission to enter, sir,' he said, as also instructed.

'Come in, poor soul. Why so wan? "*. . . We fear, to be we know not what, we know not where.*" Shut your mouth, there's a poppet, you look like a guppy – or worse. So, it can't be bad, can it? We know where we are but we know not what – what for, what how, what ho! Guthrie Everyman, your lord and master for the next two sets – take a pew.'

'Thank you, sir.' Jamie sat on a high-backed armchair upholstered in fading dark green damask and had consciously to shut his mouth which had opened again. Guthrie Everyman was huge, over six feet tall and with the muscular build of a rugby international, which always made him laugh since he'd refused ever to set foot on a pitch. 'Tiddlywinks is more my style,' he'd say. He seemed, to the small boy, to fill the room with his presence – a room which was decorated with silk wall-hangings, a fine Burne-Jones painting over the mantelshelf, incense burning in a censer in the window which was framed with elaborately swathed curtains which exactly matched the damask on the chairs. It was the room of an aesthete, not a schoolboy. Not one item of school paraphernalia marred its style; no bats, photos, or colours.

'Tea? Earl Grey? Splendid.' Guthrie sat on a matching chair opposite and began to pour the tea into bone-china cups from a fine Georgian silver teapot. On the table was a plate of paper-thin cucumber sandwiches and one of chocolate éclairs. 'From now onwards, my dear fellow, this will be your task – I wanted you to see how I like things done.'

'Yes, sir.'

'Exactly *comme ça*, you understand? I can't abide vulgar sandwiches. They give me indigestion.'

'Yes, sir.'

'And call me Guthrie in here, when no one else is about.'

'Yes, Guthrie,' said Jamie, his heart sinking, sure as he was that this implied a degree of intimacy he'd rather do without. He had thought that if he was propositioned sexually he would resist, but Guthrie was so big and strong he doubted if he'd be able.

'So how was prep school?'

Jamie shrugged his shoulders.

'Ghastly, no doubt? Don't worry, things get better now.

> *"Strange is it not? That of the myriads who*
> *Before us passed the door of darkness through,*
> *Not one returns to tell us of the road,*
> *Which to discover we must travel too."'*

Guthrie declaimed while sugaring tea and stirring it. 'Quite apt, if not as the poet intended – the old *Rubaiyat*, heard of the *Rubaiyat*? No? You must. It comes in jolly handy at all manner of times. But you're in luck, Guthrie will explain. My dear boy, what you must realize is that the whole point of prep school is to ensure you can cope with virtually anything in life. No doubt you've learnt to endure being beaten and not by a sob to allow anyone to know the pain you'd suffered. Am I not right? You've had staff and older boys sniffing about for a touch of sexual abuse and you haven't told a soul. You've been lonely in a crowd and yet no one knew what you felt. You've learnt to appreciate the value of friendship but you've realized

quickly that it's unwise to trust such friends when authority beckons, they'll always rat on you. Now you can
concentrate in a din, stomach awful food and not throw
up. I bet you find it impossible to be late for anything. And
you've learnt to smoke. See? Right on all counts. That
school has done you a favour; if another war comes you
could survive it – that or prison.' Guthrie guffawed. 'My
dear Grantley, you've been prepared for life – or that's the
theory.'

Jamie was quick to learn that he could not have been
more fortunate in ending up with Guthrie. His friends
were shouted at, beaten, abused, but Jamie never. Guthrie
treated him with courtesy, was concerned when he had a
cold, tipped him handsomely and never once touched him
in a manner that could be suggestive. He enjoyed teaching
Jamie about art, music, literature. Jamie adored him and
when Guthrie left to go to Cambridge, Jamie locked
himself in a lavatory and cried buckets – school was never
quite the same again.

4

England – 1965

The summer of Jamie's sixteenth birthday was a momen-
tous one.

He had returned from school for the long summer
holiday feeling quite pleased with himself – he'd done
reasonably well in his end-of-term exams. He hadn't
expected to do very well, he knew he never would, he
wasn't bright enough. But by plodding along, doing
enough work – not too much – he felt he could always
stay about the middle in any results. He knew his father,
who had never shone academically either, would be
content.

A letter was waiting for him on the hall-table. He recognized the handwriting immediately – large and confident swirling loops in blackest ink on the thick white envelope. He ran up the main stairs to his bedroom before opening it. It contained an invitation from his mother to join her and some friends in a villa she was renting for the summer at Rimini. The letter had come too late for him. He might have been curious to go, he hardly ever saw her these days. He felt he was probably old enough now to hold his own with her sophisticated friends. He was also getting to an age when the thought of the parties his mother was addicted to was an attractive one.

Not now, though. Not since the end-of-term celebrations at school when, after an absence of six years from his life, she had arrived unexpectedly and disgraced him in front of his friends. She looked as beautiful as ever and was perfectly groomed, the sort of mother any boy should have been proud of. At first she had been gracious and charmed his young friends witless so that all of them found it easier to ignore her companion. The long-haired man she clung to was young enough to be her son, which for Jamie was bad enough, but even worse was the ludicrous powder-blue velvet suit he wore. And Jamie wanted to die when he saw the large lump of gold, a diamond flashing in the centre, he wore on his little finger.

As he saw his friends laughing and bantering with her, all wallowing in the high voltage of her charm, Jamie began to relax a little, however. Maybe her friend did not matter too much, maybe they envied him having such a 'with-it' mother. She was talking a little too loudly and laughing too often, and it had crossed his mind that she might be drunk. But then, what the hell? He joined in the chat.

It was the boys falling silent which made him swing round to see why. His father stood behind him, tall, dignified and cold, and Jamie found himself wishing he was not always so punctual.

'Good morning, Poppy, James.'

'Father.'

'My darling Harry . . . how handsome you look and so well. Wouldn't you say my beloved ex-husband looks divine, Wayne, my love?' She slipped her hand through her companion's arm. 'Wayne Devereaux, my ex – Lord Grantley. Wayne does my hair for me, don't you, darling?'

Jamie was aware of a snigger and then another rising from his group of friends.

'Mr Devereaux.' Harry Grantley held his hand out politely.

'M'Lord.' Wayne laughed inanely.

'And how are you, Harry?'

Jamie did not know why, but his body tensed. He felt certain that behind the innocuous question there was a chill, a feeling of danger.

'Extremely well, thank you, Poppy.'

'How's your whore, Harry?' Poppy laughed shrilly. 'Still bovine?' she virtually shouted.

'Would you like to see the picnic I've brought, James?' his father asked.

'Very much, sir,' Jamie replied, turned his back on his mother, and together with his father walked away from the group.

He looked at the letter in his hand . . . he'd had to cut her, his own mother, it was the only decent thing he could do in the circumstances. And now this invitation, what was it for? An apology? He did not even know if he should answer the letter, he'd have to ask his father's advice.

He touched the black sprawling writing with a finger, outlining her signature. Momentarily he felt sad. A long-lost but lingering memory rose to the surface – it was the smell of her. He sniffed the page, that was why, the notepaper was impregnated with her perfume. It was the same scent he had loved to smell as a small child when he lay in his bed and she would come to him all dressed up and pretty, her jewels sparkling, and kiss him goodnight. He'd read that Winston Churchill had said of his mother that she had shone for him like the evening star and he had loved her, but at a distance. He knew what the man had meant, that's how he had felt when small.

'Come in,' he said in answer to a tap on the door, stuffing the letter into its envelope.

'I was wondering if you would prefer dinner in the breakfast-room, Master James?' the butler asked. 'The nights are chilly for the large dining-room.'

'My father's not dining at home?'

'Why no, sir. His Lordship left for the United States yesterday,' Fenton said, not quick enough to disguise his surprise that James did not know.

'Of course, stupid of me.' James slapped his forehead with the palm of his hand. 'I'd forgotten he'd planned to go.' He lied to cover his own hurt. His father had not even thought to tell him. 'It's hardly worth it just for me. Perhaps cook could make me some sandwiches and soup in a thermos? I'm going out, I'll eat later.'

'As you wish, Master James.' Fenton bowed slightly and reversed out of the doorway, an ability which James had always admired.

He changed quickly into jeans and a tee-shirt, slung a sweater over his shoulders and was soon walking quickly across the park. As a small child he'd always turned to Lou when he was upset. Nothing had changed. He might be sixteen next birthday, six feet tall and a promising rugby player, but still, when hurt as now, he wanted Lou.

'My, you grow bigger and taller every time I see you. Come in.' Lou held the door of her cottage wide open for him.

'Don't I get a kiss?' he asked, standing in her narrow hallway.

'Hardly seems proper, a great lolloping lad like you.'
She smiled up at him, a small, almost secret smile, he
thought, and as she stroked his bare arm he suddenly felt
a quick flash of excitement and had to look away from her
for fear she might have seen it reflected in his eyes.

Awkwardly he turned and walked into her sitting-room.
It was a pretty room with chintz curtains, matching sofa
and a friendly clutter.

'If I'd known you were coming I'd have tidied up,' she
said, moving a pile of magazines and books from the sofa
and patting it for him to sit down.

'It wouldn't be the same if it was all neat.'

'S'pose it wouldn't. I always say there's more important
things in life than housework.'

'I like to think of you here, like this . . . your books and
the television, and the light from that pink lamp shining
on you,' he said gruffly, unsure as to why he was telling
her that.

'Do you now? That's nice.' She smiled at him again, the
strange smile she had first given him. It wasn't like her
usual grin – this was a quiet, dreamy smile which seemed
to hold a message for him. 'Fancy some cider? Or I've a
bottle of wine?'

'Wine, please, if it's no bother,' he said quickly, for he
loathed the local brew.

'For you, Jamie, what's the bother? I'll just go and get
it.' He had not sat down but was still standing. He felt
huge in this small room, as if he was filling it with his
presence, as if he had strayed into female territory where
everything was the wrong size for him, a man.

Lou returned with the wine and two glasses.

'Will you do the honours? I'm no good with these
corkscrews.' She giggled and handed him the bottle. In a
strange way he felt immensely proud to be opening the
bottle for her.

'Well, isn't this cosy, then?' She sat on the sofa and swung her legs up under her.

'You should always wear blue, it suits you,' he heard himself say.

'And there I was thinking you never noticed what your old nanny wore.'

'Don't be silly, of course I do.' He sat down on the edge of the sofa beside her.

'You seem a bit down, what's the problem?'

'Nothing, really. I must be getting sensitive in my old age.' He grinned.

'Come on, out with it, this is Lou you're talking to.'

So he told her of his mother's invitation and why he couldn't go. And how hurt he felt by his father.

'I reminded him, I said, "Now you are sure you've told Jamie you're off and he's going to have to amuse himself all summer?". Your father's got a head like a sieve – he'll forget his own name one of these days.' She topped up their glasses.

'Nice wine,' he said.

'It was a present.'

'From an admirer?' He grinned again.

'Cheeky thing . . .' She pushed him playfully.

'Do you see much of my father?'

'On and off.'

'Wish I did,' he said sorrowfully.

'Look, Jamie, if there's one thing I've learnt in life it's that you never get all you want and if you did you might regret it.'

'There are days when I think I might just as well be an orphan.'

'But you're not, are you? Your dad's there, mark my words. He's there if you need him, you know, if something big happened. He loves you, Jamie, he's told me.'

'Then why doesn't he tell me?'

''Cause he's not like that. You can't change people, Jamie. I know he appears a cold old sod half the time but you know what it is? I reckon he's shy.'

'Of me?'

'Are you shy of him?'

'Well, yes, but that's different.'

'What's different about it?' She looked at him, her head on one side.

'You know, Lou, you're so pretty,' he blurted out and wondered what on earth had induced him to say that, and what on earth had got into him this evening.

'Well, then, thank you very much, young man. Fancy a bite? Come and give me a hand.'

He followed her into the minute kitchen and there he felt even bigger and clumsier as she quickly and efficiently made them corned beef sandwiches.

'Don't forget the OK Sauce,' he reminded her.

'As if I would.'

'It's odd, Lou, I feel fine now. Talking to you always helps.'

'Glad to be of service.' She whacked the bottom of the sauce bottle. The brown sauce spurted across the sandwich and a dollop landed on Jamie's tee-shirt and slithered down on to his jeans. 'Whoops. Silly me. Sorry. Take your tee-shirt off, Jamie, I'll rinse it out – you've got that jumper.'

He drew the shirt carefully over his head so as not to get the sauce on his hair and gave it to her. She stood in the small kitchen clutching the shirt to her and stared at him for what seemed a long time.

'You certainly have grown . . .' she said in a husky voice which seemed to Jamie to have hidden laughter in it. He felt himself blushing. 'Oh, look, you've got it on your jeans too. Hold on.' She turned and rinsed a cloth under the tap and came back to him and knelt down and began to dab at the sauce on the front of his jeans.

Jamie stood as rigid as any soldier on parade as he felt her gently working away at the stain. Great waves of an almost unbearable excitement flashed through his body. He did not know where to look as he realized that his penis was hardening.

'What have we here then?' Lou said quietly, and to his mounting horror he felt her begin to unzip his jeans. She'd know! She'd see! he kept thinking.

She held him as gently as she would an injured bird. The sensation of a woman's soft hands holding him was almost more than he could bear, he felt he would explode.

'Such a big man you've become,' he heard her say with difficulty for he seemed to have lost all senses, all feeling was now centred in that one place between his legs. And then, unbelievably, the one thing he had dreamt of, convinced that that was all it would ever be, a dream, happened. She took his swollen member and her mouth closed around it and she began to suck and every nerve was alive and he felt his blood gorging beneath the outer skin and he grew larger and larger . . . he was shaking, his legs bowed, he could not . . . he must . . . he arched his back . . .

'Oh, God, I'm so sorry, Lou,' he cried in shame as his semen spurted into her.

'Never mind, my darling.' She looked up at him, her large blue eyes smiling. She stood up. 'You come with me . . .' She took his hand and led him to the stairs. 'I think there's a bit of tutoring needed here.'

5

England – 1965–1966

That summer, Jamie knew, even as it was happening, was to be the happiest of his life.

It seemed to him as if he was newly born. He felt different, he was sure he looked different. Loving Lou, as a woman, had changed everything. He looked at life in a different way – he was no longer alone, he had someone to care for and protect and a person who really loved him. He was so happy and full of emotion that all his senses were more finely attuned; he could listen to music and be more affected than ever before; he found himself more aware of the simple things he'd always taken for granted like a sunset, a flower, a butterfly. When he awoke in the morning it was with a hunger and curiosity for the day ahead rather than, as in the past, a sluggish beginning.

He was enveloped in love, obsessed by it, cocooned in a new and, he was sure, a safer world.

'You won't feel like this about me when I'm old and sixty-five.' Lou giggled, pleased with her own cleverness, and sank back into the bed, her full, naked body relaxed and satiated with sex.

'Of course I will, Lou. I'll love you till I die.' He leaned up on one elbow the better to see her. 'Hell, I'll be old myself – I'll be . . .' he mumbled as he worked the sum out. 'Why, I'll be forty-nine, fifty. As old as Methuselah.' He laughed at the very idea in the way of the young, who may speak of age but not truly comprehend it will come to them.

He stroked her full breasts, marvelling at the smoothness of her skin, still amazed that he was allowed to touch this woman's body.

'You're so Rubenesque.'

'What's that when it's at home?'

'A painter who did these lovely women, all flesh and wonderful peachy tones.'

'Fat, you mean.' She laughed.

'Oh, no, Lou. You're not fat, you're . . . you're . . . bloody marvellous!' And he searched for that wonderful secret place of hers.

'God, you're insatiable, Jamie. You'll wear me out the number of times you want to do it.'

But he knew from her laugh that she was pleased with him.

Back at school in the autumn he could not forget her and the hours they had spent in her big bed with its lumpy mattress in the tiny, misshaped bedroom of his father's cottage. Nothing in his life mattered but her and that precious four-foot six-inch wide bed – his personal paradise.

Work went by the board as he mooned in his study, day-dreaming, doodling, thinking of her. Sport lost its attraction and he began to skive off, preferring to be alone to think – but always of the same thing.

He thought he would go mad with longing, that his body could not deal with this endless ache of frustration that nothing he could do would completely alleviate.

His marks began to slide, questions were asked, advice offered – he heard none of it. Sports captains shouted at him, cajoled, begged – he ignored them. The warnings began – he shrugged them off.

One weekend he could stand it no more and, after chapel, he walked out of the school and kept on walking. He caught the bus for London, the train for home and a taxi for Lou's.

'Don't you ever do that to me again.' Lou, to his great distress, was angry with him.

'I thought you'd be pleased.'

'I don't like people just turning up unannounced.'

'Even me?'

'Especially you,' she said enigmatically. 'Oh, well, you're here now.' She shrugged her shoulders. 'It could have been worse.'

By Monday he was back at school. He hadn't wanted

to go, she had made him. Of course his absence had been noted. He was punished and given the most severe warning of all – if he did that again, and if his marks did not improve, then the school no longer wanted him. He tried to buckle down, and with the prospect of the Christmas holidays looming he managed a small improvement.

On his return to Grantley he was devastated to find Lou was not there, that she had gone away to spend Christmas with an aunt. She had not warned him, that's what hurt. All he had was the short note, all formal, not loving, which she had left him.

The holidays and his sanity were saved for him by the arrival of his Uncle Frederick and Aunt Joan. Jamie had not met his father's younger brother and his wife more than a couple of times and then when he had been so much younger that the memory had faded. Fred had been a member of the Diplomatic Corps and had been stationed around the world the whole of his career; he was rarely home, having long ago decided he preferred foreign parts to his homeland. His wife was a general's daughter and so was used to a peripatetic life.

Jamie sat at the long dining-table the first night of their arrival and marvelled that here were brothers. His father sat at the head of the table, upright, austere – with them but not one of the party. His brother, who sat opposite Jamie, had the same good looks and the same handsome features, but with the added blessings of charm and humour.

Jamie was entranced. When his uncle cracked some jokes, he glanced furtively at his father who, he saw, did not smile, but his Aunt Joan, sitting at the other end of the table, was holding her sides with laughter.

During that holiday Jamie and his uncle became firm friends. Jamie had learnt poker at school; now Fred taught him chemin de fer, bridge, backgammon.

'Forget the roulette, old chap, only mugs play roulette.'

Jamie learned about wine, brandy. He smiled inwardly when Fred evidently felt it his duty to teach him about sex. It gave him an added enjoyment to sit apparently agog with curiosity, all the time knowing he'd found the perfect teacher in Lou.

'Why did you leave the Diplomatic, Uncle?'

'It was a case of them leaving me.' Fred roared with laughter. 'Two little problems. First there was a bit of a fracas over a dusky maiden in Sumatra. Then a rather unfortunate matter of a gambling debt in Hong Kong – never mess with the Chinese when it comes to gambling, Jamie. They're a mite excitable.'

'And Joan didn't mind?'

'Which, the gambling or the maiden?' Fred grinned mischievously. 'She was a bit put out by the amount I lost. But the maiden? No trouble. Take my advice, Jamie, only marry an upper-class woman from a family where there's never been a divorce. She'll see whatever you do as her duty to bear.'

'Really?' Jamie could smile, knowing full well who he was going to marry.

'And you, Jamie? What do you want to do after university?'

'I haven't the foggiest idea, Uncle. Nothing, preferably.'

'Don't think your father would be too happy with that, old boy. Think of the old Diplomatic, it's not a bad life. Don't do what your stupid uncle did, and you could go far.'

There was only one difficult moment in the whole holiday and that was at dinner when the subject of Jamie's mother came up.

'I sat next to her in the hairdresser's in London. Of course she had no idea who I was – I haven't seen her in years and I haven't worn as well as she,' Joan said good-naturedly.

'Did you?' Jamie's father said in a bleak voice, an indication that he did not wish the conversation to go further.

'She looked marvellous. Tanned, blonde, obviously very happy with her new husband.'

'New husband?' Jamie looked up with interest. There were times when he despaired of the lack of communication in this family. 'I didn't know she'd remarried.'

'Oh . . . you should have told him.' Joan quietly remonstrated with her brother-in-law. 'Six months ago – a vastly wealthy man – older of course, but then perhaps he won't mind . . .' She looked down at her plate intently.

It did not matter, it appeared, that Jamie was sixteen. Just like when he was a child, as soon as a conversation became interesting he found himself shut out.

'You should think of remarrying, Harry . . . you're still a young man,' Joan said unguardedly.

'I would prefer it, Joan, if you wouldn't regard my affairs as your business,' Jamie heard his father say icily – he heard him, only he didn't dare look up.

But when the jolly couple had left, Jamie felt bereft. Several times since meeting them he had wished they could have been his parents.

Back at school work began in earnest as A levels were studied and university entrance considered.

Jamie was working again. He had not forgotten Lou but had realized, just in time it seemed, that he must learn to compartmentalize his life. He also worked because that way he stood less chance of being noticed by the authorities. He couldn't bear the thought of losing his precious exeats. These were important for he always arranged to meet Lou in London, where they booked into a hotel and spent blissful nights together.

Holidays were a problem. Lou had pointed out to him

that his father would not be too pleased with him should he find out about their liaison. So when his father was in residence at Grantley they did not see each other. But when he was away on business or visiting friends, they fell lustily into each other's arms.

Just before the long summer break trouble loomed when Jamie received a postcard from Lou to say she would be visiting a sister in Henley. He did what he had promised he would never do again and did a bunk.

Upon his return the threat of expulsion was made more forcefully than before.

6

England – 1966

A week later Jamie sat on the edge of the bed in his small, cell-like study and his hands shook as he re-read the letter, unable to believe what he had first read.

He had been so happy when he had seen the envelope with her badly formed, almost childlike handwriting. She rarely wrote – she found it tedious, she explained – and when she did it was normally to tell him she might not be able to get away to see him.

But not on this occasion. The letter was to tell Jamie they were finished. That she was sorry but she had decided it wasn't right – only she had written *write* – that the difference in their ages was too great, that she was not being fair to him.

Tears blurred the page as he read it. His dear Lou, always thinking of him and not herself. He quickly scribbled a reply to say she had written nonsense, their love was too great to discard so lightly. He found a suitable poem from one of the Metaphysical poets for her and felt better once he had posted it.

The reply was short and brutal. '*I don't want to see you again, ever,*' she had written.

At the sight of the cruel words, incomprehension making him wild with pain and fear, he packed a small holdall without thinking and, in the middle of the week with exams looming, he absconded again.

He felt sick with misery and apprehension as he stood waiting for Lou's door to open, in the soft twilight.

'I wrote a letter to you,' Lou said upon seeing him.

'I received it, that's why I'm here.'

'I said I didn't want to see you.'

'I think you owe me an explanation.'

She looked round him as if looking for someone else. 'You can come in but only for a minute . . .'

He stood in the small sitting-room where once he had been awkward, then confident. Now he felt huge and clumsy again.

'What's happened, Lou?'

'I don't have to explain myself to you,' she said shortly, and she did not look pretty as she spoke, her face marred with anger.

'But you do . . . we've shared so much happiness. Lou, you can't make me this unhappy. Please. I need to know. What is it? Is it something I've done? I love you, Lou. I always will . . .'

'I'm pregnant,' she said shortly and sat down abruptly on her sofa.

'Pregnant?' he repeated, an inane expression on his face as he absorbed this information.

'You going deaf?'

'But Lou, that's wonderful. God, I never imagined . . . Lou . . . my darling.'

'I'm not having it.'

'But Lou, you must . . .' he knelt down in front of her. 'You can't get rid of it. I won't let you. I'll marry you. I'll get a job . . .' The words were tumbling out of him in a verbal torrent of excitement.

'I wouldn't if I were you. It's not yours.' She sat primly in her bright floral dress, her knees together. Her hands were neatly folded in her lap but it was as if she was forcing herself to sit this way.

Jamie sat back on his heels. His heart lurched at her words, disbelief flooded his mind.

'No, that can't be so. You told me how much you loved me. I believed you.' His voice was wavering in distress.

'And I did. I don't lie. I did love you . . . maybe more than you know. Now go, for Christ's sake.'

'There's someone else?'

'Yes, there's someone else. Me!'

Jamie swung round at the new voice and despair filled him. He scrambled to his feet.

'Father!' he said in astonishment. And then a red mist of jealous anger passed in front of his eyes. 'You?' He snorted with disbelief.

'How long have you been standing there?' Lou was standing now, shaking.

'Long enough. Since when have you been cheating on me, Lou?' he asked in his controlled way.

'We've been in love a year,' Jamie answered for her.

'You keep out of this.'

'I won't. It's as much my business as yours!'

'You think so, do you?'

'Yes, I do. I love Lou . . .'

'Shut up.'

'I won't.'

'Jamie, please. Why don't you just go?'

'And leave you with him? Lou, how could you? My own father . . . when?'

'For the past seventeen years,' he heard his father say.

'No, that's not true.'

'Tell him, Lou.'

'It's true, Jamie. I fell in love with your father when I first came to work for the family.'

Jamie looked about him blindly. This cottage, the good wine she always had, the nice clothes, the many trips – it was all explained. He swung round to face her.

'Don't say that. How could you love him? He loves no one . . .' He felt his voice catch on a sob and fought to control himself.

'You don't understand your father . . . you never have, no one does, only me. He's good and kind and gentle.' Lou had begun to cry.

'Fine, you loved him so much that you wanted me in your bed,' Jamie shouted.

'Jamie, you go too far,' Harry Grantley said with quiet menace.

'I don't go far enough . . .'

'You've been expelled. I had a telephone call . . .'

'I don't give a fuck about school. I belong here with Lou. Not you. I love her, I'm going to marry her. She'll have our baby . . .'

'Your baby? Are you certain?'

The red mist appeared again.

'Undoubtedly.' Jamie turned on his father. 'It has to be. Do you know how often we did it? She couldn't get enough of me, could you, Lou?'

His father moved so quickly that Jamie did not even see his hand as the fist smashed into him.

Cannes – autumn 1992

'Shit!' Jamie looked at his watch. Guthrie. He mustn't be late for Guthrie of all people.

He swung his legs off the side of the bed. How odd, fancy lying here day-dreaming of all those years ago

instead of dressing. Poor old Lou, he smiled to himself.
How old would she be now? Fifty-nine? Sixty? He couldn't
remember and yet once, he'd thought he'd never forget . . .

Jamie was waiting in the large salon of Guthrie's impeccable villa. It was no problem to wait for there was much
in the room to admire. The Picasso abstract for a start, the
Matisse. He sat on a wide, white-upholstered sofa and
looked about the room. Nothing in it jarred. Everything
was placed with such precision and with thought to colour
and balance; even the vases of white flowers were perfectly
arranged. He sipped at the black coffee a servant had
brought him.

'Dear heart, apologies . . .' Guthrie bustled into the
room, dressed in a long white, tan-trimmed kaftan and
followed by six pugs and an extremely handsome young
man in Gucci jeans, loafers and an Armani jacket. 'Takes
the old body longer and longer to get going these days.
Nothing stronger?' He nodded at the coffee.

'No this is fine.'

'Have you breakfasted?' asked Guthrie, choosing to
ignore that he himself had. Today was no day for diets, he
had told himself whilst showering.

'Well, no.'

'Then join us . . .' He spoke in perfect French to the
young man, ordering him to have another place set. 'We've
wonderful blinis . . . delightful little arse, hasn't he?' he
said as he watched his latest lover leave the room.

'If you say so.' Jamie grinned.

'And how's the delectable Mica?'

Jamie looked at Guthrie closely. There would be no
point in lying to him, Guthrie always seemed to know
things before they had even happened.

'I haven't the foggiest. She was fine when I last saw her
two weeks ago,' he answered truthfully.

'I gather she was having fun at Taki's last week.'

'No doubt,' Jamie said, failing to keep the misery out of his voice.

'Ditch her, old fruit. She's bad news for you.'

'That would be hard . . .' Jamie replied, and realized that if anyone else had said that to him about his wife he'd have duffed them one.

'Only initially – you'd meet someone else. You're still divinely handsome or didn't you know?'

'Getting a bit bloated, I reckon.'

'And why misery over a woman who doesn't deserve you?'

'Why do I let you talk to me like this, Guthrie?'

'Because you know I'm fond of you and because I always speak the truth . . . Oh, I'm sure Mica loved you once, any fool could have seen that. The problem is, does she still? Mmm?' Guthrie steepled his podgy fingers and looked at Jamie with an intent stare. 'I just get the teeny impression sometimes that you've been well and truly shafted – used up to the hilt, my dear chum.' Jamie didn't answer but shook his head as if shaking away the words he was hearing. Guthrie was only saying what he himself sometimes thought, but preferred not to, and certainly did not wish to hear said by someone else – that made the nightmare more real. He looked up as the young man re-entered the salon. Jamie frowned: talking to Guthrie was one thing; in front of someone else, and a stranger, was another. 'Don't worry about Jean-Pierre – he's a peasant, can't understand a word we say, can you, my dear child?' Guthrie smiled expansively at Jean-Pierre who smiled back. 'Found him in a bar in Marseilles, he's cleaned up beautifully, don't you think?'

'Don't you ever worry about AIDS, Guthrie?'

'Good Lor', no. I don't ever do anything that would put me at risk. I've never been one for gunging around in other people's orifices.'

The breakfast was wheeled in by a pretty Filipino maid. It was some time before Guthrie, concentrating on his blinis and caviar, washed down with Buck's Fizz, began to get down to talking about why he had invited James.

'You can stay?' he asked.

'My pleasure. I'm not exactly relishing returning to England.'

'I heard about your cousin and the roulette the other night. Your money, I presume?' Jamie nodded. 'You're a mug, Jamie.'

'I know.'

'Any chance of you stopping this gambling?'

'If I could get straight, maybe.'

'Not wishful thinking?'

'No, I don't think so. I'd promised myself that if this coup came off, it would be the last.'

'I've heard that little tale before,' Guthrie said, but kindly.

'No, I meant it,' Jamie said firmly, sensing that something to his advantage might be in the air. 'I want to get straight. Mica for one has had enough.'

'How's your dear brother Esmond?' Guthrie asked with an innocent expression.

'Rich.' Jamie laughed good-humouredly.

'Don't you resent him getting all the money?'

'No, not really. I've Grantley — luckily for me it was entailed or else Esmond would have got that too.'

'But it must be hard keeping up a huge house and estate like that with no fortune behind you.'

'I've sold bits and bobs — and of course my film work helped enormously.'

'Ah, yes, your films.' Guthrie heaved himself from the comfort of his armchair and padded across to a large circular white marble table on which books were piled in precise piles. He returned with what Jamie recognized, with mounting excitement, as a script. 'I wondered if you could cast a beady eye over this for me. I've been approached to invest in it and I know bugger-all about the film world. I need an expert to advise me. Of course, meeting you last night . . . a gift from the gods, dear boy.'

Jamie took the script, trying to hide his disappointment as he agreed to help.

'There's a part in there that would suit you to a T.'

'Honestly?' Jamie perked up again.

'Of course, I'm not the director . . .'

'No, of course not.'

'But the odd word in the shell-like of he who is . . .?'

'Of course.'

'Provided you can help me.'

'Anything.'

'What do you think of Dieter and Walt?'

'One's a Kraut and one's a Yank. Says it all, doesn't it?' Jamie replied with the arrogance of the English.

'Quite.' Guthrie laughed. 'But honestly, what do you think?'

'I think they're both greedy. Dieter isn't what he says he is. Walt, for all that he appears a civilized chap, always makes me feel that he could be a bit of a bruiser if he let go, as if he's keeping his violence in check. And to be honest, I wouldn't want to be in business with either of them – especially Dieter.'

'Exactly – filthy business he's involved in.'

'Then it's true he's an arms dealer?'

'Oh, undoubtedly. I have it from an impeccable source – the horse's mouth, so to speak.' Guthrie smiled, remembering his long conversation with His Excellency – a sinister cove but a useful contact. 'Now, this treasure hunt of mine.'

'You meant it?' Jamie laughed.

'Oh, yes, dear boy. I've been planning it for some time.'

'With them?'

'But yes. Meeting them last night was fortuitous, otherwise I'd have floated the idea at my ball. Now I need your assistance.'

'How can I help? I mean, I haven't that kind of money.'

'Provided you promise not to gamble with my money I'll stake you. I want you to keep an eye on the other two for me. I don't trust them, don't trust them an inch ... Meanwhile, if you wouldn't mind casting your lovely blue eyes over this script for me ...'

4 Jamie

1

Cannes – autumn 1992

Jamie, sunk into the billowing comfort of one of Guthrie's armchairs in his sumptuous salon, was excited. It was an excitement such as he hadn't felt for years. One that was making his heart pound, the hairs on the back of his neck stand up, a physical tingling as he mentally took stock.

He looked at the ring-bound script on his lap and patted it gently, almost caressingly. He smiled to himself at his sentimentality. It was good. It was better than good, it was bloody marvellous. It was the sort of script he'd spent recent years praying for. This was hot, damned hot.

Everything about it was right for the audiences of the nineties. A psychological spine-chiller far removed from the fantasy films of James Bond and his own Peter Ascot. It had a powerful ecological message, essential these days; the women in it were strong and not used – not as Bond and Ascot had used them – which was equally essential; the dialogue was crisp and punchy; the characters were believable; locations not so far-fetched that production costs would be out of sight. It had to be made.

His excitement over the work was genuine but its intensity was fuelled by the conviction that the hero – Bernie Lewis – had been written for him. Guthrie was right, Bernie fitted him to a T. He should and could play him.

He stood up and wandered across to the large plate-glass window and looked out on to the calm scene of Guthrie's garden dappled in winter sunshine, a light breeze barely rippling the plants and trees – almost as if the storm of the night before had been a dream.

If he got the part . . . surely Guthrie would not let him down. It was a gift. He was the right age to play the world-weary, slightly battered-by-life-and-booze Bernie who had a philosophical, thoughtful side to him which had been totally lacking in the heroes he'd played in the past. They had been empty-headed studs leaping athletically from one gun battle to the next. Ascot, Private Eye had made him famous but Jamie would be the first to admit he was too old, too battered himself to ever contemplate playing him again.

And after the Ascot series what had there been? Pale imitations that hadn't fooled the fans for long – you couldn't fool them, never. They had known he was past it, that his private life had caught up with his performing one.

Maybe he shouldn't allow himself to be so excited. Perhaps his flops had been too mega for any likely backers to accept him in the lead. But he knew he'd do anything to get this part – mortgage Grantley again, flog all the bloody paintings, sell his soul. He was hungry for it – he'd kill for it . . .

'What do you think, then, poppet?' He turned from the window at the sound of the voice to see Guthrie sallying across the wide room towards him. He still wore his copious white kaftan but for once was alone – except for the six snuffling, snorting pug dogs padding along behind him.

'It's good – bloody good,' Jamie said without hesitation.

'I felt it was – me nether regions go aflutter and they're usually right.' Guthrie did not seat himself on the large sofa but stood in front of it and simply flopped back on to it; big as it was, the piece of furniture creaked and groaned. The pugs leaped up beside him and lay in a neat row, their intelligent black eyes in their small black faces watching Jamie intently as if they too were interested in his opinion.

'Is it adapted from a book? I'd like to read it.'

'No, it's a film original. Do you know the writer?'

'Roger Marshall? Yes, a real pro. I worked with him on a *Lovejoy* years ago. Did he send you the script?'

'No, a production company — Spiral Films or some such. The chairman is an old friend of mine though I should think he's just a figure-head, past it for anything useful.' Guthrie made a motion of bringing an imaginary glass to his hands. 'A little too much of what he fancies, if you get my drift.'

'Are you intending to finance this yourself, Guthrie?'

'Good God, no! If we were wrong — and I know how easy that could be — then I'd be down the Swannee for millions, wouldn't I? That, dear heart, would make Guthrie weep buckets. No, I'll make a contribution, might be fun.'

'I know a couple of people who might be interested in a flutter.'

'Go find them, then, sweetness. Pull that bell-rope, I'm gasping, what about you?'

'There's just one thing.' Jamie looked at Guthrie slyly, at least that was his intention, but on his open-featured and handsome face it merely emerged as a sideways glance with an accompanying small smile.

'What's that, then?'

'I'll go and see my contacts if I can play Bernie.'

'I told you, I think the part's perfect for you but you know the business better than me — it wouldn't be my decision.'

'Oh, come on Guthrie, if you agreed to put up a chunk of the money only on the proviso I played Bernie, I'd be home and dry. These are hard times, it isn't easy to find the finance for a TV series, let alone a major movie.'

Guthrie steepled his podgy fingers with their immaculately manicured nails and studied them admiringly. 'Tell you what. You win the treasure hunt – and you put that money in and we've a deal.'

'But I thought you just wanted me to go along for the ride to keep an eye on the others.'

'Of course you must take part too. Otherwise it would be cheating on the others, wouldn't it? Not cricket, a rum do – all that crap. Ah, Jose – champagne and some nibblies,' Guthrie asked of a small, deeply tanned, flat-faced servant who had appeared, and spoke to him in a language Jamie did not understand.

By late afternoon Jamie was on the plane returning to London. He looked about the first-class compartment and was irritated to find there was no one he knew – he liked a natter when flying, but not with strangers, they might be boring. It was also irritating having to pay out for the first-class fare instead of travelling tourist for a fraction of the price. But if there was one rule a failing star had to adhere to, it was not to let anyone know how skint he was.

He settled back in the seat. It would have been nice to have lingered at Guthrie's for the few days hc had been invited, but this project was more exciting. He could kill two birds with one stone if they pulled it off – he could get his career back on track. And, with money to spend, maybe Mica would not wander so much. Ah, Mica, he sighed. He looked down as the aeroplane banked. He was not sure but he thought that villa down there with lawns sloping down to the azure sea was one his mother had rented years ago . . .

France – 1966

'What on earth did you do, darling? Your papa is incandescent with rage.' Jamie's mother's voice purred down the telephone from her villa, this year, in France. 'I couldn't get one word of sense out of him.' Poppy laughed. Jamie was pretty certain he could hear the racket of a party in progress in the background.

'I'd rather not say,' he said stiffly, reddening with embarrassment even though he was alone in his father's London flat.

'Oh, come on, sweetie, do tell. It's your mother here. Heavens, I've been delinquent enough in the past. Who better to understand?' Her laugh bubbled throatily – such a happy sound, he thought.

'Are you having a party?'

'A party? No. Sven's gone out for the evening and left poor Poppy by herself.'

'I thought I heard the sound of a party,' he said, but puzzled, for now he couldn't. 'Who's Sven?'

'My new husband, darling, you'll adore him – so rugged and Nordic.' She giggled. 'Come on, Jamie, tell Mummy . . .'

'I've been expelled.'

'Oh, I know *that*. That's why I called after all this time. I was *so* excited to hear such news. But why? That's what I'm dying to know.'

'Mother, honestly. It's difficult . . .'

'You can tell me . . .'

Jamie took a deep breath, still undecided as to whether he should tell or not. Perhaps it was too rich even for Poppy . . .

'I'm waiting . . .' his mother cooed.

'He found out I'd been having an affair,' he said in a rush.

'Good Lord. What on earth's wrong with that? You're

grown up now. Or was it . . .was it *who* you were having an affair with? Oh, Jamie, you're not queer, are you?'

'Don't be silly, of course not. It was Lou.'

'Lou? Do I know a Lou?'

'My nanny. Remember her?'

There was a momentary silence from France. 'Say that again, darling, but slowly . . .'

Jamie repeated himself.

'Oh, darling, that's priceless. What a gas! Listen, everyone . . .' Jamie heard her say. 'My darling son's been *doing it* with his nanny whom my ex has been banging away at for years!'

Jamie's blush deepened as he heard the great roar of laughter which greeted his mother's announcement.

'Mother! How could you?' He suddenly felt sick.

'But precious, this is so divinely funny. You mustn't be cross with me, telling my friends. I'm proud of you, such a joke.'

'It wasn't a joke to me, Mother. I loved her.' He knew he was close to tears.

'Of course you did, sweetie. What a silly thing for me to say. You must come here this instant. I insist.'

'I don't think so, Mother. I think I'd prefer to be alone . . .'

'You think you want to be alone, but that's the worst thing for you. There are thousands of women here far prettier than that old cow Lou . . .'

'She's not a cow,' he said angrily.

'You come, darling. Please . . . I'll send your fare . . .'

'No, Mother,' he said firmly.

But he went.

It was a good move. On the flight over he had decided his heart would never mend, that life without Lou and her love was pointless. He'd be far better off dead.

Within three hours of arriving at his mother's elegant villa he was having a wonderful time at a hastily arranged party. He danced to exhaustion, he drank, he was sure, to oblivion. But he was wrong. By one in the morning Jamie was happily thrusting himself between the thighs of the prettiest, sweetest, most compliant young blonde woman he had ever hoped to meet.

'Better now, darling?' Poppy smiled up at him from the breakfast table on the terrace and held her smooth cheek up to be kissed. Jamie shyly greeted his new stepfather who lowered the *New York Herald Tribune* – European edition – for long enough to smile and nod his head, before retreating behind it again.

'Breakfast?' Poppy patted the vacant seat beside her. 'Now, about today. I thought we should pop into Cannes and get you some clothes. We're meeting friends for drinks in the Carlton at noon – we can lunch there. Sven's playing golf this afternoon and wondered if you'd care to join him, didn't you, darling? Then this evening we're off to Monte, dinner with Ari and then the casino. What do you think?'

'Sounds splendid.' Jamie grinned.

'Perhaps your son and I should talk about his future . . . possible options.' The paper rustled and Sven's blue eyes looked closely at him.

'Don't be so pompous, Sven. You sound like his father – the last thing the boy needs. If you're going to talk business with the dear child then I forbid him to play golf with you.' Poppy pouted prettily and Jamie felt a mite relieved. When he had been at school he hadn't the vaguest idea what he wanted to do; now, with no chance of getting his A levels and going to university, his mind was even blanker.

'I just thought the sooner . . .' Sven said in his sing-song Swedish accent.

'And we're grateful, Sven darling, aren't we, Jamie? But

let the dear creature have a tiny holiday first?' She smiled in a practised, coquettish way at her husband – was he number three or four, Jamie thought, he couldn't be sure. The butler appeared, followed several paces behind by a shortish young man with dark hair.

'Ah, von Weiher, my dear chap.' Sven jumped to his feet. 'Darling, might I introduce Herr Dieter von Weiher.'

Poppy proffered her hand over which the young man bowed, at the same time clicking his heels, and Poppy smiled a secret smile at him, looking pointedly into his fine blue eyes.

'I just love Teutonic charm.' She laughed, and the others laughed too. Jamie found his hand being crushed in a vice-like grip which he thought a mite over-done.

'Are you here for long, Mr von Weiher? We've a lot of parties . . .' Poppy waved her hand in the air in a vague gesture.

'Just today, unfortunately. I've business with your husband.' He held his wrist as if he feared he might be rude and look at his watch and so offend.

'Sven, how boring of you. Handsome men are thin on the ground this season. Do your business quickly and then let this charming young man join us for lunch.'

'I'm most grateful, Madam, but unfortunately I have to leave.'

'Poppy, darling, some people have work to do, appointments to keep.'

'How ineffably dull for you.' Poppy pouted.

'Dieter, if you'd care to come this way . . .' And Sven collected his papers and after more ceremonial bowing they departed.

'It will probably surprise you, Jamie, but I just adore all that German formality,' Poppy sighed.

'I thought he looked a cold fish. Gave me the shivers, those icy blue eyes – like a mass murderer.'

'Oh, Jamie, how droll. He had the most divinely sexy eyes.' She stretched her neck, the sun falling on her fine features.

'You're so beautiful, Ma,' Jamie said shyly, but he said it all the same.

'Sweetness. How kind. I try.' She chuckled, patting her hair. 'Don't tell a living soul but I'm forty next year,' she whispered.

'Oh, I wouldn't dream of it. You don't look it. More like thirty.'

'Of course, with you around it's going to be harder for people not to guess. I'd hoped I could pass you off for fourteen or fifteen. Not a hope – just look at you, so tall and big.'

'Sorry.' He grinned sheepishly.

'Maybe everyone will think you're my lover – I wouldn't mind that one little bit.'

It was only then he remembered that last night he could not recall her introducing him to one person as her son, just Jamie.

The next month passed by in a welter of excitement for Jamie. He had found where he belonged, he decided. He liked the partying, the bright, fun-loving people. Everyone here, it seemed, wanted only to be happy, and it was easy, when with them, to think oneself happy too.

He learned so much in that time, which he decided was far more valuable to him than the boring French and history he'd been plodding with at school. He learned about food, the like of which he had not known existed. His Uncle Freddie had given him a grounding in wine but not wines like he drank now. His French became fluent far faster than at his lessons. His mother taught him about clothes and what went well with what and how to be smart but never flash. He learned that he excelled at making polite, light conversation. He discovered he had charm and that in these circles to be young *and* charming was a great asset. He had been sure Lou had taught him all he ever needed to know about sex — but not so. The girl of the first night never appeared again, even though he asked his mother to invite her. Soon it did not matter as she was quickly replaced by a friend of his mother's — younger than her but older than Jamie. And Laura teased and tutored him into joys beyond his imagination.

Then, to his great excitement, he learned that Guthrie Everyman, now, at twenty-three, a multi-millionaire since the early death of his father, a steel tycoon, had bought a villa close by. One telephone call and Jamie had been invited for lunch.

'Prepare yourself for a shock, my sweetness, Guthrie's done the unthinkable, Guthrie's in love.' The man had laughed his slightly high falsetto laugh. So, as Jamie approached the villa, he was curious on two counts — to see how his friend had changed in the past five years and who he was in love with.

The shock was real, for Guthrie was in love with a woman when everyone had presumed . . .

'I know exactly what you're thinking — "I thought Guthrie was a fairy" — go on, admit it.' Guthrie, blond, tanned and, if possible, even larger, gave Jamie a playful push.

'Well, be honest, Guthrie, you do mince about a bit.'

'Oh, the English, is there no hope for them? Just because a feller's a bit artistic and likes to explore the whole gamut of life's experience on offer, they immediately jump to all manner of conclusions.'

'Then I'm sorry.'

'Don't be. I was never quite sure myself what I was. I've dabbled about a bit either way. Now it would appear I've opted for a woman — Sita.'

'She's certainly stunning,' Jamie said, watching as the

graceful Sita walked in the garden below the terrace on which they sat.

'I could spend the rest of my life just watching her and die a happy man.' Guthrie sighed and smiled with the satisfied and contented look of one who thinks only he has found the secret of love.

Sita, tall and lithe, with long, shining jet-black hair and kohl-rimmed eyes of deepest brown, was a great beauty. She had long ago forsaken the sari and now dressed elegantly but casually in Western clothes. She was a professional artist of some success and, much to Jamie's disappointment, she was a very serious person.

He'd gone to Guthrie's villa expecting a marked degree of jollity. Instead he found the place gloomy – curtains pulled against the sun, a rather depressing line in purple and black wall hangings, and some awful tuneless music twanging non-stop in the background. The house guests were equally darksome. The men, bearded for the most part, were dressed in the dullest, dun-coloured clothes. Their womenfolk wore black, with heavy black eye make-up in pale, sorrowful faces. They sat in deep discussion in huddled groups.

At one glance they had decided that the blazered, polished shoes and short haircut image of Jamie encased a person who was of no interest to them, and so they ignored him and returned to their earnest talk amidst clouds of cannabis smoke. Had it not been for Guthrie, who fussed over him, Jamie knew he would have left long before lunch was served. But he couldn't hurt Guthrie and sat it out, even enduring a showing of Sita's paintings. The reason for her success eluded him as, with as attentive an expression as he could muster, he found himself looking at painting after painting of what appeared to be large vulvae. Somehow he managed to make the requisite right remarks – but with effort.

He left as soon as decency allowed, with vague promises of meeting up and phone calls to be made lingering in the air. Rum set-up, he decided as he set off for what now seemed the normality of his mother's villa. He did hope Guthrie would be safe with Sita.

He soon recovered from this letdown, however, for there was a new excitement in his life, one which confused him for, he sometimes felt, he enjoyed it even more than Laura. This was when he sat at the tables in the ornate casino in Monte Carlo and gambled with the money which Sven gave him each time they went. There was nothing in life, he concluded, to match that heart-racing, palm-sweating thrill of the turn of a card, the frequent rush of adrenalin which kept him permanently high. The memory of the happiness of success always got him past the disappointment of failure.

He was happy, how could he not be with every sense satiated with pleasure? And he had found his mother; after all this time the bright shining star was close at hand. Now she touched him constantly, smoothing his hair, kissing him, linking arms with him, whispering with him, sharing private jokes. She loved him, wanted him near her!

Sven, who he learned owned oil tankers, was extremely rich. He had to be, the way he indulged Poppy, and she in turn indulged Jamie and her many friends.

'What happened to Wayne?' Jamie asked one day.

'Wayne who?'

'The bloke in blue velvet you brought to my sports day.'

'Oh, that Wayne.' She laughed at the memory. 'A little interlude between husbands, darling. But my goodness, you were pompous that day – I thought I'd lost you for ever, that you were doomed to be like your boring father.'

'I was rather, wasn't I?' He moved uncomfortably in the chair at the thought of that day and his embarrassment.

'But you're not the teeniest bit like Harry. You're my son . . . every bit of you.' She blew him a kiss.

The next morning when he awoke late the villa was strangely quiet. He threw on a robe and wandered out on to the terrace. The table stood laid for one.

'Where is everyone?' he asked the steward, who had appeared the moment he approached the table.

'Madam Johanssen left you this.' He handed Jamie an envelope.

'Left me?' Jamie's voice brimmed with surprise.

'She left this morning, sir. For Beirut, I believe. Your usual scrambled eggs, sir?'

'Yes . . . thank you . . .' Jamie sat down at the table and ripped open the envelope. There was a stack of dollars, an airline ticket to London and a scrawled note.

'Sorry couldn't say goodbye – you looked too sweet asleep to awaken you. This is to tide you over . . . Poppy.

'P.S. Write me c/o my bankers Pictet in Geneva.'

2

England – 1966–1970

Jamie arrived in London with a tan, two suitcases of expensive clothes, a Patek Philippe watch, a Minox miniature camera, a Zenith radio and the dollars which had converted into almost £500.

He was tired as he entered his father's flat to find another note, this one from the family's lawyer which told him he was not to take up residence, that if he did so legal proceedings would be set in motion to have him evicted and that the porter was in possession of his effects.

He checked his room – it was empty of everything that

belonged to him. He stood for a moment looking about him at the familiar room which had once been his nursery. And he remembered Lou, recalling her with a sharp pang of longing which he thought the summer had buried.

The porter seemed embarrassed when he knocked on his flat door and asked him to guard his luggage while he searched for somewhere to live. After calling on two estate agents it was obvious to Jamie that he was not going to be able to stay in the Mayfair region – his money would not go far here. He wondered if Chelsea would be cheaper.

The King's Road was a revelation to him, he came so rarely to London. There had been a revolution here while he'd been cloistered away in school and at Grantley. The street was heaving with the young, parading proudly by, dressed as brightly as parakeets. Every other shop appeared to be a boutique competing with its neighbours in darkness and noise. In his blazer and slacks and with short hair, it was Jamie who was stared at. It was he who was the odd one out.

A stop for coffee and a quick chat-up of the waitress who looked like Julie Christie's double, and he was on his way to look at a room which *might* be free. She had said this rather dubiously, evidently taking in his clothes. He thanked her, pocketed the address, tipped her generously and went into the first boutique he came to.

He still couldn't quite bring himself to buy the soft pastel suit the epicene boutique owner raved about – it was a bit too much like Poppy's friend Wayne's style. He settled on a black velvet one instead, with a scarlet embroidered waistcoat and a pair of black leather boots.

'Scrumm-eee . . .' The shop owner clapped his hands together with delight as Jamie emerged from the changing-room.

It proved to be a sound investment. Within the hour Jamie had paid a month's rent on a top-floor room in a tall white house in a leafy square off the King's Road. The house was chaotic, noisy, reeked of pot and curry and was rented by two young girls who said they were models and wore the smallest mini-skirts it had been his privilege to leer at. He was sure his new clothes had helped him be accepted. As it was, they asked him if he had just come out of the army because of his short hair.

'No, I've been away,' he explained.

'Oh, how exciting. What for?' the taller of the two asked.

'Drugs?' queried the second.

Jamie merely smiled and touched the side of his nose, pretending to have a secret. And the two girls squealed and hugged each other with evident excitement. Rum old world, thought Jamie, if their thinking he was a jail-bird was an advantage.

That evening Jamie returned to the restaurant in search of the pretty waitress. She was there. He had a bowl of spaghetti, a bottle of execrable and over-priced Chianti, and by midnight was cosily tucked up in bed with his Julie Christie lookalike.

This is the life, he thought, as he drifted into sleep.

The months that followed were an odd mixture for Jamie.

Times were good and yet bad. He was happy and yet sad. He had more friends than at any other time in his life and yet he'd never felt lonelier. He revelled in his new-found freedom and yet sometimes felt frightened by it.

His money seemed to slip through his fingers. He couldn't *live* in his black velvet suit, he reasoned, and so he bought jeans, flares, sweaters, jerkins, waistcoats, boots, shoes and belts until finally he was one of the trendiest, most colourful of those who paraded up and down King's Road admiring each other.

He swapped his small room for a much larger but more

expensive one which became vacant on the first floor. He bought kelims for the bed and to cover a couple of chairs. He fell in love with a Persian rug. He purchased lamps, a painting, posters and stacks of brightly embroidered cushions for sitting on the floor.

Like an over-friendly puppy longing to be liked, and mistaken for a wealthy dropout, Jamie was soon regarded as a soft touch. He lost count of the money he loaned and never saw again as, frequently, he never saw the 'friend' he had loaned it to either. He preferred not to think of the many bets on the horses which had gone down the drain – a temporary unlucky streak, he reassured himself.

His blond attractiveness and muscular body attracted women in droves. He loved a lot but he was never in love. He would have liked to have fallen for someone and lived in hope that he would. He had never felt so alone and longed to have a woman to care for.

He waited for his mother to contact him. He had, as instructed, written to her bankers in Switzerland with his new address. He had purposely made the letter amusing, making light of his father throwing him out, skilfully covering a hurt which at first he had not realized was there, but which, as the weeks passed, grew within him.

When he heard nothing he wrote again, and then again, and sent a telegram and waited. With his money depleting rapidly, his mother's lack of response took on a greater significance.

He finally pocketed his pride and burgeoning hurt and telephoned his father who refused to take his calls. Into the hurt filtered anger. This was crazy, he told himself, here he was, worried sick over money, untrained to do anything to help himself and with two rich parents who obviously didn't give a stuff for him.

He unpacked one of the suits he now never wore, polished his old lace-up shoes and washed his hair – but could not quite bring himself to have it cut from its new fashionable length. So dressed, he sallied forth to the family solicitors in Welbeck Street.

Fortunately for him, even William Mottram whose sap, if he had ever had any, had long since dried up, still had an eye for a pretty girl. A mini-skirted dream, with mascara-ringed eyes and hair bleached nearly white, sat at reception. Her appreciation for Jamie equalled his for her, and his lack of an appointment was no obstacle, she assured him.

After a ten-minute wait in her company he was shown into Mottram's office which, no doubt, had not changed since his grandfather's day. William Mottram, while sympathetic, felt none of this was any of his business. But Jamie now knew that he could charm anyone when he put his mind to it. He left the office with a date arranged with the receptionist and a promise from William that he would try to persuade Lord Grantley that some sort of allowance was required.

He succeeded. Five pounds a week paid monthly! It would barely cover the rent for his room – but then it *was* something. There was nothing for it, he'd get a job. But what job, with a stash of not very good O levels and no ambition or even ideas as to what he wanted to do?

Over the next three years Jamie had many jobs. Since they were all fairly mundane ones he lost interest easily and became bored and flippant. He invariably walked out rather than waiting to be sacked, as would have been inevitable.

Many times he was grateful for the clothes his mother had bought him on that holiday in France. For to his surprise, when the Season began each year, he found himself still on the list of eligible young men which was annually circulated round the debs' mums.

Once, his parents' divorce, the fast set in which his mother moved, and his own expulsion from school would have excluded him from these circles. But a new breed of mothers had evolved, with new money and massive ambitions for their daughters, who themselves, in the old days, would not have been regarded as acceptable either.

During the Season Jamie ate well and drank copiously. He danced himself fit. He even managed to feed whichever girl was sharing his room at the time by taking a doggy-bag to every ball and shamefacedly filling it, saying he had a ravenous Labrador waiting at home.

He lied a lot to the debs and their parents too. His stint in the household goods department at Harrods became a job in public relations. When he worked as a barman in a wine bar he metamorphosed himself into a wine importer. When employed as a door-to-door encyclopaedia sales-man, he said he was in educational publishing. When trying, rather unsuccessfully, to sell insurance policies, again door-stepping on uninterested housewives, he had only to hint at Lloyds. He nearly came unstuck when, instead of confessing to being a road-sweeper in Oxford Street, he said he was a Rhodes Scholar at Oxford. One father, quicker than most, said he didn't realize an English-man could be one, so Jamie gave up the job since he couldn't think of a better lie.

He was always short of cash. He always paid his rent on the dot – he'd seen too many people thrown out for late payment. He was still extravagant with clothes. But the main reason he never got straight was that if he had any money left over he frittered it away on the horses. He never played cards these days – none of his group did. But with the new betting shops popping up in every high street, the temptation proved too much for Jamie. He won occasionally, just often enough to maintain his optimism when he lost.

He smoked pot, not because he particularly wanted to but because everybody else did. It was all right, he decided, but, being a gregarious soul, he found it made him and the others isolated in each other's company, so he much preferred to drink. He tried acid once but scared himself witless and never did so again; he could not understand his friends who did.

His women were legion. They were never the debs whose parties and balls he attended – he could never have afforded to take them out on dates. No, he chose waitresses, barmaids, shop girls, nearly all of them aspiring models and actresses longing for that lucky break, and as skint as he was. They were fun. It was a great time to be young and free. One-night stands were the order of the day. No commitment was the golden rule. Fun, we must have fun, aren't we having fun? was the clarion call.

Was it? he asked himself an uncomfortable number of times. Many were the occasions when Jamie lay awake in the dark of night, his latest bird breathing gently beside him, and he would feel physically whole but wish it could have been different. He knew now that there were two kinds of sex – this and the other. That other – with Lou. When their coupling had not been just their bodies but their minds and souls too. Would it ever be like that again for him?

And then he met Sally.

3

London – autumn 1992

Mild turbulence made the plane lurch as it approached Heathrow. Jamie sat up and looked at his watch, amazed that the time had passed so quickly since Nice airport. It wasn't like him to dwell on the past, yet for the whole trip he'd done nothing else. He peered out of the window and shuddered as he saw the murkiness beneath him. London in November was not the best place to be. Already the morning's sunshine at Guthrie's seemed like a dream.

The plane taxied to a halt. Jamie stood up, collected his overnight bag from the locker above him and waited patiently for the other passengers to sort themselves out and begin to file off the plane. He smiled to himself as he thought of the times he had arrived here to be whisked off to the VIP lounge, where customs and passport control were painless, where baggage arrived by magic, where he would not be bothered by the curious. The truth was he had rather liked to be bothered and resented being borne away. Now he could come and go and no fans waited, only the paparazzi in the hopes he might be drunk and fall over or be with someone who was not his wife. He doubted if they'd show any interest in him today.

He was right. Clutching his bag of duty-free, he was quickly through and with only one case was soon out of the building. For once he'd be sensible and take the bus to central London to save money.

'Taxi, Lord Grantley?'

'Thanks,' he said to the cabbie and, having been recognized, resigned himself to paying. He climbed into the taxi and was about to give his address.

'No need for the address, sir. I drove you years ago you know, when you was famous.'

'Ah, right,' said Jamie, settling back into the seat and managing to smile. 'Those were the days,' he said, out of embarrassment more than anything else.

'You've given up the acting, then, sir?'

'Good gracious, no. I've a big project in the pipeline.' He was relieved not, for once, to have to lie.

'Bet it won't be as good as them Peter Ascot films – great they were. I catch them when they're on the box – if I'm working I get the missus to video them.'

'Great,' said Jamie and wished he could hit the fellow

over the head with something sharp and messy. Why had he taken this cab he could ill afford and then have to listen to the driver droning on? Did it matter? Who, if he was honest, would care or comment at Jamie Grant, fading film star, on a bus? Maybe if he could come to terms with what had happened, everything would be easier. Still, he'd decided that if this project came off he was determined not to slip into the old ways – blowing money as soon as he got it, demanding, expecting and paying out for star treatment.

Not next time – those days were over.

He watched the ribbon development of houses through the pouring rain. Things could be a lot worse – hell, he had a decent flat and Grantley. Sometimes he despised himself for how much he moaned. And at least the cabbie had recognized him. For the rest of the journey he politely listened to the man's opinions – freely given.

He let himself into his flat. Of course she wasn't there, he hadn't really expected her to be – Mica spent less and less time in London. At first he had thought it was because she did not like the city; these days he began to wonder if it was him she was avoiding.

He quickly showered and changed, then called his agent.

'Ruthie, I must see you.'

'Jamie, I'm sorry, I've nothing for you – I've tried, God knows I've tried.'

'That's not why I'm calling – I've got something to show you. I'm coming over.' And he replaced the receiver before his agent could say she was too busy to see him.

On the street he hailed a cab – his resolution to travel more economically must wait awhile and certainly not be put into practice until the weather improved.

The receptionist at the agency in Soho welcomed him effusively. Jamie was one of her favourite clients. Small wonder when, after kissing her cheek, he presented her with a bottle of 'Miss Dior'. Giggling her thanks, she buzzed Ruth Cohen's assistant Miriam whose welcome was as warm and was rewarded with a bottle of 'L'Air du Temps'.

'You're always so thoughtful, Jamie.'

'Can't forget my favourite ladies, can I?' He twinkled at them and flirted effortlessly. They knew it meant nothing but still they responded.

At last he was let into Ruth's small office which was a chaotic jumble of scripts, photo portfolios, books, letters to be read, letters to be answered – Ruthie was always behind on both.

'You look well, Jamie.' She smiled at him and thanked him for the 'Calèche' he always bought her and which she'd never had the heart to tell him didn't suit her. These days she dreaded to see him when she had no work to offer him. Recently there had been a directive from the chairman. Ruth knew the memo by heart – any actor bringing less than £1500 a year into the agency was to be dropped. This year, so far, that meant Jamie. But she hadn't the heart to tell him to go, not when one considered how much money he'd earned them in the good old days.

'God, you're not representing him, are you?' Jamie pointed disdainfully at the photo of a young New Zealand soap opera actor who'd recently arrived in town. 'He can't act – I was better than him on a bad day.'

'He's an insufferable little shit, cocky and ungrateful. But there you go, Jamie, that's where the money is these days – TV.'

'Or here.' From his briefcase, Jamie took the script Guthrie had given him.

'Oh, not another one . . .' She gestured wearily at the stack of unread scripts on her desk.

Jamie scooped them up and shoved them under the sagging springs of an ancient sofa on which lay a somewhat smelly pug which hadn't even had the courtesy to acknowledge him. Christ, even the dog knew he was a has-been, he thought.

'Ruthie, if you never do another thing for me – please. Please, read this script. It's perfect for me.'

She leafed through it idly.

'See the production company? They're at Pinewood.'

'Spiral Films, never heard of them. Jamie, you know as well as I do these companies spring up from nowhere and disappear just as quickly.'

'No. No, this is different. Guthrie Everyman's involved.'

'Guthrie? You're joking.' She looked up at him with interest.

'He's going to collaborate. Write the music.' He lied through his teeth, but as he did so he thought what a great idea and why hadn't he come up with that before?

'Really?' She looked at the first page.

'And he's got pugs, too.' He grinned.

'Ah, well, that's it then, isn't it?' She grinned back.

'Thing is, Ruthie, I just wondered if you'd ask dear Miriam if she could run me off a few copies to tout around.'

'It's got no backing then?'

'Yes, some . . . just a little more needed.'

'How much?'

'A little.'

'Jamie!'

He told her reluctantly.

'Oh, Jamie, darling, don't get your hopes raised.'

'But I can't help it. I just feel it in my bones, Ruthie – this one's a runner.'

'And how many times have I heard that?'

'Don't piss on my fireworks, Ruthie, there's a love.'

Ruthie saw the hunger in his handsome face, saw the longing, the need. She picked up her phone.

'Miriam, I've got a script here, I need some copies. How many, Jamie?'

'Five, no, make it six.'

'Six?' Ruthie shook her head at him as Jamie calculated how much money he'd saved in photocopying.

'You'll read it tonight, promise?'

'I promise.' She laughed at him and hoped the script was all he said it was.

Back at the flat he began to make calls. They were not easy to make. Once he would have been put through immediately to whoever he wanted to speak to, not have to charm, prevaricate and argue with defensive secretaries and personal assistants.

Out of the twelve calls he made to people he thought might be interested in backing the film he only managed to speak to five. The rest were stone-walled. Four weren't too keen-sounding and only one – Archibald McNeil – agreed to see him there and then, and that was probably because they'd been to school together.

Jamie didn't give him time to rethink but raced from his flat and straight round to his office in a merchant bank off Fleet Street. It was a pleasant hour of reminiscences over good malt whisky and he left with a promise that Archibald would read the script that night and discuss it with his partners by the New Year.

Better than nothing, he thought, as he let himself into his flat. And then there was Walt – why hadn't he thought of him sooner? – one of the richest men in the world. Yes, he'd give him a buzz tomorrow.

He checked his answer-machine. There was one message.

'Jamie. I need to talk to you, please call.'

She'd left no name, she didn't need to, he'd recognize her voice any day.

But why should she be calling him after all these years?

They hadn't spoken for ages. And why did she sound so upset, as if she was crying?

He had to look up her number. He dialled it and let it ring and ring but oddly there was no reply. Couldn't have been that urgent, he reasoned.

He poured himself a large scotch. In the freezer he found a pizza which he stuck in the microwave. He rejected the resultant mess and instead poured an even larger scotch, found a jar of lumpfish roe and a stale biscuit. He returned to the sitting-room, put on a Louis Armstrong CD and relaxed in his favourite chair.

Now there was a blast from the past, he thought. Why should Sally, his first wife, be calling him? Of all people she was the last he'd ever have expected to hear from again.

Poor Sally, he thought, he should never have married her.

England – 1970

Jamie was twenty-one when he met Sally, got her pregnant, married her and knew he had made a dreadful mistake.

It wasn't Sally's fault. With heart-sinking guilt he knew it was his.

Sally was tiny and slim with beautiful legs which suited the boots she nearly always wore. She was dark with thick, almost black hair which shone like the fur of a healthy cat. She had large, soulful brown eyes, guarded by two rows of false eyelashes and heavily kohled which made them look even bigger. When she looked at him with those eyes full of love and longing for him it made him feel ten feet tall with pride.

She wanted to be a film star, wanted it with a hunger which amazed him with his total lack of ambition. She had an Equity card acquired from her only job so far as an extra in a *Carry On* film. She worked as a typist to make ends meet while she waited for that lucky break with the same conviction as a born-again Christian waiting for the second coming. To his surprise, Jamie found that he wanted to look after her in case she was disappointed.

The one-night stands ceased. She moved in with him. She liked his friends, the staying up all night with cheap plonk, setting the world to rights. As he had cut his swathe through the young women of London, Jamie had learned that despite appearances, most of them longed for marriage and the conventional life, even when they tried to hide it as being uncool. But not Sally – she wanted a career. This suited Jamie fine. He might be happy to look after her, but he wasn't ready to settle down.

She didn't take the pill, which was a nuisance. She said it made her fat and she'd never get a part then. Nor could she manage a Dutch cap. He'd told her not to worry, that he'd be careful. And he was. Until one night, a bit too fuddled with drink and frustrated with the need to always have to whip himself out of her, smartish, before he came, he threw caution to the wind, managed to ignore her little worried cries and with a shuddering joy allowed his sperm to spurt into her.

'It'll be all right,' he said, cuddling her afterwards. 'Hell, we've only done that once. Don't worry,' he counselled.

But it was not all right, and two weeks later when she told him her period was two days late, which it never usually was, he knew, he knew it had happened and he had no one to blame but himself.

'I'll never break into films now,' she wailed.

'Of course you will. I'll see to it.'

'How?' she snapped. She'd never been cross with him before.

'I've been talking to this bloke at work, his cousin's girlfriend . . .'

'Jamie!' She sat up on the bed where a moment before

she had been inconsolable. 'You're not suggesting . . . ? How could you . . .'

'No, don't be silly. Of course I'm not suggesting anything,' he said lamely as he realized an abortion was to be out of the question.

'Then what did this bloke say?' she said sharply.

'Oh, that University College is the best place to have a baby,' he lied.

'Oh, Jamie. How sweet of you. You want me to have it?'

'Of course.' And he marvelled at how easy such lies were to tell.

'You must see my parents.'

'Wonderful,' he said, but his voice failed him at these words, so dreaded by young men. She looked at him quizzically. 'What about this Sunday?' He recovered himself quickly.

When he saw the neat detached house in Luton, with the Volvo in the drive, the tidy herbaceous border and the chiming doorbell, he wasn't surprised she wanted London and fame in the cinema.

Her accountant father and housewife mother welcomed him warmly. There was one sticky moment when Sally and her mother, who had been closeted in the kitchen for a good half-hour finishing off the cooking of the roast, emerged with red eyes, both clutching hankies, and Mrs Walters had asked for a quiet word with her husband.

'You told her?'

'I had to, Jamie.'

'I suppose you did.' He looked out of the french windows at the neat parcel of lawn. 'Was she cross?'

'Disappointed, more like.'

'Yes, she would be.'

'But she feels better about it knowing we're getting married.'

'Yes,' Jamie said blankly.

'Of course she wants to meet your father. It made it easier telling her with him being a lord.'

'Why?' asked Jamie genuinely.

'Oh, Jamie, don't be so silly . . .'

Jamie was surprised that the Walters wanted a large white wedding which, in the circumstances, he thought was a bit hypocritical. He had written to both his parents with the news – though not about the baby. To his surprise both replied. This cheered Jamie: maybe by marrying he was getting back into his father's good books.

His father hosted a dinner in London where the three parents seemed to get on famously and where Jamie met his brother Esmond for the first time in years and found he liked the quiet fifteen-year-old.

He was gratified by the hefty cheque his father gave him.

'You'll need somewhere to live,' his father said gruffly as they parted for the evening. 'She seems a nice girl,' he added as he got into his taxi outside the restaurant.

Poppy's reaction was perplexing. She announced her arrival in less than twenty-four hours and they met in her suite at Claridge's.

The evening had gone well, he was sure, his mother was charming to Sally, asking her all manner of questions but nicely and in a concerned manner. He was not prepared for her comments when she took him out for lunch alone the following day.

'You can't marry her, Jamie. I can't allow you to.'

'Why ever not? I thought you liked her.'

'Of course I like her – there's nothing to dislike, is

there? She's a nice girl. But she's totally, utterly wrong for you! She'll smother you. She's too suburban.'

'Sally? Why, she's running away from all that.'

'Is she?' Poppy arched one perfectly plucked eyebrow.

'Yes. She's not into marriage, cars, houses – keeping up with the Joneses, that sort of crap.'

'Then why is she marrying you?'

Jamie looked everywhere in the crowded restaurant rather than at his mother.

'She's pregnant, isn't she?'

'Yes,' he said miserably.

'Get her to have an abortion – I'll pay.'

'She won't. She's very anti.'

'Then let her have it but don't marry her.'

'Ma, I couldn't do that,' Jamie said, shocked at such a notion. 'It's my responsibility too.'

'She didn't have to sleep with you.'

'No, but she did and it's done and I'm left with no option.'

'I think you're bloody mad. What are you going to live on? Is your father helping?'

'He gave me a cheque and he gives me a fiver a week.'

'Mean sod.' Poppy picked up her handbag and fished inside for her cheque-book and quickly wrote Jamie a cheque. 'You'll need somewhere to live.'

'Thanks, Ma.' He glanced quickly at the cheque and felt his heart miss a beat at its size. 'There's just one other thing, I'm going to need a job – a proper one.'

'Doing what?'

'Oh, I don't know, in a bank or something.'

'You'd die in a bank.'

'Maybe, maybe not.'

'Call Sven, he'll sort you out. And, Jamie . . .' She put her hand across the table and touched his gently. 'When things go wrong, remember I'm your mother.'

'Thanks,' he said, but at the same time marvelling at her lack of tact.

He banked the cheques and they started to house-hunt. He was surprised when she said they should move to the suburbs.

'What on earth for?'

'It'll be better for the baby.'

Sod the baby was what he wanted to say. He had no intention of burying himself out in the sticks, he wanted to stay where they were.

'You should be near the centre of things – get the gossip, close to your agent,' he said instead and clinched the argument. They searched in Fulham.

'Do you think we have enough money for a little car? We could pop out to lunch on a Sunday with my parents – just so they get to know the baby.'

'A car?' He stopped walking in his tracks.

'Yes, why are you looking all goofy like that?' She laughed at him.

'I've never been into cars much – more trouble than they're worth.'

'Oh, it would be nice to have one. Come on.' She tugged at his arm. 'Let's go to Peter Jones or Harrods and look at the three-piece suites.'

As the lists of what Sally felt essential items grew in length, he congratulated himself that, for reasons he was not sure about, he hadn't told her about his mother's cheque, or that would have gone too. He'd keep it as a handy nest-egg.

The wedding drew closer. He felt he was being sucked into a trap and one of his own making. The Walters' were seeing to everything, all he had to decide was where to honeymoon – he'd lied about that, Sally thought it was booked when it wasn't.

In a pub a week before The Day he met an old friend

from his school-days who now worked for a bloodstock agent. It was this friend who gave him a tip he could not ignore. Using a sizeable chunk of his wedding present from Poppy, he decided on a four-horse accumulator.

The next day he was as nervous as one of the thoroughbreds who carried so much of his money. He couldn't relax, couldn't go to work – this time as a projectionist's assistant in the Essoldo – he couldn't stay at home, not with Sally asking him every five minutes what was wrong with him.

He went to the betting shop. There, surrounded by others of a like mind in the smoke-fugged atmosphere, he watched, waited and with mounting excitement heard on the landline his first horse win, then the second. Then heart-stopping moments as he waited for the course officials' decision on a photo-finish for the third and he could barely stand from excited exhaustion when the fourth romped home.

He picked up his winnings. For a moment he thought about doing the same thing tomorrow, then ran from the shop and raced down the road as if all the devils in hell were after him to the travel agent's and booked flights and hotels for two in Cannes. The honeymoon was safe.

4

England – 1971–1974

Long afterwards, Jamie made a joke of how his marriage had broken up on his honeymoon. It was easy to joke years later, it was not so funny at the time.

It made a good story, how one week into their honeymoon he had bumped into Busty Mortimer, a fellow ex-deb's delight, now a banker and married to a biscuit heiress. How in one evening's play at backgammon he'd lost all his mother's gift to him. How, on the second night, determined to recoup his losses, he'd gambled a third of his father's money too. It was Buster, with a surprising – for him – surge of conscience that he might be taking Jamie for far too much, who called a halt to the game with a lame excuse that he'd promised his wife an early night.

They'd returned to London, Sally with a thicker waist and a sour expression he'd never seen before, and Jamie contrite and vowing he'd never do anything so stupid again. The little house they had planned with a garden for the baby's pram became a small two-bedroomed flat. The orders for the furniture and the Silver Cross pram were cancelled and they bought second-hand, which made Mrs Walters purse her lips with disapproval.

Sally had to work because Jamie wasn't. He'd lost his job as a projectionist when he'd popped out to the pub for a quickie, without realizing he'd put the wrong film on. He couldn't find another – his many jobs made employers suspicious.

He lounged around at home becoming increasingly bored, waiting for a letter from Sven which never came. The rest of the time he brooded on what a mess he'd made of everything and planned wild schemes to get them out of this muddle. But the schemes were fantasy, nothing concrete, nothing practical. The dreams of a floundering man.

Jamie changed the day his daughter was born. He looked at her through the glass which separated him from the babies in the nursery, and quite simply fell in love.

He had never thought a baby could be beautiful – his could. He experienced an unfamiliar surge of pride and love, a need to protect her. He had to change his ways, Fiona had to be cared for.

He'd wanted to call her Emma, but Sally and Mrs Walters wouldn't have it — the arrival of Fiona Charlene was duly announced to the world.

As the weeks slipped by, Jamie became aware by a look here, a silence there, how angry the Walters family were becoming with him for not finding work. He dreaded Sundays and the trip to Luton in a mini given to Sally by her father when it was obvious they could not afford a car. He was mortified by the bags stowed in the boot for their return. Food parcels for the needy, he tried to joke.

Sally was tired. It was difficult in the small flat with the baby and him cluttering up the place. He started going for long walks round London just to keep out of her way.

One day, half-way down Regent Street, he thought he saw Lou. He raced along the crowded street, weaving through the throng.

'Lou!' he called when within hearing distance.

She turned round.

'Jamie!' She smiled, the same heart-warming smile. 'Jamie, what a wonderful surprise.' She put up her cheek for him to kiss.

'God, Lou. You haven't changed a bit.'

'Oh, come on, Jamie. No need to fib. I'm nearly forty.'

'I'm not fibbing. You look wonderful.' And he was not saying it to please her, she did. Her skin was smooth and with no wrinkles he could see. Her blonde hair might now be helped, but subtly. She wore a smart trouser-suit in navy blue, a large Paisley shawl was thrown round her shoulders and pinned by a brooch.

'Trendy, aren't I?' She smiled at him. 'Let's pop into Liberty's, have a cup of tea and a natter — it's been too long.'

She waited, making small-talk, until the tea was served. 'Why don't you ever come home, Jamie?'

'I don't think I'd be welcome.'

'Don't be silly — lots of water's careered under the bridge since then. Your father misses you, you know.'

'You still . . . you know . . .?' He grinned sheepishly.

'Still his bit on the side? Yes. Amazing, isn't it? And my mum, God rest her, said it would never last.' She laughed.

'You love him, don't you?'

'Very much. And I loved you too, you know. It is possible.'

'Then why?' He had to ask, had to know even after all this time why she had been so cruel to him.

'Because he needed me more than you. You were a baby — your whole life ahead of you. I should never have allowed us to happen — stupid, but I couldn't resist you — do you know what I mean?'

'Yes, now,' he laughed.

'I had to push you, you see. I knew how you felt. Why, sometimes I thought you wanted to marry me.'

'I did.'

'See? See how wrong that would have been?'

'And the baby?'

'I got rid of it.' She did not look at him as she said this but seemed to find the sugar bowl of inordinate interest.

'Oh, Lou, poor Lou.'

'No. Nothing like that. It was my choice, Harry offered to support it. It wouldn't have been fair. What if I had the poor little bastard and he had to watch you and Esmond having everything? No, not fair at all.'

'Father could have married you.'

'And made himself a laughing-stock in the county? Come on, Jamie. Talk sense.'

'It wouldn't matter now.'

'Wouldn't it? Then you don't know much about your own class, Jamie. And you? How's married life and fatherhood?'

He wasn't quick enough to disguise the expression of sadness on his face.

'Not good? Tell Lou,' she said, and he was suddenly back in the nursery and he had a problem, and Nanny made him tell her so she could make things better. He told her about getting Sally pregnant, about how she had changed, about the honeymoon and Buster and the money.

'What did it feel like, losing all that?' She leaned across the table, her face alight with interest.

'Bloody wonderful – silly, isn't it? You'd think I'd have been in tears but it wasn't like that. I felt totally reckless, on the edge of an abyss, and I felt so alive and it was bloody marvellous. Still, I've learnt my lesson. I won't do that again.'

'Won't you?' She put her head on one side and smiled secretly at him.

'Don't smile like that, you'll get me all worked up again,' he joked – or half-joked.

'And you a married man,' she said archly. 'Got a job?'

A week later he received a summons from his father. And a week after that he had a job in a firm of stockbrokers in the City. He knew he had Lou to thank, still looking after him after all this time.

The Walters' were happy, so was Sally. She began to smile again and began her plans for a house with a garden, and the furniture brochures came out once more.

Everyone was happy except Jamie. He hated his job, he left the prison of the flat for the prison of the office and felt life sapping away from him. If it hadn't been for Fiona he sometimes thought he'd have done a bunk long ago.

For two years he'd been earning good money. His charm and contacts made him a valuable member of the team of stockbrokers; his commission grew.

He enjoyed time spent with Fiona, he was proud of her,

liked to play with her, but — and here was the rub — he felt there should be more to life. The baby, the house, the shopping, TV was all Sally could talk about. After a quick supper — usually something out of a tin, Sally was too tired to cook most evenings — the television went on and stayed on until bedtime. Soaps and quiz games were her favourites. Had she always been like this and he hadn't noticed?

Sex was something he dreamed about now. Oh, they made love — but *there* was a misnomer. They coupled for convenience. There was no excitement any more, no mystery. He knew every inch of her body and some nights, as his hands wandered over her, he wondered why he bothered, with the lack of response his efforts created.

He managed, with a mortgage, the house with a garden, but within twelve months Sally was angling for a house in the country.

'Dunstable way would be nice, close to Mum. Better for Fiona.'

It sounded like a death knell to Jamie.

It was the Magi-mix which changed his life. Sally's parents had brought her one home from France. Now all she could talk about was the damned machine and all their food was like pap, indistinguishable from Fiona's baby food. He'd taken to working late in the office and grabbing a bite on the way home.

He was about to enter a steak house for a large T-bone when he heard a familiar voice.

'Jamie Grantley, my dear boy, how are you?'

Jamie swung round to see Guthrie, but a changed Guthrie — the magnificent body had run to fat, the handsome features were now hidden in excess flesh.

'Guthrie! Good God, when was the last time I saw you?'

'Aeons ago, old sport. Care to join us at my club?

Eating alone is such a bore and my other guests are rather jolly chappies.'

Guthrie was host to a large table of friends – an assorted bunch from France, America, Germany. Some worked in films, others were writers, others painters. Jamie revelled in their varied conversation – and no one mentioned money.

As the conversation ebbed and flowed, Jamie listened avidly, enjoying himself enormously. And then he became aware that Guthrie, sitting beside him and usually the life and soul of the party, seemed to be detached from them all.

'You all right, Guthrie?' he asked.

'Me? Couldn't be better.' Guthrie grinned.

'No. Something's up. You're here, but not here, and you look sad.'

'Gracious, what a perspicacious little puppy you are.' Guthrie laughed but Jamie realized it was just a noise, his eyes had not joined in the merriment.

'Tell me.' Jamie put out a hand and took hold of one of Guthrie's and squeezed it. Guthrie sighed deeply and to his horror Jamie saw he looked as if he was about to cry. The noises of the restaurant appeared to fade and it was as if it were just the two of them – alone.

'Don't you know?

> *"Birth, and copulation, and death.*
> *That's all the facts when you come to brass tacks:*
> *I've been born and once is enough."'*

'Oh, Guthrie, what are you going on about?'

'I did try with you, dear boy, but I knew your looks would always preclude you enjoying a decent education – Eliot, sweetheart, says it all.'

'All what? Why are you so depressed?'

'Death is beautiful, they do say. Well, listen to me,

Jamie. It's no such thing. It destroys beauty, it does not create it. Death is pain and fear, putrefaction and stench – death is oozing orifices, death is hell.' He spoke urgently as if he was afraid Jamie might not understand.

'Who's died, Guthrie?' Jamie said quietly.

'You really didn't know, did you? And there I was stupidly thinking all the world must know, must share my grief. Sita died.'

'Oh, no. God, how awful.'

'Yes, it was rather. I expect you'd like to know how and are too polite to ask. Very commendable, Jamie. So silly, she had a tummy-ache and everyone was so stoned no one took much notice. It was her appendix and she had peritonitis and she just burned up with a fever and there was nothing I could do. All my money, and nothing.' He looked at his now very podgy fingers. 'We were married, you know, just before she died – pretty ceremony.' He smiled but Jamie saw the tears glistening in his eyes. 'She was happy with that. Now me?' He shrugged. 'I know I'll never find another woman, she was the one and only. Now I eat, I drink to excess, with a bit of luck I can accelerate my own end.'

'Please, Guthrie, don't talk like this.' And Jamie had to wipe away a tear from his own eye.

'Sweet Jamie. I always knew I was right to like you so much. All those snotty little fags and you were the only one with a soul.' He suddenly got to his feet. 'Too depressing for words. Come on, everyone, let's go to the Elysium, let's waste some money.' And he'd changed and was jolly again and Jamie was aware of the others and the noise surrounding them and felt he'd imagined their conversation.

At the gambling club Jamie played, it was inevitable. By the end of the evening he'd lost the building society account which was the beginning of the dream house near Dunstable.

There was more. Guthrie introduced him to a film producer – Forrest Ellingham.

'You're my Peter Ascot,' he said, pointing excitedly to Jamie.

'I beg your pardon?'

'Seen any James Bond films?'

'Of course.'

'I'll let you into a secret – my Ascot movies will wipe Bond off the screen. All that's been holding me up is who was to play Peter.'

'But I've never acted.'

'Oh, don't let that bother you, Jamie, my sweet. If Forrest here says you're right for the part, grab it in both your little paws and light a candle of thanks,' Guthrie advised. 'But in any case, Forrest, the dear boy's a natural. You should have seen his Juliet in the Lower Fourth, brought tears to the eyes.' Guthrie laughed.

'Give up your job? You're mad, you're bloody mad!' Sally was screaming at him the next morning.

'It's worth a try,' he said, beginning now to feel a bit foolish.

'A try? You have to want to act, die for it – not give it a try!'

'I think it's rather a case of it's my pretty face and body they're after.' He grinned sheepishly.

'Beefcake's two a penny. There are thousands of actors out there who could do it better than you.' She was angrily folding washing. 'Well, you're not going to do it and that's flat. I won't let you. You owe it to me and Fiona to carry on in your job. It's just like one of your stupid gambles. Just the same. If you resign then I'm leaving – that's a promise.'

'Then you'd better go,' Jamie said quietly.

'I mean it, Jamie.' Her voice was still raised.

'So do I.'

'And what about Fiona and me?' She stood arms akimbo, her once pretty face bitter now.

'For three fucking years all I've thought of is you and Fiona. Well, this is my chance and I'm taking it.'

'You're such a useless creep, Jamie.'

'Yes, aren't I? And you know what else? I gambled the building society account tonight and I bloody enjoyed doing it!'

'You bastard!' she screamed. 'I hate you!' she yelled as she flew out of the room.

In the morning Sally and Fiona had gone.

5

England – 1977–1984

Not everyone knew that Jamie had a daughter. It was not something he talked about, and in his entry in *Who's Who* he had omitted to mention his marriage to Sally. He sometimes wondered if he had excluded this information because he could then pretend to himself it had never happened and he could expunge the guilt that lingered – he couldn't, of course.

To those who had known him long enough to be aware of Fiona's existence, it was as if, after nearly seven years' separation from his daughter, Jamie had recovered from the distressing incident. He had not. It was all a feint. If anything, it was worse.

It was a rare day when Jamie did not think of Fiona and long to see her with a physical ache. Some nights he dreamed of her. It was always the same dream, she was still the four-year-old he had left, lying snuggled safe in his arms. When he awoke to find it a dream he was capable of weeping silent tears.

It was six years, six months, two weeks and three days since her small hand had held his, trustingly. She had been five when he stopped seeing her. It hurt badly, still did, but being with her for a few too short hours as they ambled around the parks and zoo and then having to say goodbye to her pained him even more and damaged Fiona. She clung to him, cried, screamed when it was time for him to leave. He loved his daughter far too much to put her through this weekly trauma. Better, he decided, to bow out of her life and let her forget him as she undoubtedly would. He would not forget her, he would keep the love safe and one day, he hoped, when she was older and curious, then one day she would come and find him again.

His hope that Sally would meet someone else had been realized barely two years after she left him. From refusing to countenance a divorce she was suddenly badgering him for one. For several weeks, knowing there would be a new man in Fiona's life, he suffered from a jealousy that he had never felt over a woman. Then reason prevailed and he told himself it was good for Fiona to have a new, responsible father, one who would give her stability and security – he was an accountant, after all.

Of course his intention not to see Fiona, although carefully explained to Sally, had been misinterpreted. Any call from her intoned his shortcomings as a father. He had stiff letters from Mr Walters, tearful ones from Mrs Walters. He sweetened their disapproval by never faltering on his maintenance payments and paying way above what the courts had demanded.

His firm resolve not to interfere in Fiona's upbringing took a severe knock when Sally wrote to inform him – not to ask – that she was to take her stepfather's name, with the lame excuse that it would make it easier for her at school. His threat to stop all maintenance if they did so scotched that idea. He was not surprised when a couple of years later a formal adoption was requested. He'd fight that if it cost him every penny, he informed them. Sally dropped the idea but not before letting him know, yet again, how selfish and neglectful he was. He was not. He wrote to Fiona regularly – not easy, for he loathed writing letters at the best of times, and made no easier since he no longer knew the girl to whom he wrote. He contrived chatty letters about his acting, his travels. She never replied. He sent presents every Christmas and birthday even though they were never acknowledged. He never failed to pay his maintenance, her school fees, anything Sally asked for. But he'd done more than that.

By the time he was thirty Jamie Grantley was Jamie Grant, a six-foot-four, dense-muscled, blond, blue-eyed, international movie idol. World-famous and richly rewarded.

Forrest Ellingham had been right and Sally had been wrong. Jamie had passed his screen tests with flying colours. Within eighteen months the Peter Ascot film was a box office hit, as were the four sequels, and the one now in production would undoubtedly be as well. With each film his fee increased until he was one of the highest-paid actors in the business. Jamie earned a fortune but was not rich.

Jamie knew himself and to ensure Fiona's future had put aside a goodly sum from his earnings to set up a trust fund for her. After that he felt his money was his to do what he wanted with.

And he had.

He lived in the fast lane. He had a spacious flat in London; he was about to buy a villa in Switzerland; he was always in the lists of best-dressed men, English and American; his girlfriends were legion and not one ever complained he was mean; he ate in the best restaurants, drank the best wine, drove the fastest, latest cars. He had everything.

And he was miserable – the one person he truly loved he rarely saw and never spoke to.

He began to roister. He became equally famous for his escapades in bars and nightclubs around the world. When not working he could go for weeks and never be sober and in such condition the fights were frequent, with reporters always in evidence. His exploits were splashed over newspapers in every language of every country where his films were shown.

The production company had initially worried and he'd had the riot act read to him time and again. When this happened he always felt as if he was back at school and being warned that if he did it again he'd be expelled. He always apologized, admitted the error of his ways, smiled the crooked smile that made women swoon in their millions, and went straight out to continue living in the only way he knew to keep the haemorrhage of pain at bay.

Then the studio bosses woke up to the publicity phenomenon that their star's wild ways produced. And since, when about to go into a production, he always took himself to a health farm for a month to sober up, tidy up and get back into form, and since, when working, he never touched a drop, the studio jumped on to the band wagon and gave press releases on escapades he hadn't even been involved in.

Spain – 1984

Jamie was tired. He was proud of his claim that he never used a double in his films – in fact he did, but only when a stunt was so dangerous that the insurance companies wouldn't countenance it, not that the fans knew. Everything else he did himself. Today he could have wished stunts did not exist. He'd spent most of the day in the saddle of a black-skinned brute with an equally black heart, as Peter Ascot galloped across the sands of what was supposedly the Black Sea but was in fact in Spain – cheaper to shoot – being pursued by a member of the KGB. He was tired, bruised from a series of tumbles, hot and, unusually for him, for he was famed for his easy nature, teetering on the edge of bad temper. And wondering if at thirty-five, with five and a half Ascot films in the bag, he wasn't getting too old for quite so much athleticism.

'Jamie, fancy a party tonight?'

'You have to be joking, I'm knackered,' he said to his co-star Shene Storey as his dresser struggled to remove his skin-tight boots.

'Oh, come on. It's at this fab castle – some Greek shipowner's bash. Everyone who's anyone will be there.'

'Not really. I'd imagined a Radox bath and bed.'

'Christ, you're getting old, Jamie. Don't be such a bore. Take me, I don't want to go alone.' Shene flicked the mane of red hair which was her trademark and pouted her bee-sting lips which were her other.

'Okay, then – just for an hour. It'll make publicity happy.'

For the duration of the shoot publicity had been building Jamie and Shene up into a romantic number. This had everyone in the know in stitches since Shene was one of the most notorious lesbians in the profession.

She was right about the castle – it really was fabulous. It was built of stone of a strange pink and yellowish hue, as if over the centuries it had been soaking up the hot Spanish sun until its original colour had faded, like a fresco. It was square, forbidding and yet beautiful. Moorish, Jamie presumed.

The party was large but then it would have to be to fill the huge, echoing rooms of the castle – a small soirée would have rattled around like peas in a pod, he decided, as he mounted a long stone staircase, the stunning Shene on his arm, to meet his host for the first time and be greeted as a long-lost friend.

One thing fame had ensured for Jamie was that he need never be alone. As soon as he and Shene entered the large hall they were surrounded by people, all of whom appeared to think they were close acquaintances, and yet, for the life of him, Jamie could not remember meeting them.

'Excuse me, Jamie, but I wonder if I might introduce my wife. She's just longing to meet you.'

'Walt! Nice to see you,' he could say quite genuinely, for here *was* a face he remembered. He'd met Walt at several charity dos in New York and had even posed for some advertisements for a natural products shampoo he'd manufactured – not out of friendship but for the huge cheque Walt gave him, most of which he'd lost on the Kentucky Derby.

'Lord Grantley, this is such a pleasure.' Charity Fielding held out her thin, claw-like hand which looked too fragile to support the weight of gold and diamonds on it.

'Oh, call me Jamie, please,' he said in his lovely seductive voice which made Charity giggle girlishly so that for a moment she lost the acid expression on her face, which normally looked as if she'd sucked a lemon and had forgotten to spit it out.

'Why, how cute. I'll call you Jamie if you call me Charity.' She continued to simper and to hold on to his hand longer than necessary. 'I just don't understand why we've never met before, Jamie.'

'Yes, odd, isn't it, Charity – such a shame,' he lied smoothly.

'I was saying to Walt we'd be just so honoured if you cared to join us on a cruise we're taking in this little boat we've borrowed,' she gushed.

'It's not so little,' Walt said – wearily, thought Jamie, as if the idea was probably his wife's and not his.

'I'd be honoured too if you could put up with me being sea-sick.' Jamie always accepted such invitations: it helped his cash flow to be a guest for as much of the year as possible.

'Tell me, Jamie. The rumour is that Guthrie Everyman is coming. Do you know him? Could you introduce us or, better still, persuade him to come on the cruise with us?'

Jamie looked at the woman, as thin as a stick-insect and as predatory as any praying mantis. 'Oh, I'm sorry to disappoint you there – Guthrie never leaves dry land, he won't even fly.'

'Really? How peculiar. How does he get about?'

'By car and train.'

'But the Channel?'

'He's waiting for the tunnel to be built.' He began to look over her shoulder, already tired of her, and Walt, as if sensing it, pointed out that the King of Spain had just arrived. In Charity's book monarchy took precedence over any film star and she was happy to be led away.

He looked around for Shene just in time to see her floating off arm in arm with a stunning blonde German countess. Since Shene had taken a shine to her, Jamie was glad he had not come on strong with her, as he might have done.

'Times are difficult, aren't they, dear boy? You never know who is gay and who isn't these days!' A voice behind him spoke his thoughts for him.

'Guthrie! Wonderful to see you!'

'I always get such a welcome from you, sweetness.'

'Because I'm always glad to see you. I think you're my guardian angel.'

'How droll! Me an angel – I've been called some things, dear boy!' Guthrie laughed his wonderful rumbling laugh that seemed to start in his nether regions, rattled around his rotund stomach, gaining strength as it barrelled about his chest, to emerge loud, triumphant, but gloriously falsetto the other end.

'Quite a bash, isn't it?' Jamie nodded at the throng below the gallery they were standing on.

'Demetrius likes to show off.'

'I thought you didn't like crowds and big parties.'

'I don't. But sometimes duty calls, dear boy, haven't you discovered?'

'Duty?'

'I work on and off as an ambassador for UNICEF – I wanted some loot out of our little Greek friend. He collects celebrities, I collect money.'

'I didn't know that, Guthrie – about UNICEF, I mean.'

'We've all got to do our little bit in this wicked, wicked world – try to set the balance right.'

'Yes, I suppose so.' Jamie agreed but a little unsurely. His own charitable commitment stretched to the odd contribution, usually at Christmas, to the Retired Jockeys' Fund. And no doubt, in a roundabout way, to his wine merchant's pension plan. 'By the way, there's an American woman here – you know, New York socialite desperate to meet you. Her husband's loaded, he might be of use to you.'

'Thank you, dear boy, but I don't think so. I'm allergic to that sort of woman – they bring me out in a rash, I swear to it – they're all always dropping squeaky farts from eating too little food and they *all* try to put me on a diet. No, I've done my bit for the kiddies today, I was just leaving when I saw your handsome lineaments.'

'Why don't you speak English?' Jamie laughed.

'But I do, sweetness, it's yobs like you who don't.'

'Jesus! Who the hell is *that*?'

'There, see what I mean? Such abuse of language.' Guthrie tutted. 'Who? Where?' he said, and craned his neck to see.

'Over by the fireplace. The tall girl.'

'That's Mica.'

'Mica who?'

'Just Mica. Want to meet her?'

Every day of his life Jamie was surrounded by beautiful women, but never in his life, he decided immediately, had he seen, let alone met, anyone like Mica.

She was six feet tall, as willowy as the stalk of a lily, and as graceful. Her neck was so long and slender it looked too slight to hold the weight of her proud head. Her black hair was scraped back severely from her hauntingly beautiful face which was so perfect that it was impossible to know which feature to praise the most. Her eyes appeared black, but a soft black like velvet or the centre of a pansy, and then she turned and the light reflected in her eyes and they were the brown of an autumn leaf. Her cheek-bones were high as if sculpted, making the hollows of her cheeks deep, and they seemed to lead the eye to her full and generous mouth above a perfectly rounded chin. She stood slightly apart from the crowd around her, their noise swirled about her and she gave the impression of an oasis of calm amidst the social racket. She watched the other guests with a serious expression, appearing to assess them, as if she did not quite approve.

'Mica, love. Meet my great chum Jamie Grantley.'

'How do you do,' she said politely in an attractive, light voice, almost like a child's. She did not smile but looked solemnly at Jamie as she shook his hand. He felt she was looking into his soul.

'Nice party,' he said, his mind seemingly having gone blank and unable to think of anything smart or witty.

'Noisy,' she replied.

'You don't like big parties?'

'Not much.'

'Neither do I,' he fibbed, feeling once more on firmer ground. 'Would you like to go somewhere quieter?'

'Yes, I would.' She turned on her heel, glancing once

over her shoulder to indicate, he presumed, that he was to follow her. He did. She wove through the crowds with a smooth, gliding walk of such elegance but such sensuality that Jamie found his mind rattling with comparisons — like a leopard, a panther, a cheetah, a snake. Shit! What a woman, he thought. Like Salome, he eventually preferred.

He drove her to a small restaurant the crew had discovered high in the hills and away from the hubbub of the busy coastal towns. She said little but sat upright opposite him, her gaze rarely moving from his face, listening intently as if she was learning everything he said.

'You don't smile much.' He smiled at her, encouraging her to do the same.

'I do when there's something to smile about.'

He wasn't sure how to answer that as he wasn't sure how to talk to her, how to amuse her, how to get her interested in him. Except he knew he must. He wanted desperately to entertain her, to keep her with him. He felt hypnotized by her.

So he talked non-stop — a gush of words, a torrent of inconsequential chat. He told her about the film, about himself, about his life. A monologue which she listened to intently, always with the large, almost sombre eyes watching his face.

He felt he was talking to a child. Despite the expensive white gown, the gold at her slender neck and wrists, there was an air of innocence about her as if the world she moved in had not touched her.

He wondered aloud if she had been discovered in some wasteland or jungle and was a stranger in the Western world. No, she told him with no laughter at the idea. She came from Peckham. But nothing more was forthcoming.

'Do you ... are you ... Mica, do you belong to someone?'

At this she reacted, bridling like an angry colt. 'I belong to no one.'

'Of course. Silly question. It was just . . . I'd like to see more of you.' Jamie, seducer of hundreds, felt like a gauche schoolboy.

'Thank you,' she said, and he was not sure if she would or she wouldn't agree to it.

'With your looks you should be a model.' He knew it was crass as he said it, knew it was something she must have heard a thousand times before. But at his words she leaned forward, animated, excited.

'It's what I want to do.'

'Then why don't you?'

'I tried. In London. I did get some work once but it was tacky — not what I dreamed of. The photographer presumed I'd sleep with him. He didn't like it when I hit him. He put the word out that I was trouble and I got no more work and my agent dropped me. And I earned so little for my trouble.' Ingenuously, she told him how much. 'Everyone says to really succeed I need to go to America.' She sat back as if as surprised as he at the amount she had said. She smiled for the first time, a small, tentative smile showing her perfect white teeth and just the tip of her very pink tongue.

'And are you going?'

'I don't know. I'm a bit scared to. There are such creeps around.' She shuddered and he wondered what had happened to her to make her this way.

'Scared of what?' he asked kindly.

'The unknown.'

'I'll go with you. Hold your hand,' he heard himself say.

'I'd like that.' And then she beamed at him and the distant look disappeared and she was even more beautiful, and Jamie knew he was falling in love.

'I'd better go now,' she said abruptly, suddenly standing.

'Of course, where?'

'The castle.'

They drove back in silence most of the way. Once or twice Jamie tried to get her talking again but she seemed lost in thought.

'What are you thinking?' he finally asked.

'If you meant it . . . about America, or whether it was a joke.'

'I wasn't joking.'

'I see,' she replied, as the car drew up outside the castle where he could see the party was still in progress. He started to get out of the car. She put one long, slender hand on his. 'No, it's better you don't come. I'll call you . . .' And like a sinuous shadow she slid from the car.

Mica was Demetrius Papadopoulos's mistress — one of many. Jamie discovered this uncomfortable fact the following day. Not difficult to do for Shene was all agog to know where he had been with Mica, as had most of the party.

'But he's so old. She can't be more than twenty,' he said aghast.

'Nineteen, actually. I agree with you, a lovely creature like that with that old goat.' And Shene shuddered. 'Such a waste.' She sighed.

'I didn't think.'

'Men rarely do!' Shene laughed. 'Didn't you twig the dress? It reeked of Paris — and the gold — must have been a pound or two of it slung round her.'

'She seems sad.'

'Can you blame her?'

'I think I want to marry her.'

'Wow! You don't hang about, do you? It might be more difficult than you think. I shouldn't think the Greek will let her go without a fight. He could be a dangerous man to cross.'

'How? How could he hurt me?' Jamie laughed.

6

1984–5

'But she's black!'

'So?'

'You can't marry a negress.'

'You were right the first time, Father. She's black – that's how you describe her. And as far as I'm concerned the colour of her skin is irrelevant.'

'It might be to you, James. Nothing about you surprises me any more. But society won't like it and neither do I.'

'Stuff society. I don't move in those circles.'

'Your children would be half-castes.'

'Yes, but I'd prefer you to say of mixed blood.'

'But a half-caste in the House of Lords!'

'Oh, Father!' Jamie laughed but it was a mirthless sound. 'What the hell does the House of Lords matter – there probably won't even be one by the time my son is old enough to take his seat. And what if he did? Wouldn't it be a good idea? We're a multi-racial society – or supposed to be. What better? This is the eighties, Dad.'

'You've left it a bit late for any such pronouncements to be taken seriously. You are a tiresome son, James. Your marriage to that strange little suburban creature a failure. You have a child you never see. Your publicity brings only shame to the family. You're a drunk, a gambler, a waster.'

'I made more last year than your investments brought in five,' Jamie said proudly, beginning to feel a bit heated and wishing his father would stop, for he didn't want to argue.

'And I hope the money lasts for you, James – though I doubt it. And what then? What use have you made of your ludicrous earnings? What investments?'

'I enjoy life.'

'Don't you think there's a little more to life than that?

Responsibility for the position you hold? Examples to be set?'

'Oh, for fuck's sake, Father! What sort of example are you to me? Who's kept a mistress tucked away down here for years – just because she wasn't socially acceptable, might embarrass you? Eh? Tell me, Father. Why didn't you marry Lou? Because you're a snob. Well, I'm not.'

'You'll apologize for speaking to me in that manner, James. What I do with my private life is no concern of yours.'

'Then neither is mine of yours, Father. I love Mica, and whether you and your society accept her or not, I don't give a stuff. And no, I won't apologize – now or ever.'

'So be it,' his father said coldly, turning in his chair, and for what, to Jamie, seemed an age stared out of his study window at the immaculate gardens and parkland of Grantley beyond, land which had belonged to his family for centuries.

'There's nothing I can do about this,' he said, more to himself than to Jamie who allowed himself a small smile of triumph. His father turned back to face him. 'Don't rely on me for anything more, James. I fear you go too far. I wish I could congratulate you on your intended marriage, but I'm afraid I can't.' He picked up his pen and returned to the papers on his desk. The interview was evidently over.

Jamie had seen Mica only twice since their first meeting, and though on a weekend business trip from Spain he had informed his father of his intention, he had yet to speak to Mica. When he did propose she was afraid, there was no doubt about it. At his words, formally delivered on one knee, ring in hand, like a scene from a movie, she had not smiled, laughed, shown any joy. Instead she looked nervously over her shoulder as if checking they were not being watched.

'Look, Mica, I know about you and Demetrius. It doesn't matter to me, if that's what's worrying you.'

'No, it's not, it's Demetrius himself. You don't know him.' And her great dark eyes, filled with fear, looked at him and he felt such an anger and concern for her well-being.

'He can't hurt me and once we're married what can he do to you?'

'He's like a spider, he collects people. He likes to own them.'

'Well, you're one who's getting out of the collection. I'll go and see him.'

'No . . . please don't do that. It would not be wise. I'll tell him. I'll tell him tonight.' She put out her hand and grabbed at his arm almost desperately. She was pleading with him in her voice, her eyes.

'All right, I don't like it, mind you. Until tomorrow. I'll collect you and we'll return to London – we've wrapped up the film here.'

'No, I'll meet you. I'll meet you in London,' she insisted.

He was nervous as he waited for her to arrive at his flat. He chain-smoked and paced up and down, back and forth, unable to settle. As the hours ticked by he worked himself into an anxious state. Why should she come to him, why give up all Demetrius could offer? How could he have been so conceited? Hell, she hadn't even accepted his proposal of marriage. Come to think of it, she'd said little, had shown no pleasure – well, that put him in his place and no mistake. He'd presumed too much. Normally women came when he called. Women fell into bed with him at the earliest opportunity – any other woman would have quickly accepted his proposal, before he changed his mind. Not Mica. He shook his head in disbelief at himself. Here he was, hopefully on the verge of marriage with a woman he'd met four times – each time a stolen few hours – a woman he hadn't even slept with. And yet, deep down inside him he knew he was doing the right thing.

The morning became afternoon and then evening. With each phone call he prayed it would be her – it never was. He felt sick with apprehension, miserable with despair, angry at her for playing games with him. And then at ten at night the bell rang, and when he opened the door she was standing there. He scooped her into his arms and held her so tight, he could have wept with relief and all his anger disappeared.

'I thought you weren't coming,' he said as finally he let go of her and helped her remove her coat.

'I said I would.'

'But I thought this morning . . .'

'It was difficult . . .'

He led her down the long, dimly lit corridor of his mansion flat and into the drawing-room.

'That's better, now I can see you, darling.' He turned her towards him. 'Shit!' he shouted. 'Who did that to you? That neanderthal oaf Demetrius? I'll fucking kill him!' Gingerly he touched the swelling at her temple.

'I fell down the stairs.' She winced at his touch.

'Mica, don't lie to me. He hit you, didn't he?'

'It was nothing.' She looked away from him. 'This is a nice room,' she said haltingly, and then without any warning she put her hands to her face and began to cry. 'I'm sorry. I'm sorry,' she kept repeating.

'Shush, there. Why are you apologizing?' He placed his hands each side of her face and kissed her eyes, her nose, her mouth, every part of that wonderful face – kissing the hurt and the sadness in her eyes away.

'You're safe now. I love you, I'll look after you for ever,' he whispered.

'I wish I could believe that.' Her voice was muffled by his jacket. He pushed her gently from him the better to see her.

'What makes you say such a thing? Of course I will.'

'I'm tired of being hit. I'm weary of it all – I've had enough.'

'I'd never hit you. I couldn't imagine hitting a woman, but especially you.'

She looked at him as if she did not believe him. He felt hurt by her attitude but at the same time wondered what could have happened, what had been done to her to make her, at nineteen, talk as if she'd had enough of life. Not knowing what to say, he held her to him, gently stroking her hair in long, rhythmic strokes.

'I'm sorry,' she said again. 'Sorry for making a fuss.' She pushed herself away from him.

'There's no need to say that ... ever ... not to me. Drink?' He poured her a large brandy. 'Have you eaten?' he thought to ask before handing her the glass. She shook her head. 'Then you can't have this, not on an empty tummy – whatever next, as my nanny would have said. Come, I'll make you an omelette – you have no idea how good I am in the kitchen. I've often thought that when the looks go I can become a celebrity chef.'

'You'll always be handsome.'

'You think so? Or are you kidding?' He laughed and pulled her with him towards the kitchen.

While she ate hungrily he went to collect her bags and then remembered she'd had none with her.

'You've no luggage?' he said when he returned with a bottle of wine for them both.

'I wanted nothing of Demetrius's. Nothing.' She shuddered.

'Great. Tomorrow we'll hit Bond Street with the plastic. I like shopping with credit cards – it makes me feel I'm getting everything for free.'

'Jamie, you are silly!' And finally she was laughing.

'Mica!' he sighed, and lifting her gently from the chair held her to him. He kissed her hair, the arch of her eyebrow, her closed eyes. He covered her face with soft, tender kisses, murmuring his love for her, his need for her. Her lithe body relaxed in his arms. He caressed the nape of her neck, his hand inching down her spine, slowly unzipping the smart black dress. Suddenly she wrenched herself from his arms, knocking his hand away from the zip, and she was tearing at it herself. She stepped from the dress, kicking it to one side, revealing her naked, fine lean body. Her nipples were erect, darker even than the rest of her. Her brown eyes were open wide and never stopped looking at him as if gauging his reaction. She hid no part of herself but stood proudly in front of his admiring gaze.

'I want you,' she said in a low and husky voice. She stepped towards him and twined one long leg around his and began to rub her black-as-night pubic hair against the roughness of his jeans. She writhed on his leg, panting, sighing. She arched her back, making her breasts jut out, and she was pulling at her nipples, crying out at her own self-inflicted pain.

Jamie had to stand with legs apart to keep his balance as she rocked him with her convulsive movement. With one hand she swept her meal clattering to the floor and lifted herself easily on to the table, never missing a beat as she continued to rub herself against his leg as if she wanted it inside her.

'Now!' she cried out and her hands were at his flies like little birds of prey, frantically searching for him, cradling him, pulling him free. She bent forward with the litheness of a ballet dancer and her full lips caressed him, sucking him. Her mouth darted along his penis, one moment with the touch of a butterfly, the next with such strength he thought she intended to suck him dry. He felt his legs weaken, was afraid he would fall, knew he could not hold out much longer. As if seeing his need she leaned back, raising her pelvis to him invitingly, and guided him towards her, her hips moving rhythmically up and down even before he entered her.

Finesse left him. At the feel of her labia enclosing him, the ripple of muscle in her vaginal wall against him, he plunged deep inside her, rode into her hard. He pumped himself in, out, in, out, feeling massive, feeling supreme, feeling as he never had before.

He shouted her name as he came, clinging to her as she clung to him. And then he could stand no more and collapsed on top of her and a wine bottle toppled over and a glass crashed to the floor and they laughed with happiness and joy in each other.

The following morning, as he had promised, he took her shopping. He was so proud of her as in shop after shop she tried on clothes which looked as if they had been made for her. Mica stood calmly, almost regally, as the exclusive shops' assistants fussed about her; tweaking a pleat, rearranging a bodice, a hemline – making what looked perfect sublime. When he asked her if she liked a particular garment or if she wanted it, she simply looked at him solemnly.

'If you like it,' she said. He wished she could have shown a little more enthusiasm but put it down to her natural shyness.

Later at home he sat on the bed sipping a glass of wine and watching as she neatly put away the dresses, trousers, sweaters, underwear, handbags and shoes he'd purchased for her. She moved with such grace and precision that it was a pleasure to watch her.

'You're very tidy,' he said.

'I like looking after my things.'

'Happy?' he asked.

'You're being very kind.'

'It was my pleasure.' He bowed his head. For some time she continued her task, saying nothing, and he watched her silently, wishing he could think of something else to say.

'When was the last time you lived with a woman here?' she asked suddenly.

'I haven't,' he said simply, but with lifting heart: did such a question mean she was jealous of his past as he of hers? 'After my marriage broke up I didn't want to live with someone again on a temporary basis, only if I remarried, and I didn't think anyone would have me.' He grinned but she said nothing. 'I suppose you could call me old-fashioned,' he said, feeling silly, in this modern age, to think in such a way.

'Then if you had a girlfriend where did you take her?'

'Well, here. But I didn't think that was what you meant – I thought you were talking about long-term relationships. I haven't really gone in for those. Odd nights, odd weekends, I've entertained here.' He felt silly again using such a euphemism for screwing, getting laid, fucking – it had never been making love. He would have liked to explain that to her but felt too shy to do so. Stupid! He crossed and then uncrossed his feet and stared with rapt attention at his black silk socks. 'Hope you don't mind. I'd loathe to have to change the furniture. Mind you, I will if you want.'

'No, that's not necessary. I like it. Swedish Biedermeier, isn't it?'

'Why, yes,' he said, and realized too late how surprised he must sound and how patronizing. He deserved the scathing look she gave him as she returned to her tidying-away of things.

'Tomorrow, how about us venturing into distant Peckham so that I can ask your parents for permission to marry

you – all proper like?' He lapsed into cockney, he supposed, to cover his further embarrassment at just how
conventional he could be.

'No!' she shouted, and stood, a new dress slipping from
its hanger in her hands. 'No. That won't be necessary,' she
said hurriedly.

'Are you afraid they won't approve of you marrying a
honky?' he laughed, confident in his love.

'Whether they approve or not is of no importance to
me. I've left, I'm not going back.'

'What about your mum, won't she be worrying about
you? We can't keep this quiet for long, you know – with
me involved the publicity will be enormous.'

'My mother is dead. I care nothing for my father and
brothers, they no longer exist for me.' And she rearranged
the dress on its hanger. It was the cold way she had said it,
so matter-of-factly as if she spoke of objects rather than
people, that made him shudder.

'What goes with your folk?' he asked.

'I don't wish to discuss it.'

'But I do.' He jumped off the bed. 'Tell me.'

'You don't want to hear.'

'I want to know everything about you, then I'll be able
to understand you better.'

She looked at him long and hard, her beautiful face
with no emotion he could discern upon it. 'Really? Does it
help you to know my father fucked me from the age of
eight, and that my mother knew and did nothing? And
that my brothers as they grew took turns with me too?
That's my family,' she said, almost defiantly.

'Jesus.' He stood wide-eyed, mouth slack with shock
and speechless.

'Bet you wish you hadn't asked now.'

'My poor darling. Oh, Jesus, my love. What can I do?
What can I say? I want to take the pain away from you.'

'It's probably a bit late for that,' she replied, turned on

her heel and walked as elegantly as ever to the bathroom. He heard the key turn in the lock and no matter how he entreated her, she stayed there for the next two hours.

They flew to America to marry. He had some post-production work to do but first he had an aftershave endorsement that he was keen to tie up in New York. Upon their arrival at their hotel, the Pierre, Walt Fielding was one of the first to call.

'Charity and I wondered if you'd care to dine with us tonight – if you're not too jet-lagged?'

'How very kind,' Jamie said in his best English style, for he knew it was what his American friends liked to hear.

They did more than dine. Charity enthusiastically took Mica under her wing and took her to shop for her trousseau. She arranged a shower for her in her Park Avenue apartment and Mica received wonderful presents from people she'd never met before. Charity's greatest disappointment was that Jamie had already arranged the venue for the wedding – that was sad, it would have been such kudos for her to have a star of Jamie's calibre marry in her weekend home in Connecticut. But still, there was compensation in Walt giving the bride away, even if it meant they had to fly to California. Charity loathed the West Coast – for her it lacked the chic of the East, she was fond of saying.

In the Green Room on the Johnny Carson show, Jamie met up with Guthrie.

'Good Lord, what are you doing here?' he asked him.

'I've a show opening on Broadway – got to do the old publicity bit, you know. The days when things just lifted of their own accord are over, more's the pity.'

'How did they get you here? You never fly.'

'Sedated and on the QE2, and never again – my poor old tum will never be the same again – and worse, my steward was ugly.'

'Oh, Guthrie, you twit.'

'Dear heart, so sweet, still speaking the Queen's English, I hear.' He cupped a large podgy hand behind his ear. 'And what are you here for?'

'I'm getting married. It's news, believe it or not.'

'Really? And who's the fortunate or rather unfortunate blushing bride?'

'Why, Mica. You should, by rights, be giving her away – you introduced her to me.'

'Did I? How remiss of me.'

'What does that mean?'

'I hate to be responsible for you taking such a mistaken step.'

'We're not all queer.' Jamie tried to laugh but found it difficult to do so for he was beginning to feel angry with his old friend and was not sure why.

'No, we're not, are we? Have you thought about this long and hard, Jamie?'

'Of course I have.'

'But if I'm not mistaken the last time I saw you was what . . . barely three weeks go. And now you tell me you're getting married.'

'That's right. So what?' he said defensively.

'Sounds to me as if you need the sane voice of an old friend. You don't know the girl.'

'I don't need to – she's all I've ever dreamed of.'

'Looks, yes, but intellect?'

'That sounds close to being offensive, Guthrie.'

'Does it? Then I apologize. I don't mean to be so, just wise. I've seen it so often. Are you sure you haven't fallen in love with her beauty? She is ravishingly beautiful.'

'That's a shit thing to say.'

'What, that she's beautiful?' He laughed and then,

suddenly serious, he grabbed hold of Jamie's arm and held it tight. 'Listen, Jamie. You can marry out of your class, your financial stratum, but the one thing you can't do is to marry out of your intellectual sphere. You're not the brightest bulb in the great chandelier of life but you're megawatts ahead of the lovely Mica. She will bore you senseless.'

'Fuck off, Guthrie. Who the fuck do you think you are?' He wanted to lunge at him.

'Promises, promises.' Guthrie stepped nimbly back.

'Jamie. Guthrie. My pleasure – are you on the same programme?'

'Why, Dieter von Weiher. What a surprise!' Guthrie took the proffered hand limply. And why are *you* here – a little light relief? Surely not.'

Dieter looked puzzled. 'No, I've just paid a record price for a rather fine Italian triptych of the fifteenth century. I—'

'Oh, spend, spend, Dieter. What a profligate little Teuton you are!' And Guthrie playfully patted Dieter's hand.

Their residence qualifications fulfilled, their blood tests in order, they were married in the garden of Forrest Ellingham's wonderful mansion in Beverly Hills. And Jamie knew he was going to live happily ever after.

At least, of his family, Poppy was overjoyed when she read of his marriage in the newspapers. She resurfaced, sent a long telegram of excited congratulations and insisted they visit her at the earliest possibility.

Jamie only saw his mother at rare intervals. In the whole of his thirty-five years, excluding the first six, he reckoned he'd visited her a dozen times at the most. She was really almost a stranger to him, he saw his friends a hundred times more often. But whenever he arrived it did not seem to matter, she welcomed him as if she had been waiting anxiously, longing for this reunion. He never stayed long for he had learnt, over the years, that Poppy tired of other people as quickly as she tired of husbands. He had seen Sven go and had not been surprised; he had felt he was too serious for his butterfly of a mother. Once there had been River, an Australian as stupid as his name, in Jamie's opinion, and redeemed only by his colossal wealth. Now finally there was Philippe, an urbane, sophisticated, impoverished, noble Frenchman. Not that his lack of money was a problem, for Poppy, with the help of an astute lawyer, was a wealthy woman from her various divorce settlements.

She was now the elegant, still beautiful, fifty-five-year-old mistress of Philippe's château in the Loire valley – and she appeared to be enjoying every minute of it.

'I think your mother is happy you married me to spite your father,' Mica said as they walked through the winter grounds of the château. She was looking delectable in a long fox fur Jamie had bought her in Paris.

'I don't understand.'

'I'm black, which has made your father furious, so she approves and welcomes us just to annoy him further. No doubt she will make certain he knows of our visit.'

'But I think she likes you.'

'Do you? I don't think your mother likes anyone except herself.'

'Perhaps,' he replied and looked away, pointing to a pheasant flying low, so she could not see the expression in his eyes. How stupid of me, he thought, a grown man still wanting his mother to love him.

'Do you gamble, Jamie?'

'Why do you ask?'

'Everyone tells me you do.'

'Oh, I enjoy the odd flutter. But I'm not how I used to be. There was a phase when I'd bet on two flies.' He laughed at the memory. 'But no more.' He was not lying. He backed the odd horse and still enjoyed an occasional game of backgammon but something had happened. Now he could afford to gamble he did so rarely.

'Good, I'm glad. I wouldn't have liked that. Money isn't for throwing away.'

'No, you're right.' He was amazed now, four months into their marriage, that he had thought her a child when he had first met her. In so many ways he had to admit she was far more adult than he, and far more self-contained than he would ever be.

'By the way, next week, after Christmas is out of the way, I'm flying to New York,' she announced as they continued their walk.

'Really? Well, I'm free. I'll come too. Why are you going?'

'I made some modelling contacts while we were there. Charity introduced me. I've people to meet.'

'But you'll need me to hold your hand.'

'No, that won't be necessary.'

'Oh, I see,' he said, and felt intolerably hurt at how distant she always seemed to be with him, as if she had no need of him.

In bed at night he could forget how self-contained she was. At night she became his enthusiastic lover. At night all was well. With her he enjoyed sex in a way he never had before. He who had bedded hundreds of women and thought he knew it all found himself constantly surprised. She desired him and had no inhibitions in showing him how much she craved him. In bed she was liberated and free, and in bed she made him feel the most important man in the world.

'Do you love me, Mica?' he asked, after they made love one night.

'Why do you ask?'
'You never say.'
'Is it necessary to?'
'To me it is.'
'I love you,' she said, almost obediently.

When she left for that trip to New York he waited in London, in fear that she would not return to him. He tried to rationalize his fears — why, after such a short time, should she desert him? There was no need. She returned triumphant, her career had begun.

It was her aloofness and detachment he feared most and yet it was these very traits which fascinated him more than anything. He felt there was a wall she had built about herself. And how, with her past, could he blame her? It was a wall he would like to tear down with his bare hands. He hated her father with an inarticulate rage. He had to help her, longed to do so. It was why they had met, he often told himself. He was there to help her, heal her. One day she would be different. One day she would be whole again. She would relax with him and be totally his.

7

1987–1992

Jamie did not like to think about how he felt deep inside him in those secret recesses of the mind. He believed quite strongly that such thinking was a dangerous pastime, that too much self-analysis could lead to trouble. He was in a profession which was obsessed by self and motivation and he did not share many of his colleagues' faith in shrinks. But all the same, even he had tried to analyse why, once Mica was in his life, he thought less about his daughter.

He never discussed this with his wife, he did not want her to misunderstand and think she was a replacement child – no way. And in any case they did not talk on that level. He still sent Fiona presents but the longing for her seemed to have disappeared. Maybe, he thought, he had only enough love for one person and that was Mica.

He loved Mica, he was sure – he was proud of her and her beauty, he missed her when she was away. But in the night, traitorous thoughts had recently begun to surface. Could what they had be love? What, after all, did they have in common? And how was it possible to love someone who was so cold in return? He felt sad and horribly alone when this thought won through.

There was another thought which would worm its way into his mind when, worried, he could not sleep – he could trace the disasters that had happened to him in recent years back to the day he married Mica. It was quite a list.

The Ascot films were invariably made in Europe and Forrest Ellingham, the producer/director, always took up residence in England during production. They were planning another film – *Hong Kong Story* – in which Jamie as Peter Ascot was to take on the might of the Chinese Triads. It was to be the biggest, most lavish production yet.

Then, one night, Forrest was driving home down the M4 after a long dinner in London when a tyre burst. Fuddled by drink, he was unable to control the large, heavy car which turned turtle three times before crashing into a motorway bridge. He and his new starlet wife were killed outright.

Jamie was devastated. He respected Forrest who had been the mastermind behind his career. Without him he knew he would feel lost and uncertain. Jamie was the first to admit he wasn't an actor, that it was his looks, his body and his charm which, miraculously for him, the cameras were able to catch, that had made him a star.

'Just point me and tell me what to do,' he used to joke.

'I can't act for toffee.' And the fans had loved him for his honesty.

Gently, patiently, Forrest, an actor's director if ever there was one, had coaxed performances out of Jamie which, when he saw the finished product, amazed him. Now he was dead and unnecessarily so – Jamie's grief turned to anger at the waste when he learned that Forrest was one of those strange people who, to save a few dollars, had fitted re-treads to his car.

For a week after the funeral Jamie went on a bender – no one could stop him pouring the vodka and brandy down his throat. He drank from fear: how could he act now without Forrest to guide him?

There was no meeting, no consultation. A hand-delivered letter informed him that while *Hong Kong Story* would continue in production it would do so without Jamie. The time had come, he read, for a younger actor with younger audience appeal to take the part of Ascot. Mike Derry, ten years younger and ten years fitter, was to take his place. There was no point in suing and making a fuss. They paid him off handsomely to release him from his contract.

That night Jamie went to the Elysium, once his favourite casino, and blew the lot. The look of loathing on Mica's face when he confessed what he had done made him promise to her it was the last time – and he meant it.

For a year he could not find work. He initially turned down a clutch of scripts, all too close to the part that had made him famous, he decided. He did one TV play which the critics slated and a voice-over for dog food, and was bored witless.

Mica was patient with him – when she was around. If he could not find work, she was turning it down. At the very beginning of her career Serge de la Pointe, the French couturier, had taken a shine to her and she featured as his main model in both his spring and autumn shows. From such an honour work poured in and she spent more time on assignments around the world than she did at home. Jamie fretted when she was away, always afraid he would lose her to a richer or younger man. But he could not have been prouder of her as he waited for the perfect script to arrive to resurrect his own career.

With Mica away so much and with time on his hands, he began to think of Fiona again. He took to driving over to Dunstable to sit and watch her as she left school each day. He could sit and be proud of her for she was beautiful – it was not just because he was her father that he thought so, it was the professional actor in him that could judge her. She was taller than her mother, blonde as he'd once been, and there was more of him in her face than her mother, he noted smugly. He longed to hear her talk or laugh but she was usually alone as she hurried past his car and it was agony to him to feel he was so close and yet dared not call out to her.

And then one day as he sat there he thought, why not? She was an adult now, nearly eighteen. He'd been protecting a child all these years, there was no need any more.

'Fiona,' he called as he stepped from the car. 'It's me, your father,' he said, and thought how ludicrously dramatic he sounded.

She turned round slowly. He was looking into blue, blue eyes – his eyes exactly. 'I just thought it was time we met up,' he said, feeling awkward. She stood silent, clutching her schoolbag to her as gaggles of girls swirled around them. 'It's been so long . . .' he added.

'And whose fault was that?'

'There's a lot you don't understand.'

'And don't wish to.'

'But, Fiona . . .' He took a step towards her and she took one back. 'But, Fiona, I'm your dad.'

'No, you're not. You've never been my father. I very much doubt if you can even spell the word.' And she turned on her heel and ran down the suburban road and Jamie was left feeling sick, as if she had attacked him physically. And he suddenly felt frighteningly alone.

He never went to try to see her again.

The following year Jamie's father collapsed and died of a massive coronary while awarding a cup for the best bull at the local agricultural show. He would have been mortified by his very public death.

When Jamie got the news he could barely believe it. It was too soon, his father was only sixty-four. He had not expected to face this situation yet. He was not ready for it. Although they had never managed to achieve the closeness that Jamie would have liked, he now felt bereft again. It did not matter that he had Mica and he had friends, he suddenly felt isolated in the world as if part of him had died too. Who would he ever be able to turn to now? For despite their estrangement over his marriage, Jamie had always felt that if anything catastrophic occurred, he would still be able to turn to Harry. Now his father had become the catastrophe.

Some nights he dreamed of his father and when he awoke for a few moments he felt he was alive and all was well – and then the realization that his father had gone sank in. He did what he always did when unable to face reality – he drank.

On the day of his father's funeral he stood on the hill above the house and knew that it was his now – and the thought did not give him the pleasure he had presumed would be his, all those years ago when, as a small boy, he had first realized what his future inheritance was. Rather, he looked at the house which he undoubtedly loved and saw it as a terrifying responsibility to deal with.

When he returned to the house he could have wished he'd lingered longer on the hill. The family lawyer waited for his return to read his father's will. He had been disinherited! All his father's money was to go to Jamie's brother Esmond. Grantley, the house and its contents, was Jamie's. It had been entailed years ago by his great-grandfather for just such a situation – to prevent an angry father giving the house to someone other than the eldest son.

To give Esmond his due, he was as shocked as Jamie and embarrassed beyond words. 'I'd no idea, Jamie,' he said, when the lawyer had packed away his papers and the brothers were alone.

'That's all right, Esmond. I'm sure you didn't.' Jamie smiled at his brother and clapped him on the shoulder. He did not know the man – they lived in different worlds. Esmond worked in a merchant bank in the City and at thirty-one was a rising star in the banking world, married to the pretty but rather dull daughter of an earl, with two children, a nice house in Notting Hill and a small farmhouse in the Dordogne. No, if he thought about it, his father had been right to do what he had, the money would be safer with Esmond.

'Do you know why?' Esmond asked, relieved that Jamie was taking it so well.

'My past habits and lifestyle, I suppose – he didn't approve.'

'And Mica?'

'That might have been the last straw.'

'She is rather exotic,' Esmond said awkwardly. 'If you know what I mean,' he added, colouring with embarrassment. 'Will you be able to manage the estate?' he said hurriedly, thinking he had presumed too far.

'Christ knows. I don't even know what it costs to run. Still, there's my film work – that'll come in handy,' he said, with a confidence he was far from feeling.

Strangely, he did what he had done as a child. As soon as the mourners had left and Mica said she wanted to lie down and Esmond and his wife had gone for a walk, Jamie walked quickly across the park to Lou's cottage and a warm and comforting welcome.

'If you ask me it was a right shitty thing to do. He never let on to me,' she said angrily as she poured him a glass of wine.

'At least he saw to it that you'll be all right, Lou.'

'You can have it back – I don't want it.'

'Don't be silly, Lou. You'll need that money. Invested, it'll give you a nice income.'

'But it was wrong. I'd be happier if you had it to help with the house.'

'Dear Lou, I don't think the amount you've been left will make any difference. But thanks all the same, I'll never forget your offer.' He felt he was about to cry and managed, in time, to turn it into a laugh. 'And you mustn't worry, I've got plenty of dosh.' He lied to spare her.

'Well, that's a relief. It was that Mica did for you, wasn't it?'

'No, not really. A lot had gone before.'

'The gambling?'

'He didn't like it.'

'Hypocrite. He liked a flutter himself.'

'You're joking?'

'I'm not. And I'll tell you something else, if it hadn't been for me he'd have lost a packet – but luckily he listened to my advice where the horses were concerned.'

'Lou, you're priceless.' He laughed and accepted a top-up to his glass.

'That Mica of yours is a bit superior, isn't she?'

'No. It's just her manner, she's a bit shy of everyone,' he said defensively.

'You could have fooled me. Right aloof minx in my

opinion ... I thought, at the funeral, she was secretly laughing at us. You are all right with her, aren't you?'

'What on earth do you mean?'

'Happy, is what I mean. She seems so cold and you need someone warm, someone who adores you and can give you confidence – you've always lacked that, and I've never understood why.'

Jamie shrugged his shoulders, feeling more than a little embarrassed. He never enjoyed people talking about him to his face, let alone analysing him like this.

'Here, you don't think she's married you because of who you are, to give her own career a lift?'

'Lou, what a thing to say! I love Mica – she means everything to me and I'd be happier not talking about her in this way,' he said, beginning to feel uncomfortable at the turn in the conversation.

'Loving someone doesn't necessarily mean you're happy with them. Good in bed, is she?'

'Dynamite,' Jamie grinned, knowing he shouldn't have answered such an impertinent question, but also knowing he could not help boasting.

'Well, that's something, I suppose.' Lou opened them another bottle of wine and, apparently satisfied by his reply, did not pursue the subject further.

Was he happy when he was with her? He told himself he was, Jamie was good at telling himself how fortunate, how lucky in life he was. But still, after over four years of marriage, the barricade she had erected about her was still in place, not one stone of it had he been able to move. He realized he knew her scarcely more than he had the day he had first met her. And she knew as little about him, but with her he often feared it was because she was not interested enough to want to know. Was Lou right? Had he just been a stepping-stone for her?

Her beauty was still one of his greatest joys. To watch her lovely face, her exquisite body, filled him with such pride. Sometimes, if he'd gone to watch her on the catwalk, he wanted to stand up and shout to everyone, 'She's my wife! Isn't she beautiful? Mine all mine!' But was she?

She still fascinated him, so that not knowing her was a constant draw to him – he always hoped that this was the day, the hour, the minute when she would allow the defences down. And when her lithe and sensuous body writhed against his and her wonderful mouth sucked at him till he cried with shuddering joy – then it was easy for him to forget his doubts and fears about her. Then he gave even more of his body and soul to her.

To keep Grantley going he sold some of the land which bankrolled it to gain a breathing space. Although Mica was now earning a small fortune each year he was far too proud and old-fashioned to ask her to help. And deep down he had a nasty suspicion she would refuse, even though she derived such pleasure from the house.

He wished his father was still alive to see just how well Mica handled being the titled mistress of such a house. Her natural dignity carried the day and it was as if she had been born for just such a role.

Nothing delighted her more now, when she was home, than to fill the house with people and to wine and dine them and party them until they dropped. They were not necessarily the people Jamie would have chosen to invite, but if they made Mica happy, that was all right by him.

The house was changing around him as Mica and her designer friends took a hand in its revamping. And the bills mounted and there was not enough income to pay them.

Back to the comfort of the bottle he went, so that there were many nights when he could not have made love to Mica even if she'd joined him in their bed, which frequently she didn't, preferring to party the night away.

Jamie began to take small pieces of silver and porcelain to London to sell. Like as not, the money in hand, he would go to the tables, and sometimes he was lucky, sometimes not – they equalled each other out. He needed a long run of losses to make him stop.

The drinking, the late nights, the worry began to etch on to his face – the last thing he could afford now that he'd passed his dreaded fortieth birthday. He started to use Mica's creams and lotions, anything to keep age away.

During the next three years he was up for two films – big ones, important ones, financed by large American studios. New hope blossomed, a restart to his career beckoned. He was so close when each time he was told the part had gone to someone else.

He learned later why. Demetrius Papadopoulos had come back to haunt him. Demetrius had large shareholdings in both studios. His arm was long, his memory even longer. No one, Jamie learned, could cross Demetrius.

One of his worst moments had been seven years into his marriage and weeks after his forty-second birthday when, out of work, he was in a hotel in London preparing to wait for yet another producer to appear and to try to persuade him he was the actor he was looking for. He passed two women and sat himself down behind a pillar – he hated to be on show.

'Wasn't that Jamie Grant, the film star?' he overheard a woman whisper unconsciously loudly to her companion.

'You know, I think it was. He's looking old, isn't he?'

'That wife of his, no doubt. You know she's taken up with that ghastly Greek again.'

'No! Who told you?'

'My cousin's husband saw them together in New York.'

Jamie felt sick. He had always feared she might find someone else, but not Demetrius, not after what he'd done to his career. He felt doubly betrayed. He forgot the producer, the film he wanted to be in, raced from the hotel and home to his flat. Mica was there.

'Is it true?' he shouted at her.

'Don't be stupid.' Mica continued filing her nails.

'You wouldn't lie to me, would you?'

She looked calmly at him. '*I* choose my friends, Jamie. I don't expect to be questioned. You don't own me.'

'But you must realize how I felt.'

'You shouldn't listen to other people's conversations, should you?' She snapped the drawer of her dressing-table shut. 'I'm going to New York tonight.'

'Again?' he said despairingly. 'You've just got back.'

'An assignment,' she announced. It was only after she had left that Jamie realized she hadn't really answered his questions.

He finally got parts but only by lowering his sights and appearing in second-rate films with low budgets, most of which were not even released in the circuits but turned up on videos and late-night television viewing. He also made small guest appearances in TV series. His career was disappearing fast.

He needed money, he needed a part . . .

London – autumn 1992

Jamie looked at his watch. He must have dropped off, he thought, or been day-dreaming. It was too late to phone Sally again, better to try to get some sleep. It would be difficult, though, for he felt elated, lifted in spirit like in the old days. He was glowing with hope that this time . . .

'Mica?' He looked up from the night-cap he was pouring himself, sure he'd heard the front door slam.

'I'm back,' she called. He couldn't believe his luck, she was home!

'Darling, I've the most wonderful news.' He bounded to the drawing-room door waving the precious script Guthrie had given him.

'You've been a right berk, haven't you?' Mica said as she swept past him into the room, shrugging off her coat and flopping down on the sofa. 'Shit, I'm tired.' She curled her long slim legs up beneath her, to leaf through the glossy magazine she'd brought with her, on the cover of which was her photograph.

'Sorry?' He stopped dead in his tracks.

'Little matter of a mega-loss on the tables in Monte Carlo? Don't bother to deny it as you usually do. I heard about it.' She did not even bother to look at him.

'Mica, I can explain. I was desperate. The bank is getting difficult. I had to do something.'

'Gambling is for idiots.'

'I know ... I'm a fool. But I've got to give the bank something. That last party you gave at Grantley – I'm still paying for it.'

'I'm getting tired of your habits, Jamie.'

'Couldn't you help?'

'What?' She sat up straight and stared at him in disbelief.

'I mean, I'm earning bugger-all and you're doing so well.'

'You expect me to bail you out of a mess of your own making? I've more respect for my money.'

'Mica, please, just this once.'

'Jamie, do me a favour, get lost.' And she turned her attention to the magazine.

'Then if you won't help me, will you do something else for me? Will you ask your friend Demetrius to lay off me this time? If I don't do this part, I'm finished.' He stood clutching the script, feeling defeated as he begged.

'I can't imagine what influence you think I have over Demetrius,' she said coolly.

'I'm sure you have, Mica. Please, just speak to him.' He listened to himself and loathed himself, despised himself.

'Don't talk like that, Jamie – I hate it, it makes you sound even weaker than you are.'

'What the hell do you mean by that?'

'You understood.' She yawned and stretched lazily.

'I don't understand. I'd no idea you thought like that about me.'

'Didn't you? Then you're not very observant, are you?'

'Mica, please stop this.' He took one step towards her, a look of despair and incomprehension on his face. 'I'm sorry about the money, it won't happen again, I promise.'

'Haven't you been listening to one word I've been saying? I'm sick to death of you, Jamie. I've had you up to here.' And she patted the underside of her neat and pretty chin.

'Why are you suddenly like this? Why are you speaking to me like this?'

'Maybe I should have spoken to you sooner. Perhaps then you wouldn't have thrown your money and me away.' She looked at him now with such an expression of loathing that he stood transfixed, shocked as the meaning of her words sank in.

'You don't love me any more?' He floundered with the words.

'Did I ever?'

'I thought you did. I loved you.'

'Did you now? Really? Wasn't it more the case that you liked the feeling I was yours – like a possession? A beautiful face. You liked to be seen with me. Perhaps it was a bit more, perhaps I was an obsession with you like all the others.'

'What others?'

'What do you know about me? What do you care about me?'

'You won't let me know you.'

'Don't give me that, Jamie. You're interested only in yourself. All you ever talk about is you and your career. What interest have you taken in mine? When do we ever sit down and talk? When have you ever wanted to know what interests me? Why, you don't even like my friends.'

'Who would? Epicene twits.'

'There you are, you see. And yours are an improvement?'

'You're not being fair, Mica. My friends have always been nice to you—'

'Patronizing, more like. Be nice to the nigger—'

'Mica! What the hell's got into you? I've always been interested, always been proud of you. I've tried to help you get over your hideous past the only way I know how, by loving you gently.'

'When was the last time?'

'Only because you didn't want to. I don't want to argue about that. We were talking about your past—'

'Correction. *You* were talking about it. I don't give a shit about the past. In any case I made it all up. My dad pissed off years ago.'

'You mean your mother isn't dead?'

'Oh, yes, she's dead.'

'Your brothers?'

'I've two sisters and I hate them.'

Jamie sat down, his head in his hands, not knowing what game she was playing, what was true or false. 'Then why did you tell such lies?'

'To make you feel sorry for me. To make sure you would marry me and not just screw me. I knew you would be useful to my career – and you were.'

Jamie cried out involuntarily, a harsh wailing, 'No!'

'Shocked, aren't you? But if you'd bothered to get to know me you wouldn't be nearly as surprised. But you, you're too self-obsessed to know anyone truly. You don't give a damn about anyone but yourself, you're like your bloody mother.'

'Mica, this just isn't true. Please stop this. Stop saying things you will regret.'

'I'll stop.' She stood up. 'I'll stop for the simple reason there is nothing else to be said.'

'Why have you stayed with me then, if you feel like this?'

'It suited me. I like being the mistress of Grantley – I like having a handle to my name.'

'You bitch, Mica.'

'No more than you're a bastard.' She walked elegantly across the room to the door and opened it. She stood for a second as if weighing something up. 'I tell you what, Jamie. I'll pay for the last party, okay? And that one only because a friend of mine did the catering and I don't want to see her out of pocket. Nothing else, is that understood?'

'Thanks, Mica, you're a brick. But don't you think . . .'

But the door had already closed and he was talking to himself. He realized he was shaking. He crossed to the drinks tray and poured himself a large whisky which he downed in one. He felt chilled to the bone. Were they really finished? Was this it, was she leaving him?

It was the way she had spoken which was the worst to take – so matter-of-factly, no raised voice, no passion or feeling in it, as word by word she had begun to destroy him, to take his happiness away, his reason for living. But then, was that not how she always spoke to him, he thought, as he poured himself another drink, faced the fact that he'd been living a dream for all his years with her.

5 Walt

1

New York – autumn 1992

Walt was fully aware that his abortive trips around the world searching for miraculous cures were a source of concern to his accountants at WCF and, behind his back, of amusement to his employees who considered such expeditions as useless as the search for the Holy Grail.

Walt could not agree with them. As he was fond of pointing out, if the educated had listened to the old wives' tales, then penicillin, digitalis and a host of other drugs would have been discovered centuries sooner. The destruction of the Brazilian rainforest was losing mankind God alone knew what drugs, what cures. Time, in this modern world, was running out unless people like him were willing to invest the considerable sums of money required for constant research and experiment.

His employees, had they not been so scared of him, would have agreed wholeheartedly about the drugs but would have pointed out that it was his obsession with cures for baldness and impotence which were the time-wasters. And he could have countered that any company which manufactured such products would have money in abundance for research into other diseases.

His trips so often ended in disappointment – like this one to Bombay and Cairo – that he himself wondered if he would bother to go charging off across the world next time, only to find yet another charlatan hoping to con him.

Even as he thought this he knew the answer – of course he'd go. The hunt itself was like a drug to him. It was also his way of remembering his grandfather – the old man's memorial in a way.

One of the sadnesses of Walt's life was that his grandfather had not lived long enough to see the extent of the company's – WCF's – success; the enormous herb farms, production units, the laboratories, the research teams, the nationwide chain of drug stores. At the beginning he had been so busy building everything that he'd only had time to write once a month – more a report than a letter. Then when his grandfather died he'd regretted he had not written proper letters, had not made the time to visit him more often. He had not even visited his grave. He must go one day, he told himself as he put his key into the front-door lock of his Park Avenue duplex.

He hung his coat in the huge hall closet disguised by trompe-l'œil to resemble a vista of Versailles. From his pocket he took a small black leather notepad and wrote down the time of his arrival home, as he always did. He was often asked why he made a note of every hour of every day. He gave no explanation. He merely said he liked to be able to see that every hour of his day was neatly accounted for – even though he had had to devise a code to prevent Charity from snooping into his affairs.

'Is that you, Walt?' she called from the living-room which she preferred to call the salon. It had once been three large rooms but was now one immense one with windows looking down on Central Park, windows which were hung with drapes of such fussiness and frills that Walt had often wondered what the point was of having paid hundreds of thousands of dollars extra for such a view if the windows were blacked out with fripperies. Charity was sitting writing at her French eighteenth-century escritoire. A fire – an enormous expense in an apartment this high – burned in the grate. Still, he thought, it kept her happy, and wasn't part of his life entirely devoted to keeping Charity content?

'Any luck?' She looked up from the list she was making.

'Nope. I might investigate the balding thing further – interesting, though. An extract from mangoes. But the impotence thing was the usual – some poor rhino bit the dust – when will they learn?' He sat down on the pretty, elegant gilt chair beside the fire – it was a thing of beauty, not of comfort. He'd talk to her for five minutes then escape to his own den where he could crash out on the worn but cosy sofa he loved and she abhorred. 'What's the list?' he asked, but out of politeness not interest.

'A lunch I'm arranging to raise money for AIDS-infected and crack babies.'

'Very commendable.'

'Are you being sarcastic?'

'Nope. I mean . . . something should be done for the poor little creatures.'

'With you in the business it only seems right . . .'

'Of course.'

'You wouldn't like to speak to my ladies, would you? About the research you're doing.'

'Nope. I'll get Winter Sullivan to do it, if you like.'

'Oh, her . . .' Charity sneered. 'I don't think having someone so young goes down well at all, it doesn't give the subject sufficient gravity.'

'You mean someone so young and pretty.' He smiled to himself, imagining the reaction of Charity's skeletally thin and rigidly face-lifted friends to glorious, young, well-rounded Winter.

'I mean no such thing. I don't want my friends to feel they are being pawned off with a secretary or some such.'

'Winter is the best PR we've ever had. She's excellent, she knows what she's talking about and puts it across well. If I asked one of the chemists they'd bog them down with data – the professionals don't necessarily give the best lectures.'

'It's such a stupid name.'

'I like it. She tells me it was because she was born in January and her mother was reading *Rebecca*.' He smiled, but Charity looked more sour. She'd no idea either that she had every right to look sour, given how much Walt liked Winter. How he felt about her, he thought, almost bordered on a schoolboy's crush. He smiled to himself at that thought and sighed inwardly – he doubted if it would go any further now.

'We've been invited to a ball in Paris in January.'

'We can't possibly go.' She laid down her gold fountain pen with an emphatic gesture. 'We promised the Coleridges we'd go to Aspen with them.'

'It's at Guthrie Everyman's,' he said simply.

'Guthrie! You've met him?' She swung round to face him, her face alight with interest and excitement. 'But he never socializes.'

'It's his fiftieth birthday.'

'I'll call Jilly Coleridge and explain. She'll understand . . . Guthrie Everyman of all people. The whole world will be there.' She clapped her hands, heavy with rings, together with excitement. Walt smiled at her and not for the first time marvelled at the difference expensive clothes, hairdressers, jewellery and a clever plastic surgeon could make to a woman.

'What shall we buy him as a present?'

'Something simple, he's got everything.' Walt stood up. 'I've some work to do. See you shortly.' He crossed the elegant room with its faux Roman pillars and clutter of gilded furniture and with a sense of relief let himself into the leather and mahogany comfort of his own room.

He poured himself a drink – a small one, Walt never made the mistake of drinking too much, not with his past experience of men and alcohol. He chose an Ella Fitzgerald CD and sank on to his well-worn sofa to relax for five minutes before he began the paperwork which always piled up when he'd been away.

At least the thought of meeting Guthrie had pleased Charity – not always an easy task. Still, he had to admit, he was as bad as her. He could still get a buzz of excitement knowing he knew someone like that. They were both the same, the way they enjoyed the company of the famous.

It was an odd weakness in his character, he acknowledged, if only to himself. And he thought he knew the reason – it was another way of showing what a success he was, a boy from the backwoods hobnobbing with the famous. But – and this thought he'd never share with anyone – even more importantly, it was a way of making *her* notice. With such acquaintances his name and picture were frequently in the glossy magazines and the social columns of the newspapers. This way, his mother must surely know of his standing in society, his great success. He laid his head back on the cushion – one worked in *petit point* as a present from his wife. *Money is everything* was worked neatly on it, and, in a rare show of humour for her, she had signed her name *Charity* beneath the lettering. He felt tired, dreadfully so. He closed his eyes – just for five minutes, he told himself.

Despite his intentions not to think about his mother he often, too often, did. As now. He wondered how his mother was, what she looked like – she was still, in his mind's eye, the same as the day he'd last seen her . . .

Oregon – 1966

'Marriage? At your age? Walt, have you lost your senses? You're barely twenty. It's too soon.'

'No, Mom.' He concentrated on his slice of the angel-food cake which his mother always baked for his home-coming – it had become a ritual between them.

'But you never even said you liked Charity, let alone loved her.'

'I know, Mom, but these things happen.'

Rosamund, still in her widow's weeds which did not suit her and made her look even more wan and pallid, looked at him with a sad weariness.

'How long has this been going on?'

'Since Dad died,' he could answer truthfully.

'Ah, then I wouldn't have known,' she said sadly, only too aware of how those dreadful months had passed her by without her even noticing. How even now the days were an agony to get through, life an endurance. For over two years she had carried this grief inside her, a great burden of pain. She had felt it grow in her, like a baby, never, it seemed, to diminish in size and, unlike a child when the first nine months were up, never to come to term. The only high spots in her life were when Walt managed to come home from the university for too short a visit.

'I wish you could get home more often, Walt,' she said in a tired-sounding voice, apparently wanting to change the subject as if the previous one exhausted her too much.

'So do I, Mom. But I can't risk my job in the drugstore.'

'You don't have to do that job. Your grandfather would pay all your costs, you know he would, he's said so often enough.'

'But I can't let him, Mom, and that's that. Maybe if I'd gone to UC as we planned, but not now, not when I'm at Westlake – it's expensive, Mom, we can't ask more of Grandpa.' He spoke emphatically, if gently. It was, after all, her fault he'd had to turn down his offer of a place at the University of California, the best pharmaceutical school in the country, and transfer to Westlake – a private university, expensive and, if he was honest, not the best.

Its advantage was that it offered a course in pharmacy when many colleges did not, and it was only a hundred miles from home and his mother. She had not made a fuss to his face but he'd heard her crying at night, and when he had tentatively mentioned the possibility of Westlake she had wept with happiness and hugged him and thus had sealed his scholastic fate.

He could not blame her totally, the decision finally rested with him, for if he had not been the cause of his father's death he would not have had to change universities. It was a pointless exercise to think about it, he would never know what the alternative might have been. And at least for the six years of his course he would be closer to his mother.

His grandfather had agreed immediately, such was his love and concern for his daughter and his realization of the dreadful burden Walt carried. But Walt, knowing everything was his fault, insisted on getting a job to help pay his way.

He worked in the only drugstore in the small town of Westlake, a mile from the college. He was there five evenings a week and all day Saturday. It made finding time to study hard. Most nights he studied after his stint in the store and it was rare for him to get more than four hours' sleep. On Sundays, despite the thin-lipped disapproval of his Presbyterian landlady, he slept all morning and used the afternoon and evening to catch up with his books. He maintained his grades and, now into his second year, was doing well but was constantly exhausted.

He was aware that his mother fondly imagined him dressed in a smart white overall helping the pharmacist dispense his pills and potions. It was not so. Despite his many hints, and a great show of interest, Walt had so far only been allowed to dispense milk-shakes, ice-cream sodas and sundaes.

Most of his fellow students were rich, with cars and hefty allowances from doting parents. Walt rarely socialized with them, he could not have afforded to nor was there any question of him joining a fraternity. He often felt like an outsider looking in at the others at college who had time to have fun and whose lives were so different to his own hard-working one. He watched them drinking too much, smoking pot, dropping acid, experimenting, and found their actions incomprehensible. Work and good grades were too important to be risked by such indulgences and so he rejected all offers to take part. After a few friendly overtures in his first week he was regarded as a boring hick and was left alone. He had even had to forgo his dream of a place on the football team.

Every six weeks or thereabouts he managed to swap his Saturday shift with another drugstore assistant who was saving to get married, and come home. And every six weeks he tried to avoid Charity, but to no avail. She always knew when he was coming, even when sometimes he wasn't sure himself if he would make it. At times he found himself wondering if she had somehow locked into his psyche and knew everything he did.

Charity had not given up on her plan to marry him and the last time he had seen her had threatened him that unless he told his mother of their intention on this trip, she would tell her herself.

'That's blackmail, Charity,' he'd said wearily.

'Yes, of course,' she had answered matter-of-factly.

Hence this uncomfortable interview now.

His angel-food cake finished, he sat and wondered how to get out of the house without upsetting his mother further and also whether he had the energy to walk the long way round through the forest to the town so as not to pass Charity's house and be able to see his friend Gubbie, in the army now but on embarkation leave, in his mobile home the other side of town.

'Gubbie's had another baby boy,' his mother said, wiping her hands on a towel, the vegetables finished.

Walt grinned with relief that she had obviously decided to drop the talk of his marriage. 'I was just wondering whether I had the energy to go and see Gubbie. Sometimes, Mom, I think you can read my mind.'

'Not always, apparently. Otherwise I'd have known about Charity, wouldn't I?'

'Oh, Mom . . .' He sighed and tried to avoid her gaze as she sat down at the pine table opposite him.

'You're throwing yourself away on that girl. With your brains you could have anybody you wanted. She's spiteful – no one likes her. Why? She's not even pretty.' Rosamund was nervously pleating and unpleating the pristine white table-cloth. 'And there's something wrong with that family – everyone says so. Mrs Hornbeam's sister is in a mental institution and two others died young,' she said darkly.

Walt sat silent.

'I mean, Walt, listen to me. You don't want to be encumbered with a wife – like poor Gubbie, a mechanic, living in a mobile home and with no hope. Maybe a baby . . .' She put one work-roughened hand over her mouth. 'Oh, no. How stupid of me. That's it, isn't it? She's pregnant. You've *got* to marry her. Oh, Walt, you stupid, stupid boy.'

'No, Mom. She's not pregnant. I haven't even slept with her.'

'Then what is it?' Her voice was rising now and he was not sure if it was from anger or pain for him. 'God, how I wish your father was here.'

'I can't tell you.' He looked up, expecting her to be crying, but she wasn't.

'Walt, my angel, you can tell me anything. You know that.'

'Not this,' he said, and looked at a point over her

shoulder at nothing. How often he'd imagined telling her what he had done, asking her forgiveness, relieving himself of the guilt. And his mother making it all right for him, just as she had bathed his bruises and made them right when he was a small child.

'Walt. You know I love you more than life itself. Walt, you must realize there is nothing you can do in this whole wide world that will stop me loving you.'

'Nothing?' He half-smiled.

'Nothing,' she repeated. 'Talk to me. Tell me. Let me help you. Let me get you out of this mess. You don't want to marry Charity, do you?'

'No,' he said, almost with relief to be admitting it.

'Then what hold does she have on you? Come on, Walt. I'm your mom.' She smiled gently at him and patted his hand.

'She saw me do something and she says if I don't marry her she's going to tell on me.' He knew as he said it how pathetic, how childish it must sound.

'Glory be.' Rosamund laughed. 'What on earth can it be? She saw you kiss someone? Steal an apple? Break a law?' She was still laughing, shaking her head at the absurdity of it.

'She saw me kill my father.' He felt as if the words had escaped from him unbidden, he was sure he had not meant to say them. He heard them like stones falling into a deep well. He watched as his mother sat rigid in her chair, the laughter stopped, the smile fading.

'Oh, no.' She sighed more than spoke. 'No. You're just saying that.'

'No, Mom. It's true. I didn't mean to — it happened. It was an accident but . . .' He could not tell her about the oar, the look of surprise on his father's face, or could he?

'How do you mean?' she said remarkably calmly.

'I think he was having a seizure — you know you told

me it could happen any time. And . . . and . . . I don't know why but . . . I hit him, Mom. Instead of pulling him into the boat, I hit him.'

'Why? Tell me, Walt, why?'

'Because of what he did to you, Mom. The beatings, the abuse, I couldn't take it any more.' He looked down.

His head rocked back with the force of her hand across his face.

'You couldn't take it? What was it to do with you?'

'But I love you, I couldn't see it all happening again . . . not like it had been . . .'

'You love me? You sit there and dare to say you love me when you have taken from me the one man I ever loved?'

'You couldn't have. It's not possible.'

'Who are you to tell me who I loved or not? He never meant it; it only happened when he was drunk. You knew that.' She was standing now, her palms flat on the table as she leant across it, thrusting her face into his, thrusting her anger at him.

'He could have killed you.'

'You fool. You stupid fool. He would *never* have killed me, he loved me! When he was fine I could not have been happier. The bad times were fleeting and getting less and less. What have you done? Jesus, what have you done to me?' She sat back in the chair in a listless, defeated manner.

'Mom . . . I'm sorry.'

'Sorry!' she shrieked. 'What a little meaningless word for the enormity of what you have done. You have doomed me to a life of unhappiness, that's what you've done. And you say you love me?' She laughed then, a dreadful sound to hear – a shrill, harsh travesty of a laugh. He sat at the table and felt the waves of her laughter assault him, knew he would never forget this sound.

Suddenly she stood, the chair toppling over behind her.

Swiftly she crossed the kitchen, picked up his bag and hurled it at him.

'Get out, Walt. Get out of my house and my life.' She was shouting.

'Mom, I never meant this to happen.'

'But it has, Walt. These are the consequences. Go. I never want to see you again as long as I live. Go and find your Charity and I pray God you live the rest of your life in as much unhappiness as you have condemned me to. I hate you, Walt, I'll go to my grave hating you.'

2

Oregon – 1966–1967

Walt sat in the cab of the large lorry which was giving him a lift back to Westlake, feeling empty. He gazed through the windscreen at the road ahead as if hypnotized. The driver, who was breaking company rules in giving him a lift in the first place, had given up trying to get his companion to talk and sulked as he expertly drove his huge cargo north.

Walt would have liked to sleep, he was so exhausted, but his tumbling thoughts, the misery he was in, prevented him. His head was throbbing. He placed one hand on his temple.

'Heavy night?' the driver asked with a spark of interest at the sudden movement.

'Sorry?' Walt turned his head to look at him so slowly it was as if his neck was rigid.

'Had a rough night?' The driver mimed putting a glass to his mouth.

'Yeah, something like that,' Walt said – it seemed simpler to agree. In fact, the man was not too wrong. He hadn't drunk last night, not a drop, but his body felt as if he had. He felt nauseated, his head was pounding, his body ached, he was dizzy – all the symptoms of a hangover but one induced by emotions and the chemicals they released.

The driver interpreted Walt's acknowledgement as meaning he wanted to talk. He didn't. But with an occasional 'Yeah' or 'Gee' or 'Wow', he gave the man the impression he was listening.

The miles sped by as Walt sat hunched, cloaked in shock and disbelief. He'd thought he'd known his mother, believed she loved him, was certain she disliked her husband even if she did not hate him as Walt had done. He was wrong on every count. He had killed his father and his mother's love for him at the same time.

For a week he stayed in his room in the lodging-house. He did not venture out once but subsisted on black coffee, cookies, dry cereal and two Hershey bars, which was all his small food cupboard contained.

That week he waited. Now his mother knew what he had done, Charity could do no more harm in that quarter than he had done himself. That left the police. He waited daily for them to come and get him but they never did.

Charity came instead. It was his precious Sunday, and he was woken by Mrs Chaseman, fresh from her religious duties, banging on his door.

'There's a young woman downstairs, says she's your fayancie – or somethin' like that. Says you're expecting her.'

'Charity?'

'She didn't give no name. I suggest you put some clothes on, respectable like. You need not think you can entertain her up here – not in my house, you don't.'

'Of course not, Mrs Chaseman,' he said, and wondered why she always wore such awful large hats.

Charity was waiting for him in Mrs Chaseman's parlour. She was tall but the thinness was now fashionably slender. Her mousy hair was streaked with blonde and she wore it shoulder-length, kept in place by a headband and back-combed to give it body. She had learnt about her hazel eyes which were now ringed with black eyeliner, so taking the emphasis away from the heavy jaw. But the braces had worked on her teeth which were white and straight. She would never be beautiful or sexy but she was passable.

'What the hell are you doing here?' Walt snapped, as with alarm he saw the case at her feet.

'Come to join you.'

'But you can't. Your schooling . . .'

'I've graduated. I don't want to go to college. There'd be no point, not when we're to marry. I've never wanted to be like some of the girls and do a job, I've always dreamt of being a full-time wife and mom.' She smiled confidently at him.

'Oh, Charity.' He sank on to the chair opposite hers. 'How the hell do you think I can support you? I'm twenty, I've another four years of college to go. Charity, it won't work.'

'But it will, honey. I've worked it all out. I'll get a job. I'll help you. You won't have to work nearly as hard as you do.'

'But your parents?' he said, grasping at straws. 'Your father must be furious.'

'Not at all. He's always liked you and he says you're so clever you'll be rich and what better for his little princess?' She beamed at him. 'I've explained what I wanted to do – and they don't mind. I said I'd get a room – they wouldn't like us to live together, not until . . .' She raised one eyebrow archly. 'They trust me to be good,' she added to baulk all argument.

'I can't marry you now . . .'

'No, of course not. Next year will do fine, when you're twenty-one and I'll be nineteen.'

'But when I graduate, I'll be drafted . . .'

'Not necessarily. My uncle's a member of the state legislature, didn't you know?'

'But Gubbie's going to Vietnam.'

'Only because the fool wanted to go – probably to get away from Mary-Lou.'

'I couldn't do that. Of course I don't want to go and fight – who does? But I'm not getting out of it that way.'

'We'll see,' she said, and sat primly opposite him. 'In any case, if you do go, I'll be waiting for you home here. Give you a real hero's welcome.'

'I told my mother what happened,' he said defiantly, feeling anger at her smug confidence in her plan.

'I know. I saw her. It wasn't pleasant – a bit creepy really. She wanted to know everything about that day as if she was checking with me.' Charity shuddered. 'It was like she didn't believe you'd done it.'

'So you can't hurt me there.'

'No, but there's still the police . . .' She smiled again. That infuriating, confident smile. 'Look, Walt, why not accept it? We're to be married. There's no way out for you. I know you don't love me – but you will. I know with your sex appeal you can have any girl you want but I don't look as bad as I used to, do I?'

'No, you're really pretty now,' he said, suddenly feeling sorry for her.

'You mean that? Gee, far out, you've made my day!' She giggled. 'So, see. It won't be too bad and I'll help you, I'll be a good wife to you. Marry me, Walt. Please . . . next year . . .'

*

In the year before their wedding Walt could not fault Charity. She had found a room of her own in a rooming-house a block from his. During the day she had a job as a clerk in an attorney's office and an evening one waiting at tables at a hamburger restaurant popular with the students from Westlake College.

In a way he enjoyed her being at Westlake. She did his washing and ironing without being asked. On Sunday she cooked him a pot roast and he'd go to her room to eat it. It was, he admitted, pleasant to sit and talk about home with someone who knew it. He could relax with her in a way he couldn't with his fellow students. Charity under-stood him. He could talk to her but he never touched her, never kissed her.

For a whole year she scrimped and saved sufficient for them to put down a rent deposit on a small apartment she had found, but Walt thought the two rooms with a kitchen and shower-room were dark and dismal.

'It's within our budget,' Charity had said firmly.

With the wedding seemingly inevitable, Walt himself had saved a little too towards buying furniture and to ensure they had a small cushion of money to fall back on – *in case money*, his mother would have called it. There was not enough for a honeymoon.

Walt's mother, though invited, did not attend the wedding the following year. Such an absence caused a buzz to circulate around the community which showed no sign of dying down for some time to come.

The Hornbeams were mightily hurt by her action but Mrs Hornbeam, being a kindly soul, persuaded her hus-band, the marshal, that Rosamund's odd behaviour was undoubtedly caused by her grief for Steve which, even after three years, she seemed unable to shake off. Though she could never come up with a satisfactory answer even for herself as to why Walt never went to see his mother, and him such a caring boy too. She'd tried to pump Walt but without success.

The wedding was everything a girl could wish for, held at the local hotel, a wooden affair like a grand Swiss chalet set in beautiful grounds above the lake – a perfect setting for a marriage. Walt and Charity were joined together under a pretty rose-decorated canopy of fine muslin which wafted in the gentle breeze. They had eight bridesmaids, one page, a four-tiered wedding cake, a string quartet and 150 guests, but no one from Walt's side.

Charity, in an organza dress with a heart-shaped neckline and a full skirt under which were four stiff petticoats, with white and pink rosebuds in her hair, managed to look a picture, which took everyone by surprise. Mrs Dewer from the hardware store was not the only one unable to keep the astonishment out of her voice when she complimented the bride on looking so pretty.

Walt felt uncomfortable at the reception – there were too many whispered huddles and too many sly glances in his direction. He knew what they were all thinking – why had the devoted son stopped visiting? Why had the devoted mother boycotted the wedding?

At any time he would have been pleased to see his old friend Gubbie, and in this atmosphere, even more so. But one look at him, gaunt and ashen with weariness, and Walt knew he saw the face of a man who had been to hell and had not yet returned.

'Does it hurt?' Walt pointed to Gubbie's right leg which had been shattered by a Vietcong bullet two months after his arrival in Vietnam. It had kept him in hospital for six months and he still needed a cane for support.

'Sometimes, usually when I need a beer.' Gubbie laughed and Walt knew he was lying, would have bet money it was giving him gyp now. 'Hey, man, can't complain,' Gubbie added hurriedly, as if aware Walt had rumbled him. 'Not when you think of the alternative.'

'What's that?'

'A body-bag home. That's what happened to the rest of my platoon – this leg is the best thing that ever happened to me.'

'It really is that bad, then?'

'Worse than you can imagine and more. Walt, promise me one thing. No fucking heroics. If you can get out of the draft – grab at it. It's fucked out there.'

'Charity said you'd an uncle who could help. But I don't know . . .' Walt's face showed the wrestle he was having with his conscience and would, no doubt, continue to have. 'What are you going to do now?'

'Oh, I'd great hopes of becoming that lawyer I dreamed of being, remember? There's a vet's retraining programme but the red tape has to be seen to be believed. It's almost as if they put obstacles in one's way – anything to save money. When this shit's over they'll forget we ever existed, they'll wipe out the shame of Vietnam.'

'No way!' Walt objected.

'Want to bet?' Gubbie smiled with his mouth but it did not transmit to his eyes.

'I hear it's congratulations time again – number three on the way.'

Gubbie looked at Walt closely as if studying his face to see if he was laughing. 'If it's mine,' he said bleakly.

'What the hell does that mean, Gubbie?'

'Haven't you heard about my Mary-Lou . . . if it moves, screw it?' He laughed a short, bitter laugh and Walt wondered what had been worse for him, the war or his homecoming.

'Shit, Gubbie, I don't know what to say.'

'Say nothing, man. Probably safest.' He put out his hand and took hold of Walt's arm. 'I'll tell you one thing, Walt. Charity can be a pain in the butt, I'm the first to admit, but she'll be a good wife to you – no doubt about it. You'll go far together. You've kept your side of the bargain, she'll keep hers.'

Charity must have told him, Walt thought with a start. But, he realized, he was not afraid that Gubbie knew, instead he felt oddly comforted.

'Tell you what, Gubbie. When I'm rich and famous, I'll put you through law school myself. How's that for another bargain?'

'It's a deal, man.' Gubbie laughed as they slapped their palms together in agreement.

As Walt and Charity drove back to Westlake in the small Ford the Hornbeams had given them as a wedding present, Walt acknowledged there weren't many women who would accept not having a honeymoon with as good a grace as Charity had.

'We've a life to build,' she said. 'Time for a honeymoon later.' He was glad. In the circumstances it would have been a stupid charade.

'Close your eyes,' Charity ordered as she opened their new apartment door and led him in. 'All right, you can open them now,' she said excitedly.

He looked about him, amazed. The dark brown paint was replaced with gleaming white. The floorboards were stripped and waxed. Pretty flowered curtains hung at the windows and a sofa and chair had matching covers.

'Charity! How the hell . . .?'

'My mom lent me her sewing-machine.'

'But everything else? The paint. I mean, honest, is this the same apartment?'

'You like it!' She hugged herself with excitement.

'I love it. But how did you manage?'

'When you were at them boring old books I was painting and scraping away.'

'But you've two jobs.'

'I made the time.'

'Charity, thank you, it's wonderful.' He turned and for the first time kissed her and it was a genuine kiss of thanks.

That night he made love to her. It was not very good. He had slept with only one girl in his whole life – two years ago, after a party. He really had no idea what he should do. And Charity, a virgin, had even less. She clung to him and whimpered as he entered her – too quickly, too soon, he was sure. And she wept with happiness as he came in her. Afterwards, he held her close and felt ashamed. She had cried out her love for him but he could not respond. She deserved better. He wished she didn't love him. Almost wished he could love her.

3

Oregon – 1970–1978

Walt graduated with honours. Waiting to accept his degree at the awards ceremony he smiled at Charity. She had pushed her way to a seat at the front and sat there in a straw hat with cherries on it, grinning like a Cheshire cat with as much pride, if not more, than the many parents present. She had a right to be, there was no doubt of that. Without her hard work, relieving him of his evening shift at the drugstore, he would not have graduated with such high marks. He was grateful for all she had done. He'd still worked Saturdays, despite her protestations, he felt he had to do something for himself.

He stood in line and looked at the rows of proud parents and a wave of nostalgia washed over him, as it occasionally did if he was not careful, and he felt as bereft as any orphan child. He'd told himself that if he was to survive, then he had to cut loose from the past, but it was a hard thing to do. He knew Charity had invited his mother to the ceremony but she hadn't seen fit to come. It saddened him but now that the future, his future, beckoned, he'd bury the past – he must. He shrugged his large shoulders as if easing himself into his dark blue gown – an image of his father loomed into his mind. No. Go. Leave me, he ordered to himself. He shuddered – he must not dwell on that.

He looked out for his grandfather. If anyone should be here it was him. It was not until the end of the ceremony, with the photographs over and Charity clinging to his arm like a limpet, that she told him that Dolly, the old man's housekeeper, had telephoned to say he had a nasty chill and could not come. Charity had kept the news to herself so as not to spoil his day – Charity thought of everything.

To the world he and Charity seemed a happy couple even if the female element marvelled at how she could have caught such an attractive man. 'She must be good in bed,' they decided among themselves.

Charity was not good in bed but she was not bad either. And Walt had a sneaky idea the same could be said of him. They made love once a week, unless Charity had her period, which was the only time she was moody with him. They made love not because Walt desired her but because he was young and needed to. Still, it wasn't as he imagined it could be, not how he had hoped. Certainly he'd never been lifted to the realms of ecstasy in her arms; the earth had not creaked let alone moved; and the stars remained firmly rooted in the heavens. Making love to his wife was more a bodily function like his other needs. He presumed it must be the same for her – a weekly romp to get rid of an itch – but he didn't know for sure since she never said, never complained.

Sometimes he wished she would complain, for he felt

enormous guilt about Charity. She worked hard so that he was free to study. Her management of their household accounts was little short of miraculous. She had few clothes and only one hat. If only he could love her in return and relieve his guilt. He'd tried, God, he'd tried. But he didn't, and couldn't, love her. He felt she deserved better of life than this.

They had rowed seriously only once and that was when, with his graduation over, he had reported to the draft board.

'But I told you, my uncle . . .' she whined.

'I know, the one in the state legislature. No, I have to go.'

'But why?' She stamped her foot.

'I don't know. I suppose it's just I feel I've got to do it. How could I ever look Gubbie in the eye again if I dodged the draft?'

'Gubbie would be the first to congratulate you on showing some sense. That goddam war has ruined his life.'

'Then maybe I owe it to Gubbie to go out there and wham one at the Vietcong just for him.'

'Don't talk so stupid! Jeez, how could you – after all I've done for you do you think I want to get a goddam telegram telling me it was all a waste of effort?' She stood in the middle of their small sitting-room, her angular face white with anger, twisting the handkerchief she held in her hands into shreds.

'I thought you did all that because you loved me?'

She hurtled round to face him. 'I did. I do. Don't you understand anything? Don't you see, you son of a bitch?' She was shouting at him now.

'I'm going,' he said to her with an awful finality. 'You can't stop me.'

'You don't feel anything for me, do you? I might just as well be dead.' She began to sob. 'I hate you, Walt,' she burst out.

'Really? I thought you said you loved me?' He grinned at her, satisfied with himself for besting her.

'Oh, no . . .' She turned on her heel and ran to their bedroom, wailing as she went.

Walt did not feel proud of himself after she'd left him alone. He should have handled that better, he told himself. He wondered why he was making a stand over this when nearly everyone he knew of fighting age was pulling every string they could to avoid going to fight. Was it just that he wanted to be away from Charity for a couple of years to give himself some space? Or was it that in some perverse way he wanted to go because he hankered after the excitement of war?

He never saw Vietnam, never heard a gun fired in anger. He was sent to Fort Orde to work in the pharmacy and for two years dispensed the GIs' prescriptions and was furious with himself at the waste of time, the delay in his plans.

Finally discharged, he got a job with a large pharmaceutical complex near Westlake. The work was routine and uninteresting and the pay was not nearly as good as he and Charity had hoped for and relied on, so Charity, who was desperate to have a baby, put such ideas on hold and continued to work. They had a plan: of an evening, Walt was to refine his grandfather's recipes to make them more acceptable to a mass market. But he found, as so many had before him, that when a job is dull and boring the fatigue it engenders is great. His ambition to be rich faded. In the evening he preferred to slouch in front of the TV with a beer and, like as not, sleep. He preferred sleep for, despite his determination to forget his past, it had an unfortunate way of slipping into his mind without warning, in the shape of his mother and father. There was another problem; on the West Coast every other person seemed to be into producing alternative medicines and cures, and Walt began to think he'd missed the boat with his insistence on joining the army. And he had come to a far more alarming conclusion: he hated being a pharmacist.

After a year of watching Walt begin not to care, it was Charity who suggested they move east to New York.

'Maybe what you have to offer won't be as common as here with all the hippies,' she suggested.

'Oh, yeah, and how do we get started?'

'Well, for a start you don't work for other people, only yourself.'

'Great. Good idea,' he said sarcastically. 'And how do you suggest we live until Grandaddy's miracle cures are welcomed by the great American public?'

'No problem.' She uncurled her long legs from under her, leaped up from the sofa and crossed to the small desk at which, laboriously, she did their household accounts and wrote weekly to her mother. From a small drawer she took a notebook. 'See.' She held it out to him.

'Ten thousand dollars! Where the hell's this from?' he said in amazement, having only a hundred dollars in his checking account.

'Savings, and then my Aunt Peggy left me a couple of thousand and Uncle Mark a thousand dollars in his will. Handy, them dropping off like that.'

'Your family seem to die early,' he said.

'What does that mean? You hope I'll go early too?' she said sharply.

'Don't be silly. It was just a comment. But why didn't you tell me about the money?'

'I thought you might want to spend it on something useless like a vacation. I put it away and decided that when my account got to ten thousand dollars that was the time to do something.'

'Charity, you're a wonder.'

'I am, aren't I?' She grinned at him. 'I've planned it all. We'll sell this stuff.' She gestured with her arm at the furniture her hard work had slowly accumulated in the past seven years. 'We'll trade in the car and get a station wagon with a roof-rack. That'll take what we decide to keep, and our clothes.'

'Won't it upset you to let these things go?' he asked, knowing how she had scrimped to buy each item, how excited she had been at every new acquisition.

'No. Why should it? They're only things, after all. We can soon replace them. The car is the important thing – then we can go east.'

'Charity, it's a great idea and I appreciate it. But if you buy a new car – and I know you'll want to buy it outright, no downpayment and instalments . . .'

'No way,' she said, shocked at the very idea of borrowing.

'Well, then, the money won't last long, not in New York of all places.'

'It will. I promise. We'll rent a cheap apartment with a good-sized kitchen – you can work there. I can work, just like I'm doing here. When you think the products are ready – and I suggest we start with just two and add to them, say the eczema cream first and the feverfew for migraines – I'll go out on the road to sell them in the car, plenty of room for samples, see. Couldn't be simpler.'

That was the beginning of WCF Inc. – their initials, Charity's idea.

'It's better, sounds more professional, as if there's a huge factory complex behind it. Some of the outfits into herbals want their heads examining. I saw one lot the fools had called "Whispering Glade Products".'

'I saw an "Aquarius".'

'Exactly – too hippie, too amateurish. Now, WCF Inc., that gives confidence. But in our literature we'll use that quote of your grandfather's that you like so much: *"The old ways are the best ways."*'

'You're the boss.' He'd smiled at her and her enthusiasm. He was frequently amazed by her and the myriad ideas she had for them.

It had been hard at first. Their apartment on the lower East Side was a cold-water walk-up with only one room. The kitchen, far from being 'a good size', was a minute, curtained-off portion of the main room.

Soon the kitchen had spilled into the main room and on every surface were pots, bowls, retorts. Dried herbs hung from the ceiling. The heat was intense since the gas stove was rarely off.

Walt had got to stabilize his grandfather's products. Sold from a wooden house in the backwoods to committed believers in alternative medicines, the appearance of the creams and lotions did not matter too much.

'Give it a quick stir,' his grandfather would often say.

'What's a bit of mould? Do you good,' Walt had often heard him advise.

'Of course it tastes awful – the worse it tastes the more good it does,' was another.

Selling on the open market against stiff competition and with the blessing of the American Food and Drugs authorities was another matter. Creams had to be smooth, without impurities and stable – lotions the same. Linctuses too had to stop dividing into their separate components and had to taste more palatable. And mould of every sort had to be eradicated.

They had found a good and reliable source of fresh herbs, and at weekends, when Charity was not working, they drove up into New York State and combed the woods for other necessary barks and plants.

It was expensive, time-consuming and tiring. At least during this period, with a diminishing bank balance as a spur, Walt was able to block his memories of his mother and father. He did not enjoy the work any more than he had before but he was aware that it might just be the key to his original ambition to become rich.

Charity had had the packaging designed professionally.

'We've got to spend the money to make it. Good packaging is the key. Something eye-catching, memorable.'

'I'd wondered about something in brown and sepia – you know, nostalgia,' Walt had suggested.

'Everyone's doing that, I've seen cakes, syrups, now pharmaceuticals packaged that way. No, I think we should go for something white, maybe silver lettering if we can run to it – crisp, clean-looking. Smacks of "Laboratory tested",' she said, and Walt, looking round the incredibly cluttered room, burst out laughing and even Charity saw the joke.

After eighteen months Charity had three products – stabilized, checked and passed by the FDA. It had not proved as complicated a procedure as they had feared, since all the products contained natural, non-harmful ingredients. She took to the road in a brand-new, navy-blue suit, a crisp white blouse, new patent leather shoes and a large black attaché case which she'd had fitted out to carry her samples.

'You look like a nurse,' Walt said.

'Exactly, that's what I intended,' she replied, as she prepared to leave.

'Good luck.'

'I don't need luck. We've a good product. I believe in it. It'll sell,' she said confidently. He frowned, worried she might be disappointed.

Charity was right, but then, he told himself, Charity was always right. The orders came flooding in and Walt worked night and day in the one room to try to keep up. Money was coming in, but at what price? He had no life outside that kitchen. He had not even had time to explore their surroundings.

They needed proper premises, he insisted, arguing that he would go mad if they did not. It was a long search and a time of disagreements since Charity vetoed everything as too expensive. In the end, exasperated with her and her indecision, without consulting her, he took a lease on a small unit and, to Charity's fury, paid for it with a bank loan.

'How dare you do this without me!'

'If I'd waited for you to make your mind up I'd have been an old man,' he snapped in reply.

'I don't like it.'

'Too bad.'

'I hate being in debt,' she complained.

'All businesses have to borrow,' he explained shortly, though still surprised at how simple it had been – the bank had taken one look at their order book and had offered twice what they needed. He had been tempted but had said no, the smaller loan would do – 'For now,' he heard himself add confidently.

'But we were doing all right here,' she insisted, as if refusing to accept that it was too late. She was still shocked that Walt had acted on his own. She was the one who controlled the money, not him.

'Well, I wasn't,' he snapped back. 'I'm doing the work. I'll say where I work.'

'And what do I do?'

And what had seemed such a simple idea deteriorated into a full-scale battle which simmered between them for days. But then fighting was becoming a way of life to them; Walt hardly noticed.

His working conditions might have improved but he

still worked every waking hour just to fulfil the orders which grew as Charity moved further and further afield on her selling trips.

'We must think of national advertising, maybe mail order,' she suggested.

An assistant was required, then another. And to give Walt time to develop further products a third was employed. Within a year he was back at the bank and an even larger loan was given for a bigger work unit.

During this time his grandfather had fallen ill and Walt hadn't had the time to go and see him. And then the old man died, and he could not spare the time to fly to the funeral. Gubbie's leg was amputated but a visit to him could not be fitted in either. Walt worked and worked until he thought he would drop and found at the end of the day that it was the figures in the ledger that excited him: the laboratory was becoming a loathed prison.

And then Charity became pregnant and everything changed.

4

New York – 1979

It was not an easy pregnancy. Poor Charity – her body swelled up like an inflating balloon. Her feet doubled in size so that she was only comfortable in slippers. Her hair when newly washed was still so lank that it looked as if it had not been tended for months. Her face was doughy and broke out in spots. She developed varicose veins and heartburn, and to top it all was one of those poor unfortunates who was sick not just for the first three months but for the whole of her pregnancy.

'Isn't there anything of your grandfather's that will make me feel better?' she pleaded.

'I've tried them all on you,' Walt answered apologetically. He really did feel sorry for her, and was at a total loss as to how to help her. She looked pathetic and she stopped going out and shuffled around the depressing and inadequate flat, spending most of her day watching television and reading trashy magazines.

'I'm sorry, I can't work – I can't let anyone see me like this.' She was in tears.

'It's all right. I understand. I'll do the selling.'

'But you don't know how.'

'I can learn.'

'But the lab . . .'

'Andrew and Scott are quite capable of keeping production going,' he said, referring to the two senior assistants out of the five they now employed.

'But then they'll know what's in them, they may pinch our products.'

'Honey, any competent chemist could find that out.'

'Oh, Walt,' she sighed dreamily. 'You called me honey, you've never done that before.' Her eyes filled with tears and Walt wished he'd meant it.

He often rationalized his position as a form of comfort to himself. He liked the good things – he was to be a father, something he wanted desperately; Charity was a good and caring wife – careful with money, his health, his clothes. He could understand her present predicament and it would pass once the baby came. He thought of how life had turned out for his friends – Gubbie long divorced from Mary-Lou and saddled with alimony payments he could ill afford on a mechanic's wage, and two other friends from college had seen the inside of the divorce courts too. And yet he and Charity, with no love on his part but a mutual respect which had built over the years, stayed together. Maybe he was luckier than he realized. On the debit side the thought always rankled that since this marriage had not been of his choosing, for he didn't love her, he must be missing out on a real relationship. He was in an abnormal, almost sterile partnership. He wished he was in love, wished he knew what real love could be like.

Walt did two things. He visited the bank again and had a long talk with his advisor. He went straight from there and rented a spacious two-bedroomed flat at Kipps Bay Plaza on East 30th Street with a view of the East River and, if one moved far to the right of the sitting-room window, the United Nations building.

Charity was too depressed and low to complain about the added expenditure. She merely burst into tears of gratitude at his thoughtfulness and perked up sufficiently to begin to plan the furnishing of her new home.

The second thing was, he discovered a new world. He found he loved to sell, that he was good at it. He made business contacts easily and above all enjoyed the haggling and dealing as percentages and grosses were argued about and delivery date penalties were batted back and forth.

As he climbed into the car each morning, the day was a new challenge and full of excitement – nothing like his days at the lab bench. He didn't ever want to go back to that. The problem was that Charity was already talking of returning to work when she had had the baby. He had, therefore, six months in which to build orders to the point that the firm must expand enough for both of them to be needed out on the road.

The bank called him and wondered if he would be interested in a conventional pharmaceutical company out at Queens which had gone bust and which the bank was insisting be sold. Walt walked around the airy production line, the well-fitted laboratories, with a mounting sense of excitement. This place was perfect. Here they could quadruple production on the herbal remedies – he'd need more staff but the extra costs would be easily covered by the increased sales. And as he talked to the chemists employed at the factory, all anxious to please him if he was to be the new boss and ensure their jobs, he reached another conclusion. He'd keep on the current conventional lines as well. He'd been worried for some time that the alternative medicine craze was just that – a fleeting fashion which could quickly disappear. Concentrating on the herbal remedies only, he could easily be sunk. Not now. This company's main production was a comprehensive line of vitamin pills and dietary supplements. The Americans would *never* give up on their vitamins, Walt told himself.

Why had it gone down the tubes, then? He didn't have far to look. In the car park was the present owner's car, a large, expensive, imported Jaguar; beside it stood his own beat-up Chevrolet. If Walt had learnt anything in the past couple of years it was to take a small salary, drive a modest car and to plough everything else back into the company.

He went straight back to the bank to discuss financing. He sweated a bit at the commitment he was taking on but was buoyed up by the obvious confidence which the bank had in him; why else would they be lending to him? He agreed the purchase that very same day.

When he returned home to his nice new flat with, at last, some decent furniture, he did not tell Charity what he had done, he did not want to worry her, he told himself. But even as he conned himself he was fully aware of the real reason – he didn't want her to know, he wanted this to be his deal alone. Until this last year she had been the decision-maker, but Walt had discovered that he liked making his own decisions.

The pregnancy creaked on, with Charity's complaints becoming shriller and more continuous, and Walt found it harder, each day, to be as sympathetic as he intended. He began to go to work earlier and come home later. It wasn't just to escape her endless whining, he needed to put the hours in to get the new business up and running, to nurse the accounts they already had, and to make contacts for new ones.

'You've got another woman, haven't you?' she accused him one night when he returned, bleary-eyed with fatigue, at eleven.

'Oh, hell, honey. Don't be silly. When would I have the time?' he asked as he made himself a cup of coffee – Charity would not make it for him, the smell made her nauseous, she said.

'You'd make time. I know you. You've been waiting for something like this to happen so that you could go out on the hunt.'

'Something like what?'

'Getting me pregnant.'

'Honey, you're pregnant because you forgot to take the pill.'

'You don't want it, do you? You never did. You hate me even more for getting pregnant.' And she began to cry, an ugly, gulping sound as if she was fighting for breath.

'Charity, this just isn't true.' He turned from making his coffee to face her. 'I'm pleased you're having the baby – if it's what you want.'

'See, I'm right. If it's what *I* want. You don't mention yourself.' She sobbed.

'Look, Charity. I'm tired. I've had a bummer of a day, do we have to have this scene?'

'Who is she?'

'There's no one,' he replied, as patiently as his fatigue would allow.

'Then why all these late hours?'

'Because I've been working. Without you there's extra to do.'

'You said Scott and what's-his-name could manage.'

'Andrew. Scott and Andrew – yes, they do manage. But

. . .' This was it, he was going to have to tell her, silly of him really not to have done so sooner. 'The thing is, Charity, I've bought us another business.'

'You've done what?' She stood in front of him. He stirred a spoonful of sugar into his coffee. 'It's a handy little pharmaceutical company – vitamins mainly – and at Queens. We can continue . . .'

'How dare you!' she spat out at him. 'How dare you, you son of a bitch.'

'Charity, I didn't tell you because in your present condition I didn't want to worry you unduly. That's God's honest truth.' He stood in the centre of the small galley-like kitchen, his cup of coffee in his hands.

'That was ours. That was what we had . . .' She began to cry again.

'Honey, I don't understand what you mean. It's still ours . . . I'm doing it for us and the baby . . .'

'You bastard! You pig! You're taking it away from me.'

'What, for Chrissakes?'

'The business. It's what we had together. It was my only link with you, you shit!' And she leaped quickly at him, grabbed the cup, hurled the hot coffee into his face and ran screaming from the room.

Ten days later Walt was fucked for the first time in his life.

It had all been an accident. Working late, he had not realized that Yolanda, his secretary, was working late too. This secretary was something else he was going to have to tell Charity about – but not yet, not until after the baby. He certainly did not have to make an excuse for employing her, he needed her. No, it was the way she looked that Charity might have difficulty accepting. He'd inherited Yolanda from the previous owner whose taste in women was as exotic as his taste in cars.

Yolanda was tall and full-breasted, with well-rounded

hips which she made sure everyone noticed by wearing tight clothes. She had long, luxuriant red hair which could not be natural, Walt realized, and huge grey eyes which were always moist, as were her full red lips. She had a soft Southern drawl which made many a man's spine shiver. The rumour was that she had been the original owner's mistress, though why, with her looks, she remained a secretary was in everybody's mind at the works – the men because they lusted after her and the women because they'd have preferred her not to be there.

'Why, Mr Fielding, I'd no idea you was still here.' She stood in the doorway of his small office.

'Walt, please call me Walt. I was just finishing this paperwork. But what are you doing here?'

'I've been organizing a new filing system, what with all these wonderful new products – thought you'd like to keep them separate, see how they're doing, and all.'

'Yes, I would, really. Keep an eye on the old and the new – see which one is keeping ahead.'

'Would you like me to explain it all to you?'

Walt glanced at his watch, it was past seven-thirty. 'Well, if you don't mind staying on, I'd like that.'

'Oh, I've nothing to do but wash my old hair.' She flicked her copper mane which shone with cleanliness.

It took them an hour for Walt to inspect and understand the new system which he had to admit was logical, blindingly simple and a vast improvement on Charity's filing system. It seemed only polite to ask the young woman out to dinner after she had spent so much of her time with him. She was pleased to accept and told him she knew of a nice Italian restaurant a couple of blocks away.

Yolanda was easy company. Walt liked the way she listened to him, leaning slightly forward on her elbows as if waiting eagerly to hear what he had to say.

'Why on earth's a beautiful girl like you a secretary?'

'Now, now, Walt. Is that kind? You meant to say *just* a secretary, now didn't you?' She smiled at him, taking any sting out of the reproach. 'You need brains to be one – a good one, and I'm the best.'

'I'd endorse that. I'm sorry, I didn't mean to be rude – it's just, you're so beautiful . . .' he started and then, realizing what he had said, stopped in confusion.

'Why, thank you, Walt. That's mighty kind of you to say,' she replied, with the ease of a woman used to such compliments. 'I did hope to model, once, but I'm the wrong shape – you have to be razor-thin, not look like a woman.' She laughed a delightful sort of laugh. 'Then I was a man's mistress for three years, until he dumped me. After that I thought, never again, I'll be independent.'

'I'm sorry . . . I didn't mean to pry.'

'I don't mind you knowing, Walt. I like you.'

'And I like you, Yolanda.'

An hour later, back at her apartment, to get into bed with her seemed the natural thing. He felt awkward and clumsy at first; being with such a sexy woman made him realize how sexually naïve he was even before they began to make love. He need not have worried. He was putty in the hands of this experienced woman. Once aroused, it was as if his body had been waiting for her and knew exactly what to do even if he himself didn't.

To compare what happened that night with his dutiful coupling with Charity was impossible. With Yolanda he experienced total passion. He had not realized how much he needed a woman until she began rapidly to remove his clothes and he found himself tearing at hers. There were no parts that he felt he could not touch, explore, kiss – unlike Charity who did not even like the light on. Yolanda made his erection larger than he had thought possible, made him feel more masculine, more in control, capable of more passion than he was aware was in him. For the first time in his life he experienced real raw sex.

Charity knew, as soon as he stepped into the apartment. He realized it wasn't just the time – two in the morning – but the expression on his face that gave him away also. He braced himself for the scene to come. But it didn't.

'I've been expecting this for some time, Walt,' Charity said to him coldly. 'But I don't expect it to continue. Whoever she is, this was a one-off, is that understood? And you tell her that, get it? You're mine, you always will be. For Walt, I promise you, you can never divorce me – I know too much, remember? And I'll still go to the police unless you toe the line. I'd prefer it if you slept in the nursery. Good night.' And she turned and waddled to her bed in her long white cotton nightie.

Walt shuddered. They'd been together for nearly twelve years now, during which time he had looked after her, been faithful to her, lain with her as best he could. Whenever he relaxed, allowed himself to think the past was behind him, Charity would remind him, threaten him. What he had done was like some fearful baggage he was doomed to carry with him for life. And when he slept, there was no respite, he often dreamed in sweat-making clarity every detail of that fateful day.

He turned and walked into the nursery, newly decorated for the baby. He undressed and lay down on the unmade single bed beside the waiting cot. Charity had hung a mobile of baby elephants from the ceiling, his movement had made them dance. The big, rugged-faced man lay watching the mobile, aware of his wife's sobbing in the next room.

Had he been so wrong? He'd never lied to Charity. Never told her he loved her when he didn't – called her honey sometimes, that was all. He'd fulfilled his side of the bargain – now, apparently, there were other conditions to be fulfilled. He hadn't expected this to happen with Yolanda, but it had, and by Christ it had been wonderful and he wanted it to happen again and again. He'd felt liberated tonight – he'd tasted freedom, a fleeting happiness, a forgetting, and he'd liked it. He turned to switch off the light and put a pillow over his head to shut out Charity's weeping.

5

New York – 1980–1989

It was the arrival of Gubbie in New York which set Walt on a path from which he was never to stray.

The baby, a boy called Hank after no one in particular, was a year old. Charity, much to her own surprise, had become a devoted mother, content only when she was with her child. There was no question of her returning to work. Walt never mentioned it, nor did Charity.

There had been a change in her, there was no doubt about it. She seemed softer, and physically she was – the extra weight she had gained suited her, made her look less angular. With another person to adore she paid less attention to Walt, which suited him enormously. And since she had the baby to love – his baby – he began to feel less guilty about not loving her himself.

Without Charity at work he needed a right-hand man, someone he could rely on totally. That was when he called his brother-in-law Gubbie.

They sat in a Manhattan bar, Gubbie drinking martinis with enthusiasm, Walt slowly sipping a beer.

'So you're heading for the big time at last, Walt. What took so long, man? I'd given up on you when you weren't a millionaire by thirty.'

'I don't know. I seemed to get stuck in the labs, which I didn't like. I really didn't know I liked the business side so much until Charity was pregnant and I had to go out selling.'

'You're not stopping with this outfit, then?'

'No. You'll see – I won't let you down, I'll be a millionaire in five years or I'll go bust! I've been talking to my bank. I've found an outfit near Boston, purely by chance. There's a lot of garbage with it – couple of shops, gas station badly run down, stuff I wouldn't need. But the nucleus of the firm is fine – pharmaceuticals, of course. I'm planning to jettison the rubbish but keep the labs and build it up from money made selling the rest off, and the bank agrees.'

'Asset-stripping.'

'I'd prefer to call it rationalization.'

'Why not in a big way?'

'Come on, man, give me a chance, I've only just started.' He laughed and sipped his beer. 'But next time perhaps,' he added.

'Charity tells me she reckons you've got a woman stashed away.'

Walt looked up sharply from his glass but Gubbie was grinning at him. 'Yes, I have as a matter of fact. I thought she didn't know about this one.'

'Women sense things. This chick, has she got a sister?'

'Phew . . . I thought I was in for a brotherly bawling out.' Walt laughed with relief.

Gubbie leaned across the small table. 'Look, Walt, my sister's all right – she's got a nice flat, nice clothes, nice baby. You never loved her, she blackmailed you into marrying her. I don't recall she demanded life-long fidelity as well. Good luck to you, man.'

'I've tried with Charity, I really have. I'd like to feel differently, it would be less complicated for a start . . .'

'And less expensive?'

'That too. But I got to thirty-three and I realized I didn't really know what love was – I needed to find out.'

'And this one blows the wax out of your ears in a way Charity doesn't?'

'Couldn't have put it more succinctly myself.' He laughed.

'I don't understand the love bit. It's all bullshit to me. I loved Mary-Lou, look where that got me. Now I just fuck 'em and leave 'em.'

'Understandable . . .' Walt waved to a waiter and ordered more drinks.

'Do you ever think about your father?' Gubbie suddenly asked the sort of blunt question only very old friends can.

'I try not to. But he creeps up on me. I can be driving along feeling fine and wham . . .' Walt hit the front of his forehead with the palm of his hand. 'There it all is, like watching a movie. There's never any warning, no trigger I can make out. And I have nightmares but that's to be expected. I guess it's my punishment or some such crap which will always be with me.'

'I reckon you did your mother a favour. I know she doesn't see it that way but I reckon she'd be dead by now if you hadn't.'

'I'm sure of it. He was an evil bastard. Do you or your mother see much of mine?'

'No. She's become very reclusive, especially after your grandfather died. My mom tried to get her out and about but she didn't want to know. My mom says she's enjoying her grief.'

'Oh, I don't know . . .' Walt began defensively and then thought, what if it was so? Then his guilt would be totally exonerated.

'Do you have any contact?' Gubbie broke into his thoughts.

'No. I've only been back a couple of times. I went home – you know, to see the old place. Sentimental journey . . .'

He laughed. 'I stood outside, didn't knock or anything, but she must have seen me. She never came out. I write, she doesn't answer. Not even over the baby.'

'Sad and stupid.'

'You can say that again, Gubbie. Still, if that's the way she wants to play it . . .' He shrugged.

'You're hardening up.'

'Am I?'

'It's about time. You were too soft for your own survival at one point.'

'Life teaches you, though, doesn't it?'

Over the next five years there were many changes. Walt, though he had not kept his promise to Gubbie to put him through law school, had done the next best thing. Gubbie was vice-president of WCF Inc. with special regard to sales. Gubbie loved his job, the expensive car that went with it, the women it helped pull and the generous expense allowance Walt gave him. Walt could not have chosen better. Not only was Gubbie good at his job, able to motivate the workforce and talk to them in a non-patronizing way, but he was an invaluable sounding-board for Walt's own ideas.

When a new acquisition appeared, or Walt heard the rumour of a new remedy, it was always Gubbie he discussed it with. Any worries, it was Gubbie who shared them. All major decisions were debated with Gubbie.

Charity, who Walt would have expected to object, did not seem to mind at all. Maybe because it was her brother, maybe because she was still enjoying domesticity. They lived in White Plains now, in a fine four-bedroomed house with integral garage, large garden and pool. They still tended to pinch themselves to believe that such a house was theirs, just as they did with the two imported cars in the garage with its automatic up-and-over door. Charity had friends in the neighbourhood, other wives whose husbands commuted into the city. She had coffee mornings to attend, fund-raising lunches to give, PTA meetings to go to. She appeared to be happy.

So was Walt. After a wobbly start life had been good to him, there was no doubt about it. He was proud of his home, his large Mercedes. He was doubly proud of his business which had grown with such speed that by the age of thirty-nine, if he stopped to add everything up, which he never did since he hadn't the time, he was becoming seriously rich. But most of his pride was reserved for Hank, blond and blue-eyed like himself, with every sign that he was going to be big too and bright as a button.

If Walt had one complaint it was that he did not see enough of his son. Frequently he had left in the morning before he was up and invariably returned when he was asleep. But Walt tried to keep Sundays clear. That was the day of the week he devoted to the boy, teaching him to bat, to fish, getting to know him.

He had a mistress. He had always had one since Yolanda. He still missed her, and of them all she was probably his favourite. They'd been together for nearly a year when she left Walt for someone else. She'd been quite honest with him, the new fellow was richer, that was all he had going for him, but time was moving on, she'd said, and she had to look to her future. She needed money. Walt had got as close as possible to a broken heart over her. He lost his concentration, his pleasure in his work, for several weeks until he pulled himself together. He had made the mistake of thinking Yolanda loved him as he was sure he loved her. But she hadn't, and since he recovered within the month he was led to the sad conclusion that he hadn't really loved her either.

It was a mistake he did not repeat with the women who followed Yolanda. They used him as he did them – that was the ground-rule from now on.

Gubbie had married again, a girl in the office, and was blissfully happy. Sometimes he would bring his wife to White Plains for a weekend and they were happy times.

Richer, a father, more riches to come, with his reputation as a manufacturer and a ruthless wheeler-and-dealer growing, with a non-complaining wife and a compliant mistress — Walt was a happy man.

'Charity, have you noticed Hank's dragging his foot — the right one?' Walt pointed out one day when father and son returned from a hike in the woods which Walt had curtailed when he noticed the boy was having difficulty keeping up.

'Yes, he said he twisted his ankle falling over when playing ball.'

'When did he do it?'

'I can't remember. Let's see . . . must have been a week ago.'

'And you didn't get it checked?'

'Walt, really, it was only a little twist.'

'Then I think you should get the paediatrician to take a look at it.'

'Oh, Walt, don't be silly. Children often hurt themselves, they soon get better. Hank's just a clumsy child, he's always tripping up and dropping things. If I took him to see Dr Bouzkic every time he did, then I'd live in his office. His head's in the clouds, that's his problem.' Charity laughed.

'He needs a check-up,' Walt said calmly enough as he placed a pile of papers in his briefcase. 'And keep him off school.'

'Walt, what is it?' Charity had stopped laughing. 'You're never normally like this, what's worrying you?' She was anxious now, twisting her hands.

'You're probably right, I'm an old fusspot. He's probably pulled a muscle or something simple like that – but I'd like Bouzkic to take a look all the same.'

'You going back to work?' she said a shade sulkily. 'But it's Sunday.'

'Yes. I've some figures to check with Gubbie before tomorrow – we're going to Michigan, there's a business proposition there I need to look at. I'll stay in town.'

'With your mistress?' she said bitterly.

'No, with Gubbie – you can call and check if you like.'

'Fine! You're worried about Hank and you leave me to deal with it. Great. Just great.'

'It's nothing, we've agreed. Must go . . .'

As he drove he felt icicles of fear around the pit of his gut. What he had not told Charity was that just recently he'd noticed one or two things about Hank which, if taken in isolation, were unimportant but, if considered together, took on a totally different significance.

The clumsiness which Charity joked about was, he was sure, getting worse. At school Hank had been in trouble for day-dreaming and refusing to concentrate – but was he being difficult or could he not help it? There was the slight rigidity in his limbs which Walt had pointed out to Charity and which she took as an explanation for the clumsiness, blaming the school for making the child play too many games and straining his muscles. But when she wrote requesting he be rested from games and all physical exertion there was no apparent improvement. Hank had always been adroit with his fingers but Walt, after their return from their walk, had seen that the boy was unable to fit the pieces of a jigsaw puzzle together.

When he added all these factors together and regarded them as symptoms, then, Walt thought, there was a problem. But symptoms of what?

As the miles sped by, he thought and worried at this problem. Why did he feel so afraid for the child? There was something in his mind, a shadow of a meaning which he could not grasp at, could not recall, but which he knew, instinctively, was the key to what ailed the boy. It was like a faint warning bell. For once Charity need not have worried: it was his medical textbooks, his scientific papers, his research laboratory files he was driving towards.

Several hours later, in his office, surrounded by books and papers, he found the barely remembered research paper and the faint worrying bell became a clarion call.

A couple of years previously at a big scientific conference in Atlanta, one of Walt's biochemists had given a paper on an extremely rare hereditary disease. As always in these matters, they had debated whether to continue this man's programme of research. They had decided, and Walt, as chairman, had agreed, that given the rarity of the disease and therefore the low number of cases per capita throughout the world, it would not be a sufficiently lucrative subject to justify the considerable outlay always required when researching an intransigent and mysterious illness. The project had been shelved and the biochemist, disappointed at their decision, had resigned and moved on. Walt knew immediately that he must find him.

He tried to calm down, telling himself that he was probably panicking unduly. His medical knowledge was inevitably greater than most people's but still not as good as a qualified doctor's. Any knowledge unless total could be dangerous. But all the same . . .

He did not go to Michigan as he planned, Gubbie went for him. He sat in his office, work on his desk untouched, and waited for the call.

'Walt? It's David Bouzkic here.'

'Yes,' Walt said, aware his voice was faint.

'I thought it best to talk to you rather than Charity at this stage.'

'Is it Huntington's chorea?' he forced himself to say.

'Hey, Walt! Not so fast. Is it what?'

'Huntington's chorea . . . You know. It's a genetic . . .'

'Walt, hang on, man. Yes, I've heard of this condition, but let me reassure you – I've never seen or known of a doctor who's had to deal with a case. It would be highly unlucky if—'

'Hank's got all the early symptoms.'

'Walt, my friend, calm down. There could be a list of things wrong – probably minor. Why this one?' The doctor spoke in soothing tones.

'I don't know, Dave, it stuck in my head and it won't go away. You know me, I don't panic unnecessarily – maybe I'm being illogical, I pray to God I'm wrong. Call it instinct. I'd like tests run.'

'Of course, Walt. I'll do every test known to man.' He laughed but it sounded false to Walt. 'Meanwhile, don't worry, it's probably a streptococcal infection we can deal with.' He continued to reassure but he too was concerned.

'And, Dave, there's something else I thought of. Charity's family – they have a nasty habit of being institutionalized as insane, or of dying young, or are regarded as alcoholics. That was common once in affected families – before the illness was recognized.'

'Come on, let's face it, Walt, with a kid of six it could be a whole range of things. Don't let's jump to any conclusions – not yet. Let's do the tests first. Look at it this way, I've never heard of a child that young developing Huntington's.'

'I have,' Walt answered bleakly. The doctor did not reply. 'How's my wife?'

'She's fine. I diagnosed a twisted ankle, which is what she wanted to hear, and I said he looked a little peaky and I'd like to run some tests. Don't go rushing home now, will you, it will only alarm her.'

'Okay.' He replaced the receiver and fought with himself. His inclination was to rush home, not to Charity but to scoop Hank into his arms and run for the hills with him and keep him safe.

It was Huntington's chorea, that rarest of illnesses that cut an obscene swathe through whole families. Now his mother's warning of insanity in the Hornbeam family, of members dying young, began to make sense. They hadn't been mad, they had just appeared so – falling down, unable to coordinate, eventually unable to communicate, all because of a faulty gene. What was even crueller was that, rare as the disease was, almost unheard of in a child of Hank's age, Walt had been right, there had been another case in Canada. That angered Walt perhaps even more. Why, if the boy carried the defective gene, why could it not have waited, why hadn't God let him have twenty-five, thirty good years first, as most sufferers enjoyed? And cruel also was that, perhaps because he was so young, the disease was working faster on him than on an adult. The muscles were packing in fast, he was becoming helpless before their eyes.

For two years Charity was like a demented woman. So great were the stress and anxiety created by Hank's illness that she could not sleep, lost interest in everything – house, garden, friends, her appearance – and devoted every waking hour to Hank and his needs. She was smothering the boy with her maternal fear.

'Charity, you've got to let him have some space. He has to go to school – he wants to go while he can. Don't you see? As long as possible we must try and treat him as a normal child,' Walt said to her across the breakfast table where she sat unkempt and bedraggled, chain-smoking in accompaniment to her black coffee breakfast.

'He might hurt himself. What if he fell over? What if the other kids pushed him?'

'Charity, the school knows to watch him, they'll make sure he's safe. You know that, we both went to see them.'

'You don't care, that's your problem.'

'That's not fair, I do care.' He banged the table.

'Then why don't you do something?'

'What can I do?' He spread his hands in despair.

'All these laboratories, all those scientists working for you. If you weren't so mean you could make sure they found a cure for your son.' She began to cry, she often did.

'All the resources at my disposal are working flat out. This is life, Charity, not a Hollywood movie – cures aren't found overnight. It takes years of painstaking research.'

'We haven't got years,' she snapped back, quick as a flash.

'But a lot of research has gone on long before you or I were even aware of this disease. We're liaising with these scientists worldwide, we're doing all we can. I can't do more. Don't you think if I could, I would? He's my son too.'

'And it's your fault. All your fault. This is a punishment on you for the wickedness in your life – this is God's answer to you for killing your father.' She was shouting now, agitatedly buttoning and unbuttoning her dressing-gown with one hand, shuffling for another cigarette with the other.

'It's no one's fault,' he said wearily, standing up to collect his briefcase and car keys. He turned to face her. 'Look, honey, I know what you're going through, but letting everything go like this isn't going to help Hank.' He gestured towards the chaotic kitchen. 'Let him go to school, he's desperate to be like the other kids.'

On the freeway into New York Walt tried to control his despair. He sat behind the wheel of his car, smartly suited, impeccably groomed, the epitome of the successful man he was, and tears slid down his tanned cheeks, tears he did not even bother to wipe away.

Often, safe in the capsule of his car, this time of privacy was the time he let go. Sometimes he screamed out loud as he drove, screamed and roared like a wounded lion with hatred at this obscene disease. Other times he planned and schemed for his son. Yet others, as today, he wept silently and alone.

What else was there to do? They'd been to London, Toronto, Vienna, Stockholm, everywhere they thought there might be a specialist who could help them. They'd tried every alternative medicine known to man short of a witch doctor. Hank had had every crank diet Charity read about tried on him. Walt had spent a small fortune on travel alone, not counting the large fortune going on research. And all with no result. Each month Hank was losing more and more of his muscular ability until eventually they had been warned that the best scenario was that he would die, the worst that he could remain a helpless cripple, unable to talk, for years. Some specialists told them he would know nothing, that his brain would slowly die. Others told them that they felt he would be aware, that his brain would be locked in his crippled body, no longer able to communicate with the outside world.

Walt didn't pray much, unlike Charity who had grabbed at religion in the hope it might help. But when Walt prayed it was to ask that his son be given a little longer of the good times and then to die. When he prayed thus he always felt guilty afterwards as if he'd betrayed his son, as if, in an odd way, he was killing him too. Then he'd storm into his research laboratories, berating the research chemists, the biochemists for not coming up with any clues.

One thing Walt never told Charity was that far from it being his fault it was hers. Hank suffered from one of those rare diseases transmitted at random through a parent's genes. So far Gubbie and Charity had not succumbed, but that didn't mean they wouldn't. Charity's genetic make-up had doomed her son. Strangely, Charity, although reading widely on the subject, had not as yet put two and two together to realize where the problem lay. But was it so strange? Was the truth too painful to contemplate and so her brain had pulled down a shutter on the parts it felt it was ill-advised she should know about – like terminally ill patients who believe they are getting better?

It was imperative she and Walt had no more children. But this would not be a problem, nor need the subject be discussed with her, because about the time Hank became ill Walt and Charity moved into separate rooms and sex between them was now just a memory.

Walt continued driving, blinking the tears from his eyes so that he could see better. Here he was, about to do a deal for Dewling Pharmaceuticals which would give him the platform to bid for America PC and make him the largest production unit in the States, with a chain of drugstores coast to coast. All this work, all this success, all the money which now poured in had been his dream, a dream he was to hand on to his son – but a dream that lay in tatters. He no longer knew if he had the strength or desire to go on.

By the third year of his illness, Hank was in a wheelchair. Soon he became totally bedridden.

'Am I going to die, Dad?' he asked Walt one morning.

Walt looked at his son, his heart lurching at the question. Hank's body was wasted now by the disease within him. How the hell did you talk of death with a nine-year-old child? Walt made himself smile. 'I hope not, son, 'cause I tell you what, I like living but I don't know if I'd want to hang around in a world you weren't in.'

'Then I'd better fight this thing. I don't want you to croak it, Dad.'

'That's right, Hank. We'll fight it together. We'll be

fishing again before you know it.' He hung on to his emotions until out of the room when he hit the wall with his fist in frustration.

And the child did fight, and Walt had nothing but love and admiration for his uncomplaining courage. And then Hank caught a viral infection and his fever soared uncontrollably until his small body was racked with convulsions. Walt's prayer was half answered. Hank lived but his brain had been damaged. He was not doomed to live a prisoner in his crippled body. He was no longer aware of the predicament he was in. It was a blessing of a sort, Walt told himself time and again to keep his own sanity.

Then one day Walt returned from a trip and Hank had gone. His room was empty, his toys packed away, even the walls had been redecorated.

'I've put him in a home,' Charity said, almost coldly, Walt thought.

'Oh, Charity, no.' He stood dumbfounded at this news.

'It's all right for you. You're not here half the time. It's I who bore the brunt of this. Well, I can't do it any more. He's gone, he might as well be dead. We've got to get on with our own lives . . . start anew . . . start as if Hank had never existed,' she said in a sob.

He did not comfort her, there was no point, they had moved away from such gestures long ago. In his study he sat and thought. Maybe she was right. Maybe it was better for Hank who'd be more comfortable in a proper nursing home. Perhaps wanting him here all the time he was being selfish.

He went to visit his son every Sunday, not dutifully but because he wanted to. Charity never went.

6

They grieved, but not together. How Charity felt Walt did not know, he had not inquired, just as she had not inquired of him. He did not want to be asked, did not want anyone to enter into his sadness which was painfully private. He assumed she felt the same. They dealt in different ways with the tragedy of their son, which was strange.

For Walt, since he had no contact with his mother, the only person he knew with whom he could share this horror, the loss was greater. The only two people he loved were living and yet lost to him. Perhaps it would have been easier to bear if they had been dead instead of his son's living death and his mother's rejection of him. He began to think that everything in his life would be easier when both his mother and son were dead. Initially he had felt his work had become pointless and he seriously considered whether he wanted to continue if there were to be no son to hand everything over to. It was as well he had not taken this course, for work was to prove to be a panacea for him. His home, without Hank in it, felt less like a home, so he began to work even longer hours, with the result that he amassed even more money. Now he was always featured in *Forbes* magazine as he climbed its ratings of America's richest men. To keep his sanity, to keep himself constantly occupied, he had set himself a new goal – he wanted to be right at the top of that list.

He would never understand his mother. His father had been dead for over twenty years yet she had made no contact with him when Hank was born, nor was there any response to his letter that the child was ill. He was angry with himself now for even bothering to write – totally against his resolution to bury the past – it had been a weakness on his part. But then he had every right to presume that someone who had loved as his mother had in the past, would finally care about her grandson. Maybe she did, maybe she too grieved alone, but by not sharing in his pain she continued to punish him.

He supported Rosamund financially. The old wooden house on the edge of the forest was still her home but totally changed — it had a new kitchen, new bathrooms and furniture, and it was redecorated every year. Walt knew all this since his lawyer told him what expenditure had been made — he insisted on knowing, right down to the smallest detail. To the lawyer's perpetual amazement, he even wanted to know the colour of each new set of drapes. He could still remember every detail about the house and he liked to keep it fresh in his mind's eye. His mother changed her car every other year for a new one. And each year she took a holiday, usually a cruise. The lawyer reported on her admirers, who they were and their financial status. Rosamund was attractive, well off; it was hardly surprising she should have admirers, but none of them was ever invited into her house. So, he could conclude, no one shared her bed. Walt was told she was happy — he wished he was.

His mother did not know that the money which kept her in such comfort came from him — that would have been a disaster, for no doubt she would have refused to accept one dollar of it and her subsequent poverty would have added to his guilt. The lawyer had spun her a tale that investments made by her father and left in a trust for her benefit alone were producing large sums of money. Walt could not help wishing that one day she would know it was his hard work, his success which kept her. He might long for her to know but he knew he could never tell her.

In a crowded, busy life he felt lonely. He was aware that his staff were friendly to him because he was the boss, not because they liked him as a person. He realized they were afraid of him. He had himself to blame for that, for as the years ticked by he became more irascible. He knew why it had started; with the realization that their friendship was false, that they agreed with him because of who he was. It had annoyed him and made him put up further barriers between himself and them. The only one who came half-way to being a friend was Beth, his secretary; sometimes he allowed himself to think she liked him for himself alone.

He had women by the score, that was his reaction to Hank's predicament. He found when coupling with a woman in bed that, for the length of the act, he could forget, the pain decreased – even, sometimes, disappeared.

So apart from a permanent mistress set up in an apartment, he also made use of escort agencies, call girls, an army of women he used ruthlessly to help relieve his agony. He was not particularly proud of this behaviour and tried to make amends by being generous with presents and money and handouts even when he had finished with a woman.

It was this appetite for women which prompted him to note each hour of every day, what he had been doing and where he had been. For a simple reason. A call girl had been savagely murdered, by a client, it was presumed. His name and number, along with many others, were listed among her papers, but written down in a code of her own making which had taken the police a week to crack. Since there was a long list of customers to be interviewed it was a further week before it was his turn. He could not for the life of him remember where he had been or with whom on the fateful night. He had become so agitated by his inability to recall his whereabouts that the police, desperate to make an arrest, had kept him in custody for an uncomfortable night and day. From his office diary it was confirmed that, unfortunately for him, he'd been in New York all day, but the evening? It was Gubbie who came to the rescue, for Gubbie kept a diary. The two of them had dined together and then gone to a nightclub; later Walt had gone off with a girl called Roxy who was traced and gave him an alibi. It had been a frightening experience, one he was determined never to repeat. From that day he had kept his notebook with its coded entries, of every move he made.

Charity's reaction to Hank's illness surprised everyone who had known what a devoted mother she had been. She acted as if he had never existed. She put away all photographs of him, she forbade his name to be mentioned. She had erased Hank from her life.

It was a strange way for anyone to grieve, but Walt was sure that was what she was doing – she had loved Hank too much not to. Walt wondered if in an odd way by pretending the boy did not exist she could eliminate the horror and with it his pain. It was only a theory since they never discussed Hank, for Walt too was banned from mentioning the boy.

Soon after Hank had gone to the home for incurables he had suggested she come with him on one of his weekly visits. 'It's a fine place. The nurses are so kind. And you know, I reckon I see an improvement in Hank. I'm sure last week he reacted to my voice,' he said kindly. 'Why don't you come? It's a nice day for a drive.'

'No, thank you, I'm afraid I've things to do,' Charity said quite politely, as if he had invited her to join him for lunch.

'Can't they wait?'

'No, Walt. They can't. It's better this way. Please never ask me again.'

So he hadn't, but continued with his own lonely vigils.

Instead Charity embraced a social life with enthusiasm. She had decided that the house at White Plains was no longer big enough nor grand enough for her new ambitions, especially given the money Walt was making. He was glad to sell up, the house held no happy memories for him.

They moved to New York and Walt purchased a duplex

on Park Avenue. They had arrived, he should have been happy but he wasn't. The gilt had gone.

Charity began the decorating and furnishing of the apartment with enthusiasm. He gave her carte blanche – he felt it was the least he could do, he felt so sorry for her. At least he had the business to use as a balm and until now she had had nothing to occupy her.

As the apartment was being worked on, Charity made herself over as well. She dieted to lose the little weight which Walt had thought an improvement, until she was fashionably thin. She had her teeth capped. She had plastic surgery on her jaw and nose. She visited the best couturiers where she spent a fortune on her clothes, and passed hours at the beauty salon. Her hair was styled and coloured blonde. She was a changed woman, she could pass for attractive now.

The social whirl eddied around her and embraced her enthusiastically. For the New York society Charity and Walt moved in was less interested in where you came from than the size of the bank balance you brought with you. Charity persuaded Walt to support museums, art galleries, ballet and the opera generously. In return they were invited to parties, dinners, balls and receptions, and finally Charity achieved her most heartfelt ambition – she was approached to sit on various charity committees.

She became addicted to meeting famous people – collecting them, almost. A film star hit town, a politician arrived, minor European royalty holidayed in New York, and Charity invited them to dine, to stay, to shop with her and showered them with presents.

At first Walt had watched this with amusement, then he found himself being sucked in as well. He got a kick out of having a famous face sitting at his table. And what he liked most was his picture in the papers, in the society columns. Maybe, just maybe, back in Oregon a certain lady would see them and realize just how rich and famous her only child was becoming. He joined the head-hunting with enthusiasm.

Walt had given up the idea of ever being in love now and could laugh at himself as he had been in his thirties when he had so desperately wanted to love and be loved – like a lost child, he often thought.

He had his work, that was his love now.

7

America – spring 1992

Walt had one unwritten rule, he never messed with anyone who worked for him. No matter how attractive a woman was, nor how strong the come-on, it was a trap he was determined not to fall into. He called it a trap advisedly. He had seen the consequences of such behaviour too often. It wasn't just that he regretted losing Yolanda – no, a good secretary could take years to train to be just right, then one lovers' tiff and she was gone, and with her the business secrets to sell or give to her next employer. And wives had an uncomfortable way of finding out about staff romances. A wise wife had a good friend in the company who fed her such information. And even if this were not the case, it was more difficult to use work as an alibi if a member of the staff was involved. No, far better not to touch them.

When Beth had come to work with him, with her smart good looks and neat figure, he'd been tempted, as any man would have been, but he had not touched. Now he was glad he hadn't. He had a marvellous working relationship with Beth based on mutual respect. She understood him, was not afraid of him, and next to Gubbie and himself probably knew more about the workings of his empire than anyone else. Sex might have mussed all that up.

The day Winter Sullivan was shown in for her interview,

Walt was standing at the window of his ultra-modern office, looking down on the fleets of vans and lorries which transported his pharmaceuticals nationwide. Beyond them was the railway line with his containers on it, bearing his logo, which carried them even further afield. He turned round, saw Winter and his heart turned turtle.

She wasn't beautiful in the conventional sense. Her large grey eyes were a fraction too wide apart, her face a little too broad, her mouth was smaller than fashion demanded and her nose had a tiny bump in it. It was a face where everything was infinitesimally wrong and yet the overall effect was of enormous attractiveness. Her shining blonde hair was straight and as smooth as water on a pond, and Walt wanted to touch it, just to feel the silkiness of it. She was neither tall nor short, fat nor thin. Most appealing of all, there was a vitality about her, a joy in living which shone from her face even before she smiled. Such a smile was not a polite, or simpering, or diffident smile. It was broad and genuine and bordered on a grin.

'Miss Sullivan.' Walt held out his hand in welcome. 'You appear to be just what this company is looking for.'

'You haven't interviewed me yet,' she said, and her voice was soft and bubbling with laughter and he realized his error.

'This meeting is really just a formality – to welcome you,' he lied, and wondered why he did and what the hell had got into him. 'My personnel people have been very impressed with you and your résumé.' He tapped the file on his wide, state of the art, steel and glass desk. And he sat down on his black leather and chrome chair and tried to look serious.

'Quite a grilling they gave me.' He heard the laughter in her voice again and felt he could listen to that voice for hours at a stretch.

'It's an important position you would be filling. Pharmaceuticals are a sensitive subject with some people, we need good press and public relations. I see you've worked for the past five years for Zeigals. Why change?' He felt more in control now but realized he'd much rather be telling her how lovely she was, how exciting he found her.

'I suppose working in conventional pharmaceuticals I've been able to see the pros and cons. If you remember, we had that problem over the lawsuits and Zeigals' Meridian tranquillizer?' He nodded, he remembered it well, even if he had forgotten how many million dollars they'd had to pay out when a couple of pregnant women lost their babies. Probably not the drug, but in this day and age it was cheaper to pay up, withdraw the drug, and then reconstitute it a bit and relaunch it with a different name and a label advising pregnant women not to take it.

'Well, anyway, during my years there I found myself getting more and more interested in homoeopathic and herbal remedies. That part of your work interests me.'

'It's only thirty per cent now,' he pointed out, and then wished he hadn't – maybe she'd lose interest in the job, perhaps he should say they were about to expand in this area.

'I realize, but a very important thirty per cent of alternative medicine,' she replied, before he'd made up his mind whether to lie or not.

'My old grandfather used to say that herbal medicine wasn't an alternative, that it's the real one, the original.' He laughed. 'And true when you think of the vast number of modern drugs which are based on herbs. Did they take you to our own herb farm up in Connecticut? No? You must go, it's very interesting.' With me, he thought.

'I'd love to. What I want to do for people is point up that "alternative", for want of a better word.' She smiled and spoke with such conviction that he longed to kiss her. 'And orthodox medicine should be going hand in hand. That's the message I want to get across.'

He leaned forward. 'I wish my grandfather was here to

hear you say that. I sometimes think he would be horrified by the path I've taken. He'd have no truck with orthodox prescriptions, he'd pour them down the drain. But it's not that simple, not that simple at all.' He glanced quickly at his watch. He'd like to suggest lunch but thought that was going a little too far, too fast. 'Tell you what, we've an excellent canteen here if you would like to take lunch there. I'm going to Connecticut this afternoon to the herb farm, maybe you'd like to come and see it with me?'

'I'd love to. Thank you, Mr Fielding.' She stood up and he wished he could join her in the canteen. But if he was to sneak off unplanned to the farm then he'd have to work through lunch to clear his desk or Beth would be on the warpath. After Winter had gone he summoned Beth to his office.

'Beth? Arrange for someone else to interview the other applicants, will you? And order my car for two and inform Miss Sullivan to be in the front hall at that time.'

'Yes, Mr Fielding.' She grinned at him.

'What's that grin for?'

'You've decided then? On Miss Sullivan?'

'She's good. The best.'

'Yes, of course, Mr Fielding.' Beth turned and glided from the offices and Walt felt like a little boy who'd been caught with his fingers in the cookie jar.

That had been nine months ago. In that time Walt had not touched Winter once, even though he longed to. He knew why. He didn't want to lose her, nor the friendship she gave him so generously. From the looks she sometimes gave him, the way her hand would sometimes linger on his, he was sure she felt something for him. It could have been so easy and yet it was so difficult.

If they became lovers how long would it last? How long before she became discontented with the arrangement and wanted more? He would have divorced Charity in a trice to be with Winter, but how could he? Not when Charity knew so much. No doubt the law could be bypassed with a clever lawyer – too much time had gone by and it would be her word against his. But what would his friends say, those important famous friends that he liked to have around him? He knew what they would think – no smoke without fire. His cultivation of the famous was a weakness on his part, he was aware of that, and he did not like it about himself. But then these people were part of his life now, turning his back on them would be going back to the past.

From the moment he first saw her he'd known she was different, and her time with him had not made him change his mind. Proof was not needed, but if it had been, it would have materialized when Winter accompanied Walt to Hank's nursing home. They were flying out to a conference in London and Walt was then travelling on alone to India and Cairo. He'd said he had somewhere to go first.

The chauffeur-driven limousine sneaked through the pleasant grounds of the home.

'What a pretty place, what is it?'

'A nursing-home,' he said shortly.

'Oh? It looks an expensive one.'

'Very, but it's the best. Has to be the best,' he added gruffly.

'Who's here, Walt?' she asked gently, using his Christian name as she did when they were in private.

'My son.'

She sat quiet, said nothing, did not pry but simply put her small hand into his large one.

'May I come in with you?' she asked, as the car came to a halt.

'If you like. It's really rather boring,' he said, and instantly regretted sounding so unfeeling. 'I mean, it might be boring for you,' he added clumsily to make amends, wishing he'd refused her offer – he preferred to see Hank alone.

'I'm sure it won't be.'

They entered the nursing-home which, with its lack of hospital smell and bustle, was more like a country house than an institution. They were greeted by the elegant receptionist who accompanied them, chatting brightly about nothing in particular, along the carpeted corridor to Hank's room where, at the door, as if waiting for them, stood a nurse. It was a pleasant room, well furnished with antiques, and with french doors with glazed chintz curtains opening into the lovely garden.

'Good afternoon, Mr Fielding. Hank's got a little bit of a cold so we thought it best to keep him in bed today,' the nurse said conversationally, not in the normal brisk tones of her profession.

Walt crossed the thick-pile carpet, pleased to note that his orders were being respected: the television was off and music filled the room. He stood looking down on his son. Hank was thirteen now but looked like a small child of six. His body was thin and immature but it was his face which was the most striking. Nothing of life had touched it. The expression was as fresh and innocent as the day his brain had stopped functioning. His eyes were open and stared at Walt with complete incomprehension.

'Hi, Hank!' He took hold of his son's hand and squeezed it. 'Thought I'd just pop in. I'm off to London for a few days. What do you want me to bring you back? I thought about a Burberry, for when you go out for your walks. How about that? And I'll bring you some postcards . . .' He carried on a monologue for a good twenty minutes. He talked about a baseball game he had not been to and fishing trips he had not taken. He talked of pop bands and music he never listened to and movies he had not seen. 'Right, Hank. Time I was pressing on.' He bent and kissed the sweet child's face. 'See you, Hank,' he called from the door, and Winter, who had been standing by the window the whole time, crossed to the bed and bent and kissed him too.

''Bye, Hank, nice meeting you,' she said.

They walked in silence to the car, got in and drove off. Neither said anything as they sped to the airport. Walt sat lost in thoughts of what might have been, feeling the immeasurable sadness he always associated with Sundays. Winter put out her hand and held his.

'Walt, I'm so sorry.'

'Bitch, isn't it?'

'Such a lovely boy, too.'

'Yes,' he said, tucking his chin down, controlling emotions that came easily to the surface on Sundays.

'Hard for you too. All those drugs, all that research, all those chemists and biochemists you employ. Harder for you to accept.'

'It is.' He looked up at her tentatively, not sure if he could hold on.

'Am I intruding? Do you want to talk?' she asked.

'Yes,' he said, and sobbed with an agonizing sound. The tears, for years suppressed, were freed, and she put her arms around him and held him while the storm of pain and frustration swept over him. And then he talked as he'd talked to no one else, not even Gubbie.

'And only you go to see him?' she finally asked when the storm of emotion had passed.

'Yep. I guess Charity can't ... I don't hold it against her. It's hard. Damned hard. She's banished him from her life. Made him not exist. That's her route to sanity.'

'And you can't do that?'

'No way. All the time he's lying there I live in hopes. They tell me he doesn't know me, probably doesn't comprehend a word I say to him. I can't believe that. You never know ...'

'That's true. So true. No, you couldn't leave him. I bet he knows you. Love like that can get through, I'm sure.'

He smiled at her. 'Sorry, letting go like that.'

'No, Walt, I feel privileged.'

While in London, Winter had gone out shopping and had returned to their hotel with a Burberry carrier bag.

'For Hank,' she'd said simply. That had been two weeks ago and Walt had known that he could not go on much longer as he was . . .

America – autumn 1992

'Are you going to moon in here on your own all day?' Charity stood in the doorway.

'Hell! I must have been asleep.' Walt yawned and stretched. 'Must be jet-lagged.'

'We're out to dinner tonight at the Shropshires. Robert Redford might be there.'

'Really?' he said and felt enormously weary and uninterested.

'What's got into you? You've got an hour to sort yourself out,' Charity said sharply.

He swung his legs to the floor and sat up straight. 'Charity, tell me. Why won't you visit Hank?'

Her face tightened, as if by tautening her muscles she could shut the question out.

'We've been through all that.'

'But we haven't, Charity. You know we haven't. Maybe we should talk,' he said kindly enough.

'You know how I feel about the whole catastrophe – that it's a judgment on you. I don't want to see him now or ever.'

'I think you should. I don't think we should forget him.'

'Oh, I haven't forgotten him, Walt. I never forget anything.' And she had gone, and Walt sat alone and remembered the wonderful release and comfort he had felt talking to Winter. He felt sorry for Charity that she had not experienced the same.

A week before Guthrie's party in January, Charity was shopping. She had bought the dress and was now busy purchasing the right accessories. She must have been thinking of something else when she stepped out into Fifth Avenue and was hit by a yellow cab.

Walt was in his office when Beth brought him the news. To his shame Walt realized his first reaction was one of enormous relief. Was he free? And then he shook himself and reined in such thoughts.

'Is she all right?' he forced himself to ask.

'I don't know, Mr Fielding. I'll order your car.'

He stood by the hospital bed.

'What happened?' he asked.

'God knows. I must have been miles away. Damned nuisance – look at me,' Charity complained.

'That's a fine bruise on your forehead.'

'It's my damn leg. The doctor says it'll be a good three months before I'm mobile again. And you'll have to get me out of here and home – I hate hospitals.'

'Yes, honey.'

'And then there's Guthrie's party. I was so looking forward to that. You must still go, Walt.'

'On my own?'

'You'll know nearly everyone there. And I want to hear all about it.'

He got out of the room as quickly as possible. He did not wait until he was home. He used one of the hospital payphones.

'Winter, it's Walt. I'm due at a party in Paris next week. Would you like to come?'

6 Dieter

1

En route for Germany – autumn 1992

Dieter was surprised. He had completed a satisfactory deal with His Excellency. A large sum of money, part of his commission, had already been transferred to his Swiss bank account and more would follow when the transaction was complete, yet he felt a total lack of interest in the whole affair.

He had sat in the Spanish villa drinking interminable cups of sweet coffee and had watched His Excellency poring over the specification of guns, armoured personnel carriers, missile launchers, all the hardware of war that the saner countries in the world had decided his volatile country should not have access to, and he'd longed to say to him, 'For God's sake make your mind up, take them or not, I don't give a damn one way or the other!' That had shocked him. He'd never thought like that before. He was invariably excited, describing his wares with pleasure. Not this time.

Instead of being elated he felt nothing. He was not happy, he was not excited, yet he was not bored. It was an almost *couldn't care less* feeling he was experiencing, and that was not like Dieter at all.

As the miles between Spain and his German home sped by he felt an increasing feeling of foreboding. So strange was it that he did not stop overnight in Cannes as he had planned but pressed on. So strong was it that it

kept him awake and kept fatigue at bay. Something was
wrong.

It was dawn as he swung the powerful Mercedes
through the narrow streets of the village with the expertise
of familiarity. He slowed for the sleeping policemen he'd
had installed in the gateway between the tall and intricately
worked wrought iron. Nor did he drive quickly up the
drive for fear of hurting any animals which might stray on
to the roadway. And he slowed almost to a halt in the
curve in the drive that gave him his first glimpse of his
beloved home. At the sight of it he sighed with relief.
During the last hundred miles he had become obsessed
with the idea that harm had befallen this, his proudest
possession. The small castle stood below him in its parkland. The mountains behind, with their winter browns and
sagey greens, provided a fitting background to the sparkling white of his own schloss – his very own, which never
failed to give him a thrill. At least that emotion remained,
he thought, as he put the car in gear and made the steep
descent to his home.

Magda appeared on the steps at the sound of his car.
He had known all along that she would be there to
welcome him. When he could not give her an exact time
of arrival, it was no matter, she would always be waiting
for him, the time of day or night of no consequence to her.
In all the years of his marriage to her he had never once
returned to an empty house.

'*Liebling.*' He kissed her cheek. He would have liked to
scoop her into his arms and smother her face with kisses.
But he never did – it would not be fair to her since it could
go no further. He always maintained this detached cool-
ness with her, it was better by far.

'Dieter, I've missed you,' Magda said simply, as she
always did. Given the circumstances, one could presume
that she was merely being polite. But this was not so, she
was always genuine.

'Some breakfast, or do you want to try to get a little sleep?'

'Breakfast. If I go to sleep now I won't wake up until tomorrow and I've an appointment in Munich.'

She led the way to the small breakfast-room which overlooked the water-meadows. It was, he often thought, his favourite side of the castle. The table was laid perfectly as always, with a Christmas flowering rose in a silver vase which Magda told him she had picked that morning from the bush they had planted together when she had first come here. She disappeared into the small kitchenette she had had installed in the butler's pantry beyond. It had been her idea so that whatever time Dieter returned from his travels she could feed him and make him coffee without having to disturb the servants. Magda was considerate like that, it was no wonder that the staff who worked for them would have died for her.

'I'm sorry about the other day,' Dieter called, raising his voice so that she could hear in her kitchen. He had already apologized on the telephone but he had purposely chosen a moment when he could not see her face to apologize personally for hitting her. It was easier, he hated apologizing.

'Oh, that ... You've already said sorry. I'd quite forgotten, it was nothing,' she called back. He was pretty sure that was what she would say even before she said it. Too often he had to apologize for his sudden flare-ups of temper and she always forgave him. But a temper was one thing, violence was another. The reason for it was plain to both of them but still, in his book, his behaviour was unforgivable – gentlemen did not hit their ladies. Maybe he wasn't a gentleman? He shook his head to reject that unpleasant thought. Sometimes he wished Magda wasn't so understanding; perhaps if she screamed and shouted her own frustration at him he would be able to feel less guilty at not being able to make love to her. He played with his knife, wiping its spotless surface on his napkin – how often he thought in this way and how often it got him nowhere.

'I've had the strangest feeling all the way home that something was wrong. I was almost afraid to look in case the house had burnt down,' he said, his voice still raised but happier now he had got the apologies over.

'Really? How strange,' she called back. He sat at the table, his hand stroking the fine damask table-cloth. He flicked open his napkin and smoothed that into his lap. He never failed to enjoy, and be pleased by, the beautiful things he used daily – objects most men would not even notice.

Magda appeared with the silver pot of coffee on a tray and smiled at him.

'You look tired, my darling.'

'And you look as beautiful as ever,' he replied. It was not a husbandly lie but the truth. Dark-haired Magda with her large grey eyes, perfect heart-shaped face with its smooth, creamy complexion was a great beauty, even now in her late thirties. When Dieter had fallen in love with her he had been surprised, for having always been attracted to blondes, he had always assumed he would marry one and thus have a chance of the fair children a German should have. Instead he had fallen for dark-haired Magda and there were no children and now never would be. He frowned; this thought often intruded and spoiled the day for him.

He drank his coffee and ate two slices of toast with some Cooper's marmalade he had sent from England. There was little about that country he liked but its marmalade was an exception.

Magda sat opposite him, waiting, he knew, for him to finish eating so that she could light a cigarette. He did not like her smoking and he worried at the number of cigarettes she got through in a day. But he could not stop her, could not even suggest it when he realized that he was probably the cause of her addiction.

'More coffee?' She picked the coffee pot up and it was then that he noticed her hand was shaking.

'Magda, what is it?' He was concerned.

She replaced the pot on the silver tray with a clatter. 'Oh, Dieter, I don't know how to tell you.'

'Yes? What?' he asked with a sinking feeling. He had been right, something was very wrong.

'It's your mother, Dieter, I'm so sorry to have to tell you this but she died peacefully in her sleep last night.'

'My mother?' he repeated inanely. 'My mother – dead?' He shook his head as if clearing it to allow his mind to absorb this information. Magda interpreted the action as one of denial.

'I'm so sorry, but it's true. Your stepfather phoned.'

'How did he know my number?' Dieter said sharply.

'I don't know, my darling, but he had it.'

'But I'm ex-directory,' he said indignantly.

'Yes, darling, but does it really matter? You had to be told, didn't you?'

'Yes, I suppose so,' he said grudgingly, and looked into himself and wondered how he was feeling at this news. 'You know, I think I will go and lie down after all.' He stood up abruptly.

'That would be a good idea. I've already taken the liberty of cancelling your appointments for today. Naturally everyone understood.'

'Bless you, Magda, you think of everything.' And he gently kissed the top of her head.

He climbed the long flight of marble stairs and felt as if his legs were encased in deep-sea divers' boots, so great was his tiredness now. He quickly undressed, pulled the curtains against the weak winter daylight and was soon in bed. Despite his weariness, despite his longing for sleep, it did not come but instead teased him, allowing his eyelids to feel heavy and droop and then waking him in an instant, so that he lay wide-eyed, looking up at the canopy of the bed.

'Sophie. Poor Sophie . . .' he said aloud to the empty room . . .

Cambridge – 1957

Dieter stood in front of the bay-windowed, yellow-brick, semi-detached house in the busy street and shuddered. It was so ugly. He checked that he had locked his van door. He pushed at the rickety gate, which squeaked as if in reply, and walked up the short tessellated pathway, slippery in this damp weather. He rang the bell and pulled his coat further around him against the winter chill as he waited for the door to be answered. He'd give them ten seconds and then he'd go. Really, he did not know why he had come. Curiosity, he told himself.

A small boy dressed in the unbecoming grey uniform of countless English schoolboys – knee-length grey socks which were half-way down to his ankles, and overlong grey shorts – opened the door. He said nothing but stared up at Dieter from small, suspicious grey eyes.

'Is Mrs Clarkson in?' Dieter asked.

'You're not English,' the child replied.

'No, I'm not.'

'I can tell. You don't speak proper.'

'How clever of you to notice.' Dieter's smile was taut. 'I asked if . . .'

'Mum!' the child shouted. 'There's a foreign bloke here to see you.'

Dieter stared with disbelief at this child who, he presumed, was his half-brother.

A woman appeared at the back of the narrow hallway.

She was wiping her hands on a tea-towel and peered myopically towards her front door.

'Yes?' she said uncertainly, beginning to walk along the hall.

That's not my mother, Dieter thought indignantly at the sight of the short, plump woman with greying hair who approached. 'Dieter? Is it you? Is it really you?' And she put her arms around him and was standing on tiptoe in an attempt to kiss him. Dieter stood rigid as any soldier and waited for the onslaught to subside. 'Dieter, my darling, you came, I always said you would. Come in, it's so cold. This town is always so cold.' She ushered him into the hall where they both stood awkwardly staring at each other, the child leaning against the wall looking from one to the other with marked interest. 'You've grown so,' she said.

'Inevitably, Mama. Children do.' He found he could not keep the irritation he felt at such an inane remark from his voice.

'How silly of me. Of course, you're a man now. All of twenty. Imagine. Darren, this is the big brother I've told you about so often. We called him that to go with Dieter.' She laughed. In the laugh was his mother. 'Still, let's go into the front room, we've a fire there.' She opened the first door of the hall and he was shown into a small room which appeared smaller from the amount of furniture crammed into it. 'I'll make us some tea. Come and help me, Darren.' She ushered the child through the door.

Dieter looked about him. He could see his mother's touch in the slate-blue velvet curtains at the window and the discreetly striped wallpaper. But it was a pathetic effort in a room of unrelieved ugliness. He leaned forward and banked up the fire with more coal.

She re-entered the room with a tray. Dieter held the door for her.

'You always had such lovely manners,' she said wistfully. 'Bob will be so pleased you're here. He'll be home soon. You'll stay to supper?' She spoke in short sentences which emerged rapidly. 'You must tell me everything, what you've been doing . . .'

He looked at her blankly. What could he tell her of the past eight years? What would she understand about it?

'This and that,' he said enigmatically.

'When you ran away you can have no idea how I worried. We spent days looking for you, you know. Where did you go?'

He smiled, he'd often wondered if she'd searched for him, he had liked to think she did. 'I lived in a shack in some woods. I made it very cosy. Then, when the winter came, I moved out and into the room of a friend.'

'You live in Berlin still?'

'No, Munich. I moved there three years ago. I wanted to be in the West. My British passport made it easy for me to get out of Berlin.'

'So it did you some good? You were so angry when Bob adopted you.'

'Yes, I learned to be grateful,' he said smoothly, not letting on that he had two passports now – his English one which was vital to his business operations and his German one in his father's name – acquired with easily obtained forged papers and some hefty bribes.

'And what do you do?'

'I buy and sell.'

'What?' asked the child.

'Anything I think I can sell,' he said shortly. This was true. He had soon realized that if he could not see the need for something, undoubtedly there was someone else who did. His job had been to learn its value. But he did not tell his mother of his trading in food, cigarettes and alcohol which he bought from a corrupt sergeant who relieved the NAAFI of large quantities of goods, which Dieter sold on for inflated prices. Nor did he tell of the short time he dealt in scrap metal but having made a good sum moved out again – it was not the image he saw for himself. But he did explain how in the chaos of post-war Europe there was much to buy – furniture, paintings, silver. He let her believe it was his astute dealing that had bought the warehouse rapidly filling up with his purchases, and not diamonds.

'I'm going to open a large antique store. There's money about again.'

'Not here there isn't.'

'It's so grey here. How can you stand it?'

'You get used to it.'

'Do you?'

'Of course. I'm very happy,' she said, almost defiantly, he thought.

'Where's Bob now? Is he still in the army?'

'No, he left as soon as he could. He's a college porter – he loves the work,' she added, a shade quickly, he thought. He did not respond, he did not know quite what to say. From living in a castle with his father to this? He did not know whether to admire or pity her.

They all looked up as they heard the scraping of a key in the lock.

'Well, I never, here's a turn-up for the books. Dieter of all people.'

Bob Clarkson stood in the doorway. He was dressed in an ill-fitting suit, his belly was large and pendulous, his complexion red and vulgar. Dieter knew then that his mother needed pity.

The visit to his family was an ordeal for Dieter. He'd always despised Bob, now he loathed him for giving his mother such a dreary life.

The supper seemed interminable and the food indigestible.

'This'll stick some lead in your pencil, Dieter,' Bob

guffawed. 'Steak and kidney pudding, the food of old England,' he intoned with pride.

'Wot won us the war, right, Dad?' Darren glanced slyly at Dieter as he spoke, but to his evident disappointment Dieter did not rise to the bait.

'Now, now, Darren. We don't want no talk of war. Do we, Dieter?' Dieter stared stonily at his stepfather and brother.

'Dieter's done well, Bob. He's opening an antique shop,' Sophie said quickly.

'Well, that's nice, son. I'm surprised there's much call for that sort of thing. I'd have thought, after the bashing we gave them, it would be a long time before Germans could afford such luxuries.'

'On the contrary. My fellow-countrymen wish to return to normal quickly – as we are doing,' he added pointedly.

'Your fellow-countrymen? I thought you were French.'

'No, Darren, I'm German,' Dieter said coldly.

'Well, it's not something I'd want to brag about if I were you, mate.' Darren sniggered, pushed back his chair and left the room.

Dieter answered their questions monosyllabically after that. Bob announced apologetically that he was off to his club – a darts match he could not miss. Dieter was relieved.

'You staying?' Bob asked as he put on his overcoat.

'I'm afraid I must be going.'

'Oh, Dieter, no. I'd hoped you'd stay the night,' Sophie said.

'I'm sorry, Mama. I've an important appointment early tomorrow in Norfolk to buy some paintings. And then I'm booked on the afternoon ferry sailing from Harwich.'

'There should be a law against it. Our treasures going abroad like this, and to Germany of all places,' Bob blustered.

'But Bob, you won the war, you can't have everything.' Dieter smiled coolly. Bob looked long and hard at him and for a moment Dieter wondered if he was going to hit him, or was he searching for words he could not find?

'I'm off,' he said abruptly.

'Dieter, you shouldn't goad Bob like that, it's not fair. He's not as smart as you,' Sophie admonished him when they were finally alone.

'It's their stupid English pride, it annoys me. This country is drab, grey and finished, in my opinion. Not like Germany. Oh, Mama, you would be amazed. There is so much work being done, such pride in rebuilding. A determination to be the best again. You should return.'

'Whatever for?' Sophie laughed. 'I'm quite content here.'

'How can you be? With this family, in this house, in this country?' Dieter spoke with feeling.

'I agree we don't have much money. But so long as we are warm and have food, the other things I used to think so important, aren't important at all. I have no silver but then I don't have it to clean. My wardrobe of clothes is small – there is less to wash and iron and mend. I can clean this house from top to bottom in a day. So I have no servants to fetch and carry, but then I don't have to contend with their squabbling and prying either.'

'But England? I mean . . .'

'England has been good to me. I like the people. They'll recover – they will,' she said emphatically as Dieter shook his head. 'I feel safe here. For the first time in years. Why? Because of Bob. He makes me feel that way. I know he is a little vulgar but he is kind and good and he loves me more than I have ever been loved in my life.'

'But after my father . . .' He sounded perplexed.

'Ah, your father.' She looked down at her hands, a dreamy expression on her face. He was right, Dieter thought. No one could replace him. 'I could never love again as I loved your father, that is true. He was so charming, handsome and debonair and I was so young.

But, and this is where Bob is better than your father, I never felt safe with Heinie and he never loved me.'

'Mama, I don't believe that.'

'Then why didn't he marry me?' She smiled at him wistfully.

'He would have, when he came back from the war.'

'No, Dieter, he would not. I used to pretend to myself he would, but deep down I knew it was only a dream I held, to keep going, I suppose. I was his mistress, and no doubt when my looks had gone he would have replaced me.'

'Never!' Dieter said staunchly.

'Dear Dieter, always so loyal. But try and imagine if your father had not been killed, if he had survived like his brother, do you really think the dashing Count, finding out that I had turned to prostitution for us to survive, would have taken me back into his bed?' Dieter winced at the words. Sophie looked closely at her son who looked away. 'Never! But Bob did,' she said quietly.

'You've changed, Mama.'

'Yes, of course I have. If I hadn't, I would have been lost.'

'I can't forget, Mama,' he said, his voice choked with emotion.

'You mean, my darling, you can't forgive me. I'm sorry if that is the case but I'm afraid it is your problem, not mine. I'm not ashamed of my past. There is nothing I can do or say to make it different and if you can't accept it, then you can't.' She shrugged.

Dieter looked at her sitting under the harsh hanging lamp, an opaque bowl in which the corpses of dead flies were silhouetted against the bulb. How could anyone change so much? Where was his flighty, coquettish mama? How could that delightful creature have become this philosophically accepting matron?

'Why did you come, Dieter? Why, after so many years?'

'I wanted to see you.'

'Just that?'

'Perhaps I was curious.'

'I thought there might be another reason.'

'No, nothing,' he lied. There was a very good reason. Next week he was to sail in a small fishing boat laden with guns to an African state about to have a revolution. Up until now he had sold the odd gun and, respected for his discretion, had known it was only a matter of time before he would be approached for something bigger. That day had come. It would be dangerous. He might be captured and left to rot away his life in a stinking African jail. He might die ... Dieter had come to say goodbye – just in case.

2

Europe and Africa – 1957–1962

The shipment of arms would start from Holland. A year before, using his English papers, Dieter had been able to set up an import–export business in Rotterdam in preparation for just such an assignment. The true ownership was buried in a labyrinth of shell companies he had registered in Liechtenstein. At first it had been difficult for those he had to deal with to take someone of his age seriously but they soon accepted the proud young man as a business equal – after all, his money was as good as anyone's twice his age. He imported carpets and wood-carvings, cloth and silks from the East. He exported cheeses, office furniture and small machine parts, as stated on his licence.

Since Dieter could not spend all his time in Holland, nor wished to, he needed to employ people he could trust, not only with his affairs but also with the large sums of money which would at times be required to pass through the office. And Dieter knew the only sure way to ensure discretion was to employ people who were indebted to him.

He had met Jan in a bar drowning his sorrows. He had been imprisoned for collaborating with the Germans during the occupation. He had served his time and had emerged to find that society did not forgive, and he had become an unemployable outcast. When he realized that others who had done far more for the enemy than he had escaped from prison and prospered, his bitterness knew no bounds. A man with a grudge, penniless and yet intelligent, was ideal for Dieter. He befriended him, fed him, clothed and housed him and finally offered him the job as manager of East, West, Import, Export — EWIE for short. Jan's gratitude was unbounded.

Dieter had met Renalta, petite and blonde, sitting on a park bench crying uncontrollably. He had sat down beside her and silently taken her hand and had waited for the tears to subside.

The tale she told him was a predictable one. How she had met an American sailor who had fed her stories of Southern plantations and mint juleps which, to an impressionable girl, sounded like *Gone with the Wind* come to life and he her Rhett Butler. He had seduced her easily. When she found she was pregnant she discovered something else — that the American authorities had no record of a sailor of the name he had given her. When she had confessed, her pastor father, a godly man, had melodramatically thrown her out into the street. She had no money and was contemplating suicide when Dieter hove into sight.

He paid for her abortion in a discreet clinic and found her a clean, pleasant room. He offered her a job as Jan's secretary. He slept with her a couple of times just to make certain. Renalta was now madly in love with him and, he was sure, would die for him.

Bruce, Dieter's skipper, was a large and fearsome-looking Scotsman with a scar on one cheek and a limp which he never explained. He had had a conventionally dreadful war on the Western Approaches. So frightening had his experiences been that life afterwards seemed tame and he ended up in civvy street bored witless. He had drifted in and out of jobs which he always lost because, when bored, he drank like a desperate man.

Dieter had trawled the bars of many ports until their paths crossed. They formed an immediate respect for each other. Dieter had chosen well. The prospect of smuggling, cocking a snook at society and the large sum of money Dieter offered, persuaded Bruce that he had at last found gainful employment.

On Bruce's advice they bought a war-surplus Motor Torpedo Boat. Dieter had been dubious, it seemed to him to be all engines. But when Bruce pointed out the speed this boat could reach, outrunning anything else, he agreed. In fact these selfsame engines gave it a limited range and would need constant refuelling. Bruce solved the problem by suggesting they change to diesel, convert the rear cabin into a storage tank and sling hammocks for the small crew required.

They had cleverly contrived hiding-places for the guns behind the bulkheads, alongside the bilges, and deep under the metal plating in the engine-room. The operation had been financed by the sale of more diamonds. It had hurt Dieter to see them go, it always did.

One of the Western military attachés in Berlin had introduced Dieter to the principles of this particular little adventure. An African state, still unstable following its independence from colonial rule, was about to enjoy a bloody revolution. He would need the help of many of the contacts he had made in his early days in Berlin.

A large part of the consignment was supplied by the American government from a base in Germany, courtesy of a corrupt American stores sergeant. The shifting of the arms across the Russian zone involved a complicated and costly system of vans, cars and lorries, all with hiding places, all suitably disguised by other cargo, and helped along by a Russian diplomat who hoarded every dollar Dieter paid him to fulfil his dream of an escape to the West. They would rendezvous for the final stage of the haul at an isolated inlet on the west coast of England, where the armaments officer of a crack British regiment, who unfortunately was having difficulty in meeting horrendous mess bills, would be waiting for them.

Dieter had learnt his most valuable lesson as a child in the ruins of Berlin – that everyone had a price and traitors' hearts could beat under the most respectable tunics. He had his team.

As they finally set sail with the last of the cargo on board, Dieter felt he could relax. He lay on the bunk in the tiny cabin in the bows of his MTB. He had nearly called her *Sophie* but had changed his mind at the last minute. It was *Renalta* which was emblazoned on the smart black paintwork. Dieter had wanted to keep its nondescript colour which blended so well with the sea, but Bruce had advised differently.

'Paint it – less suspicious. Keep it grey and the sods'll be thinking, what's he got to hide?'

As they headed out to sea Dieter was exhausted. He would never, he was sure, forget the nervous tension as cargo had been smuggled on board disguised in packing-cases he himself had built, marked 'machine tools': the guns, mines and grenades were hidden under genuine parts, in cheeses, in re-sealed cans and behind anything movable. He was lying on a floating arsenal and he felt lightheaded and, strangely, happy.

The MTB had not been built for leisurely cruising, and

once they hit the Bay of Biscay she revealed the rather unpleasant yaw which was part of her repertoire of unstable and uncomfortable movements. Dieter had never been so sick in his life, a state of affairs which seemed to amuse Bruce inordinately.

'What you need is some tiddly stew,' he advised, and then boomed to the Irish mute who acted as cook in the minute galley, 'Bowl of your best Irish here, on the double for Mr Weiher.'

'Bruce, don't joke with me. I'm ill enough.'

'It's no joke, Dieter. Nothing makes you sick like an empty stomach. Eat, you'll be fine. Come up on the bridge when you're ready – there's a great sea running.'

Dieter didn't go on deck, he had no desire to see the sea running well or not. But Bruce was right, he kept the stew down and fell asleep after several large port-and-brandies.

The following day he awoke feeling normal again. He had found his sea legs. He discovered he liked the dip and yaw of the boat, the biting sea breeze which made him fit and alive, and he loved to stand and watch the restless, ever-changing sea.

The further south they went, the more Dieter became fascinated by the sky. The stars shone far brighter, seemed far nearer, and he looked at the blackness of infinity and felt that if he put his hand up he could touch it.

The voyage was uneventful. As they neared their destination, Bruce doubled the watches – the men were alert for naval vessels, coastguards, customs men, anyone who might have too great an interest in their smuggled brandy and cigarettes, which were what the crew had been told they were carrying.

The night of their rendezvous, they approached the shoreline on half-power, lights dimmed and the men speaking in whispers. Dieter felt his heart thumping with excitement as the great black bulk of Africa loomed on the starboard side.

There was no warning. One moment he was thinking poetical thoughts on the mystery of the great continent, the next he had five inches of cold black steel prodding at his neck.

'Customs,' a deep voice said behind him. 'Stand still, no harm.'

Dieter did as he was told and seethed with anger. How had the lookouts missed them? How could they fail, having come so far?

'You got guns. You give me guns.'

'I've no guns. Cheeses and machinery only. You're welcome to see the papers.' Dieter spoke calmly and courteously. 'There's no need to keep that thing sticking in the side of my neck. It's a mite dangerous, wouldn't you say?' Dieter turned slowly, marvelling at how calm and cool he was despite how angry he felt. He looked into two terrified eyes in a black face covered in sweat. The man wore a tee-shirt and shorts and his feet were bare.

'Customs, my arse!' Dieter heard Bruce bellow from the shadows. He sprang forward, knocked the gun out of the man's hand, banged him on the head with his own gun and with one swift, almost graceful movement he hurled the man over the side of the boat. 'The sharks'll see to him.'

A shot rang out, the bullet whistling so close past Dieter's cheek that he put his hand up, convinced he had been hit.

'Get down, you loon.' Bruce pushed Dieter unceremoniously on to the metal deck.

The gun battle was short and sharp. The man had three companions but none were marksmen and their bullets whistled through the night, pinging on the metal of the ship, ricocheting off other parts, crumping harmlessly into cargo strapped on deck. Bruce was not the only one with a gun. In a split second his crew had chosen their targets and three more black bodies were hurled into the sea.

After such noise the silence was so dense that Dieter felt it was almost tangible. He sat up gingerly.

'Who do you think they were?' he asked.

'Who knows? Pirates, perhaps. On the other hand it might be a double-cross on the part of your clients, I've known that happen. There's no point pretending we're not here now. It's full steam ahead and get this over quickly and bugger off sharpish, don't you think?'

'Do you think it's safe to go on?'

'Safe? Of course it's not sodding safe. What do you want to do, scuttle back to Rotterdam with this lot and no bunce?' Bruce turned on his heel and stalked back into his wheelhouse, leaving Dieter feeling stupid.

The MTB slid into the deep-water inlet where the rendezvous was to take place. They were all on deck waiting for the signal. They waited five minutes, cursing under their breath. Then they saw the flashing light. And Dieter smiled – he felt he was in an adventure war film, and then he chided himself for such foolishness.

A somewhat flimsy wooden pontoon had been built out into the inlet for them. Working silently and quickly, the men began the long task of unloading the ship.

Bruce and Dieter crossed on to land. Sitting on the running-board of a large lorry was a smartly suited gentleman with an attaché case at his feet. Smiling introductions were made.

'Any nasties around? Soldiers, police, that sort of thing?' Bruce asked him pleasantly.

'No. They've all had their dash, they won't be bothering us,' the gentleman said in impeccable Oxford English.

'Dash?' asked Dieter.

'Bribes,' Bruce explained.

'I must congratulate you on arriving so punctually,' the man said. 'I heard some gunshots – trouble?'

'Some pirates boarded us as we were coming in, but they're all nicely asleep now.' The loading was going faster now for Dieter's men had been joined by six Africans in army fatigues who moved swiftly.

'So, to business.' The man clicked his case open. By the light of a hurricane-lamp, Dieter salivated as he saw the neatly stacked dollar bills.

'If you could hold that lamp up, Bruce, I'll count it.'

'There's no need, it's all there,' the man said.

'All the same, if you don't mind.' Dieter began to count the notes as quickly and expertly as any bankteller.

A soldier came and whispered in the immaculately suited man's ear. He stood up, straightened his trouser creases, dusted sand from his shoes, beckoned to one of his men and picked up another briefcase. 'Everything seems to be in order. My sergeant informs me the goods we ordered are here. So, you have the money and I shall be on my way,' he said.

'Not so quickly, if you don't mind.' Bruce stood menacingly, feet apart. 'I should sit down again if I were you until my partner here has finished his counting.'

'Is that really necessary?'

'Very.' Bruce pushed him hard so that he sat down with a thud on the running-board.

Dieter frowned. He looked up at Bruce.

'It's only half the sum agreed.'

'As I thought. You shit!' Bruce snarled.

'Gentlemen, please.' The man waved a heavily ringed hand in the air. 'We've had a slight problem. The money we had expected from our Russian friends was less than promised and . . .' He did not finish the sentence, for Bruce shot him between the eyes and his body lolled back like a rag doll, his face looking up at the magnificence of the sky as if surprised by it.

At the sound of the shot his men came running, shouting in their own language, scrabbling for their own guns. They stumbled and screamed as bullets ripped into their bodies, blood spurted from severed arteries, its warm, slightly acrid smell filling Dieter's nostrils. They were strafed by the repeated rat-tat of machine-gun fire. Dieter swung round: on a slight rise, laughing as if fit to burst, was the tiny Irish cook wielding a machine-gun on its stand. Several men lay moaning in the sand; Bruce walked among them despatching them with single shots, with as little involvement as a huntsman destroying a wounded stag.

'What the fuck did you do that for?' Dieter swung round to face Bruce who was nonchalantly taking a swig of malt from a hip-flask which he offered to Dieter who shook his head in annoyed refusal. 'Jesus!'

'The little shit was cheating you. He was lying.' Bruce bent down and picked up the man's briefcase, apparently oblivious to the blood on it. He clicked it open, it too was stacked full with dollar bills. 'See?'

'How did you know?'

'He looked shifty and I didn't like the cut of his suit.' He grinned.

'But you can't go around shooting people because they look shifty.'

'In circumstances like this I can. You don't think our soldier chums here would have let us go with any of the money, do you? If we hadn't dropped them they'd have seen us off.'

'But there are two more shipments.'

'Then I reckon we've done this feller-me-lad a favour.' He prodded the corpse with his shoe. 'I think he was working freelance. His bosses might have killed you on the last consignment, but not the first. He was pulling a fast one on them. No, we've definitely done him a favour – nice clean death, you don't think his friends would have been so kind to him, do you?'

'But the others, did you have to shoot them?'

'Tidier this way.'

'Bruce! You're incorrigible. What would I do without you?'

'Be dead, probably. This is a filthy business you're in, Dieter my lad. I think you need some guidance if you're to survive.' Bruce slapped him on the back and put his arm around his shoulders as they walked calmly back to the boat. Dieter did not look back at the carnage they had left behind them.

That night, he and Bruce got enjoyably drunk together as the MTB sped swiftly north.

'I hate to say this, Bruce, but I've enjoyed the trip. I can't remember when I last felt so alive.'

'Fun, isn't it?' Bruce grinned.

'But what about next time? What if that happens again?'

'But it won't. You see, you've left your calling card. No one messes with Herr Dieter – that's what that elegant stiff back there is telling them. And don't worry, the word will spread where it's most needed.'

And there was no trouble on the next two trips, nor on the subsequent ones. Dieter found he looked forward to the deals, longed for them, found he had become totally addicted to the excitement of the run. Dieter, and Bruce with him, were becoming very rich very quickly.

Dieter blessed the day he had met Bruce. He trusted him implicitly and from him he learned much, not just about smuggling and gun-running but about human nature too. For five years they operated as a pair, working their way with larger boats and even larger contracts. The morality and the consequences of their actions never bothered them. Where there was a revolution, a minor war, where sanctions had to be broken, Bruce and Dieter were to be found. The politics were of no interest to them – all much of a muchness as far as they were concerned. They both wanted to be rich and they were both having fun.

*

One night in 1962, after a successful consignment had been delivered to a group of terrorists, Bruce had got drunk with Dieter, as he invariably did. He had then gone in search of a whore, while Dieter, who rarely bothered with casual sex, went to bed.

Bruce was found dead in his bed the following morning. He had been knifed through the heart, he had been mutilated and his wallet had been stolen.

Dieter was called to identify the body. When he saw the lifeless, bloody form he had to turn away to hide the tears that filled his eyes from the mortuary attendant. When finally alone he allowed himself to cry, and hard, racking sobs shook him. He felt despairing, inconsolable and alone. Bruce had been his friend, the only friend he had ever had. He realized that he had loved the man. As he cried he remembered his father and how as a child he had held back the tears, and here he was, a man, unable to contain them. Bruce had been like a second father. And he knew as he wept that he was grieving for both of them.

Dieter never went on a gun run again – he left that to others.

3

Germany – 1963–1965

The illegal shipments were intermittent. Dieter did not make the mistake of neglecting his other operations. The business transacted at the import and export company in Amsterdam initially to lull the port authorities' suspicions, grew to be an important source of his income.

Renalta, had, it appeared, finally resigned herself to the fact that Dieter was not going to make her his wife. But Dieter was aware that rational behaviour in a woman who felt spurned could not be guaranteed. Therefore to ensure her devotion he had moved her to a small, comfortable apartment on which he paid the rent. In addition he made sure he never forgot her birthday or the anniversary of their meeting and always sent expensive presents. She seemed content with this arrangement and it was a cheap price for Dieter to pay for her loyalty.

In Munich, his large antiques shop in an old warehouse was a huge success. To get to the bric-à-brac on the top floors, customers had to walk past the expensive furniture and other objects and often they fell in love with an item they did not even know they wanted until they saw it. The price of everything was clearly marked and they were saved the embarrassment of asking. Dieter encouraged them to browse and young, polite and knowledgeable assistants were available should anyone need advice.

Dieter's favourite of all his enterprises was a small shop where he sold his war artefacts – uniforms, medals, drums and antique guns. He had rapidly become a valuable contact for collectors and had begun a lucrative mail order catalogue.

His art gallery prospered. He did not bother with contemporary art, nor was he much interested in anything painted this century – his view of later Picassos was not the conventional one. It could safely be said that he was intolerant of anything non-representational, and his favourite paintings were invariably Italian, of a religious bent, which was odd since he was an atheist. But even in this rarefied atmosphere he had a bargain basement where many a portrait of an English aristocrat hung patiently waiting to be adopted by someone *nouveau* lacking his own portraits of worthy ancestors. Dieter had found that Americans in particular loved these pictures and he was seriously thinking of opening up a branch somewhere in the States. He had the name, Instant Ancestors – that amused him.

By his late twenties, Dieter was becoming very rich and

thinking of breaking into fine-art auctioneering. He saved carefully and had a numbered bank account in Switzerland, an acquisition which had given him particular pleasure. There he salted away the money from his illegal arms deals.

His increasing wealth made possible one great pleasure – a generous allowance to his mother. Initially Bob took umbrage and said he was quite capable of looking after Sophie himself. Dieter felt irritated by such proud stupidity, and he insisted. He wanted his mother to have the best. He tried to rehouse them too, but Bob refused his offer. Whenever Dieter was in England he would try to see her. They only met in London, the house in Cambridge depressed him too much and he always felt an intruder there. Just recently these visits had ceased, not on his part but on Sophie's – she was too busy to meet him. Dieter wondered what could be keeping her so occupied, and he was hurt that she did not rearrange her affairs for his visits.

When Bruce died he had been surprised by his initial mourning for the man, nor had he expected it to last so long. It was a good year before he could shake off the feeling. Now, when he remembered, he would have a frisson of regret at the loss not just of the man but also of the tingling excitement he had experienced on the boat with their illicit cargoes, outwitting the authorities of a dozen nations. But then he would sometimes remember the smell of the blood and ripped guts, the screams of the dying on that first venture into Africa, and he would shudder and be content to remain the anonymous organizer and pay others the going rate to take the risk for him.

His apartment was modest and in the old part of the city – he could never imagine himself living anywhere modern – but for the time being he did not hanker for anything more spacious. It was furnished with choice pieces of furniture and paintings from his stock. Nothing stayed there long for everything was for sale. He liked his constantly changing décor – at least he never became bored with things.

There were certain objects that he would never sell, however ... his father's possessions which had been pillaged by the Nazis. Over the years, he searched for them painstakingly, tracking them down in the auction houses of Europe, following up on leads or gossip that a private sale might be in the offing. He never asked how people had come to own these things. He merely paid the price they asked and accumulated everything he could find of his father's in a fire-proof, permanently locked room in his warehouse.

He had a passion for good clothes, his shirts were from Turnbull and Asser, he had a tailor in Savile Row as well as one in Munich, and his shoes were always hand-made, by Lobbs of London as well as in Italy. His underwear was silk with his monogram embroidered on it. Clothes sat well on him for he was slim and he made sure he kept his body in good shape.

He lived simply. A cleaning woman took care of his apartment and his washing and ironing. Apart from his early morning coffee and toast he took all his meals out.

A large black cat he had never intended to own had adopted him. He called it Moggie – in English – which amused him. He enjoyed it being there when he returned home of an evening. He would pour himself a generous malt whisky nightcap, the cat would jump on to his lap, and he would tell Moggie about his day, confiding many of his thoughts and dreams to it, things he would never tell another living person. Moggie was a good listener and no bother since the cleaning woman fed him, and Dieter grew increasingly fond of him.

He was fonder of Moggie, in truth, than of the many women in his life. He always chose small women, because of his own lack of height, and they were always blonde.

He did not like the current fashion for mini-skirts and hot pants and he insisted to any woman he took an interest in that he choose their clothes. They always obliged, yet he despised them for complying so rapidly. Some of them were intelligent, others stupid, it was all the same to him. He did not choose them for intellectual stimulus, only for the other sort.

An affair rarely lasted longer than a couple of months. Three months, he thought, was his record, and that had been with an air hostess who was constantly out of the country, so did not really count. After two months women invariably began to fall in love with him. The signs were always the same – they would invite him for a meal they intended to cook for him. He always refused such invitations; he liked good food and was not prepared to risk a meal cooked by an amateur. The minute a woman showed an interest in his laundry or offered to iron his shirts, queried the arrangement of his furniture, or the colour scheme of his flat, he knew she was preparing to move in on him. He would terminate the relationship instantly. He always did it the same way, with a large bouquet of mixed flowers and a gentle little note saying that it was over.

He had never been in love and was puzzled that so many women should fall in love with him. He did not feel deprived or sad about his failure to fall in love, he did not feel the need for it and was sure that it would be time-consuming and distracting, that it would get in the way of his work and his ambitions. In a way he was relieved that he seemed unable to love, and he never questioned the reason why.

Sex he enjoyed. He was good in bed, that he knew for certain – and he often thought this was probably one of the reasons why women loved him so easily. He despised them for that too, for how could sex be love? He might not have experienced love but he was certain that sex was an adjunct to it and not its own *raison d'être*.

He had a few friends, not close ones, not *best* friends, but people with whom he enjoyed an occasional meal. Nearly all were in the same line of business as he, so there was always something to talk about which did not encroach upon feelings and opinions – Dieter liked to keep these to himself.

He had not chosen to live in Munich just for the beauty of the city nor for the surrounding countryside, but because it was the closest large city to his father's old estate. He waited until he had a spanking new car before motoring out to his childhood home. In the early days of his life in Munich he had decided that when next he saw his home he would arrive in style. Even then he had not entered through the park gates but had driven to the other side of the valley and, from a vantage-point high on the opposite mountain, he had looked down on the pretty schloss through binoculars. He could see cars parked – expensive cars, more expensive than his own. He could see people moving about – guests, he presumed – and then he saw his uncle, Johannes von Weiher, strutting importantly about. He had sat there for a long time, consumed with the anger of one whose rightful inheritance was not his. This pilgrimage had now become a regular event for Dieter, usually at weekends.

And then one Thursday, when he was in the area buying furniture, he had decided to make a detour and had taken up his position at his vantage-point. He had not been there many minutes when he noticed a car driven by his Uncle Johannes come out of the gates of the castle and drive off at speed. Why not, if the coast was clear, he thought, and he drove down the hill, across the narrow valley and through the great gates of the castle, his heart thudding at the memories conjured up by the clearly remembered road. As he drove along, looking keenly to left and right, he did not like what he saw was happening to *his* estate. A plantation which still had several years to reach full maturity had been felled long before time. The fences were in poor repair. The hedgerows had gone wild with untrimmed growth. Fields which should have been full of crops were lying fallow. In the garden surrounding the house the lawns needed mowing, the once immaculate flower-beds had been allowed to become weed-infested, everywhere looked neglected and bedraggled by comparison with his father's time. It saddened Dieter to see his father's careful husbandry squandered by his uncle.

He stopped the car in front of the house. The castle stood white and serene but the woodwork needed painting, moss should be cleared from the lower walls, the steps to the front door were cracked and in need of repair and some windows were boarded up. Guttering hung loose, and he could see tiles missing. The house looked like a beautiful woman who had fallen on hard times but whose beauty no hardship, or need, could ever diminish. What a jewel, he thought. He experienced an odd mixture of feelings – pride, regret, sadness yet joy, and overall fury – at the sight of the neglect. He would have liked to run up the steps and knock on the great door. Caution warned him otherwise. There was no doubt in his mind that, finding him here, his uncle would order him off immediately. He was not afraid of meeting Johannes but he knew that being ordered away from what was rightfully his was a humiliation he could not bear. So he drove around the side of the house to the kitchen quarters at the back. Pulling into the cobbled back courtyard, he saw that if anything, the neglect was worse here.

Maria the cook and Willi her husband had been old when he lived here; as he knocked on the door, he doubted they were still alive. How he was to explain himself to new staff was something he had not worked out – maybe he should just leave . . .

'Willi!' he said with genuine pleasure as the door was opened and the old man stood there, not looking a day older. 'Willi, what a joy to see you.'

'I beg your pardon?' Willi said, stepping back from such enthusiasm from a stranger.

'It is I, Dieter. Dieter von Weiher.'

'God in heaven! Is it you? Really you? I don't believe it – marvellous! We thought you must be dead . . . come in, come in,' he said effusively, holding the door wide open in welcome, and Dieter, entering, smelled the same warm aromas of his childhood, and, for the first time in twenty-one years felt he was home.

Maria, red-faced and fatter, in the high button boots he'd forgotten she always wore, and her crisp, white cook's apron, swept him into her arms and hugged him as if she were never going to let go of him again. Dieter felt such a surge of comfort and warmth, the old feeling of security came back to him.

'You look just the same,' he said with amazement, when Maria eventually freed him from her embrace.

'Hardly.' Maria laughed. 'I'm seventy-three now and old Willi here is seventy-seven.'

'You don't look it,' Dieter lied gamely. How strange, he thought, they had only been in their fifties when he had left and yet the child he had been had thought they had one foot in the grave.

'And you, Dieter. Let me think. You're twenty-nine, if I'm not mistaken.' Maria beamed at him. 'Coffee? Chocolate cake? You loved my chocolate cake – do you remember? You'd have eaten a whole one if I'd let you.' She laughed happily at the memories flooding back.

'Coffee!' Willi snorted derisively. 'This is cause for celebration. Schnapps,' he insisted, going to a cupboard for the bottle. 'And something else!' he added with a grin and left the room to return a few minutes later with a small, rather battered attaché case. 'Do you remember this, then, Dieter?'

'It's my old case. The one I had to leave behind when Mother and I left in such a hurry.'

'The very same,' Willi said, blowing noisily into his handkerchief.

'And inside?' Dieter flicked the catches. 'My soldiers,' he said, almost disbelieving what he saw.

'I said I'd look after them until you returned, and I did.' And Dieter found it necessary to blow equally noisily into his own white handkerchief. He and Willi hugged each other tight and Dieter had to fight to control his emotions.

Maria fussed over him as she sat him down at her long, scrupulously scrubbed pine kitchen table. He looked about the large room with the huge dresser which covered one wall and on which the blue and white servants' china was kept, the plates in serried rows, arranged by size. Under them were the large earthenware pots for the flour, sugar, and – his favourite – biscuits. Brightly polished copper pots and pans hung on the walls where they had always been, each in its own place. The range, always hungry for wood, purred in the background. It was just as he had remembered it. Nothing had changed.

'Do I smell bread?' He sniffed the air appreciatively.

'Do you want some?' Maria was on her feet.

'Not now, dear Maria, later perhaps.'

'You'll take some back with you, that you will. And some of my jam – remember my jam? Oh, my dear boy, so much to remember.' She wiped her eye with the corner of her apron.

'This feels so good,' he said, leaning back in his chair with a contentment he had not felt in years.

'Your mother . . .?' Maria asked, diffidently, obviously afraid of what she might hear.

'She is well, thank you, Maria.' He smiled as he answered, willing her not to ask more.

'She lives in Munich too?' He had obviously not willed her sufficiently.

'No. She's *remarried*.' He emphasized this word, he wanted no nonsense about his illegitimacy in these parts. 'To an Englishman – a perfect gentleman.'

'Does she live in one of those lovely English houses with black and white beams?'

'Oh, yes. In an enormous park, twice the size of this one.' He lied glibly.

'I'm glad. Such a shame you left, so unnecessary too. We tried to tell your mother but it was no good, it was your father she was determined to find – she wouldn't listen to us. There was no need, you see. The Americans came, not the Russians she was convinced were arriving. They were surprisingly kind and treated the house with far more respect than we had expected. My, how often we have thought of you and your poor mother, wondering where you were and what had happened to you. She was always good to us – a kind woman.'

'Thank you, Maria. Of course, it took her a long time to get over my father and he will always be her great love.'

'It's always worse when there's no body, isn't it? You need a body to help you heal. More cake?'

'No, thank you.' His mind was racing as he spoke. So, his father had not been found, which probably meant the silver buried with him had not been found either. 'And how is life here?'

'Bah!' Willi made a dismissive noise. 'You'd never think this master was of the same family. He's a waster.'

'Willi! You shouldn't be saying that . . .' Maria chided.

'It's all right, Maria. I'm afraid there's little love lost between me and my Uncle Johannes. He's not like my father. Carry on, Willi, I'm interested. I could not help but notice the grounds looked rather sad and unkempt.' Dieter was leaning forward with interest. 'And I saw wood cut – long before time – and yet he drives an expensive car.'

'Unkempt . . . that bloody car – he's a fool – a bloody fool!' Willi needed no prodding, he was soon away on a long diatribe of Johannes's faults. From bad estate management to meanness with wages yet extravagant spending on himself; from ignorance on wine, and drunkenness, to poor choices of women. Maria and Willi did not approve.

'Do you know where he is now?' Maria asked conspiratorially. Dieter shook his head to show he didn't. 'In bed with the minister's wife, that's what our master Johannes is about. Disgusting!' Maria sliced more cake for them all.

'Every Thursday the minister has to go to a big meeting in Munich – stays the night, he does. Our Johannes is over there like a dog after a bitch in heat.'

'Disgusting!' Maria said again, but even more emphatically.

'And worse than that, I think he's up to no good,' Willi continued. 'He's started this timber company – he's destroying the woods – and who gets the contracts from the local council for timber for building? Why, Johannes. And wood that's green, that'll bow in twelve months. Bribes, that's what it's all about.'

'His mother's worried sick,' Maria informed Dieter.

'My grandmother's here?'

'Yes, she came soon after the war, before the Russians released your uncle – pity they did, if you ask me. That old woman managed everything better than him. She loves this place now, has grown to have quite a feel for it, not like him.'

'Did she lose her own estate? In the East, wasn't it?' Dieter asked.

'Every damn thing. Poor old girl arrived here in the middle of the night with a case and an old maid half witless with fear – she's dead now, good riddance, she was useless. That was it – all the Countess had left in the world – that case and the clothes she stood up in. Her jewels, silver . . . all gone . . .' Maria tutted.

'Of course she didn't know about your father. It was hard telling her, I can tell you – you know, that he was missing, and she should have expected the worst. It made her go a little bit potty . . .' With head on hand, Willi indicated his diagnosis of the Countess's mental state.

'Willi . . . you shouldn't be saying these things,' said Maria before launching herself into further gossip.

Dieter could not remember when he had last enjoyed a conversation so much as he sat back in his chair and let the old couple prattle, damning their employer at every turn. When he eventually looked up it was to see that the light was fading.

'I must be going.' He suddenly stood up.

'Don't you want to meet your grandmother?'

'No. Not this time.'

'You'll be back, then?'

'You know, Maria, I think I will. I think Thursday might be a good day, don't you? My Uncle Johannes doesn't exactly like me.' He laughed.

'I should take that as a compliment.' Willi laughed in return.

4

Germany – 1965–1967

Always at the back of Dieter's mind had been his resolve to have his revenge upon his Uncle Johannes. He didn't yet know how he could do this, but the older he got, the more he realized it was a rare man who did not have something in his past he would prefer to remain secret. Dieter had no intention of rushing in unprepared and thus botching the attack. He knew he would need resources. Now, with a sizeable fortune in the bank, the time was ripe.

Dieter had built up a large network of contacts over the

years. People he had done business with, people he had
done favours for. Now he wanted something back –
information.

The speed with which this information poured in
amazed Dieter and only proved to him that his uncle was
both stupid and arrogant. Stupid not to have covered his
tracks better and arrogant to think he could get away with
his misdemeanours.

A nest of nasty secrets was uncovered. Johannes had
defrauded a partner in his timber business, a man who was
now bent on ruining him. He was cheating on his taxes on
a large scale. It looked as if he could be accused of fraud
on some property deals. The corrupt building contract
deals with the local council was a greater operation than
Willi had grasped, and spread wide over this part of
Germany. Apart from the minister there was a handful of
very angry cuckolded husbands. On the estate were two
young girls; one he had raped, the second, while going to
bed with him willingly, had not anticipated the baby
Johannes left her with and refused to help support – two
fathers had scores to settle.

There was, it transpired, a small army of people who
hated his uncle. Dieter did not even have to waste his
energy hating him himself but instead utilized it by putting
the various aggrieved parties in touch with each other.
Until now, these people had thought they were alone with
their problems, but joined together they were an impressive
and united force. Dieter had nothing to do but sit back
while they consulted with lawyers and whispered in the
necessary ears and the relevant authorities went into gear.
Dieter could honestly say he had had no hand in this. All
he did ask was that he be tipped off as to the time and
place of Johannes's arrest.

In the three months he had spent collating his information he had got into the habit of visiting the castle every
Thursday – always by the back door, always when his

uncle was away on his amorous adventures. Each visit was an emotional experience for Dieter. He had always known he loved the house which held his earliest memories, but even so he had not realized the extent of this love. To own it was a physical need. He ached to live here again. His feelings for the house only underlined for him just how far from love were his relationships with the young women in his life. Such a thought did not bother him. The house, he thought, would probably be more stable and reliable; it was certainly a thing of greater beauty than any human being.

He knew now what had been behind his desperate need to accumulate and save money. The idea of acquiring the schloss had always lurked deep in his subconscious – a dream left over from his childhood. But he had consciously thought it an unrealizable dream . . . until now.

He still had not told anyone about the whereabouts of his father's remains. He had toyed with the idea of going there and getting the silver but decided against it. If caught, he would have been branded a common thief – not what he intended. So he kept this knowledge up his sleeve to use at a later date.

He had given Maria permission slowly to feed the old Countess stories about him as a little boy until she thought the time was appropriate to tell her that Dieter often visited Maria in the kitchen. At first there was no response from the old woman, then there was the occasional question about him, and whether he had visited that week, until finally the Countess was asking to meet him; curiosity had won over pride, just as Dieter had known it would. He did not accept the invitation, not yet, he was biding his time.

Perhaps, he thought, this is the happiest day of my life. He was making his way along the drive but to the front of the schloss today, not skulking around the back. He parked just as the large door swung open and Johannes was escorted down the steps by a squad of large policemen. Disappointingly he was not in handcuffs — that would have been perfect — but it was clear from his downcast walk that he was mentally shackled. Dieter leaned on the bonnet of his brand-new BMW and watched with a smile.

'Good morning, Uncle,' he said politely.

Johannes looked up. 'Who the fuck are you?'

'Your nephew, Uncle. Don't you remember me? Heinie's son. I'm the one you tried to throw out of that basement slum in Berlin, with my mother, Sophie. Now, surely you remember her, you have to, you were so jealous she chose your brother and not you,' Dieter continued with a smile which he knew, in the circumstances, must be infuriating to Johannes. He heard the small ripple of interest amongst the police at his revelations. He had never hinted to anyone of his background until now. He knew that by nightfall the whole district would know.

'Ah! The frog bastard. Come back to gloat, have you?' Johannes hit back.

'Something like that. Most importantly, I wanted you to know who had done the dirty on you, who had made sure you would be arrested. It was me, you see.'

At this Johannes lunged at him, his arm raised, fist clenched ready to punch. Dieter did not flinch. Johannes was grabbed by a large, burly policeman and was reduced to scowling at his nephew, bastard or not, with frustration.

'I thought I'd like to look over the house again. See what repairs I might have to make,' Dieter said slowly.

'You little shit! You won't get this house — never. It's mine!' Johannes was shouting.

'Don't you think that with all the possible fines coming your way, and the state of your bank balance, you might be forced to sell?' Dieter spoke in such a normal, reasonable tone of voice that Johannes became almost apoplectic with rage.

'And if I do you'd be the last sod I'd allow to buy it. You get this house over my dead body,' he screamed.

'As you wish.' Dieter laughed. 'Good luck, Uncle,' he called as he ran up the steps and for the first time in twenty-two years entered his father's house by the front door. He slammed it shut and leaned on it. He felt breathless, delirious; it was true – revenge was sweet. He knew a happiness he had not felt since he was a small child.

Dieter did not have long to wait for the next episode in his uncle's downfall. The police and fraud squad interrogations took several days and then Johannes was released on bail ... pending further inquiries. Dieter liked that; how ominous it sounded. He could imagine his uncle's fear as he waited, skulking in his castle, already disgraced, to see what those inquiries might be. It was finally decided that there were three accusations and there would be three trials – for fraud, embezzlement and corruption. The state was more interested in matters fiscal than moral.

Johannes's lawyer advised him to plead guilty, since he so plainly was, and thereby get a lighter prison sentence. Johannes's reaction to this was to tell his lawyer to go and rot in hell. He went out, got drunk, visited a mistress for a memorable night and then went home and shot himself.

'At least he was finally a gentleman,' said Dieter, with a clear conscience, to Willi.

Dieter thought it best if he allowed the Countess a decent period of mourning. He waited a further three months before finally letting Maria know that the time had come when he would like to meet the old lady, his blood grandmother.

From Maria's description of her he had expected to

meet a bent, wizened, batty old crone. So he was surprised, when shown into an upper salon, to find a very upright, smartly dressed and obviously intelligent woman who was beautiful in her old age. This was disappointing. A batty old crone would have been child's play to manipulate, this woman would be much more of a challenge.

'Countess.' He clicked his heels and bowed to her.

'Maria tells me you claim to be my grandson,' she said without preamble, barely acknowledging his polite greeting.

'I don't claim. I am.'

'Stand there,' she ordered, pointing to a position by the window. She studied him for what seemed an age. 'You have a slight resemblance to my son Heinie but he was blond and you are dark.'

'My mother was French – a brunette.'

'Ah, yes. Heinie preferred brunettes. And I remember talk of a French woman – a bar owner's daughter. Hardly suitable.'

'I agree, Countess. I fear my father was something of a romantic.'

'Not romantic enough to marry her, though, was he?' She looked at him sharply through eyes alight with intelligence, weighing him up. He smiled courteously before answering.

'No . . . but then, as you have pointed out, it was not a good match for someone in his position,' he said smoothly.

'Had he come back from the war, what do you think he would have done?'

'I've often wondered, Countess. Knowing my father, I think probably he would have given my mother a generous allowance, perhaps suggested she move back to Paris where he would have purchased her an appropriate apartment, and would have ensured my education and a start in life.'

'I see,' she said, not showing any reaction to his answer.

'And you would not have been made bitter by such an arrangement?'

'No doubt I would eventually have learnt to accept,' he said cautiously, there was no point in making himself out to be a total saint.

'Weren't you angry at what could only be regarded as abandonment?'

'On the contrary. I'm pleased it turned out the way it did. I've learnt to fight for myself. Had I been cushioned by my father's protection and wealth, maybe I would not be the success I am now.'

'You regard yourself as successful?' she asked, ignoring Maria who had come in bearing a tea tray in the English style.

'Yes.'

'How much is this success worth?' She poured the tea.

He paused, waiting for Maria to leave. His grandmother seemed to find this amusing. 'I have no objection to you knowing my wealth but not the servants also.'

'Really, and why is that?' As she spoke her voice was full of barely suppressed laughter.

'Because you are my grandmother,' he replied with quiet dignity and he told her of a portion of his worth – he had no intention of ever revealing the true total to anyone.

'You have done well.' She handed him a cup of tea.

'I've worked hard.' He added sugar.

'My second son was aware of you?'

'Yes, very.' It was his turn to have difficulty in keeping his amusement out of his voice.

'You did not like my son?'

'No. I'm sorry for you that . . .'

She held up her hand. 'There is no need for sympathy. I did not like my second son either. He had me here only on sufferance. But then, I had nowhere else to go.'

'Of course your estate in the East . . .'

'Yes, in Communist hands now. That was my real home. To my husband this was merely a shooting-box, but I have learnt to appreciate it.'

'The house in Berlin?'

'Johannes sold the land. There is now an unspeakably ugly block of flats there, full of unspeakable people. I should not care to live there even if I could afford to pay the rental demanded.'

She changed the subject then and he let her do so, for he found her stories of her youth in Berlin interesting. He had come prepared to dislike her but when he left, an hour later, it was to find he liked her, even though she had dismissed him, and quite curtly – there was no doubt of that. As he turned to bow at the door, she looked up.

'Certainly you have the look of Heinie about you. But that alone, you must realize, young man, is not enough for me to accept you. I need proof.'

'I have proof.'

'Then bring it next time you come.'

On the next visit, after the formalities, he handed her the first edition of Schiller. She took it from him and seemed to caress it.

'I gave him this.'

'I know.'

'How do you know?'

'My father told me.'

'It has an inscription from me. You could have bought it in a bookshop – our library was ransacked by the Nazis.'

On the visit after that he took the small, pearl-handled revolver.

'Your mother-in-law's, I believe,' he said as he handed it to her pre-empting her.

'Hardly my father-in-law's,' she answered, and smiled slyly at him.

On his final visit he took her the regimental tray.

'Given to your husband by his regiment, the 2nd West Prussian Field Artillery Regiment.'

'Any fool could work that out.'

'Look, Grandmama, this is all I have. These objects and my memories. I've answered all your questions, haven't I? You've been astonished by my knowledge.' He was leaning forward in his chair, exasperated by her this time. Each visit had been like sitting an examination, he had blessed his good memory and was certain he was wearing her down.

'There is a lot at stake. Any impostor could have acquired these objects.'

He stood up, rigid with indignation. 'I am *not* an impostor. I have one secret – something I alone know. I'd rather not tell you. I don't wish to distress you.'

'Mr Clarkson,' she said, refusing as always to call him von Weiher as he longed for her to do. 'I have lost both my sons. I have lived through two wars. I have lost everything I possessed. All I am left with is this house and its contents ... something, it is painfully obvious, I will have to sell if I am to survive. I doubt if I can be distressed further.'

He looked at her for a long time before answering.

'I know where my father's body is. I know how he died. I know where the best of the family silver is. Will that do you?'

'Yes, Mr Clarkson, I think that might.'

The Countess was an intrepid woman. Dressed in boots and a heavy coat, she was bundled into Dieter's car and driven to the forest. The road which once had led to the small hunting-lodge was no more – the forest had reclaimed it. This did not stop the Countess who, with Willi on one arm, Dieter on the other, slipped and scrambled her way through the dense undergrowth.

As they entered the lodge Dieter shivered and looked over his shoulder as if expecting the Gestapo to be behind him. And he was concerned. What if the soldiers had returned after the war to collect their loot? He had no way of knowing if they had survived. What if there was nothing there, what if they had decided to do the decent thing and bury his father out in the forest? How would he explain himself to his grandmother then? And what if upon seeing the skeleton she accused him of planting it? She was quite capable of that.

He and Willi manhandled the heavy oak dresser away from the nailed-up door which Willi began to work on with a crowbar. Intrepid as his grandmother was, Dieter could not expect her to go into the cellar on the dumb-waiter as he had as a boy.

Willi had a powerful torch.

'I'll go first,' said Dieter, 'in case the staircase has rotted.' His heart was thumping painfully as he led the way – what if someone had entered through the kitchen? What if everything had been stolen?

Apart from a thick covering of dust and thick cobwebs, everything was as it had been on that day in 1944. It was obvious to anyone that this place had not been disturbed for years. The discarded uniforms from which he had torn the badges lay on the floor. The boxes containing the family silver were stacked against the wall. His hand shook as he lifted the torch and shone it on the pile of rotted clothes and bones which had once been his father.

The Countess said nothing. She stood for a long time in silence, looking at the skeleton which had collapsed into an untidy heap as if thrown down. There was a loud sob –

it was from Willi. The Countess turned and stared disdainfully at him and the poor man, overcome with emotion, raced back up the stairs.

On the journey back to the castle she said only one thing. 'You knew nothing about this, Willi?'

'Nothing, Madam. That shooting-lodge wasn't used in Count Heinrich's time, it was young Dieter's play-home. The Count would have knocked it down but for the boy. I'd all but forgotten it existed. The forest hid it well. And I knew nothing about those boxes. The master must have moved them there himself. He'd told me everything was safe, not to worry about the best silver – I presumed he meant he'd put it all in a bank.'

The Countess sat silent and said nothing.

At the schloss Dieter was invited to stay for dinner and the night, if he wished. Of course, he did – this had not happened before.

It was not until after dinner when they were alone and with large brandies in their hands that the old lady suddenly said, 'I loved him.' She said it as if to no one in particular, as though she expected no response. Dieter saw her eyes were full of tears. 'Now he is truly gone.' She fumbled for a tiny lace handkerchief with which she dabbed at her eyes. It was then that Dieter realized that she had been living in hope, a hope that as the years slipped by must have become fainter. Like so many others, his grandmother had persuaded herself that her son was still alive in some slave camp in Russia. He had taken that hope from her today.

'I wish I had not shown you. I've taken him from you.'

'No, it is better I know. I want to know everything.'

He told her about the Gestapo officers, the scraps of conversation he had overheard. How he had put two and two together and had concluded that, after his father had spoken indiscreetly to his mother, in French, of the war and the German failure, he must have been tortured to reveal where his silver was, been forced to show the Gestapo its whereabouts, and had then been taken there and shot. The Countess sat in silence for a long time after this, as if assimilating the tale, filing it away.

'Dieter, we have business to decide.' She turned to face him and he smiled at this first use of his Christian name. 'I had to be sure about you, you do understand?'

'Of course.'

'I have this estate left me by Johannes. I have no money. No living relatives. I need an heir. I could adopt you, make you my legal son and this would all be yours, and your father's title as well. Couldn't I?'

Dieter thought his heart would stop beating. He realized he was holding his breath. 'Yes?' he said cautiously.

'If I do that, what are you willing to pay me?'

'I hadn't thought.'

'Then I think you should. My terms are simple. I would like to keep an apartment here for myself and a maid – I need a maid, Maria tries . . . I would expect a villa in the south of France, my old bones like the sun. I wish an adequate income for the rest of my life.'

'That could be arranged.'

'But I would also expect a down-payment – say the value of this estate. Just in case, Dieter.'

'In case of what, Grandmama?'

'In case you over-reach yourself and become bankrupt.'

'There's little chance of that, I can assure you.'

'All the same . . .'

He laughed. 'You're a hard businesswoman, Grandmama.'

'And you are a strange grandson.'

'In what way?'

'Your father was a warm person, why are you so cold?'

'Am I? I don't know. Maybe because life has treated me differently. It's difficult to trust when you're on the streets of a war-ravaged city, scrabbling to survive.'

'A pity. But you must learn to trust.'
'As you trust me?' He laughed.
'Touché.' She laughed with him.

5

Germany – 1970

His father's title, his father's schloss were Dieter's. When the adoption papers were signed he regarded them as a mere formality. He was home, and his birthright had, at last, been restored to him.

His grandmother had put about the tale to her dowager friends that Heinie's son from a wartime marriage had finally found her. So the stigma of his illegitimacy was buried with his father in the grand mausoleum which Dieter had had built, in the forest, on the site of the old hunting-lodge. The tomb was large enough for Dieter himself and his son and his son's son to be buried there also.

He repaired the fabric of the castle, set about making the land productive again. The inside of the large house was restored and those possessions of his father's which he'd been able to buy back were replaced in exactly the same position he remembered from his childhood. Then began, with renewed vigour, the search for everything pillaged down to the last porcelain figurine.

Dieter's title and his new standing in the community ensured that his legitimate business boomed. He was offered other business opportunities; he became a director of several companies, all involved one way or another in the arts field. He acquired an auction-house which he intended to build to rival Christie's and Sotheby's. He was a respected expert on Italian old masters. He had arrived. Now, he was even richer.

His social circle expanded. Often he was invited to advise on a painting the owner *might* be selling. His discretion was a byword among the impoverished minor English aristocrats who, battling against death duties, were his main source of works.

He endured many an uncomfortable English house-party – the facilities and food were never up to his demanding standards. But he endured them for the contacts he made and the gossip which could tell him who was thinking of selling. Paintings acquired were then sold to his other important clients – the Americans.

He longed for the big deals, to be entrusted with the buying and selling of important works by artists like Titian or Bellini. And then he met Guthrie Everyman and his wish was fulfilled as that upper level of society welcomed him with arms held open like the petals of a flower.

His success was such that he could easily have dispensed with his illegal arms deals. He thought about doing so for there was always the fear he might be uncovered and then his carefully built social standing would crumble away overnight. Dieter knew that a reputation was a precious, necessary, if ephemeral thing which, unless guarded, could disappear like early-morning mist burnt away by the sun, if exposed to the full glare of gossip and innuendo. But his concern was conquered by his drive to accumulate money. Like so many who start from nothing, his greatest fear was that one day the money might disappear, leaving him to scratch a living on the streets again.

At thirty-four, rich, handsome, charming and titled, he was many mothers' dream catch. He enjoyed himself with women but he did not commit himself.

'Dieter, I can't believe this, you in your father's castle, and a real count. I'm so proud of you.' His mother hugged him excitedly, but he felt awkward, unable to respond.

'Once I'd redecorated it, put everything back in its right place, I wanted you to be the first person to see it. I've restored your old bedroom to how it was.'

'Dieter, what can I say?' She looked up at him, her eyes brimming with tears — oh, for Christ's sake don't cry, Mother, he caught himself thinking.

'You took long enough to invite her,' Darren, his half-brother, now a tall, rather languid young man in his early twenties, fashionably dressed in a soft velvet suit, said pointedly.

'It has taken me over three years to restore it. It was in a dreadful state — It would have upset my mother to see it like that. I was determined it should look as she remembered it,' Dieter replied shortly, wishing his brother and stepfather were back in their dreary home rather than here. His dream had been to have his mother all to himself, as it once had been. But Sophie had insisted she bring the others, and his only consolation was that Bob Clarkson's elder son Lance had declined.

During this visit of ten days, Dieter found himself puzzled by his mother. She was seriously overweight now, something he would never have expected of her. She wore little make-up and made no effort to cover her wrinkles nor to colour the grey from her dark hair. The clothes she wore were dowdy, of man-made fibres, and looked as if they came from a cheap mail order catalogue. She seemed ill at ease in the castle, awkward with the staff, out of place somehow.

Had the Sophie of his memories been a dream? Had she ever been the chic, elegant, scatty Frenchwoman he remembered? Had she, in fact, when with his father, been gauche and unsophisticated? He was glad now that he had planned her visit when his grandmother was away in the south of France, for the Countess would not have recognized this woman as the paragon Dieter had described. No doubt the arrogant, autocratic old lady would have made Sophie feel even more socially inept.

'Mama, you don't spend your money on fine fashion?' he asked one day, aware that Darren appeared in a different outfit every day while Sophie seemed to have only a couple of dresses.

'Oh, I lost my interest in clothes long ago.' She laughed, but looked embarrassed.

'Then what do you spend the money I send you on?'

'Ah, this and that.' She waved her hands ineffectually.

'Mama?' He looked stern.

'There's so many things. I mean, Bob's wages aren't much and well . . . he's so talented . . .'

'Talented? Bob? In what?'

'No, no, Darren. He's a musician, you know, he's really good. He'll be bigger than the Beatles one day.'

'Mama, I know little about the music business but I'm sure it's hard to succeed.'

'Of course, that's why his father and I have insisted he gets a good education first. He's going to the Poly and he plays in his spare time.'

'And you're paying for his education, his instruments, his clothes?'

'Well, yes. I didn't think you'd mind.'

'I don't mind – it's your money, Mother, do with it as you wish. But I do expect you to spend some on yourself.'

'There's not enough to do that.' She had a determined expression on her face, and sat, solid and middle-aged, in the chair.

'Not enough? Mother, whole families live on what I give you.'

'Well, I need more.'

'For Darren, no doubt, not yourself.'

'He needs better equipment, he needs a better sound if he's to succeed – it's a hard business, the pop world. You see, Dieter—'

'No, Mama. I won't.'

'You're jealous of him, aren't you? Jealous because he's my son, my baby.' Her voice was shrill as she spoke and she looked angry.

'No, Mama. If you must know, I don't like him.'

'How could you say such a thing about your own brother? Honestly, Dieter, sometimes I think there's something wrong with you – you're so cold.'

'There's nothing wrong with me, Mama. It's Darren, he's indolent, he'll always be a drain on you. I doubt if he has the energy to succeed in anything let alone take over from the Beatles.'

'I won't listen to this.' She clapped her hands over her ears.

'I didn't think you would. No one can say anything against your precious, useless Darren. You're obsessed with him, Mama.'

'That's a horrible thing to say.' She had leaped to her feet. 'Why don't you admit it, Dieter – you don't want to help because you're mean. You've so much and you're too mean to help your little brother. You always were mean. Nothing's changed. Remember in Berlin, how you hid things from me, those badges – we could have had so much, much sooner.'

'And look what you spent it on when I did let you have them,' Dieter said angrily.

To his dismay, the row wound up to a frightening crescendo. His mother verbally abused him and he, to his later shame, countered her attack with accusations of his own. He was cold, unfeeling, a miser, an unnatural son. She was flippant, ungrateful, had not looked after him as a child. He was impossible, more than ungrateful. She'd never wanted him, never loved him. Having him had ruined her life, she wished he'd never been born. He never wanted to see her again. Nothing would please her more . . .

His mother packed and left. Dieter felt a deep, black depression seep over him. He felt betrayed by her as once before. And then he wondered why it mattered. Had he not forgotten her long ago, had he not then decided he did not love her? Why should he, a grown man, care? He'd visited her, yes, but out of duty only. If this was how she felt, so be it. He would forget her again. It did not matter, he told himself. But he kept her allowance on.

It was five years later and he was thirty-nine when Dieter woke up to the realization that he had almost become a recluse. The change in him had been a slow one, and since it had not been intentional, it took him somewhat by surprise. Looking back, he could pinpoint the beginning of the change to just after the row with his mother. It had depressed him, no matter how much he pretended he didn't care. Even if he had not often seen her she had been there, someone he thought he could turn to if necessary. It was obviously lucky he had never needed to, for he realized he would have found her sorely lacking.

After she had left he found he no longer enjoyed the parties that had been important in his social calendar. He began to find them noisy and futile. Then dinner parties followed – he stopped going to, and giving, them. They had become pointless also – always the same people and, he realized now, invariably the same conversations. Soon the only appointments in his diary were those concerned with business.

He was finding that he was happiest at home in his castle. The restructuring of the estate and turning it into a viable proposition gave him immense pleasure. He had spent too long alone as a child to be afraid of solitude. Instead he discovered that he had missed it. An evening alone with a perfect meal, excellent wine, music of his choice or a good book to read, suited him very well.

The last pursuit to be given up were his casual affairs. He was never sure why but one day, in bed, he had looked down at his latest conquest and found he could not remember her name. Nor could he be bothered to find out. Once the affairs had been to relieve the ache of sexual need. Now the need seemed less important. He found he could manage without sex for long stretches of time. He could look at how he had behaved with women and was not proud of how cavalier he had been, how self-seeking. Now he did not seek a woman, if it happened it happened – but it was rare. And when he slept with a new woman he never felt quite as replete as he had in the past – there was always something missing, he was not sure what.

The realization of how much he had changed and how unbalanced his life had become struck him forcibly the day Moggie died. Though old, the cat had died in his sleep without any warning. Dieter dug the tiny grave himself in Moggie's favourite place, the rose garden. He stopped digging, leaned on his spade, and sobbed. Bruce, Moggie – the only times he could remember crying. Had he gone too far? Had he isolated himself too much? Why, when he'd had friends, were none of them close? Why, now, could he live without any of them? Had his mother been right that he was incapable of love? If, at the age of thirty-nine, the only true friend he had was a small black cat, then maybe she was right.

'Dieter, I want you to meet my new companion, Magda,' his grandmother said as she stood in the great hall of the schloss, briskly removing her gloves, her glance sweeping the floor and furniture and checking that all had been well cared for in her absence. She had arrived in the usual flurry on one of her visits home. She would only stay a month before becoming restless, before needing the sun again.

'How do you do?' Dieter and Magda spoke in unison. And then they both laughed.

Magda was small in stature and slight of build. Her long, straight brown hair was caught back in a band. She had large grey eyes and one of the sweetest expressions Dieter had ever seen — not a hint of the cynicism or worldly sophistication which normally attracted him to a woman. Her voice was attractive with a slightly husky catch and her laugh was low and pleasant to hear. He took her hand.

'Welcome,' he said, and found himself aroused by her beauty and interested in her in a way he had not felt for some time.

During the month of his grandmother's visit he fell in love. At least he presumed that was what had happened for this was a new experience to him, a totally unfamiliar range of emotions. He felt as if he had been hit by an express train of feeling which, since it had never happened before, he took to be love.

He found himself almost breathless with pleasure if he glimpsed Magda in the garden, even at a distance. When she entered a room he felt his pulse race. He found himself lingering on stairways or paths, just in the hope of seeing her. He had almost to sit on his hands when in her presence, so great was his longing to touch her, to smooth that long, shining hair, to bury his nose in it, to smell it — he knew it would smell wonderful. Nights were intolerable knowing she lay only a few doors away along the corridor and that he was fearful of approaching her, in case she rejected him, a thought which made him shudder with despair. But what really took him by surprise was that he longed to look after her, provide for her, keep her safe. He had never felt that before for anyone other than his mother. It was all a new and confusing experience for him. He thought he had been discreet, that only he knew of his turmoil.

'Why on earth don't you woo the girl and put us all out of our misery?' his grandmother asked one evening as they took their customary aperitif together. He had been jumping at every sound, hoping it was Magda's footfall he was hearing, and slumping back in his chair with disappointment when it wasn't.

'I don't know what on earth you're talking about.' He looked away from her acute expression, embarrassed; it was as if his grandmother was reading his mind.

'Yes, you do. You're smitten with the girl. It's obvious to everyone.'

'Does she know?' he asked, knowing he would be mortified if she did.

'She'd have to be remarkably dense not to.' She laughed. 'Of course she does. And the signs are she's in the same state – she's becoming useless to me, forgets the post, my books, buys the wrong cigarettes. She's *mooning* over you too, you stupid boy!'

'But what do I do? What if you're mistaken and she doesn't even like me?'

'Why should she dislike you? Ask her out – go and dine somewhere, just the two of you. Propose.'

'Propose!' he said in amazement. His obsession had not taken him that far, only a vague longing to care for her.

'She's quite suitable. Good family – ruined by that damned war, of course. But that's no problem when you're always so busy amassing money. You're an excellent catch, Dieter, she'd snap you up.' His grandmother's voice bubbled with amusement.

It was not to prove as simple as his grandmother had made out. Magda did like him, even he realized that from the way her face had lit up when he invited her out to dinner. He had enjoyed the evening immensely. They had far more in common than he had thought – shared interests in music and literature and art. She liked to talk of art and politics; he was happy to oblige on the first, less on the second. He found her surprisingly serious for one who smiled and laughed so much.

They had many such dates, all equally enjoyable. Dieter particularly liked the way she listened to him so intently, her large grey eyes watching him, making him feel so important.

And then the evening before she and his grandmother were due to leave, she confided how much she loved the schloss, how she felt it was almost a living thing. Dieter was beside himself with happiness. At that he proposed. She didn't even stop to think, she turned him down flat.

'But why? We are perfect for each other,' he said, feeling sick with desolation.

'We've known each other such a short time, Dieter. A month. Not long enough.'

'It's long enough for me, I've no doubts. You're everything I could have wished for.'

'That's very sweet of you, Dieter. But if I marry it has to be for life, I have to be certain.'

'For me too. This isn't a flippant proposal.'

'I'm sure it's not, Dieter, my dear. But only time will tell us if we're right for each other. And there's something else . . .' She shook her head at his questioning expression. 'Oh, it doesn't matter. I'm being silly.'

'What, what is it?' He tentatively took hold of her hand.

'You haven't said you love me.' She glanced down at her hands.

'Oh, Magda. Oh, my darling. I'm sorry. I forgot. I do, I really do.'

She laughed.

'What are you laughing at?' He frowned.

'You still haven't managed to say it.'

'Didn't I? I meant to . . . I love you, Magda.' He stumbled over the words.

'And I love you, Dieter. Please ask me again in six months' time.'

But it was a year of endless journeys beween Germany and the south of France, and innumerable proposals, before she finally said yes.

'Could you say that again?' he said with disbelief.

'Yes.' She laughed at his amazed expression.

'You're absolutely sure?'

'Totally.'

'Why so long, Magda?'

'I wasn't sure if you really loved me, if you knew what loving someone involved. I wondered often if you weren't mistaking your feelings as love because you wanted to be loved so very much. You struck me as someone who has not known much love in his life and often such people can't love – not as the rest of us can because they have not learnt how to.'

He was taken aback by this for he did not even know it about himself. He glossed over it since it was a thought which made him feel uncomfortable.

'You're not worried about the age difference? Hell, I'm forty-one next year.'

'What's eighteen years' difference? When you are truly in love it can't possibly matter.' And she put her hand out to touch his. 'If I have a doubt it is still that it might be difficult for you to give of yourself totally but I've decided I have enough love for the two of us.'

Dieter, that evening, felt his life was complete.

Unusually for a relationship in the 1970s, they had not yet made love. They had kissed, and passionately, but they had not been to bed. Right at the beginning Dieter had decided that this was not to be like any other affair in his life. He respected Magda too much, there was such an air of innocence about her that he was loath to be the one who took it away.

Perhaps it was a mistake.

'Magda, darling, I'm so sorry. I don't know what's happened.' Dieter flung himself back on to the pillows of their marriage bed and was mortified.

'Darling, it doesn't matter. We're both so tired after all the excitement of the wedding. Let's just cuddle up and sleep.' And she opened her arms wide for him and held him tight as she drifted into sleep, but he lay through the night staring at the ceiling, horrified by what had happened.

The next morning it was the same. In the evening, the morning and on and on through the honeymoon on the yacht he had hired and which was sailing the romantic Caribbean. Try as he might, he could not make love to her. It would begin perfectly but each time, as he entered her, he felt himself become flaccid. As miserable day followed day, the crew, who until now Dieter had not even been aware of, all appeared as large and lusty men. He began to feel afraid.

On their return from their honeymoon Dieter used his business as an excuse to go to Munich for a couple of days. He looked up an old girlfriend and fucked her until she begged him to stop.

On the way home he felt elated, he had the radio on full blast and sang at the top of his voice. Whatever had been the problem was cured. He bundled Magda into his arms, smothered her with kisses, rushed her to their bedroom, undressed her with desperation as his erection swelled. And then the unbelievable happened again; as he entered her he became impotent. He slumped with despair.

So the course of their marriage was set. His longing for a son would never be fulfilled. This woman he adored, whom he had set on a pedestal way above all other women, he could never make truly happy.

Magda said she was. That it did not matter. That the love of their souls was more important than physical love. That he must not worry, nor despair, that the more he worried the less likely the problem was to be resolved.

He took a mistress – he had to, his needs remained. Nothing, to him, was worse than waking in the morning with an erection and to be too afraid to turn to the woman he loved for fear of knowing he would fail her again.

Sometimes he wished Magda was not so patient and sweetly understanding. It made the abnormal even more so. He wished she would shout and scream her frustration at him, tell him of her anger, how cheated she must feel, blame him – punish him in some way. She never did, always she was placid and apparently content.

He was not kind to his mistress. He almost felt he hated her. Why could he make love to her all night if he chose, yet not to his wife?

As if Magda did not suffer enough, worse was to come. It was she who had tentatively and with such sensibility suggested that, given the circumstances, they might try to conceive a child by artificial insemination.

For Dieter it had been a brutally humiliating experience explaining, or trying to, to her doctor why it was necessary, and getting a load of clap-trap back from the man who obviously fancied himself as a Freudian analyst as well. For Magda it was to prove a bitter disappointment. Even if Dieter had been able to make love to her she could never have conceived his child. Magda was sterile.

They had talked of adoption but Dieter rejected the idea – if they were destined not to have children, so be it. But Magda continued to long for one.

The affairs continued, usually short-lived, until this latest one. Dieter knew he should be more discreet but he was not – in a perverse way he wanted Magda to find out. Why? he often wondered. Perhaps it would jolt her into the anger he felt he needed from her, perhaps her fury would be a scourge like the lash of a whip to him. Maybe, even, by finding out she would leave him – a thought which filled him with despair but gave him the hope of a form of release – punishment again. Such thinking was a mistake, for then he realized that if Magda did know, and condoned his behaviour, that would be the greatest mortification of all.

Germany – autumn 1992

'Sophie,' he said aloud again to the empty room and knew he felt nothing. He would not go to the funeral, there would be no point. He had buried his mother in his mind years ago.

Or had he? Sometimes he had a thought, a thought which would never quite leave him. Was it something from his past which prevented him being a true husband to Magda? Had he put her on a pedestal to love, and did he feel that if she was touched by lust the love would die as it had with his mother when he had discovered the truth about her?

He lay on the bed and faced this thought, would not let his mind release it. Was this a dreadful form of legacy which his mother had left him? Was her betrayal of him as a child to continue to haunt him for the rest of his life?

7 Guthrie's Party

1

France – January 1993

Guthrie, as he had said himself many times, was more than a little surprised to have attained the age of fifty without mishap. Certainly he had not deserved to get there unscathed. His ability to drink everyone under the table was legendary, no doubt aided by his serious bulk, the result of an insatiable love for good food – he'd never been known to have a hangover. After only a few hours' sleep he would write for a full day and then he was able to party the next night away. Such energy was awesome. Conventional society did not interest him. He found the fixed social rounds of the jet-setters too irksome and that of his native England too boring. He went his own way, emerging only occasionally into these groups, where his selectivity ensured he was always welcomed, sometimes almost hysterically. This manifestation particularly amused him. He had discovered early in his life that he was attracted to both sexes and had joked of what a bonus it was: 'It doubles the opportunities for a bit of hanky-panky, don't you see?' he'd often said. That was until Sita, the only person he had ever loved, came into his life. After her death it appeared to the observant that he suppressed his masculine side and encouraged his feminine one to emerge with abandon. It was as if he knew he would never find another like her, and he closed his mind to women. Thereafter his love life had been varied and his choice of partners, at times, dangerous. But he was held in such affection by his lovers that he had been able to discard, on a whim, gypsies, small-time crooks and big-time ones also, yet none of them had harmed him, and not one of them would have a word said against him.

Despite his size, he could out-swim most people, but exercise was not one of his favourite pastimes. He lived for pleasure and he gave it to others in abundance. His party would be one of those special events which Guthrie occasionally offered society. He was about to return, in one fell swoop, the hospitality he had enjoyed, the favours he had been given, for about the last five years. Since he entertained on the grand scale so rarely, an invitation was a sought-after thing; reputations could be made or broken on whether a person received an invitation from Guthrie, or not.

Like many men with his sexual proclivity, he had a genius for planning such occasions. He had an acute eye for the minutiae which ensured sublime comfort, food and drink, and created an elegant atmosphere. To ensure perfection he had been planning this particular party for a good year.

'But do you think it wise, Guthrie, to be spending so much? There is the most appalling recession on,' a friend had counselled.

'All the more reason, dear heart. Spread the loot around a bit, circulate it. The crime would be to keep it in the bank or under my mattress. Never let it be said old Guthrie here is not a good socialist.' He laughed hugely at this little joke and thereafter repeated it many times.

His home in Paris, he had decided, would be too small for the party and so he had bought a château, a short distance from Paris, to use instead. Such an act quickly passed into legend.

'Did you know Guthrie's bought a bloody great château just as a venue for his party?'

'Good God, the man's mad.'

He wasn't. He'd been looking for such a place for some time so that he could fulfil another plan which had been fermenting in his mind for several years. That a suitable château should come on to the market at just such a time merely meant he could kill two birds with one stone.

Guthrie was often asked what nationality he felt he was.

'European, of course, old love. What else? I can't be doing with all this nationalistic stuff.'

'Will you ever return to England, to live?'

'Good God, no, too bloody wet, darling.'

France, he had long ago decided, was where he felt most at home. He admired the Frenchman's indomitable independence, his pride in being French. He enjoyed the hedonism of a nation where wine and food were masters. He liked the disregard for authority. He regarded the whole nation as eccentrics. He loved them.

He had been twenty when he decided this was the country where he wished to spend most of his life.

'That last traffic light was red,' he had said, with admirable self-control, to the French companion who was driving him around Paris.

'So?' his friend asked.

'Well, shouldn't you have stopped?'

'Why? Tell me why? What is this thing?' The Frenchman waved at another set of traffic lights. 'It's a collection of wires only. And this electronic thing, has it the right to tell me, a free Frenchman, what to do? Never!'

Guthrie admired such an anarchic philosophy and had bought his villa the following week and had never, for thirty years, regretted it.

At the news that Guthrie had bought an enormous, empty château, the owners of antique shops, galleries and the *brocante* of Paris went on red alert, expecting a sharp increase in their turnover. Disappointingly, Guthrie did not appear to cut the expensive swathe expected of him.

Instead, the old house teemed with masons, plasterers and plumbers. Guthrie was concentrating on the plumbing, building bathrooms, shower-rooms, lavatories and a new kitchen. The rest could wait, he told the curious. But all the same, workmen and tilers toiled late into the night and the clatter of the seamstresses' sewing-machines as curtains and pelmets were fashioned echoed around the tall, proud rooms.

The theme for his party had occupied him for some time. It had to be a costume party – Guthrie loved dressing up. A gold or silver party was out – they'd been done to death. And if he just said fancy dress, people would come in all fashions from all periods and he didn't want that – it would look too messy and Guthrie could not abide that.

It was a book on Cecil Beaton featuring one of his illustrations for the set of *My Fair Lady* that decided him. Edwardian – so elegant. Black and white only – even more elegant. It was symbolic, too – black, in mourning for fifty years ill spent, and white for, hopefully, another fifty years, but different ones, he'd decided.

When the invitations were finally delivered they caused much consternation – there were so few of them. Since Guthrie knew so many people it had been expected that a thousand at least would be invited. Instead Guthrie had invited only four hundred – a measly number, it was agreed, and one that left many people throughout the world disappointed and four hundred smugly jubilant.

The castle was a good hour's drive from Paris and Guthrie had had four London buses shipped over to join a fleet of luxury coaches to transport guests who preferred to stay in Paris. There was little local accommodation and what there was Guthrie had already booked.

The buses were waiting in the Place de l'Etoile, special permission had been given by the police, which was convenient for most of the great hotels where Guthrie's guests would be staying. He had dickered with the idea of the buses calling at each hotel in turn but, given the tardiness of many of his female guests, he had decided a central pick-up point was best. Each bus had *Guthrie's* as its destination.

A pipe band was in attendance, though why was a mystery, since Guthrie frequently declared he loathed the bagpipes and tartan in equal measure and boasted he'd never set foot in Scotland in his life. The skirl of the pipes, the soldiers in their colourful kilts caused great excitement and soon a large crowd had gathered to watch the comings and goings.

Those who were guests were, for the most part, finding it difficult to maintain their sophisticated air. Since some had never been on a bus and others could not remember when they last travelled on one, they were as excited as small children. Among them was Winter Sullivan, New York sophisticate, elegant in a tight-bodiced dress of black silk, a panel of small black and white check set in the front of both top and skirt, and with a small bustle, also in check.

'A real London bus! What a gas! What say we ride on top?' Winter's eyes were shining with a genuine joy Walt found attractive. He was glad she was here and not Charity. Not for an instant would Charity show such uninhibited animation, and she would probably have refused to board the bus in the first place, regarding it as vulgar. He took hold of Winter's hand. 'The top it shall be.'

What had started as an orderly queue of guests was rapidly turning into a mêlée as the normally polite social-ites began an unseemly push and shove, spurning the luxury air-conditioned coaches in favour of the red buses. Using his considerable bulk, Walt pushed his way to the front and helped Winter up the steep step on to the platform of the bus and then followed her up the stairs, admiring the undulation of her bustle as she climbed, and realizing for the first time why that fashion had been such a success.

'Walt! Walt! I've saved you a place.' Dieter was waving from the front of the bus where he and Magda had saved four seats. 'I saw you on the pavement.'

'Hi, Dieter. Wow, what a scrum that was! And Magda too! We don't see nearly enough of you these days, Magda.' He kissed her cheek, and not for the first time wondered what such a sweet woman was doing with a cold fish like Dieter. 'And this is Winter Sullivan, my public relations officer.' Walt noticed the sardonic smile on Dieter's face at the introducion. 'She graciously agreed to accompany me; my wife has broken her leg but insisted I came,' he said, pointedly, and then kicked himself, annoyed that he should be bothering to explain himself to Dieter of all people.

'Hold on tight, everyone p-l-e-a-s-e!' a voice called out in an exaggerated and rather bad attempt at a cockney accent. The bell pinged and the large red vehicle inched out into the Place, turned into Avenue Foch and headed for the Bois de Boulogne.

The excited hubbub from the guests had reached a new high, akin to a primary school outing. The enjoyment was catching.

'Fares, p-l-e-a-s-e, I thank you!'

'Jamie!' both Walt and Dieter said in unison. 'You're the conductor?'

'Great uniform, isn't it? And see this.' He tapped a large metal machine at his front. 'A real old-fashioned ticket machine. Wonderful, isn't it? I've always wanted to be a conductor, maybe I should take it up, perhaps I could make a success of that at least.' He grinned but Winter was certain he'd meant it. 'Right, fares, please.'

'How much is it?' asked Walt, producing a bulging wallet. He knew from past experience of such gatherings that one might be an invited guest but would invariably be called upon to shell out for something or other.

'As much as you want to pay. It's all for charity, UNICEF, you see,' Jamie explained, and Walt was not surprised.

Jamie stashed the five hundred American dollars Walt gave him into the large leather money bag he had slung over his chest. 'That's just for the one, is it, sir?' he asked cheekily as he handed over the single ticket which he rang up from his machine with a flourish. Walt laughed and produced another wodge of notes. Not to be outdone, Dieter, having quickly assessed the amount Walt had donated, doubled his own offering.

'For two tickets,' he said pointedly. Jamie touched the peak of his cap.

'Thank you, Guv.'

'Jamie, I wrote to Guthrie but received no reply, apart from my invitation. Do you know if the treasure hunt's still on?'

'As far as I know, Dieter. Still interested?'

'Perhaps,' Dieter said noncommittally.

'I am, most decidedly,' Walt announced. 'I reckon it could be fun.'

'A treasure hunt, can anyone join?' Winter asked with interest.

'It's a mite expensive to join.' Jamie laughed.

'Maybe you can just come along for the ride?' Walt looked up at Jamie to see his reaction.

'It's all right with me if Winter comes.' He smiled charmingly at her and Winter, who had expected that a film star would smile in a slick, professional way, was taken by his genuine warmth. 'What do you say, Dieter?'

'We would be charmed.' He bowed his head but Winter was not nearly as impressed with his smile.

'I'd like to come too,' said Magda. 'If that's possible,' she added, and Winter thought she sounded downtrodden.

'I don't think so, my sweet. We don't know what it entails. What if it were dangerous? Far better you stay at home.' Dieter patted Magda's hand. Winter thought that if she were married to him she would clock him one for being so patronizing. But then, she wouldn't have married him in the first place – too smooth by far for her taste.

'No, in that case, I should want to be with you,' she replied, and Walt thought what a lucky bastard Dieter was to have such a wife.

'That's settled then. Great.' Walt squeezed Winter's hand and then immediately apologized, certain that if he'd been younger he'd have blushed.

'Don't apologize, please. You're my friend as well as my boss, aren't you?' Winter looked at him and Walt felt his heart knock in an unusual and unfamiliar way. And he wondered why, and what was different about this young woman from all the many others.

'What's the treasure and where?' Magda asked.

Both Walt and Dieter looked embarrassed at her question. They had both spent enough time telling themselves what a ridiculous notion it was without having to say so to someone else.

'We don't know where we're going. Guthrie reckons he's found the Elixir of Life, the hunt is to find it,' Jamie explained to the women, without a hint of embarrassment. He spoke as though looking for such an impossible dream was a normal, run-of-the-mill thing he did every day. 'We've got to put up an ante – winner takes all.'

'So what is in it for this Guthrie fellow?' asked Winter.

'If we fail he cops the lot.' Jamie grinned, for the first time realizing from Winter's expression how far-fetched it all sounded.

'An Elixir of Life. An ante, presumably large . . . sounds like a con to me,' Winter said matter-of-factly.

'No, not Guthrie,' Walt said, but realized he sounded somewhat unsure.

'But anyone who'd found such an elixir would make a fortune. Why should he give it up?' Winter persisted.

'Guthrie isn't interested in money — he's got so much of the stuff.'

'I've never met anyone who has so much he doesn't want more,' she said, and Walt wondered if it was his imagination, or was Winter looking at him with a pertinent look?

'Guthrie's different . . .' Jamie replied emphatically, but looking with renewed interest at the attractive woman. He found himself wondering if it was just Walt's money she was interested in. Who was she and was she Walt's mistress, or could anyone try? 'He's not like other people . . .' he finished lamely, aware of the way his thoughts were going and not wanting them to. The last thing he needed now was another involvement: it was too soon, he was still bleeding from pain for Mica.

'Have you managed to raise the ante, then, Jamie?' Walt asked, but not in such a way as to cause offence. All the same, when Jamie answered that he had, he could not help wondering how he had managed it.

'I sold the odd painting,' Jamie said airily, as if reading his thoughts.

'What will you do when they're all sold?' Dieter said with a smile, not believing Jamie for one minute. If anything of importance from the Grantley collection had come on to the market he'd have heard on the art world grapevine.

'Then I'll have to start on the family silver, Dieter, shan't I?' Jamie answered with a lop-sided but attractive grin.

'I'm surprised you've any left to sell,' Dieter drawled, still smiling.

Winter looked at him with surprise. The German had been charm personified, now there was a distinct edge to his voice. The Englishman seemed extremely pleasant, so what was causing this unpleasant undertow between them? Magda, her cloak covering her hand, squeezed Dieter's thigh as if warning him to stop.

'Quite a bit to go yet, Dieter. You know how it is with we English – there's always the odd treasure stuffed away in the attic to keep the big bad wolf from the door and the little dealers like you busy.' This time the grin was sardonic. 'Still, mustn't stand here gossiping. I've work to do. See you at the party.' He doffed his conductor's cap. 'Fares p-l-e-a-s-e,' he called out in his hammy cockney accent and moved back along the swaying bus. Winter found she was sorry he had left them.

At first, out in the depths of the countryside when the bus driver lost his way in the warren of secondary roads, the mood on the bus remained happy. In his capacity as conductor and feeling this made him rather like the captain of a ship, Jamie organized a sing-song from the top deck.

'Fun, isn't it? Like a good old East End knees-up.' Jamie grinned, enjoying himself enormously.

'A what?' asked Walt.

'It's a rowdy pastime of the English working classes,' Dieter answered for him.

'Oh, dear, Dieter, you never did like us much, did you?' Jamie asked good-naturedly.

'I don't like or dislike, I have little time for a people living on past glories. And I never bother with second-rate nations.' Dieter smiled coldly as he spoke.

'Is that so? I thought you were quite buddy-buddy with second- and even third-rate nations. Banana republics your speciality. Anything, in fact, with a wallet.'

'You seem to be remarkably devoid of your so-famous British humour tonight, James.'

'How the hell would you know if I was devoid of it or no? In all the years I've known you, Dieter, I don't think I've ever heard you laugh.'

'Oh, but I do, James. I laugh most uproariously when

Germany beats you at football. Imagine the great English race beaten at their national sport!' Dieter spoke to the passengers in general.

'Nothing new in that, old chum. We beat you twice at yours.' There was a roar of laughter from the passengers at this and Dieter, never having mastered English humour and not quite sure what Jamie meant, sat back feeling disgruntled.

'Who the hell does he think he is?' whispered Winter to Walt.

'He's an English lord.'

'No, not him, the German.'

'He's a count,' Walt replied.

'He's not got very good manners, then, has he?' Winter remarked.

With a squeal of brakes the bus stopped again. A great groan went up from the passengers.

'This is totally ridiculous!' Dieter declared, jumping to his feet. 'I'm going to speak to the driver.' He raced down the aisle.

'Poor son of a bitch,' said Winter loudly.

Jamie reached the driver's cab to see Dieter angrily shouting at the driver who sat, a large Michelin map over the steering-wheel, gazing into the night through the windscreen, with an exaggerated look of patience on his face. Dieter finally lapsed into silence.

'Right. You finished, mate? Well, let me tell you I don't like being lost any more than you do. I'm hungry. I'm thirsty. I'm knackered, and what's more I've been given the wrong sodding map. If you're so bloody clever, you sort it out.' And so saying he opened the door of his cab, slid out and nonchalantly sauntered to the back of the bus.

'You! You come back here this minute!' Dieter shouted.

'Well, thanks a bunch, Dieter. You've really done it now,' Jamie said.

'Get that man back here,' Dieter ordered.

'I will. But you just get back in that bus, take your seat and shut up. Leave it to me.' It was Jamie's turn to be issuing the orders.

Fuming with anger, Dieter returned to the bus and swept up the stairs to a disgruntled chorus from the other passengers who had already been briefed by the driver.

Jamie, using all of his considerable charm plus delving into his leather bag for some money, set about persuading the driver to have another go.

Armed with a satisfactory sum, Jamie's autograph, and the good wishes of his passengers, the driver returned to the cab and this time he was successful. The château was found.

2

'Isn't this something!' Winter exclaimed as she looked over the stone balustrade of the balcony at the noisy throng below in the great hall of the château. Long, narrow banners of alternating black and white silk hung on the buttermilk-coloured stone walls and lifted gently in the warm draught caused by the movement of so many people, so that the walls seemed to move too. The floor of the hall consisted of large black and white marble tiles, and as the guests, in their monochrome costumes, moved about, they resembled large animated chess pieces. All the flowers were white, in giant black vases. Guthrie's request had been met to the letter, not one scrap of coloured fabric marred the effect.

'It's the same in the dining-room,' said Jamie, who had joined them. 'It's done up like a huge tent, a bit like eating in a giant Bassett's liquorice allsort.'

'It's just so neat! It's the Ascot scene in *My Fair Lady* all over again.' Winter swung round to face him.

'I hope we're not supposed to be mourning something,' Walt said.

'Hell! Fifty years gone by is enough to send one into a terminal spin, I'd have thought.' Jamie smiled as he spoke and Winter thought how handsome he was, far more so than on the screen. And Jamie thought she was really quite lovely, even if her face, if analysed, was all wrong.

'Shall we go and join the party?' asked Walt, taking hold of Winter's arm in a proprietorial way and pointedly leading her away from Jamie without more ado.

In the ballroom they found the walls swathed in black velvet which was stretched taut over the ceiling where small lights flickered like distant constellations.

'It's like dancing in the universe,' said Winter as Walt led her on to the floor where not for the first time he rued the modern dancing and longed for an old-fashioned waltz so that he could take her into his arms. After two numbers, which left him feeling deafened, he suggested they sit the next one out. She complied, even if, Walt thought, a little reluctantly. Despite a search they could find nothing to sit on, the few chairs in evidence having been taken by those elderly guests brave enough to stand the ear-splitting beat coming from the group's speakers.

Winter would have liked to ask Walt how much he thought it would have cost to hire the world-famous group but refrained. It would be gauche to ask, she thought, and, given his age, he probably didn't know anyway. It was only at such times that Winter gave Walt's age a thought. He was so vital, with more energy than a lot of the friends of her own age. He carried himself like a younger man too, so it was not something that habitually crossed her mind. Still, she thought, he must be a good fifteen years older than she was, and she hoped she would manage to wear as well.

'Let's find somewhere quieter,' he said, linking his arm

in hers, and they entered the hall. It was no quieter, they
had exchanged one noise for another. So many people
greeting each other and talking created quite a din. They
merged into the throng as they wandered about, glasses in
hand, and Walt introduced Winter to one group of
acquaintances and then another. Winter felt uncomfortable at the men's knowing glances. She liked even less the
somewhat detached responses of the women which told
her she was of no importance to them; but all the same
she was aware of their sly but none the less intense scrutiny
as they took her measure, inspected her looks, and assessed
the price of her dress and the jewellery she wore; finding
neither expensive, they then proceeded to ignore her. She
did wonder what their reaction would have been had she
been dressed by Versace and dripping in diamonds.

'Walt, they think I'm your mistress,' she whispered to
him.

'What on earth gave you that idea?' he looked suitably
shocked.

'The looks they keep giving me.'

'All in your imagination, Winter,' he said, feeling rather
guilty since it was very much part of his own imagination.
And he knew full well that in this group any young woman
on an older man's arm would be so labelled.

They finally found a space to sit on the wide steps of
the stone staircase which swept regally to the floors above,
and which was crowded with people, like themselves, who
couldn't find anywhere else to sit.

'You're not bored?' Walt asked anxiously when he
realized they had been sitting in silence for some time
watching the constant movement of the party-goers.

'Gracious, no. I get great amusement looking at people,
don't you? I like working out their nationalities and seeing
if I can guess what they do. And I mean, why are rich men
so ugly?'

'Are we?' He smiled at her.

'Not you.' She gave him a gentle push. 'You're attractive in a nice worn, rugged way.'

He smiled at her back-handed compliment. 'But you're rare. The rest — they're either bloated or muscle-bound and tanned like kippers.'

A statuesque blonde in a dress so tight it was unlikely she could sit down even if she found a chair, paused to say hello to Walt, pointedly ignoring Winter.

'At least you can't say all the women are ugly,' he said, as he watched the woman undulate away. 'And she's rich — married to one of the biggest retailers in the States.'

'Then she's not rich, her husband is the rich one.' And she would have liked to add that she doubted if the stunningly turned-out woman looked half as good in the morning without the thick make-up she was wearing. She grinned at him. 'Do you think those women over there once looked like her?' She nodded towards a group of Charity's friends, face-lifted, skeletally thin, but rich. 'I mean, what goes with the rich? It's either women looking like that, like clones, almost, or else young birds, young enough to be their daughters, with the wealthy men. Do rich men only go for dumb-looking bimbos or X-ray women?'

'What a cynic you are, Winter.'

'No, I'm not. I'm a realist. No one looks real here, everyone's so artificial.'

Looking at her face, almost devoid of make-up, he could concede she had the right to make such a remark. 'But you're young and naturally beautiful. What about when you get older, won't you want to use whatever means are at your disposal to stay young-looking?'

'You mean when gravity begins to do its worst? I'll let it. I intend to grow old gracefully — looking like them would be awful. My mother would knock spots off that lot, with her wrinkles and all!'

Dieter and Magda walked by. 'Well, this one disproves your theory. Dieter's rich and handsome.'

'No, he's not. He's like a statue, he's so cold. You've got to have warmth and humanity to be truly handsome. As it is, he gives me the shivers. Do you know him well?'

'I met him years ago but I wouldn't say I know him. I don't think anyone could say they do. He's a bit of an enigma. Maybe his sweet wife does.'

'I wonder why she stays with him.'

'Perhaps she loves him – it can happen, you know, even to the rich.' He laughed at her.

'Still, pretty difficult, I'd have thought, with a case like him. What's he do?'

'He's an art dealer,' Walt said, preferring not to relate the rumours of Dieter's other business; he could just imagine Winter's reaction to that.

'Of course. I thought the name Weiher rang a bell. Then he's seriously rich, I read an article on him which said his personal collection is worth billions. So much wealth is obscene for one person. Odd, isn't it? He loves art and yet he looks like a serial killer.'

'Oh, Winter, my dear. I think you should be careful who you repeat such slanders to.' He smiled at her and wondered whether, even if he finally took the plunge and tried to seduce her, he was going to succeed with this one. Normally his riches got him whoever he wanted. It would be a real bummer if the one he wanted turned him down for that very same reason. Still, he found her somewhat naïve outspokenness refreshing: most people kowtowed to him because of his money, he was fully aware of that.

Jamie had almost not come to the party, he'd been feeling so depressed. First there was his misery over Mica and the certain knowledge that he had lost her – a thoughtful friend had felt it her duty to let him know that Mica was back on Demetrius's yacht. He knew one of the reasons he had forced himself to come was the hope that Guthrie might have invited her. He thought that if he could just get her on her own for a few minutes, explain things, if necessary beg her to come back to him, then all would be right. The other cause of his depression had been his abject failure in his efforts to raise any backing money for the new film. He'd set out with such high hopes, especially after meeting the writer of the script, Roger Marshall, who had told him that his dream was for Jamie to star in it, that when he'd been writing it, it was Jamie he'd imagined in the role. The few contacts who had initially shown interest had faded. He was not sure why – was it his reputation for boozing and roistering which was frightening them off? Or his lack of any starring vehicles for so long – had he become that unsaleable object, a fading star? Or was it the long arm of Demetrius cocking up everything out of spite? That last possibility really stuck in his throat. Wasn't having Jamie's wife enough for him without continuing to ruin his career as well?

So he had had to make himself come to the party, and now he was very glad he had. The film was on again. The news, which he himself had not heard, was out – Guthrie had decided to collaborate as a consultant on the film and was indeed writing the music. Finding backers was no longer a problem, for Guthrie's name and power outclassed even Demetrius. Jamie found himself in the pleasant position of parrying those desperate to invest in the production. They seemed to be queuing up to speak to him, virtually flapping their chequebooks under his nose. Jamie fenced with them, not sure what the hell was going on, but suggesting they talk to Guthrie about it – he was an actor, not a money man, he explained politely, giving a passable impression that he was totally *au fait* with the situation.

It had been some time since Jamie had enjoyed such

popularity as a film idol: his title always ensured he was accepted but, with stardom once again a possibility, he found himself sought out whichever way he turned. This particular circle admired success and abhorred failure as if it were a contagious, terminal disease. He was wiser now and knew that if the film flopped, they would be racing away, breaking contact with him, searching out the next potential star.

In the years when he'd been desperate for work he'd dreamed of this happening again and regretted he had not been careful and appreciative of his fame when at the top of the tree. He had anticipated enjoying it. Instead, he found himself beginning to back away now, to find himself viewing his admirers with a marked degree of cynicism.

He had finally hidden himself behind a large pot of madonna lilies whose perfume was rapidly giving him a headache. He stood watching the crowd forming and re-forming groups like giant amoebae and he wondered what he'd ever seen in them, and why their approval had once meant so much to him.

There was no change in his hunger to do the film, he wanted it desperately. He needed to prove to himself that he could succeed again, and this time he would not slip back. He'd show Mica. He smiled at that thought – so who was he proving himself to? No, he shook his head, he needed to restore his self-respect. There was nothing wrong in showing Mica as well.

Something was wrong, though, he was bored ... that was unusual, he was rarely bored by anything.

It wasn't the party's fault – it was undoubtedly a success, judging by the level of noise. And he'd met some interesting, different people for a change. The bus ride here had been fun, despite Dieter – a new experience, he supposed. No, he was bored. He'd found himself talking to a group of bankers and their wives and had had an almost uncontrollable urge to tell them that he didn't give a monkey's what they thought of him. He'd suddenly felt jaded and old and he didn't like either feeling. He shook himself; maybe he'd caught a bug. He slipped from behind the lilies. He'd find himself a drink – a real one this time.

Dieter, after a lengthy conversation with a smart-suited young man about the state of French politics and the GATT talks, had, to his consternation, discovered that he had been talking to Guthrie's plumber.

'This is such an interesting mix, Dieter. So unusual. Why, I've met a carpenter, two nurses and Guthrie's gardener . . .' said Magda.

'Bloody stupid mix,' he said shortly.

'Oh, I don't know. It's right we should meet people from different walks of life – we never normally do.'

'What on earth for?' Dieter asked her in astonishment. 'If I wanted to talk to a gardener I've got plenty of my own at home.'

Magda lapsed into silence, always the best thing to do when Dieter was like this. He was very edgy tonight, ever since the bus trip. And she wondered why. Maybe it was the treasure hunt, maybe in his mind it had already begun and Jamie and Walt were already the enemy. She'd often seen him like this when in competition against another auction-house to acquire an important painting to sell.

'And do you realize that he's put all those ordinary people up, either here or in the local hotels, while his friends have had to come and return on those stupid buses?'

'I enjoyed the bus ride.'

'You would.' He took another glass of champagne from a passing flunky. 'At least there's one good thing.' Magda looked at him with expectant relief. 'He's not furnished this place yet. It'll cost a small fortune. No doubt we'll be in line for that.'

'That'll be nice for you,' his patient wife said quietly.

'And where is he? Peculiar host, if you ask me – no one's seen him all evening.'

'I'll just go to powder my nose,' Magda said, excusing herself. There were times when nothing could please her husband and, much as she loved him, she realized this evening was one of them.

Where was Guthrie? That was the question on everyone's lips. Guthrie's request that he did not want presents, that those who wanted to give were invited to donate to his beloved UNICEF, had been ignored by many. At one side of the hall was a long table on which stood an enormous silver soup tureen already full of envelopes with cheques and money inside. But beside it was also an increasingly precarious pile of parcels, which, in compliance with his instructions for dress, had all been wrapped in black, white and silver paper.

Everyone jumped and laughed at their reaction when four trumpeters blew a mighty fanfare from the top of the stone staircase. Half a dozen young priests in long black soutanes and black-brimmed hats appeared, and with eyes downcast, scurried down the steps, to all appearances like a flock of theological students rapidly crossing St Peter's Square from their seminary.

There was another great burst of the trumpets and suddenly Guthrie appeared to spontaneous applause, for he was dressed as a cardinal, in scarlet from head to toe. He paused on the steps and, old ham that he was, gave a gracious wave to his guests below. Everyone sang 'Happy Birthday' with varying degrees of success and in varied accents. 'Speech! Speech!' came the cry.

Guthrie looked at his watch and then raised his hand as if in blessing. 'In exactly thirty seconds, I shall be fifty!' he declared. A drum-beat marked the seconds ticking by. The trumpets shrilled, the crowd cheered, a colossal cake was wheeled in and the curtains were pulled back on an alcove showing the largest champagne fountain anyone had ever seen. 'Speech!' his guests clamoured. Guthrie raised his hand again for silence.

'In those immortal words . . . not tonight, dear hearts. Too fatiguing by half. But . . .' he encompassed the hall in a theatrical gesture: 'Enjoy!'

He descended the stairs regally and began to move among his guests, graciously accepting their good wishes – a red island in a black and white sea.

An hour later, summoned by one of the 'priests', Walt, Dieter and Jamie were shown into a room – a furnished one. There was an imposing mahogany desk, a sofa on which Guthrie's pugs lay looking up at the men with their black, beady eyes and, as a group, decided to ignore them. In a semi-circle in front of the desk were three high-backed, tapestry-upholstered chairs of great value. Thick curtains were drawn over the windows, and the sound of the party was muffled by the heavy door. A fire glowed healthily in the hearth and one library lamp, on the desk, was the only illumination.

'What a relief to sit down.' Walt sank gratefully on to one of the chairs.

'You would have thought he would have made some attempt at furnishing the place before the party,' Dieter grumbled.

'Not like Guthrie, is it . . .' Jamie began.

'Not like what?' Guthrie bustled into the room and the dogs were galvanized into welcoming him hysterically. He took time to settle them. 'Not like what?' he repeated, levering his bulk into the throne-like chair behind the desk.

The three looked embarrassed and Walt and Dieter looked at Jamie, who had known Guthrie the longest.

'You usually have everything furnished to perfection,' Jamie explained. 'We're all a bit puzzled – there aren't enough chairs, is what we're going on about.' Even as he said this he thought it was a churlish thing to say after the amount of caviar, smoked salmon and lobster that they had all consumed, not to mention the endless glasses of champagne. To complain about the lack of seating did seem a bit petty.

'Yes, I'm sorry about the chairs – a bit of a cock-up there. But the rest of the furnishings? Well, you see, this place is to be different.'

'Really? In what way?' asked Jamie.

'It's not for me.'

'No?' Jamie looked surprised.

'No,' said Guthrie and, infuriatingly, did not elaborate. 'Well, gentlemen, here we are. The three of you have turned up as promised, does that mean that you are all still on? Got your cheques?' He smiled mischievously at them.

'Could we have a recap, Guthrie? Just to make everything crystal-clear.' Dieter smiled at him, the smile that nobody trusted a hundred per cent. 'As I understand it, our ante is two and a half million Swiss francs or its equivalent at today's rate of exchange. The winner, that is, the person who discovers the elixir, takes all – the money and the elixir. The two losers have to add the same figure again which also goes to the winner, five million in all.'

'Couldn't have put it better myself, Dieter, my dear chap.'

'But who holds the money?'

'Well, I rather thought I would. Or don't you trust me?' Guthrie looked from one to the other with a serious expression but with a marked twinkle in his eyes.

'Of course we do, Guthrie!' Walt laughed, but felt embarrassed because he'd thought the same thing himself.

'And you, Jamie?'

'Guthrie, how could you even ask?' he said nonchalantly, for since Guthrie was bankrolling him, and he wasn't putting up a penny, who held the loot was of no interest to him.

'Well, I'm sorry, but I think it's most irregular. It's a large sum of money to leave in the—'

'No one's forcing you, Dieter. Don't take part if you're worried.'

'That's not what I meant, Guthrie.' Dieter looked angrily at the other two for sitting mute. They must be just as concerned as he, yet were happy to leave him to sort such details out. 'If we were setting up a business between the four of us and substantial sums of money were involved, we would want legal safeguards, wouldn't we?'

'Oh, come on, Dieter. You're outvoted,' said Walt, who was now anxious to get on with the hunt. 'You hold the money, Guthrie, it's all right with me.'

'Why, thank you, Walt. How gracious of you,' Guthrie drawled, and Walt knew he was being laughed at.

'There's just one other thing.' Everyone looked at Dieter with exasperation this time. 'What's in it for you, Guthrie? I mean, you face losing this magic elixir. On top of that you only get the money if we all fail. It strikes me that the search may be an impossible task. That this hunt is a charade.'

'Dieter, honestly. Why the hell didn't you ask all this in Cannes?'

'Because if you remember, Jamie, it was the end of a long, indulgent night. I've thought subsequently.'

'Dieter, dearest, you really are making a right old dog's dinner of all this. Loosen up, dear boy. Chill out. I really do hope that one of you is successful – I can't be doing with the flaming elixir. And by the way, Dieter, there's nothing *magic* about it – there, then, that's a free clue for you all – perhaps I shouldn't have said that. Naughty

Guthrie!' He smacked his hand. 'As to the money – I'm not interested. If you lose I shall donate it all to charity, you have my word on that. Is that good enough for you?'

Reluctantly Dieter nodded.

'And the whole point of this jolly litle romp, Dieter, is fun – you know, that tiny little word F-U-N. It means pleasure, enjoyment, amusement, even.' Guthrie smiled expansively as he lectured Dieter who, in turn, looked furious and foolish in equal measure. 'So, shall we proceed? Whatever you're holding in your clammy little paws, please.'

One Wells Fargo dollar cheque was handed over quickly; one Hoare's Bank sterling cheque, in an envelope because it was blank, followed. One bank draft – post-dated – drawn on a Swiss bank followed reluctantly.

Guthrie hauled himself from his chair and padded over to a wall-safe which none of them had noticed in the dim lighting. 'There they rest until one of you returns triumphant. And here . . .' he handed each of them an envelope. 'In there is your first clue, the second you will find when you've solved this one. I think we should put a time limit on this, don't you? I suggest three months from today – April the sixth. We rendezvous here at eleven a.m. If none of you appears then I shall assume I can deal with the money as I see fit and shall await your second payment. Now, any questions?'

The three participants looked at their hands and their feet, anywhere but at Guthrie, like students caught out at a lecture when no questions come immediately to mind.

'It starts from this moment?' Jamie asked, just to fill the silence. With no transport it would be difficult to get anywhere at this time of night.

'I did think it might be fairer if you all began at the same time, that's why I suggested you come and leave on the red bus. Then you'll all arrive in Paris at the same time, won't you?' Guthrie smiled as he levered himself up. 'Well, if everybody's satisfied I might as well get back to my party – jolly little jamboree, isn't it?'

'So we can we open these?' Walt waved his envelope.

'Anytime, dear boys. And *bonne route*, as our charming hosts say, to you all.' And he swept from the room.

Walt pocketed his envelope, deciding to look at it later – after all, they were all three stuck here. Jamie peeked into his and slipped it into his breast-pocket. Dieter scanned his and laughed.

'Well, if they're all going to be this easy, finding the elixir will merely be a logistical race. Gentlemen.' He clicked his heels and bowed.

'Cocky son of a bitch,' grumbled Walt.

8 The Hunt for Treasure

1

'Where Roses Bloom in a House that's Bad'

Dieter was not on the first red bus to leave for Paris at two in the morning, nor on the second, which departed at three. There was no sign of him on the final bus, which left at four.

'Little creep's scuttled back to Paris,' Jamie said as he, Walt and Winter took their seats on the top deck – he was not expected to play the conductor on the return trip.

'Is Paris in the clue, I wonder?'

'Why haven't you opened it, Walt?' Winter asked sleepily.

'With the amount of champagne we've consumed, I need a good breakfast before I can think straight and contemplate a solution.'

'I know how you feel, Walt. We must be getting too old for these jaunts.' Jamie grinned.

'Speak for yourself, you washed-out Limey.' Walt grinned back.

'Maybe by breaking the rules and not travelling with us he's out of the race.' Walt brightened up at this thought.

'Was it a rule, though? Didn't Guthrie just suggest it might be fairer? In a way I hope he isn't banned. It'll be more fun if Dieter's in on it. I'd like to beat the conceited bastard.'

'You talking about that little jackbooted twit?' A man

had leant over from the seat behind and was tapping Jamie on the shoulder.

'Hello, Twerp. I didn't see you at the party – where were you hiding, you old rogue?' Jamie enthusiastically welcomed and introduced the Viscount Thameside, better known as Twerp to his friends and gossip columnists.

'Sorry to hear about Mica, Jamie,' he said, his rather vacuous face serious for a moment.

'Thanks, Twerp. But there you go. These things happen.' Jamie shrugged and grinned as if his heart was all in one piece. 'Do you know something about the disappearing Kraut, then?'

'Do I? Robbed my poor guv'nor blind over a Rembrandt a few years back. Saw him coming. The provenance was a bit iffy – well, it often is when they've been hanging in the same place for centuries. I mean, ancestors didn't keep receipts, did they?'

Jamie clucked sympathetically, pretty sure he knew what was coming.

'Well, that damned Dieter bloke said he doubted if it was gen, but upped and bought it all the same, but for peanuts. Then he sold the bloody thing for millions. Evil little shit.' He apologized to Winter for his language. 'Still, I had a mini-revenge tonight. Look.' He dug into his breast-pocket and produced a wodge of notes which he waved drunkenly in the air. 'Sold him my clapped-out old Range Rover for double its value. Stupid little turd!' At which he found it necessary to apologize again.

'So now we know how he got away,' said Jamie.

'But where did he go, is more to the point.' Walt said ominously.

They had arranged to meet over breakfast in Walt's suite at the Ritz. Jamie had booked into the less expensive Hôtel du Louvre. With only four hours' sleep and a hangover which, as yet, was only hovering but if not fed a little more alcohol threatened to develop into the full-blown variety, Jamie insisted Buck's Fizz was an essential accompaniment to breakfast if they were to solve anything.

'Right. Here goes.' Walt, who had steadfastly refused to open his envelope until breakfast was served, slid a butter-knife under the flap of the envelope, slit it open and removed the thick sheet of cream notepaper within.

'What does it say?' Winter asked, leaning forward eagerly.

'"*Where roses bloom in a house that's bad,*"' Walt intoned with a puzzled expression and repeated it several times for good measure. 'I hate crossword puzzles! Why the hell did I ever agree to this stupid escapade?'

'Who got out of bed the wrong side, then?' Jamie began to tuck into his scrambled eggs, while Winter nibbled at a croissant. But Walt ate nothing, he merely looked cross.

'We're both mad. All that money for a stupid jaunt with clues that are incomprehensible and yet, no doubt, our little German friend is half-way there already.'

'It's not that bad—' Jamie began.

'At least I can afford to lose the money. Can you?'

Winter looked up from spooning jam on to her croissant and wondered why Walt should suddenly become so aggressive. 'I wonder if it means bad as in naughty or bad as in unwell?' she said helpfully, hoping to diffuse the atmosphere Walt seemed set on building up.

'Do you know any French?' Jamie smiled at her as if fully aware of what she was doing, and in thanks.

'No,' Walt barked.

'Only from my schooldays. I remember a little,' Winter volunteered.

'Well, then?' Jamie said in an encouraging tone, and she found herself thinking again how handsome he was, and marvelling that she could find a man in his forties so attractive.

'Let me see,' she said with a little shake of her head, as if to rid herself of such thoughts and the complications they might lead to. She studied the piece of paper which Walt handed to her dismissively as if he had already given up. Jamie found himself thinking how pretty she could look even when frowning and wondered again what was going on between her and Walt. Something must be, he presumed, knowing what a lecher Walt was, yet he'd not seen a sign of anything pass between them and Winter had arrived at the suite after Jamie, politely knocking at the door. It would seem she had not slept in here.

'Well, roses are easy enough,' she began.

'I'd concentrate on the end of the line if I were you,' Jamie said helpfully.

'You know, don't you?' She looked at him and he nodded that he did.

'How much money do you want to tell us?' Walt asked abruptly.

'Oh, come on, Walt. That would be cheating,' Winter admonished.

'It would save some goddam time, though, wouldn't it?'

'Come on, Walt, that wouldn't be—'

'Jamie, if you're going to say "cricket," so help me God, I'll thump you one.'

'I wasn't, actually. I was going to say "nice".' Jamie grinned.

'So bad is *mal*, or is it *mauvais*? And house is *maison* – a *maison mauvais*.' She shook her head. 'It doesn't make sense. Or could it mean an asylum or something? Weren't they called bad houses once upon a time?'

Jamie waited patiently in silence.

'*Maison mal . . . maison mauvais* or *mauvais maison* or

mal maison . . .' She kept repeating the alternatives to herself. 'Hang on! It rings a bell! *Mal maison* – it's a place, isn't it? What, where? Oh, Walt, you must know, you must have heard of it.' Walt shook his head. 'Malmaison – I've got it.' She looked up, excited. 'It's a house, a real place. But who lived there? Someone famous . . . A woman. I know!' She jumped up in her seat. 'Josephine lived there. She was a great gardener. She must have had a rose garden. We need a Michelin, a map.' She finished in a tumble of words.

'Napoleon's Josephine?' Walt asked.

'The very same.'

'I don't think that's fair. If you hadn't been here, I'd never have got it – what the hell do I know about French history?'

'But I was here, Walt.' She touched his hand gently and Jamie felt his heart sink as he saw the intimate gesture.

The minute their breakfast was finished they set off in Walt's car through a cold and drizzly Paris.

'Is it far?'

'No, about eight miles or so,' Jamie assured them as he expertly drove the large Volvo estate through the congested streets of the city towards the extraordinary modern La Défense. He'd been surprised by the car, which was not at all what he'd expected Walt to own. But Walt had explained it was mainly for his wife's convenience. When they were in Europe she liked to visit antique and junk shops, trawling for treasures for their various homes, and the Volvo made the transport of her purchases that little bit easier. But Jamie noticed Walt looked uncomfortable talking about his wife – in front of Winter, he presumed – and he didn't like that one little bit.

They drove mainly in silence since all of them were tired

from the previous night's party. Jamie decided he had to stop thinking of Winter in this way. What had he got to offer her? No money – only if his film was a box office success. A broken heart from a broken marriage. He had a house which devoured whatever money he could lay his hands on, and he had a gambling problem he was still struggling with. No, she was probably better off with Walt. His fingers tightened around the wheel. But how could she be? He was a lech, everyone knew, he went through women like a grim reaper, leaving them used and despised. That couldn't happen to Winter, he couldn't allow it.

Walt sat deep in thought and wondered what his best approach with Winter was. He still marvelled that, much as he wanted her, he hadn't tried to screw her yet. It must be a record for him. But she was different from all the rest. He respected her. He was even beginning to believe that he might be in love with her.

Winter was asleep.

'Tatty place, isn't it?' Jamie looked gloomily out of the window at the passing scene as they drove through a run-down area, past cheap shops and numerous garages and car lots.

'Sorry?'

'Odd place for an Empress to end up – still, I suppose it didn't look this grotty then.' He swung the car off the main road from Paris and nearly missed the turning up a narrow, tree-lined road signposted to the château. The lurch of the car woke Winter.

'We there?'

'Almost,' answered Jamie. 'Bloody hell!' he yelled, and wrenched the wheel over to the right to avoid a Range Rover which, emerging from a gateway to the parking lot, drove straight at them. Jamie turned the wheel, the heavy Volvo's rear section swayed skittishly on the damp cobbled road. The branches of a leafless tree scraped the side of the car. Jamie slammed on the brakes, the car slewed round and ended up facing the way it had just come.

'Shit!' He rested his head on the steering-wheel and waited for his racing heart to return to normality. 'Thank God this car's so solid. Anything lighter would have turned over.'

'The son of a bitch,' Walt shouted, slamming his fist on to his knee. 'That was Dieter. He did that on purpose, he was trying to push us off the road.'

'You sure?' asked Jamie.

'Are you blind or something? It was a bloody Range Rover.'

'They're very popular in France – very BCBG,' Jamie replied. 'You know, Preppie, Sloane Ranger-ish.' He thought he had best explain.

'I recognized him as they flashed past. Magda was with him,' Winter added. 'And it was a right-hand drive vehicle.'

'Still, how would he know we were in this car? We could have been anyone. Much more likely he's a lousy driver,' Jamie said in a very reasonable and calming voice. And Winter had the strange impression she was in the car with the fictional Peter Ascot, Jamie's starring role – Ascot was like that in emergencies in his films. Was Jamie acting now or was that how he always was and so didn't need to act the part of the private eye? She shook her head at such a puzzling conundrum.

'He knows this car. I drove him to Antibes in it last year and while I was there he borrowed it for a couple of days – and, I might add, returned it with a dent in the side and an empty tank.'

'Hardly sporting of him, was it?' Jamie put the car into gear.

'I love you English, you're so laid back.' Winter laughed from her seat in the back of the car.

'Not much point in being anything else, is there?' Jamie shrugged his broad shoulders.

Winter fell in love with Malmaison.

'It's so pretty and yet so melancholy. Can't you just imagine poor Josephine walking these paths, pining for her lost love?' she said dreamily.

Jamie said he could, but Walt said nothing because he couldn't – imagination had never been his strong point.

'Do you think Josephine planted these self-same roses?' Winter asked as they entered the rose garden.

'I shouldn't think so,' Jamie said and then, seeing her disappointed expression, added quickly. 'Not all of them, perhaps some.'

'I do hope so,' Winter said, sensing he was lying to protect her and thinking how nice that was.

'So what do we do now, look for a clue tied to a bush?' Walt asked, looking miserable in the drizzle which was turning into heavy rain. As if in answer to his question a man, sodden and disgruntled-looking, approached them from a small pavilion and wordlessly handed them two envelopes.

'You'd have thought he would have checked who we were,' Walt said as he ripped the envelope open.

'I think he had photographs of you both. As we approached, he was looking at something in his hand that could have been a photo. What does it say, Walt?' Winter was standing on tiptoe, trying to read the note.

'What do you make of that, Jamie?'

'Look, Walt, I didn't mind helping out on the first clue, I thought it was a bit unfair if you didn't know any French. But we can't keep on doing them together – it wouldn't be right and in any case, if we did, who would be the winner?'

'We could always share the prize,' Walt said reasonably.

'Yes, or we could bump the other one off,' Jamie said

jokingly, but was none too sure how much of a joke it was: he did not know if Walt was capable of killing for money; he was certain now that Dieter was.

2

'*A Caribou Stands Guard over a Field of Death*'

Dieter felt smugly pleased that he had outwitted his opponents on two counts. Firstly getting away from the ball without them; after all, he had argued with himself, Guthrie had not *actually* said they had to return on the stupid buses. And secondly he must be a good hour ahead of them, if not two.

'I thought this was to be a game,' Magda said as she sat beside him, still not fully recovered from that morning's near miss with the Volvo.

'With so much money involved it's no game,' Dieter replied, as he wound up the engine of his Porsche on the motorway north of Paris – he had left the Range Rover in the city centre and had changed to his own fast car.

'I should think Jamie thinks it is. I can't see him taking this seriously.'

'But he's a fool. Everything in life has come easily to Jamie – he has no respect for money or he wouldn't fritter it away gambling.'

'And Walt?'

'He likes money, no doubt he'll do anything to win.'

'Like trying to push his competitors off the road?'

'What on earth do you mean?'

'They were in that car this morning, the one you tried to push into the ditch.'

'Magda, my darling, of course it was not them. The car was being driven erratically, it was only due to my skill there was not an accident.'

On an empty road? thought Magda, as she leaned across to push the cigarette lighter in.

'Do you have to smoke? I hate it in the car, you know I do.'

'I get nervous when you drive so fast and on wet roads,' she replied, lighting her cigarette and inhaling deeply. With an irritated tetching noise, Dieter opened his window an inch and wind and rain blasted in. Magda took another deep puff before resignedly extinguishing the cigarette.

Why was he being so edgy with her? he wondered. Admittedly he knew he would do anything to win this treasure hunt, for he was incapable of settling for second-best in anything. No, the excitement of the hunt was not the reason for his attitude.

He was normally considerate to her, for her happiness was his pleasure. He was aware that she knew a side of him that his business associates would be surprised to find existed. He never forgot a birthday or an anniversary. Although Magda knew of his sad and lonely childhood, he had never complained about it, never used it as an excuse for anything that happened to him or anything he did. While he could be ruthless in business, he never was with her. And even if he was domineering with her sometimes, he felt from her reaction that she quite liked him to be, maybe to compensate for the fact he could not dominate her in bed. He knew she sometimes blamed herself for his inability to make love to her. They should have discussed it and been more open about the problem, but he could not bring himself to do so, the subject embarrassed and shamed him too much. But oh, how he longed to make love to her. He sighed as he drove and when she put out her hand and gently touched his, he took hold of hers and gently squeezed it.

It was Gretel, his mistress, who was the problem, he thought. He was usually discreet, but this time he feared he had not been discreet enough and that Magda might have seen them in a restaurant in Munich. There was an even sadder expression in her eyes and an almost desperate need to please and placate him. This not only made him feel even more guilty but, irrationally, made him irritated with her. He'd never felt like that before and was ashamed that he did. He had a nasty idea that even if Magda had found out she was going to let this affair continue, that in her selfless way she understood his need for Gretel. He knew her so well and could almost imagine her reasoning that if she could not make him happy she was grateful others could. And that if she didn't make waves he would always return to her. And where did that leave him but feeling even more of a heel? He pushed his foot down still further on the accelerator at the thought.

It would be best for everyone if he finished with Gretel, that's what he should do. But he didn't know if he could. Gretel was different from the rest of his women. Of course she was blonde – they all were, except Magda – but it was more than that, she was intelligent, sweet-natured, putting up with his many moods. In many ways she was like his wife. He wouldn't go as far as to say he loved her but he was inordinately fond of her.

He needed Gretel. Without his visits to her and his success in her bed, he knew he would feel half the man he was, and feared that he would then fail in everything. He was unkind to Gretel – not in financial terms, for she had more now than at any other time in her life, but he was cruel to her when he made love to her because she wasn't Magda.

He was confused, deeply confused.

If Magda knew, then he supposed he was duty-bound to give up Gretel. His greatest fear was that the two women might meet, and being so alike might make friends. Then the secret plan which he had discussed with Gretel – albeit in the loosest sense – might come out.

He wanted a son. At one time he could tell Magda that

it did not matter that they were childless and it was true. In an odd way her sterility made his impotence a fraction easier to deal with — at least they were both to blame. But, as time slipped by, the longing for a son had emerged and grew stronger in him with each passing year. Gretel would make the ideal mother. Either she could have the child and keep it and Dieter could adopt it later to ensure his inheritance, or he and Magda could adopt it in babyhood and raise it together. He was not sure which course would be best and was half afraid to suggest it to either woman. Should he pretend to Magda the child was a foundling or be honest and say it was his son? He was all at sea, not knowing what their emotional reactions might be. Not knowing if he might end up with neither of them.

Dieter could not bear to think of a life without Magda, nor did he want to lose his physical life with Gretel — hence his present irritability. He grated the gears as he changed to overtake a lorry.

'Darling, what is it? You're so edgy.'

'Am I? It's nothing.' He shook his head.

'You sure it's not something you'd like to discuss with me?'

'No — just business . . .'

She suddenly became aware that the car had slowed down. 'Where's this?'

'Albert. Near the Somme. We'll have lunch and solve the clue afterwards. You've been very thoughtful, what have you been thinking?'

'Oh, nothing. I'm tired, that's all.' She smiled at him and wondered when he'd have the courage to talk to her about the baby he wanted her new friend Gretel to have for them.

In his hotel room Jamie worked logically at the clue. A caribou must have a North American connotation. And a field of death must refer to a battlefield, he concluded. So he phoned a friend who was married to a cousin once removed who was first secretary at the Canadian Embassy in Paris and in ten minutes had his answer.

He hired a car and just after lunch was on his way to Albert in northern France.

Walt and Winter were already almost at Albert. Winter had been most impressed when Walt had solved the clue in one minute flat.

'Well, that's easy enough. It's Beaumont Hamel – there was a Canadian division on the Somme. It's a fully preserved battlefield. The caribou is their memorial.'

'How did you know that?'

'I've always been fascinated by the Great War – the greediest war of all.'

Where to look? thought Dieter as he parked the car in the car park of Beaumont Hamel, a tourist attraction in summer but deserted now. He and Magda walked towards the immaculately tended battlefield.

'They usually have visitors' books in these places,' he said to Magda when no obliging man appeared with an envelope. 'I wonder.'

He quickly found the book in its bronze case, set in a cairn embossed with the maple leaf. He flicked to the back. There were three envelopes. He pocketed all three.

'Come on,' he said to Magda.

'I'd like to look around.'

'No time. Come on . . .'

As soon as his car was out of the car park a gardener appeared from a small wood. He walked to the case, checked the book and in the back put three envelopes each addressed with a different name.

Dieter and Magda met Walt and Winter half an hour later on the road to Albert. Walt flashed his lights and hooted. Dieter ignored them.

'Just look at these fields, Walt. They're not flat, there are regular ridges in them.' Winter pointed out of the window as they sped along the straight, tree-lined road from Albert.

'Remains of the trenches – you can see the outlines quite clearly. They'll probably never disappear.'

'What a legacy to leave!'

'Sure is.'

'I suppose this road would once have been a mass of soldiers.'

'Yes, bringing up supplies, taking the wounded back, pock-marked by shells.'

They turned off the main road and were then on winding, twisting secondary roads, passing through many villages but passing even more cemeteries, the white regulation tombstones in their carefully maintained plots marching into the distance like a stone army over the dead of another army.

'Oh, my God, Walt, look. Please stop.'

They were looking at a signpost.

'Blighty,' Winter said softly. 'Isn't that England? Why Blighty?'

'Yes, poor devils. It's Hindustani for home, I believe.'

'Oh, no. How sad.' And tears filled Winter's eyes. 'The whole place is so miserably sad.'

'It *is* winter, Winter.' He smiled at his feeble joke but she, having heard it so many times before, did not respond. Walt started the car again.

'I don't know whether I like this or not,' Winter said when they eventually entered the park of Beaumont Hamel. The whole battlefield had been preserved just as it had been in that fateful summer of 1916. Grass now grew on the dips, which had once been trenches where men had fallen, wounded, screaming for their mothers. Where others had been blown to smithereens and others had drowned in the mud, too feeble to raise their heads. Gaunt, twisted pieces of metal, rusted with age, lay where they had been left. But the horror was covered by lovingly tended grass. The field itself spread out before them, its mounds and ridges looking like a sea with lush green rolling waves. There was a calm and peace about the place but it was one of infinite melancholy.

They climbed the path of a mound, neatly planted with bushes, to where a large bronze caribou stood guard. On the retaining wall a bronze arrow marked the distance in miles to Newfoundland.

'Oh, God, I want to cry,' she said, and Walt put his arm about her to comfort her, for he too was moved. And then loud laughter rang out, shockingly in such a place, they both thought. They looked down to the killing ground and twenty yards away saw a small child, her blonde hair flying behind her beneath a poppy red beret, her short little legs in scarlet dungarees pumping the air as, screaming with excitement, she ran from her elder brother who, also laughing, chased her.

'That's what they died for, so that she could run free,' Walt said, his throat choked.

'I hope they know,' said Winter and put her hand in his. 'I'd like to sign that book of remembrance we saw.'

'Me too,' said Walt, not letting go of her hand.

Jamie was already there when they reached it.

'Hi! These clues aren't too difficult, are they?' he yelled, waving the envelopes in the air as they approached. Winter frowned, finding his ebullience out of place. 'You staying in Albert or Amiens or moseying back to Paris? There's a quite decent hotel . . .'

'We thought to stay at Amiens,' said Walt.

'Good, me too. Perhaps we can have dinner together?'

'I don't want to leave them,' Winter said softly.

'Who?' asked Jamie.

'The poor dead soldiers.'

'Creepy place, isn't it?' Jamie grinned cheerfully.

'Doesn't it make you sad?' she asked, puzzled at his apparent indifference.

'No point in dwelling on it, Winter. Does you no good. I've two grandfathers, a great uncle and half a dozen cousins scattered about the place.'

'Don't you want to visit their graves?'

'No, not really. It hurts a bit, you see.' He turned away and looked out over the green swathe of the battlefield. She'd never understand the English, she decided.

3

'Where Ludwig Ran Amok'

The three men all reached the same solution to the latest clue, if not at the same time.

Dieter hired a plane to fly him and Magda home that night. Walt arranged for his chauffeur to drive the car to Germany while he and Winter boarded his Boeing with the flight plan logged to Munich. Jamie, economizing, caught the overnight train.

Dieter, on his home ground, was confident that he would quickly acquire the next clue. He had a particular feeling of affinity with the young King Ludwig of Bavaria who, he was certain, was the Ludwig of the clue. He too as a child had read and re-read *The Ring of the Niebelungen* and been fired by its stories of chivalry and courage. Had he not also desired his own dream home above everything else, just like the King, even if he had not had to build his as Ludwig had done? Had Wagner's music, which might not have been written but for Ludwig's patronage, not moved him and made him feel a great

welling of national pride? He knew well the various castles
Ludwig had built: regarded as follies at the time, they were
now one of the most important sources of income for the
Bavarian Landrat.

Ah, yes, this stage would be simple, he thought, as he
entered his own dream home – *his* castle.

Magda had been quiet on the journey home. He felt she
was cross with him but he could not think why, and since
he had plans to make he had no time to try to find the
answer. Women! She seemed to have lost interest in the
treasure hunt once he had given in and let her come.

They arrived home too late for anything but a light
supper.

'Do you think I should visit the Castle of Neuschwanstein first or last? It would seem to me to be the obvious
choice, since it's the best known of Ludwig's castles,' he
said. 'What do you think?'

'Yes,' she answered.

'But then perhaps it's somewhere more obscure – perhaps the Schachen hunting-lodge.'

'Perhaps.'

'But then that might not be fair to the others . . .
perhaps they would only know of Neuschwanstein or
Linderhof.'

'Perhaps.'

'Aren't you the least bit interested in where I should
search?' he said with a marked tone of pique in his voice.

'Of course.' She smiled politely.

'Is something bothering you?'

'Nothing,' she replied, which always annoyed him out
of all proportion.

'Do you wish to continue accompanying me?' he asked
with studied politeness.

'Of course.' The same empty smile attended her reply.

'Well, I've work to do.' He stood up, crumpling his
napkin and throwing it on the table in a gesture of

annoyance. He crossed to the door and paused. 'I don't understand you, Magda. You say you would like to spend more time with me and when it is possible, as now . . . then you lose interest.'

'It's not that. It's just that . . . I wish . . .'

'Yes.'

'I wish you didn't want to win so desperately. I'm frightened of what you will do.'

'Oh, really, Magda. How silly of you. But how sweet.' He kissed her cheek, wishing he hadn't seemed so irritated with her.

Later, in his study, Dieter was surrounded by all the books he had on Ludwig, looking for a clue to show if the King had had a more extreme fit of insanity. The obvious choice would have been Schloss Berg, where Ludwig, imprisoned in his madness, had murdered his doctor and killed himself – one couldn't run more dramatically amok than that, he decided. But then, Schloss Berg was in private hands . . . no, undoubtedly it would be one of the more popular ones. He'd go to Herrenchiemsee first, where Ludwig had tried to re-create Versailles. Slamming his books shut, he picked up the phone to call Gretel on his private line. Annoyingly, she was constantly engaged.

Walt and Winter settled into their expensive two-bedroomed suite at the Hotel Rafael. Jamie, when he arrived, found a more modestly priced hotel; he wished he didn't have to keep worrying about his image and could find a cheap gasthaus instead. He realized now that he had been foolish when he had turned down Guthrie's offer to finance his expenses as well as bankrolling his ante.

'Ah, well,' he said to himself, as he prodded the bed in the small room where he found himself, and to his surprise discovering the bed to be incredibly soft with a goose-down duvet thrown over it. He took off his hat and the dark glasses which he'd worn so that he would not be easily recognized. He could just imagine what the tabloid press would make of an ex-movie star not staying at the best hotel available. Still, he thought, he might win this hunt – it was proving remarkably simple so far. It had crossed his mind that two things could happen: either the clues would begin to get harder, or Guthrie was up to something. And then, even if he came in a poor third, there was the new film – everything was on course to proceed, with shooting starting in May in Prague. He was a lucky bugger, really, not many were given a second chance like this. And then he thought of Mica and her lovely, lithe body and wondered if he was so lucky after all.

'No good hankering after something you can't have, Jamie old boy. Let's face it, you can hardly blame the woman. Who'd want to stick around with a waster like you?' he said aloud to his image in the pock-marked mirror, and to make himself feel better, practised one of the lop-sided grins which had helped make him famous in the first place. He peered at his face with a ruthless professional eye and debated for the umpteenth time whether he should have a face-lift or not. Many did. But then he shook his head, it wouldn't seem right somehow, and he could just imagine what his father's reaction would have been to such a notion. He laughed, showing his perfect capped teeth – silly, that, nothing wrong in having your teeth tarted up but such a calvinistic barrier to doing the same to your face.

Food, he needed food, he decided. He liked German cooking, he'd go out and find a restaurant serving a good honest sausage and sauerkraut, and have a couple of beers, and then maybe he'd go to the library. He didn't know much about Ludwig except that he'd gone mad and built a castle called Neuschwanstein which he was pretty sure was used in the film *Chitty Chitty Bang Bang*. Not a lot to go on, he thought; maybe he could chat up a pretty librarian – one who spoke English – to do a little research for him.

Walt had already contacted his European agent to find him a historian expert on the subject of Ludwig of Bavaria, who also spoke excellent English and who would be able to brief him, after lunch, in his suite.

Dieter was up early, before Magda had stirred. He ate a hurried breakfast, anxious to be on his way. If Magda was going to try to restrain him he'd be better off without her. He scribbled her a note and was soon racing down the autobahn towards Lake Chiemsee.

Despite the early hour there were many tourists. He scanned their faces expectantly, but with no response. Once the castle doors were open to the public he was content to wander through the rooms, admiring once again the sheer genius of Ludwig's decorative concept. He lingered too long in the porcelain room, studying the exquisite Meissen door panels with rapt attention. So lost was he in admiration that for a time he forgot the reason for his errand until he looked at his watch and saw it was nearly noon. It had been a totally wasted morning, he thought. Obviously, whatever there was to be found was not at Herrenchiemsee. He went back to the car park, got into his car and drove far too fast up the autobahn back to his office.

His normally calm secretary was agitated when he entered.

'What on earth's the matter, Wilma?'

'Thank goodness you've come. A man has been phoning constantly and he doesn't sound very happy, Count von Weiher, in fact once or twice he was quite threatening. I told him I would give you his message as soon as you contacted me, but you didn't call as you usually do.' She sounded affronted, he chose to ignore the implied criticism. 'I really think you should phone him immediately.'

'Any mail for me to sign?' asked Dieter, having no intention of phoning anyone immediately if they were that demanding, and certainly not prepared to accept instructions from his secretary of all people.

She handed him a stack of neatly typed letters at which he merely glanced – he could rely on Wilma totally – before signing them. He leafed through another pile of mail which had arrived that morning to see if there was anything of note. And only then did he turn his attention to the small pile of notes she had given him relating to his telephone calls, looking for the ones she felt he should return immediately, the ones that had bothered her so.

He frowned, but not at the discarded six – they could wait. He was frowning at the remaining six – all from Toto. Toto should not be calling him on his office number. In all his years of dealing with His Excellency they had never contacted each other on telephone numbers that could easily be traced back to Dieter. If he was doing so, then why? Dieter looked at his telephone as if the instrument could give him the answer – maybe it would be safer to go to a hotel to make the call from an anonymous callbox. A little late in the day now Toto had called here, he thought. He looked at his watch: if he was to travel south to Neuschwanstein this afternoon, he would have to call now and take the risk.

'Toto? Dieter von Weiher here. I'm sorry I was out – business, you know,' he lied smoothly.

'His Excellency is none too happy, Count von Weiher.' Toto sounded far from his normal happy self.

'And why should that be, Toto? I checked, everything is going well.' He lied again, he'd done no such thing. He'd been involved with the party, and now the hunt, and he could not shake off his initial lack of interest in this deal.

Once it was set up he'd hardly given it a thought – all most unlike him. In coded faxes he had alerted Jan at his Amsterdam office that a shipment of machine parts was due in for urgent delivery and confirmed what the system of payment was to be. They would have long been in receipt of funds from His Excelllency – there could not be any reason for a hold-up. Weeks ago he'd received confirmation from Jan that his orders had been put in hand, that everything was going smoothly.

'So how can I help you, Toto?' He smiled as he spoke.

'His Excellency is wondering why he has not received the consignment for which he has paid such a considerable sum.'

Dieter felt the room close in on him, he realized he was cold yet sweating. Nothing like this had ever happened before. Half the arms should have arrived at their destination, with the other half still in transit. 'Toto, my dear chap. I'm so sorry, I really have no idea what you're talking about – as far as I'm concerned everything is on schedule.' He spoke with a confidence which he felt seeping from him alarmingly quickly.

'Not so far as His Excellency is concerned, Count. He has received nothing.'

'There must have been a hiccough – nothing more to it, I assure you. Perhaps bad weather en route.'

'I hope not, Count. I've been trying to contact you for five days now. His Excellency's schedule is seriously disrupted. I fear His Excellency is running out of patience.'

'Then I'll get on to my contacts immediately, Toto.'

'I'd do that if I were you, Count. In fact, His Excellency is only willing to give you exactly twenty-four hours more.' The phone went dead.

Dieter sat holding the receiver for a moment listening to the burr but not hearing it. Toto always called him by his Christian name. He had not been this formal with him for years. Dieter's stomach lurched. Something serious had happened. In the past there had been minor panics but nothing more. Dieter was too good an organizer for that. For the first time for a long time he felt afraid. He knew His Excellency was not the sort of person to expect or understand a delay of any sort, nor would he allow for any excuses. He was a professional and expected others to be so too. Dieter phoned the Amsterdam office and listened bleakly as the phone rang and rang. He redialled the number in the faint hope that he had misdialled the first time. And then he faxed them; the fax went through, the confirmation slip emerged from the machine. He waited ten minutes for the reply he had asked for. No fax came chattering back on the instrument.

He sat at his desk, steepling his fingers, staring into space. Where was Jan? The man had worked for him for thirty-seven years, his devotion and gratitude to Dieter were unassailable. Dieter had looked after him and Renalta well over the years. Both were far richer than the expectations of their official positions. Renalta had retired years before on a healthy pension and lived in a luxury flat. The thought that was burrowing away in Dieter's head was that if Jan had cheated on him, why should he have done so? Why now? The man was in his seventies, doubtless wanting to retire in the very near future. He had more than enough to keep him in comfort for the rest of his life. There would be no point in him cheating ... Dieter's fingers drummed a restless tattoo on the desk. Surely not, he thought, shaking his head. Last month Jan had asked for an increase in wages, something about covering a mortgage on a house for a grandchild. Dieter had refused, and reasonably, since Jan earned so much already. Dieter considered he had paid well in excess for his loyalty.

Since Bruce's death Dieter had employed several sea captains, none as good as him, but the current one, Al, an American unable to settle from the excitement of the Vietnam war, was better than most. And, as always, he was paid handsomely to do the dangerous work. Dieter felt he could trust him, but even if there was any doubt, he had no choice, he thought, as he dialled.

'Al, this is Dieter von Weiher here. Have you by any chance had any contact with Jan van Rentas recently?'

'Not for a few weeks, Dieter. I saw him when we docked with that consignment of rugs from India.'

'Yes, yes,' said Dieter, irritated. 'He hasn't contacted you over a special consignment?'

'Sorry, Dieter, can't help you.'

'Thank you, Al.' Dieter replaced the receiver and sat staring bleakly into space. If Jan had double-crossed him, when had he done so? If it was last week, then all was lost. Perhaps he was still in Amsterdam. He arranged to meet his customary pilot in the bar of the Hotel Ambassador. Then they would fly to Holland. He made one more call to a private detective asking him to put a tail on Walt and Jamie, to find out how they fared in his absence.

He went to the flat he kept in Munich for his assignations and showered and changed, then he realized he still hadn't spoken to his mistress, Gretel. He hadn't time now, this was more important. She was a patient woman, she would understand that business came first, and he'd sweeten her with a little present. Maybe he'd buy her some diamonds in Amsterdam, her delight in them had always pleased him in the past.

Two hours later he was standing in the bar of the hotel drinking a glass of Perrier, too tense to drink any alcohol safely.

'Dieter, how goes it?'

Dieter swung round to find Walt standing behind him, looking bronzed, casual and confident.

'Oh – fine, thanks, Walt. And you?' he replied, expertly covering his surprise: how, since he'd stolen Walt's envelope, was he here?

'Solved any good clues recently?' Walt laughed. 'Not

too difficult, are they? But I tell you one thing, I don't understand Guthrie. I mean, these clues – a child could solve them. With so much money at stake I think he's got some ulterior motive. You know him, what do you think his game is, Dieter?'

'I really wouldn't like to say. I've been acquainted with Guthrie for many years but I would not say that I know him.'

'Ah,' said Walt, 'that's what Jamie says too. You'd think the English would understand each other, wouldn't you?'

Dieter laughed. 'No, I think they're the last people to do that. And how's pretty Miss Winter?' he asked with a knowing look.

'She's tired. We went to . . . er . . . what's that place called? Herren-something or other. Bit over the top for my taste, all that gold and what have you. But there was no one there. We thought we'd take in this Neuwan-something or other tomorrow. You had any luck?'

'I haven't had time yet to search anywhere, I'm afraid – business, you know,' lied Dieter.

'Dieter, there's a hell of a crush at reception, perhaps you could tell me . . . my chauffeur was driving my car down from Paris and has had an accident. Nothing too serious but the car is damaged and it'll be a week before it's back on the road. I need to hire a limousine. Can you recommend a company?'

'Oh, no problem at all, Walt. You're very welcome to use my car.'

'But won't you be needing it?'

'No. Unfortunately I have to go away for a few days on urgent business. You're very welcome to use it; in any case I have several more in my garage,' he said with a throwaway gesture of his hand.

'That's mighty kind of you, Dieter. In the circumstances

I would say that's exceedingly kind of you, thank you very much. Winter and I appreciate it greatly.'

The pilot entered and waved to Dieter from the doorway. He made his apologies and left. Walt had been alone for only a few minutes when Jamie sauntered in.

'Hi, Jamie, any luck?' he asked.

'None whatsoever. It's a damn fool clue if you ask me. You've got a mad king who ruled the whole of Bavaria – he could have been mad everywhere, couldn't he? I presumed it meant one of the castles he built, but what if it doesn't? What if he was particularly barmy somewhere else?'

'We went to Herren – hell, I can't remember the name of the damn place – the one on an island in a lake. Winter said it reminded her of Versailles. There was nothing there, though we waited for ages.'

'I was there too. Actually, I saw you.'

'Why didn't you show yourself?'

'Oh, I didn't like to. You two seemed very engrossed.' This was not strictly true, Walt and Winter had been behaving like any other tourists there, but Jamie wanted to test him, see if he would be more forthcoming. Walt disappointed him.

'I thought we'd try the two castles close to a town called Füssen tomorrow. And you?' he said, with no mention of Winter.

Jamie had discovered from his obliging library assistant, who turned out to be an ardent fan who had seen every one of his films several times, that Ludwig had built three castles, Neuschwanstein, Linderhof and Herrenchiemsee, and there were countless others he had renovated. Jamie had decided to concentrate on the three he'd built, and it looked as if Walt had decided to do the same.

'Dieter's just turned up trumps for a change, after trying to make us crash – guilty conscience, perhaps. He's lending me a car – says he's off on a business trip – we might beat him yet.'

'Really? How extraordinary.'

'Yeah, odd, isn't it? You'd have thought with a guy like Dieter he'd try and put everything in our way to make things as difficult as possible, not give a helping hand.'

'You would. Maybe he's already solved this clue – it is his stomping ground after all, so he's got a distinct advantage over the rest of us. Maybe he isn't off on a business trip. Perhaps he's already on the next stage.'

'Somehow I don't think he is. He looked rattled to me, as if something big was bothering him. Still, that's not our problem.'

'No, and if he has got difficulties, I'm not crying for him. What about dinner?'

'What about it, Jamie?'

'Well, I don't see why we can't join up for the evenings, do you?'

'No, Jamie, I can't see one reason why not.'

Dieter arrived in Amsterdam and took a taxi to his office. It was deserted. He stood in the middle of the room, his fists clenched and his face drained of blood. He would have trusted Jan to the ends of the earth; what a fool he had been. He did not have to phone the bank to know that the money he had transferred to the office account, and the rest to a numbered account in Switzerland, to which Jan had access, would not be there. Jan had absconded with the lot – the ingrate, after all Dieter had done for him in the past. Both Jan and Renalta would be dead now if it hadn't been for him. He sat at the desk and forced himself to calm down. Wrong decisions could be made in anger.

Renalta, of course. She might know. She and Jan had always been close. He called her home number, half of him afraid she too might not answer. But she did. She was pleased to hear from him, as always. He cut through her greetings and asked for Jan. No, she explained, she hadn't seen him for over a month, she rarely went into the office these days and they seldom saw each other socially.

'Mind you, Dieter, he was furious when I did see him. Said you wouldn't help him pay a mortgage?' She spoke questioningly, obviously hoping he would explain more.

'And that's all?' Dieter asked, not wishing to explain further but finding it difficult to believe that Jan could betray him over such a paltry sum.

Dieter went to his warehouse. The packing-cases containing the arms were not there, had not even been signed in. Jan had stolen them as well and no doubt sold them on to a contact of his own – but not to His Excellency.

He returned to the office. He sat thinking and from his breast-pocket pulled his personal organizer and tapped in a number. Soon he was calling a local man he had used successfully once or twice in the past to find people who did not necessarily want to be found. He talked for some time.

'Karl, I don't care what it costs, you find that bastard for me and you bring him back here – no, come to think of it, don't bother. I never want to set eyes on him again. You've got contacts, you get them to deal with him – you know what I mean?'

He replaced the receiver, then called Renalta, asking her to come and help him. He slipped off his jacket – he had work to do.

The dinner that Walt and Jamie had enjoyed together with Winter had gone on rather longer than any of them had intended. Perhaps a little more wine flowed than was wise, and certainly the triple cognacs at the end of the meal were fatal.

When Jamie returned, slightly drunk and very weary, to

his lonely hotel bed, he realized he had agreed to go with the others to Neuschwanstein the following morning when he'd previously decided to work solo. He knew why he'd agreed to Walt's suggestion – he wanted to spend time with Winter. It was a long time since he had met a woman he found quite so engaging. When he was with her he found he didn't think about Mica as much.

It was one of those wonderful cold, crisp days with which January sometimes blesses Europe, and it was a happy party that climbed into Dieter's large Mercedes to be driven by Walt's chauffeur, who had arrived in an apologetic flurry earlier that morning. Winter had quite expected Walt to give the chauffeur a blasting for damaging his car, it was what he would normally do to an employee. That was obviously what the man expected too, judging by his frightened expression.

'Can't be helped, these things happen. Good thing you weren't hurt,' the astonished chauffeur heard his boss say. He was getting quite mellow, thought Winter, that was nice. They enjoyed the drive through the beautiful Bavarian scenery, the sun glinting on the snow-covered mountains.

'Just look at that!' said Winter. 'Isn't that the most beautiful thing you've ever seen in your life?'

They all looked out of the window and saw Neuschwanstein in the distance for the first time. The castle looked like the fairy castle of any child's dream. Its white turrets were gleaming, made whiter by the backdrop of the dark green pine forest which in turn was silhouetted against the snow of the mountains behind. The sky above was a cloudless powder-blue.

'It looks like it's carved out of ivory,' said Winter. 'It's so neat.'

They parked in the car park far below the castle. Winter

would have liked to hire one of the horse-drawn coaches but she said nothing: logic told her that the bus, though less romantic, was undoubtedly faster.

The bus took them to a point high above the castle, where they joined the jostling, pushing throng streaming down the hill towards the turnstiles. Their tickets purchased, they finally entered the castle, where they stood expectantly in the forecourt, but nobody came to speak to them. The tourists merely looked back at them curiously. There was the usual nudging and whispering of 'Is it him?' that Walt and Winter accepted as normal now when with Jamie.

'Well, treasure hunt or no, we haven't come this far not to see the inside of the castle,' said Walt, much to Winter's pleasure.

It was easy to forget the pressure on them, and they stopped wondering where Dieter was as they wandered around the gem of a castle that poor, mad Ludwig had built. The rooms were small and dark, and despite the ornate carving and decoration there was a strange feeling of intimacy about them as if they were trespassing in someone's home.

'Gosh, it felt to me just as if the poor King had popped out and would be back any minute. It was so sad in there,' said Winter when they emerged.

'Lunch, I think, don't you, before we go to the Linderhof castle?' asked Walt, obviously not as moved as she.

They motored to the nearby town of Füssen and quickly found a restaurant to their liking. Like all the meals these three had taken together, this one was long and amicable. Perhaps yet again a little too much wine was drunk, but they were learning to enjoy each other's company. Walt might wish Jamie was elsewhere and he alone with Winter, and Jamie might have thought the same, but for the two men companionship won over any jealousy. It was three o'clock in the afternoon when they finally left the restaurant and wandered slowly through the narrow, pedestrians-only street towards the car-parking area.

'Where's the chauffeur?' asked Winter.

'Over there,' said Jamie. 'He told me he was fed up with German food and wanted to find a good honest hamburger.' He laughed. They waved, the chauffeur waved back, crossed the street, climbed into the car, turned the keys in the ignition and was blown to smithereens.

4

The houses captured the explosion, the noise bouncing from one wall to the next like a wild ball of sound. The racket reverberated like thunder over the small town. Oxygen was sucked from the air so that passers-by stood with hands on their chests, gasping for breath, thinking they too were about to die. Glass fell in a noisy cascade on to the pavement, shards flying in all directions, cutting those unfortunate enough to be below. People began to crumple to the pavement, bleeding profusely. There was a momentary lull as others took stock, came to terms with the shock, and realized they were uninjured. And then there was a rush as the crowd began to race down the street towards the now flaming car while others attended to the injured. Winter, ashen with shock, turned as if to run after them. Walt grabbed her by the hand.

'No, Winter, stay here.'

'But, Walt, we must go.' She stuck her hands into her pockets, aware they were trembling.

'Where?' said Walt. 'There's nothing we can do, he's dead. Nothing could have survived that explosion.'

'But, Walt, he's your chauffeur, we must go and see the police. We must tell them we were with him, we must give them his name.' Winter spoke hurriedly, her voice trembling as her body shook.

'Winter, I don't think that's such a good idea – I think the less involved we are, the better.'

She looked at Walt with a horrified expression. 'I'm sorry, Walt, I can't agree. He worked for you, for God's sake.'

'Yes, yes, and I'll see everything's fine, I'll pay for his funeral, I'll look after his widow, but if we get involved with the police now we could be stuck here for weeks. Isn't that so, Jamie?'

'Well, I understand what you're saying, Walt, and I can think of nothing nicer than doing a bolt out of a mess like this, but I don't think we can. We'll have to see the authorities and explain it's not our car, that it belonged to Dieter.'

'Oh, hell, all right then,' said Walt, disgruntled.

'He's right, Walt. We have to do it.' Winter slipped her arm through his, but Jamie thought what a ruthless cove he was.

Although they were allowed to sleep in a hotel they spent most of the next two days with the police. They were interviewed separately, made statements separately and then were re-interviewed by different policemen and had to make fresh statements – obviously a check and counter-check on their stories were being done. Winter could not think of any enemy she might have. Jamie joked and admitted that a few husbands might like to see him dead, but the German police did not share his humour. Jamie was philosophical about it, provided he had cigarettes. Winter was slightly irritated by what she regarded as impertinent questions. Walt was incensed. 'What business-man doesn't have enemies, for God's sake!' he ranted. 'How the hell do you think I got where I am? By being a saint?'

Winter and Jamie were told they could leave town provided they left their addresses with the police. Walt was kept for another day of bad-tempered interviews.

When they finally met again, there was only one topic of conversation – Dieter.

'I still can't get over it. I mean, this is just supposed to be a fun treasure hunt. What did Guthrie say? Something to amuse. And what happens? This Kraut tries to kill us,' said Walt, shaking his large head in disbelief.

'But was it Dieter?' asked Winter. 'I mean, isn't it possible that a car could just catch fire? I've seen them on freeways a couple of times, pulled over on to the hard shoulder and people dancing frantically about them.'

'Yes, Winter, they can, but not quite as dramatically as that one did. No, that was a bomb – someone meant somebody to die,' Jamie said gently.

Winter shook, despite the sun, and wrapped her arms about herself, trying to keep warm. Both men stepped towards her to put their arms about her to comfort her, and both, embarrassed, stepped back at the same time.

'Look, let's get something to eat – Winter's cold,' said Walt solicitously.

They found a warm and cosy restaurant and sat down after ordering three large martinis.

'But who would want to? We were all having such a lovely day. You don't think it was there, all the way down the autobahn, do you? You don't think it could have gone off at any time?' asked Winter, still wan-looking.

'No,' said Walt, 'I think we were followed. I think it must have been put there while we were all at lunch. Whoever it was didn't realize the driver wasn't one of us. Easy enough to do, I suppose, not that I know much about the business.'

'But we know someone who does, though, don't we, Walt? Like dear old Dieter. Oh, he wouldn't do it himself, wouldn't soil his hands, I've heard. But who better to know who to ask to plant a bomb than an arms dealer?'

Winter's eyes rounded with shock. 'Dieter? An arms dealer? What do you mean? He's a legitimate arms dealer, of course?' she said, as if begging them to confirm this. Jamie slowly shook his head from side to side. 'Oh, how awful. And, despite not liking the English, he seemed such a polite, nice man.'

Jamie laughed. 'He just tried to kill you for the second time and you think he's a nice, polite man?'

'What do we do now? I mean, do we let the little Teutonic shit get away with it or do we put one on him?' Walt asked.

Winter sat back on the banquette. 'I don't believe I'm hearing all this,' she said. 'I mean, he tries to kill us, so are we going to try to kill him? Does that make it right? Honestly,' she shook her head, 'I feel I'm in the wrong play here.'

'I think we just ignore him. I think we've told the police sufficient. If we add this it'll muddy the water like nobody's business. No, let's leave it to them to find out,' Jamie said matter-of-factly. 'He's unlikely to try it again, surely.'

'Do you want to give up, Winter? Do you want us to go home?' Walt asked.

'No way, we'll see this through now. We've got to beat him, haven't we?'

'Tell you what, though, someone trying to bump you off is more fun in a film.' Jamie grinned and Winter could have kissed him for lightening the sombre mood.

That night Jamie couldn't sleep. He tossed and turned. Eventually he gave up trying, switched on the light, poured himself a drink, and zapped through the TV channels with the remote control in the faint hope of finding something to watch. Rejecting the soft porn channels, he paused at one where a documentary was running. It was in German, so he could not understand, but the photography was good – low-flying shots of a great forest. Then the action changed to a native village, the cameraman was surrounded by small men with the flat, fat-nosed faces of Guthrie's servant. 'Of course,' he yelled, and punched his pillow. 'We've been looking for the wrong Ludwig,' he said aloud. Then he laughed. 'Wrong continent.'

Although it was the middle of the night, he picked up the telephone and dialled the airport. An hour later he was still trying. He had tried all manner of combinations. London, Paris, Lisbon, he'd even thrown caution to the winds and tried to get himself on Concorde. All flights to Brazil were booked for over a week. If he was going to manage it, he was going to have to make a complicated journey, flying first to the States and then to the Argentine – it would take days. He sat on the edge of the bed and thought. He knew what to do. At six a.m. he was tapping on Walt's door.

'Hell, Jamie, what time do you call this?' Walt said, as he let him in.

In the sitting-room Walt called room service and ordered coffee and orange juice. Through the open door Jamie could see the rumpled bed but it was empty, he noticed with satisfaction.

'Right. We've been looking in the wrong place, Walt. I know where to go now for sure. The trouble is, I can't get a flight, everything's booked for the whole of this week. So, I was wondering, if I tell you where we should be looking, will you take me on your fine Boeing aeroplane?'

Walt opened the door to room service and while he poured the coffee he was thinking fast. They weren't getting anywhere here, and the sooner he saw the last of Munich the better, as far as he was concerned. The more miles he could put between himself and Dieter, the happier he would be. During the night he had virtually decided to give up the hunt, not for himself, he didn't mind about himself, but he felt he couldn't expose Winter to any more danger. And since she was determined to stay he felt it was up to him to stop now.

'Okay, you're on. So,' he picked up the phone again, 'where do I tell my pilot to log the flight plan for?'

'Brazil,' said Jamie.

'Brazil?' Walt repeated inanely. 'What's Brazil got to do with Ludwig of Bavaria?'

'Nothing. Wrong Ludwig.' Jamie laughed. 'We should have been looking for Daniel K. Ludwig. You remember?'

'Of course. Who's likely to forget? Dear old Ludwig – the first American ever to have anything to do with the destruction of the rainforest. The richest man in the world for a long time. Dead now.'

'Exactly. So to Brazil we go.'

'But Brazil's enormous, Jamie. I mean, the rainforest is enormous, even at the rate they're destroying it. I know, I've got people down there trying to salvage what plants they can for possible use in drugs. I've an experimental farm where we're trying to duplicate the conditions of the rainforest artificially, but we've a long way to go. Where do we begin to look in a country of that size?'

'No doubt the same thing will happen that happened before. When we arrive at the right place, a nice obliging little man will appear with the envelope and point us in the next direction. Let's go to Rio and see what happens.' He grinned.

'Well, I hope you're right. Otherwise we have a very long look ahead of us.'

After two days Dieter had still not appeared and Magda was worried. She knew all about the car, the police had visited her many times, but what was frightening was the questions they asked. Did her husband have enemies? Was there someone who hated him enough to kill him? Magda confessed she knew little of his business dealings but, she pointed out, it was unlikely that people in the art world would stoop to murder. Secretly she had to wonder if there was something else wrong.

Magda had called Dieter's secretary so many times that she realized she was annoying her. She'd called his shops, the gallery, business associates – no one knew anything. There only remained one person who might know where he was – his mistress, Gretel.

It took Magda a long time to steel herself to dial her rival's number. She had learnt about her some time ago. And she had been concerned by this mistress – she was more beautiful, more intelligent, and had lasted longer than any of the others. So she resolved to find out more about her. She had discovered her name and one day had followed her to her hairdresser. In the salon it had been the simplest thing to strike up a friendship. They had taken to making an appointment at the same time and afterwards taking coffee and cake together. Fear of Gretel had changed to terror when she had confided that her lover wanted her to have his baby.

Magda's hand dithered over the telephone – she knew who Gretel was but Gretel had no idea that she had made a friend of Dieter's wife.

Gretel's fear for Dieter's safety overcame her shock and embarrassment at discovering Magda's identity. Both women were united in their concern and it seemed the most natural thing for Magda to ask Gretel to join her at the schloss and for Gretel to accept. They would wait together for news.

Magda, normally so reserved, burst into tears the minute she saw her. Patiently, Gretel calmed her.

'Tell me what's happened,' Gretel asked gently. 'I read about the car. Horrifying, I nearly died of shock. You don't think it was meant for Dieter?'

Magda looked at her, her eyes full of tears. 'Oh, Gretel, I'm so afraid. He's been gone for two days and he always calls me to let me know he's all right. Something is wrong – very wrong. I'm afraid it's got something to do with this treasure hunt.' She explained to Gretel what had been preoccupying Dieter for the last two weeks.

'I don't think it could be anything to do with that. After all, he lent the car to the other contestants. Unless . . .'

Both women looked at each other with equally horrified expressions.

'Oh, surely not,' said Magda, her hand to her throat.

'No! What a silly notion,' said Gretel. 'Dieter wouldn't do anything as base as that.'

The day turned to evening and they continually reassured each other as they talked about their favourite subject – Dieter. Magda felt strangely comfortable with Gretel – all sense of rivalry had disappeared. They were united in their concern and love for the same man.

'Would you stay tonight, Gretel?'

'What if he comes back and finds me here? Maybe he won't be pleased.'

'He would have to know sooner or later that we've met.'

'And like each other.'

'That's right, Gretel. I'm so glad you're with me. You understand in a way no one else could.'

They sat, drinks in hand, by the telephone in case he rang. As the hours ticked by Magda became distressed again.

'You have to try and sleep, Magda. You're exhausted already.'

'But what if he telephones and I don't hear? And I don't want to be alone.'

'I'll sit with you. I'll wake you if he calls. Have you some sleeping pills or something you could take?'

'Yes, somewhere. The doctor gave them to me a couple of years ago when things were a little bit bad between Dieter and me, but I never took them.'

'But I think it's a good idea tonight, don't you?'

'Yes. Perhaps you're right.'

Gretel ordered some warm milk into which she put some brandy and she stood over Magda, for all the world like a nanny, and watched her take the sleeping pills, then she sat and waited until Magda slept. She became uncomfortable in the chair. She kicked off her shoes, took off her dress and in her slip lay on top of the bed beside Magda, pulling the bed-cover over her. She was soon asleep.

Dieter was exhausted. He had flown practically everywhere across Europe in his desperate search for weapons for His Excellency. With war in Yugoslavia, the IRA as always active, South America with its usual scattered insurrections, Russia in turmoil, he had difficulty in his task. Arms were at a premium. His bank accounts in Switzerland were seriously depleted as he withdrew money to enable him to buy goods, but still he could acquire only half of what His Excellency wanted. He'd have to wait ten days for the rest of the order to be fulfilled. He winced at the price demanded, but he paid. From a hotel in Frankfurt he called Toto, once again throwing caution to the winds, to tell him that half the consignment was on its way. Toto said he would relay the message to His Excellency but he doubted if he would be pleased.

'I hope to get the rest to him within two weeks. Please, would you ask him to give me two weeks?' Dieter grimaced as he spoke, he didn't like to beg anybody for anything.

'I'll see what I can do,' said Toto.

Dieter's hand was shaking as he replaced the receiver in its cradle. This was it, he decided. This was the very last deal he would ever do. There was no excitement any more, it had been replaced by fear, a fear he could well do without. Why did he constantly put himself at risk like this? He had enough money to last him and Magda for the rest of their lives. He was a fool.

He went back to Munich and by the time he arrived it was nearly dawn and he was exhausted. All he could think of was home and his bed and Magda. But he had one thing to do first before he could allow himself to relax. He hired a car and drove to his office. He let himself into the empty building, he did not bother to check his faxes or the pile of messages on his desk and once more phoned Toto. Despite the hour, Toto answered immediately and he sounded wide awake.

'His Excellency agrees.' The line went dead.

Dieter exhaled with relief. He sat at his desk and looked at the top note on a stack of others his secretary had left. He re-read it again. How strange. Why had Walt and Jamie gone to Brazil, and together? He called the private detective he had had trailing Walt and Jamie. The man did not sound as wide awake as Toto had nor as agreeable at being woken up at this hour of the morning.

'Yes, Count Weiher. They flew out late yesterday in the American's Boeing. I checked, the flight plan was for Brazil. Rio. No mistake, my contact at the airport is reliable.'

'Brazil?' Dieter said with sudden realization. 'Of course. Daniel K. Ludwig.'

'And, Count, have you heard . . .'

Dieter did not bother to listen to more, he replaced the telephone without thanking the man – he frequently failed to thank underlings. He looked at his watch, called his pilot and instructed him to fly him to South America later that day. He might be rich but he'd like to replace some of the money in his Swiss account with the treasure-hunt money. And there was nothing he could do here, only fret.

He could be over there and back within a week, judging by the stupidity of the clues. This would give him only one week to chase the second consignment of 'toys' but it should be time enough.

In the garage beneath the building, Dieter climbed into his car and wearily drove through the deserted early-morning streets of Munich, out on to the autobahn towards his home. His eyes were heavy with fatigue now, the lids leaden. He opened a window to keep himself awake and pushed a cassette of Wagner's music into the player and turned the volume up.

He let himself into his castle. For once Magda wasn't up waiting for him, but then he could hardly blame her, he thought with a smile. Everything would be all right now. They'd fly to Brazil this afternoon. Magda had never been to Brazil, she'd enjoy that, she'd like the shops there. He raced up the stairs and burst into their room, only to see Gretel and Magda asleep in the same bed, Gretel's arm flung out and holding Magda. He stood at the foot of the bed, his face livid with anger, which rapidly turned to despair.

Gretel was the first to wake. 'Dieter,' she said, holding out her hand, an expression of relief on her face.

'You whores.' He turned on his heel and slammed out of the bedroom, down the stairs and out of his castle.

5

Jamie was right. They had barely signed in at their hotel in Rio when they were approached by a man holding the by now familiar envelope giving them their instructions.

Their final destination, or so they thought, was a small and dusty town, Santa Anna, a tiring plane-ride from Rio in a small and noisy craft. The heat was almost intolerable, the humidity even worse. They were booked into a small and shabby hotel which had never heard of en suite bathrooms, but it was clean and the food was passable. Everything was in stark contrast to the air-conditioned opulence of their suites in the hotel back in Rio de Janeiro which, two days later, seemed another world and a dream away.

'Do you know, I don't think I've ever seen so many churches,' said Winter, flopping into a rattan chair redolent of an era long past, of planters and gin slings, but with a frayed cushion and holes in the arms. She had been for a walk and looked hot and tired. 'It wouldn't surprise me if there was one for every day of the year here. Every street corner seems to have yet another church and they all smell the same, fusty and of faded incense.'

'And as many bars, I'm sure,' said Walt.

'It's the poverty, though. It's everywhere – the unmade roads, the drains stink! It's awful. Those poor children playing in the dust cracked me up, they're all so beautiful, with those large sombre brown eyes – children shouldn't have eyes like that. And have you noticed those of the mothers? Their expressions are blank, completely without hope, and they can't be very old themselves, they just look it.'

'It makes you feel uncomfortable with what we've got at home and take for granted, doesn't it?' said Jamie.

Walt did not respond to this. He had been rich for too long and he carried his wealth like a shell of protection against any poverty he saw. To him nearly everyone he met was poor by his standards. He had long ago dispensed with the necessity of feeling guilty about it. 'I'd like to show you something which might interest you,' he said instead, 'but after we've had a beer.' He flicked his fingers at the only waiter who padded away on flat feet to fill their order.

A taxi had eventually been found for them – taxis did not abound in this place. And when it arrived it looked as if it was more often used for transporting livestock than humans. It bounced along over the rutted road, its gearbox grating in agony as its driver seemed unable to change gear smoothly. He drove with a nonchalant disregard for people or property and only the crucifix dangling from the broken central mirror gave his passengers hope that they might arrive at their journey's end. He finally drew to a halt on the outskirts of town in front of a large, low, modern building which stood out starkly against the older houses clustered around it, with their peeling shutters, shabby stonework and pretty wrought-iron balconies most in need of repair.

'What's this?' asked Winter, looking at Walt with interest.

'My laboratories,' he said with pride.

'I didn't even know you had any here. Why didn't you tell me, Walt?' She sounded a little peeved. 'As your PR I should know. What are they for?'

'As the rainforest is being destroyed, and so many possible future cures for man with it, we're in a race against time. Did you know that only one per cent of the plants here have been researched for possible medical properties we could use? So about eight years ago I set up these laboratories, close to the action as you might say, and close to the Indians whose expertise we can use and combine with that of my scientists,' he said quite simply.

'Walt, that is just so wonderful. Gracious, just imagine the publicity we could get from this, you should have told me.'

'No, not yet. I didn't tell you on purpose. Maybe when we've had a little more success with our projects. But come in, do.' He ushered them towards the plate-glass door where their arrival was causing excitement as the staff recognized Walt from photographs, and the Director was hastily being summoned from his house next door.

The next couple of hours were spent touring the modern

laboratories. Walt had not stinted on the equipment for them, even if, as Winter sensed, the scientists felt that they and their work had been neglected by Walt and the outside world for too long.

'The problem is,' said one intense young American scientist, 'that unless one comes up with something dramatic no one wants to know.'

'I do,' said Winter and smiled at him so that suddenly he felt that everything was all worthwhile again.

'This is our refrigerated seed bank,' he explained as they donned anoraks to enter a large cold store, with shelves on which were row upon row of labelled storage boxes. 'We keep these for future research and also as an insurance that these plants don't become extinct. For a start, nearly a thousand and a half plants found in the forest have anticancer properties. And many products from here are essential to the pharmaceuticals industry.'

'Walt, this is wonderful! What a project you've set up! Just think of the public relations exercises—'

'I didn't do it for that,' Walt interrupted.

'No, of course not. But why not use it all the same?' She squeezed his hand and he wished the others would disappear. He felt proud at her pleasure in his work.

'I'm thinking, quite seriously, of building a hospital here too,' he said, excited by everyone's approval but having just thought of this possibility. 'If we get out of the forest what I hope we'll get, I think we should pay something back to the country, don't you?'

'Oh, yes,' said Winter, 'that would be marvellous.' And already she was forming the glowing press releases in her mind. And she thought how modest Walt was for such a rich man, almost as if he was unaware of the good he was trying to do.

'What exactly do you hope to find, Walt?'

'It could be anything – we've only scratched the surface of what this great forest has to offer. A cure for arthritis would be nice, apparently you never see an Indian with it. And what if there was something growing here that could cure AIDS? Just think of that.' They did, but Jamie was not too sure if it was the cure that Walt was excited about or the money he would make from it. But then Walt's expression changed to a softer, sad look. 'For myself, I dream of a cure for Huntington's chorea.'

At this, Winter took hold of his hand and squeezed it and looked at him with affection, but Jamie did not understand why. When he saw the change in Walt's face he didn't like to ask, he sensed he'd be intruding on something very personal.

The following day, still in the hotel, they were becoming bored and irritated. The pilot of the plane had told them they were to wait at the hotel but had not explained what for — if he knew. So each time the doors of the hotel opened they all looked up expectantly, hoping to see a man with an envelope, as had happened, like clockwork, in the hotel in Rio. But then when the door opened and Dieter walked in, none of them was any too pleased to see him.

He strode confidently across the small reception hall to the corner they habitually sat in. He was impeccably suited in cream linen. When he took off his panama hat not a hair was out of place, as if he were impervious to the almost ninety-degree heat and the humidity. He held his hand out in welcome and was smiling.

'Hello, everyone, we meet again,' he said, clicked his heels and made the little bow which Winter had previously found so charming.

All three ignored his hand and he stood there feeling rather foolish as he looked at them with a puzzled expression. He held his head to one side, questioningly. 'Excuse me, but do I sense a hostile atmosphere here?' He was genuinely puzzled. He had thought that by loaning them his car he'd have been forgiven for trying to force them off the road in northern France, which had been a spontaneous act on his part, and one which he later realized he should not have done. 'Have I done something to offend you?'

At this Walt snorted. Winter looked at him with loathing and Jamie leaned back in his chair, stretched his long legs lazily and said, 'Well, Dieter, I reckon that's just about the understatement of the year.'

'Perhaps one of you will have the courtesy to explain to me,' he said in a clipped manner, ruffled now.

'It was very kind of you to lend your car to Walt, Dieter. It wasn't quite so kind of you to try to blow him to pieces, and Winter and me with him.'

Dieter swung round and looked at Walt and Winter, horror dawning on his face. 'I beg your pardon,' he said, 'do I understand correctly? Something has happened to the car?'

'A bomb happened to the car, Dieter, old boy,' said Jamie, languidly. 'Surely you of all people know? And we got to thinking. Walt here couldn't think of anyone in Germany who'd wish to bump him off. And we thought, who do we know who would be capable of making, or finding, the wherewithal to make a bomb? And, odd as it may seem, Dieter, your little name kept on cropping up with depressing frequency,' Jamie said sarcastically.

'My dear friends, I don't know what to say to you. I know nothing of any bomb. I've been out of Germany and returned to my home with only time to repack my case.'

'Oh, come on, Dieter, Magda must have told you. She had to deal with the police, they want to talk to you somewhat urgently.' Jamie did one of his cocked-eyebrow smiles.

'I did not see my wife,' Dieter said stiffly, but even as he spoke an image of Magda and Gretel in bed together flashed into his mind. He had to clench his fist to stop himself from crying out at the pain of the memory.

'And your secretary didn't contact you, leave you a message?' Walt asked disbelievingly. His Beth always knew where he was. 'You must have a mobile phone, everyone has one of those.'

'No, not on this trip, I didn't. And my secretary had no way of contacting me. I'm sorry, gentlemen, you must believe me. I had no idea what had happened. I lent you my car in good faith, if the bomb was intended for anyone I would say it was intended for myself. You have my apologies for the inconvenience this must have caused you, I'm afraid I can say no more.' And with this he bowed to Winter, turned on his heel and walked to the reception desk to ask for the key to his room.

He left surprised consternation downstairs. All of them were left feeling a little bit foolish: it was the one thing they hadn't thought of, so convinced had they been that Dieter was trying to kill them. But when they thought about it, it was a far more logical conclusion, given the shady businesses he dealt in. Perhaps if he hadn't tried to run them off the road in France they wouldn't have even begun to think along those lines.

Upstairs, Dieter began to shake. Without doubt, the bomb had been meant for him. Without doubt, it had to be His Excellency who had arranged to have it planted there. He wondered how communications were in this place; difficult, he thought. But he picked up the phone on the off-chance. It took him three hours to be connected to his office in Munich, and he could have wept with relief when Wilma read him over the coded faxes he had asked for. His Excellency's arms delivery was on schedule again. All he could do was pray that they arrived at the right destination this time. Maybe he should leave now and go and supervise everything personally, but the cost of acquiring a new consignment of arms for His Excellency had been so great that he needed to win this treasure hunt now, for it pained him to see the large hole that had appeared in his numbered Swiss bank account. And he did not want to return. He was still devastated from seeing Magda and Gretel in each other's arms. The memory of it still made him feel physically ill. Maybe he should think about it, but for the moment he could not bring himself to do so. It was a state of affairs he would have to address eventually but, for the moment, the pain was too great. He needed activity to keep his mind busy.

The next afternoon found all four summoned once again to the small, bumpy airstrip on the outskirts of town. Another, smaller plane with another pilot was awaiting them. Dieter had obviously been the person they had been waiting for. The plane took off and within minutes they were flying over the vast expanse of the tropical rainforest of Brazil. Beneath them lay the canopy of the jungle. It was so dense it seemed as if the clouds had fallen from the skies and become green; the great billowing mass stretched as far as the eyes could see. 'It's huge, awe-inspiring,' said Jamie. 'No destruction here, thank God.'

'Where do you think they're taking us?' asked Winter. 'Not that I'm complaining, it's wonderful to see. I wouldn't have missed this for anything. Look down there, look – a river.' She pointed. 'Is that the Amazon?' she asked the pilot.

'No, the Araguaia,' he replied.

They peered out of the small windows of the light plane to see a wide, winding, brownish river flowing sluggishly beneath them. They followed its course for a couple of hours and then the plane banked to the right and beneath they saw that a small airstrip had been prepared amongst the trees. It looked so tiny in the mass of the forest that their hearts were in their mouths as the pilot prepared to land on a runway which appeared far too small. The plane touched down with a jolt and they were all shaken as it bumped along the rough terrain. But this was not their destination, this was a stop for refuelling. They took off again and several hours later the plane banked and the heart-stopping procedure was repeated as they landed on another makeshift runway.

A guide was waiting for them, who could have been Guthrie's servant's twin. He was so short that they all towered over him, including Dieter, and he had the same flat face, high cheek-bones, dark brown eyes and squat, rather fleshy nose. He was dressed in baggy white trousers and a tee-shirt which, incongruously, had a picture of Madonna on it. He said nothing, but pointed with his stick and they followed him and began to walk along a path which had been cut for them through the cavernous greenery. The foliage was so dense that they could not see a glimpse of sky, only the intense green of the vegetation. They all noticed a strange, unfamiliar smell of damp caused by this great lung of the world as it spewed forth its oxygen. All around was the noise of animals scattering and slithering away from them. It was beautiful and terrifying at the same time and they kept close together. The foliage thinned slightly and then they could see the sky. When they emerged on to the steep bank of the river they had seen from the plane, the sun was beginning to set, a great angry reddish-golden ball reflected on the river which was no longer brown, but sparked with orange and gold. Two long canoes were waiting for them. They climbed in, but they went neither up nor down the river. Instead they were transported across to the middle where the canoes came to a halt on a large sandbank.

'You sleep here,' said the guide in broken English.

'Here?' said Walt. 'What on earth for?'

Again the guide said nothing to them but barked orders to the Indians who had steered the canoes and they unloaded rucksacks and bedding from the craft. He then indicated to them that they must dig holes in the sand to lie in.

'Friendly cove, aren't you?' said Jamie with a smile to the guide, who did not return it. 'I get the distinct impression we're not exactly flavour of the month to this chappie here.'

'Don't say that.' Winter shivered and wondered for the first time why she had come, realizing she felt afraid. 'How quaint.' She forced herself to laugh. 'I've slept in some funny places but never like a turtle in a hole in a sandbank in the middle of a river, in the back of beyond.'

'Maybe it's safer here,' Dieter suggested.

'Safer?' said Winter, looking at him.

'Creepy-crawlies,' said Jamie, grinning and walking his fingers in the air at her. She willed herself not to respond. 'Look, there's just the sand here,' he added, regretting trying to frighten her when he realized she was looking really scared.

'What about alligators?' said Dieter, as if immune to her fears.

'Alligators?' said Winter. 'Oh, my, I don't think I'm very happy here.' She giggled nervously.

'Here, you,' Walt said to the guide in the tone of voice which always resulted in action when he used it to underlings. 'What about alligators?' he said slowly, as if speaking to a child.

The guide tapped the gun on his back. 'I watch,' he said.

A fire was lit and the guide proceeded to cook their supper for them. None of them really had any idea what to expect. To go with the wild duck which, the guide assured them, he had shot that afternoon, there was rice and black beans, sprinkled with farinha, which they learned was a coarse flour and which Walt knew came from the mandioca root and was quite safe. They were pleasantly surprised to find that they enjoyed the supper. With no radio and their stomachs full, they chatted for a while, then settled down for the night; it had come upon them quickly for they were in a land of no twilight. The temperature dropped rapidly and they were glad of the sleeping bags. Everyone wrapped their faces in gauze to protect them from the mosquitoes which had plagued them since their arrival and against which their insect-repellent appeared useless. In the circumstances none of them had expected to go to sleep but all three did, lulled instead of disturbed by the strange primeval sound of the forest.

6

They were awoken by the morning chorus of monkeys who were re-establishing their territorial rights for the day. The dawn broke as swiftly as the sun had set. Their breakfast was the remains of their supper; cold duck, rice and black beans wasn't, they all concluded, as easy a meal to digest, so early, as it had been for dinner. The sleeping bags rolled up, the cooking pots cleared, they got into the canoes and this time went north down-river.

For two hours, the swift craft skimmed through the limpid water. The jungle teetered on the steep river banks as if about to fall in and engulf it. They passed an occasional village with dwellings built of foliage clinging to the banks as precariously as the trees. As they passed, groups of people and children ran out calling to them, laughing and waving excitedly.

The whole area was alive with relentless noise from animals calling to one another, with birds' calls and the persistent rustling of the vegetation itself — it was not a peaceful place. At every turn it seemed there were things to see — large white storks, with black heads bowed, strutted like a flock of clerics. Alligators slid from the banks. Jamie thought he saw a dowdy pheasant, and ducks, and at one point even a deer.

'This has to be an animals' paradise,' said Winter, trailing her fingers in the water.

'I wouldn't do that if I were you.' Walt smiled at her. 'Alligators and piranhas.'

Winter snatched her hand out of the river. 'Oh, my God, I'd forgotten. How stupid of me.' The others laughed except for Dieter who sat silent throughout the journey, keeping to himself.

Ahead a small, rickety wooden jetty came into sight, built out into the river. The canoes turned towards it. A group of natives stood in silence at the bank, huddled together as if afraid – there was no talking or laughter. The party was helped none too gently out of the canoes on to the jetty. 'Hang on!' Walt protested when it was his turn, but either the natives did not understand or they chose to ignore him. They formed a crocodile and walked along the swaying structure to the bank. A young white man in a laboratory coat stood waiting for them with a serious face made sterner by the gilt spectacles he wore. The guide, having delivered them, disappeared into the crowd.

'Good afternoon, I'm Dr Bush. I work for the Friends of Brazil Foundation. You must be Mr Fielding, Lord Grantley, Count von Weiher and Miss Sullivan.' He spoke firmly, and rather coldly, in a Boston accent. He did not proffer his hand in welcome.

They replied that he was correct and none of them admitted they had never heard of his foundation – it didn't seem polite. 'Follow me,' he said, turning abruptly and striding off at quite a pace through the jungle.

'He's not a very friendly chappie either,' whispered Jamie to Winter, which made her giggle. The doctor turned round and stared at them; he looked so shocked and pompous that it made it even harder for Winter not to laugh.

After a five-minute walk they emerged into a small clearing which had been hacked out of the ever-present forest. There were two long, low buildings built of breeze blocks ahead of them, and dotted around the compound were huts made from branches and leaves. To one side there was a kitchen garden where a boy with the face of a simpleton and with only one leg patiently hopped from row to tilled row as he hoed the soil. Standing apart was a small bungalow with a picket fence and a rose garden which looked touchingly out of place, Winter thought, as if the owner was defying the forest. They entered one of the buildings through a doorway, meshed against insects, and found themselves in an oblong room which was unbearably hot, with an unpleasant, putrid odour. The rhythmic, noisy clattering of a generator made speech almost impossible. Along both sides of the wall stood rows of white hospital beds – their paintwork was chipped but the sheets were spotlessly white.

There were children in four of the beds. Two lay on their backs, staring wide-eyed and vacantly at the ceiling while tears, silently shed, trickled down their faces. Two others looked as if they were comatose. But all four had severe facial deformities: one boy had one eye only, another just a gaping hole where his nose should have been. Walt, Winter and Jamie fought their mutual reaction of distaste at what they saw, forcing themselves to look at the children and not to recoil. At a long table down the centre of the ward sat four Indian boys, with arms missing, some lacking legs; Walt recognized the smell, it was the unforgettable stench of putrefying flesh, of gangrene. The three smiled at the patients with the embarrassed half-smiles that the fit give to the disabled, and they trooped after the doctor who had said nothing as they walked through the ward. He led them into another long room which was a replica of the first, except that here the victims were young girls.

'They're all kids,' Jamie whispered.

'How old, do you think?' Walt asked.

'I shouldn't think they're older than ten. And the youngest, about six. But it's difficult to tell, isn't it? They're all naturally small, even the adults.' Dieter stood rigid, his face devoid of emotion as he surveyed the scene.

It was the same in the second building. They said nothing as they walked through; they could think of nothing to say in the face of such sadness and disability. The doctor strode across the compound and like lambs they followed him to the small bungalow with the brave attempt at a garden.

'Have you worked here long, doctor?' Winter asked politely.

'For two years, but I leave in six months.'

'Why?' She smiled at him, but he did not smile back.

'Our bodies aren't built for these climates, it's as much as we can do to work at maximum efficiency. But it's all right, these children will not be abandoned – my church will send another doctor.'

'That was a very sad sight, doctor. I'd like to help, if I can. Perhaps you would welcome a donation for equipment and some toys, too – I didn't see any toys,' Walt volunteered.

The doctor looked at Walt coldly. 'No, thank you, Mr Fielding. We've had enough gifts from you.' A servant entered and the doctor ordered lemonade for them all without asking if there was anything else they preferred. Jamie, after what they had just seen, would have given anything for a stiff Scotch. There was a detachment about the young doctor, a sense of disapproval that they all felt, not just Walt.

'I'm sorry, doctor, I don't quite understand what you

mean. I have no recollection of having made a donation to your church.' Walt's voice sounded agitated. 'Come to think of it, I don't think I've ever made a donation to any church.' He laughed, awkwardly.

'I don't think you understand, Mr Fielding. Those children you've just seen are *your* victims – you are responsible for them and the predicament they find themselves in.'

Jamie, Winter and Dieter looked at Walt, who sat there puzzled and, now, angry.

'Don't be ridiculous, I've never heard of you. Who the hell do you think you are to speak to me like that?' Walt said furiously, but the doctor did not seem to react to him.

'Am I to take it that you are about to deny this?' the doctor asked.

'Too goddam right I am. I know nothing of these children; nothing of this place. This is the first goddam time I've been here – and the last,' he added.

'Do you remember about ten years back, one of your companies was trying to manufacture a contraceptive drug which need only be taken once every six months?'

'Yes, yes, I do. We hoped to get it developed so that it could be taken only once a year. But we cancelled the project.'

'Why was that, Mr Fielding?'

'It didn't work, that's why,' Walt snapped.

'Your tests told you so?'

'Well, of course they did. The lab tests failed – it happens, you win some, you lose some.' Walt shrugged his shoulders.

'And the field tests?' the doctor persisted.

'There were no field tests. It didn't get that far. I've just said it failed the lab tests – the animal testing. Or are you against that?' Walt said belligerently, sensing a possible anti-vivisectionist here.

'Then how do you explain what you have just seen, Mr

Fielding? These poor creatures are the reason why the first drug was cancelled,' the doctor said, but Walt looked blank. Winter felt anxious.

'Doctor, I think you owe it to Mr Fielding to explain what you mean. It's no good talking in riddles,' she said quite sharply, but slipping easily into her professional role for she was sensing danger.

'I'm sorry if you thought I was speaking in riddles, Miss Sullivan, I assumed that Mr Fielding would understand. His drugs were tested on the local native women. They failed as a contraceptive and these poor souls who were subsequently conceived were born deformed, in every way you can think of. The lack of limbs are the least of it. Some had no faces, some no brains. You've seen the lucky ones, the others died.'

There was a stunned silence. No one looked at Walt.

'Jesus, I had no idea. You must believe me, all of you, I had no idea that this was done.' He swung round to look at them but especially at Winter, a look of pleading in his eyes that she should believe him.

'Then don't you think you should have had some idea that it was? Surely since the company is yours the responsibility is yours also?' the doctor said in a frigid but reasonable tone of voice. 'But of course, you never came to check your laboratories here, did you? You sent other people. No doubt you don't bother to keep an eye on the many other laboratories you own?'

'Yes, that's so. I have facilities in many places but I haven't been to all of them. I don't have the time, it's not necessary – I employ the best staff, I rely on their professionalism and the reports they send me. I received no reports on that particular project.'

'Perhaps you'd better keep a much closer watch in future – if what you say is true.'

'Of course it's goddam true. I'm not in the habit of lying, doctor.' Walt stood up abruptly and walked to the window where he looked out on the two long, low buildings, which were full of such misery.

The professional in Winter woke up. This news was catastrophic; if it should get out, all manner of lobbyists would grab at it. The damage to Walt's firms, let alone his standing, would be immense. It could even finish him.

'Can you prove this?' she asked.

'Yes.' The doctor did not elaborate.

'But it's such an extraordinary accusation. I've never heard of anything like it in my life.'

'Haven't you, Miss Sullivan? No doubt you take the pill – it might interest you to know that, way back in the fifties, that too was tested on Indians before it was risked on Western women. Obviously certain people . . .' he glanced across at Walt's broad back, 'certain people regard the life of an Indian as of less importance.'

'That's awful!' said Winter, making a mental note to check if it was so but realizing with relief that at least Walt could not be accused of that. He'd have been only a schoolboy back then.

Walt turned from the window and faced them. 'I've just told you I knew nothing,' he thundered.

'How does it feel to be a murderer, Mr Fielding?'

'It's hell!' Walt shouted, one of his flashes of memory of his father coming to the surface to add to his confusion.

'Oh, come on, doc, that's a bit stiff,' Jamie interjected.

'Probably slanderous.' Dieter spoke for the first time.

'There's no point in me saying I'm sorry, it's too late for that, for those poor wretches.' Walt had turned from the window. 'But at least I can do something to alleviate their misery. Even if you don't want my money, doctor, I shall give it to you. No doubt your superiors will welcome it, even if you don't. Thank you for your time,' he said with dignity and turned towards the door. A table was laid with food, evidently their lunch, but no one felt like eating and the others stood up silently, embarrassed for Walt, and followed him.

'One moment,' the doctor said, 'I have something for you.' And he handed them the by now familiar envelopes with their names hand-written upon them. The treasure hunt seemed remarkably unimportant now, and none of them felt this was the time to open them.

They walked along in single file, no one speaking – but Winter leaned forward and slipped her hand into Walt's and squeezed it. He looked at her and she saw that his eyes were full of shocking despair, almost too painful to see.

They were soon back at the jetty, packed into the canoes and retracing their route. It was a silent journey. Walt was deep in thought and the others felt it seemed wrong to chatter. In any case, Dieter's mind was racing as he looked at his new clue – he was the only one to do so. It was late afternoon when they arrived back at the sandbank and the guide again lit the fire for them.

'I think I'll go for a walk,' said Dieter.

'A walk? Where? You can hardly say this sandbank's long enough for a walk.' Jamie sounded surprised.

'No. I'll just take the canoe across to the bank and walk through to the clearing, stretch my legs a bit,' said Dieter. 'Anyone coming?' he asked, but not very welcomingly.

'No, thanks,' said Jamie. Dieter wasn't his favourite person at the best of times, but on this trip he'd been so withdrawn and remote that there would be no fun in accompanying him.

'I'm tired,' said Winter. She wasn't, she would have quite liked a walk, but she didn't want to leave Walt who sat hunched on the sandbank looking across to the far side with a lost expression on his face, oblivious to them all.

Dieter climbed into one of the canoes and expertly paddled himself across to the path that led to the clearing.

'He knows how to handle a canoe,' Winter said, as they watched him go.

'He would,' Jamie replied sarcastically.

The supper was to be slightly different tonight, a fish which they had watched the guide catch, gut and pop into the pot with the rice and the black beans.

'I think I would get a bit bored with this diet if I had to live here too long,' said Jamie to Winter.

'It's a great experience, though, isn't it? I mean, it's so wonderfully beautiful here, totally different from anywhere else on earth. Just us and the animals,' Winter replied, making conversation, feeling someone should. Those animals suddenly began to shriek with fright as, from a distance, they heard the sound of an aeroplane. Jamie looked at Winter. Within a minute, the small light plane was flying above them, and they watched it turn to follow the line of the river back to Santa Anna.

'That little bastard's done it again!' Jamie exclaimed.

'Dieter?' Winter asked, though she already knew the answer. 'Can he fly?'

'It wouldn't matter if he could or he couldn't. He's bribed the pilot, I bet you anything.'

'Now what the hell do we do?' Winter asked. 'Walt!' she called. Still he gazed out across the water. She crossed to him and shook him by the shoulder. 'Walt,' she said in a raised voice, 'Dieter's taken the plane. We're stuck. Have you any suggestions?' she asked with exaggerated patience.

Walt shook himself, as if dragging himself back to them. 'Um . . . um . . .' he said and fumbled in his pocket. 'I've money here, maybe we can hire a bigger boat.'

Jamie laughed. 'I don't think these people are interested in money, Walt. You'll be offering them your platinum American Express card next,' he said good-naturedly. 'No, I think we have to give them things. What have we got?'

Collected together, they had a gold Rolex, a Cartier tank watch and one small diamond ring. Jamie produced his gold Dunhill lighter, which he looked at longingly, stroking the inscription and wondering where Mica was now. He sighed. 'You can have this too – I keep saying I must give up smoking.' He grinned, but Winter thought it was a very pale copy of his usual warm and friendly smile.

It was left to Jamie to negotiate with the guide. A larger, faster boat – a bataloas – which as far as Jamie could make out was a long clinker-built craft, was available. A Rolex was handed over. It would require several men to row it. The Dunhill lighter was pocketed in the baggy white trousers. It would take them approximately six days to reach Para Belem on the Atlantic coast and civilization. A Cartier watch was dangled invitingly. Well, maybe five. The watch glistened in the firelight and four days was agreed before it was handed over. Pleased with his bargaining, Jamie handed Winter back her ring.

At supper, neither Jamie nor Winter ate much, and Walt nothing. Afterwards, Jamie and Winter sat talking while Walt sat huddled some way from them in a world of his own. Jamie could not remember a time when he had sat and talked to a woman like this – certainly not Mica. Too often he'd been too busy working out how to seduce them. But here he was with Winter, a woman he found infinitely attractive but with whom he was content just to talk.

She told him of her childhood – idyllic, he was glad to hear, he could not have borne to hear her tell of an unhappy one. Of college, of New York, her friends – how he envied her friends!

And then an odd thing happened. Jamie began to tell her of his life. He'd never told anyone, not even Mica. He could talk to Winter of his loneliness as a child, the hurt his father's rejection had caused him. He even, rather shamefacedly, told her about his love for his nanny, Lou, but Winter did not laugh, somehow he'd known she wouldn't. He confessed his broken marriage, his last attempt to talk to Fiona and her rejection of him.

'And that was it, you let her walk away?'

'I didn't know what to say, how to handle it.'

'The poor kid, she must be so confused.'

Jamie looked at her, puzzled. What about me? he wanted to say, I was the one who was hurt.

'Parents can do so much damage, can't they? Just because they want revenge.'

'I didn't,' he said indignantly. 'I stopped seeing her because I thought it was best for her.'

'Did you? Are you sure it wasn't because *you* couldn't take the separation? I bet over the years she'd rather have spent the odd weekend with you than nothing at all.'

'Bloody hell, Winter, don't say that!' Jamie was appalled.

'The truth often is the pits, isn't it? Still, if you did stop seeing her, you can hardly blame her if she wants no contact now.'

'No,' Jamie said miserably, wishing now he'd tried to seduce her and thus saved himself from this.

'I don't mean to lecture you, Jamie. It's just how I see it. I think it's dreadfully sad. I bet you'd make a lovely dad.'

'That's not what her mother thought.'

'How old is Fiona now?'

'It's unbelievable, but she's twenty-one this year. Perhaps that's why I'm suddenly thinking of her so often – it's an important birthday, isn't it?'

'I bet you always think of her.'

Jamie sat silent for a moment. 'No, that's not strictly true. My wife helped me forget. It hasn't been so bad since I married her – I don't mean she was a replacement for my daughter.' He laughed at the very idea. 'I'm not kinky.' He laughed again.

'Why do you always make jokes when you're hurting so much inside?' Winter gently took hold of his hand.

'Oh, you know the English.' He looked away, at everything but her.

'No, I don't know the English at all. Explain to me.'

'Oh, hell.' Jamie dug his toe into the sand and studied it for an age. 'Well, it's just not on, is it? I mean, to burden other people with your problems.'

'In my country people make a profession out of it, even go on chat shows to air their problems.'

Jamie shuddered at the very idea.

'I laugh because I can't face the reality,' he said in a rush. 'My daughter doesn't want to know me, my wife is with another man. I'm alone. I've a career I might resurrect or I might be down the tubes. I'm in debt, I need money desperately. Best thing is to have a good giggle.'

'Why did you marry Mica?'

'I loved her.'

'Did you? Or was it because you wanted her to be yours?'

'Same thing, isn't it?'

'Is it? Were you friends?'

'Like we are? No, I suppose not. I've talked to you more than I ever did to her.'

'Perhaps that's why she left, because she felt lonely with you. If you weren't friends, then it would be hard to sustain a relationship.'

'I'd never thought of that. She said I bored her and I was useless – she's probably right.' He laughed and then, as if aware of what he was doing, stopped abruptly.

'Do you still love her?'

'To be honest, Winter, I don't know. When she's away I don't know the friends she's with either. It seems as if she likes to keep us all separate from one another.'

'Perhaps she likes to be a different person to different people.'

'You're a smart woman, aren't you?'

'Not particularly. I hate to see people in pain, and you so obviously are. It must be hell to be a man — lose your kids and you lose part of your soul, don't you?'

He looked at her with amazed admiration. 'That's so right.'

'Try and see Fiona again. You need her.'

'Oh, I don't know. I mean, what if she really hated me? I couldn't cope with that.'

'How could she hate you, Jamie? You're such a sweet person . . . impossible to hate.'

'I drink too much.'

'Is it surprising?'

'And I gamble. My first wife was right about those things. All my life it's been an addiction.' He paused. 'You know, that's the first time I've admitted that to another living soul.'

'Do you know why you do it?'

'Yes. It makes me happy when I'm unhappy. It makes me feel I exist again. Do you understand?'

'No, I'm afraid not.'

And he loved her for her honesty — it would have been much simpler to say she did. He put out his hand and stroked her face, outlining the contour of her firm chin with his finger, admiring the way her blonde hair shone like a sheath of silver in the moonlight. 'Winter, you're so understanding and so beautiful.'

She turned to face him. She put her own hand up and covered his and held it there for a moment, looking at him with her large, wide-spaced, honest grey eyes.

'Don't, Jamie, don't let's spoil it,' she said softly, and disengaged his hand. 'Perhaps we should get some sleep,' she added, to his disappointment.

Walt still sat huddled away from them, now staring into darkness. Winter got up and went and sat beside him. She lit a cigarette. In the flame from her lighter she could see the man being eaten alive by mosquitoes. 'Oh, Walt, just look at you. That's so silly. Come on, wrap yourself up.' She got a blanket and covered him. From her bag she took her anti-mosquito spray and sprayed them both. 'There's no point in letting the little monsters eat you, Walt, is there?'

He turned and looked at her. 'Winter, I did not know. I just did not know.'

'I understand, Walt, I believe you.'

'There's something very wrong here. I have to go back to New York. I have to find out who's responsible for this.'

'Yes. I see that. I'll come with you.'

He turned, and from under the blanket his hand appeared and groped for hers. 'Would you, Winter? Would you really? I feel so dreadfully alone. There's no one . . .' He stopped.

'No, Walt, you're not alone, I'm with you. I'll come with you.'

'I've always been alone. I've suddenly realized that, sitting here, looking out across that water. All my life, I've been alone.'

Winter put her arms around him. 'You're not alone.'

Jamie, who had been watching them, turned away. Despondently he lay down in the indentation he'd made for himself in the sand and hoped he could get to sleep.

The next morning he awoke as dawn was breaking to find Walt standing over him.

'Jamie, I have to give up the hunt – I have to go home,' Walt said.

'I understand that, Walt,' Jamie said with a smile, but his heart was sinking. How the hell would he get back to Europe from South America? But he continued to smile.

'Look, Jamie, don't take this wrong, but I am aware that you're not as, well . . . rich as the rest of us. How about I fly you back to New York and make sure you get back to England?'

'Thanks very much, Walt, I'd appreciate that. Have you looked at the clue?'

'You know, Jamie, I haven't. My heart's gone out of all this. It doesn't seem important any more.'

7

'Where Principe's Deed Ignited a Continent,
the Flames Burn Still . . .'

Jamie sat on the plane to London, once more, courtesy of Walt, in first class. It had been a confusing time in Brazil. Dieter had seemed withdrawn and less talkative than usual. Why, he hadn't even bothered to knock the English. He had behaved like a man beset by problems, but pinching the plane was unlikely to make anyone want to help him with them. Then Jamie's interest in Winter had grown even stronger, and the last thing he needed was a romantic involvement at this time. Although he could acknowledge she was Walt's, he could not shake away the memory of her, of the lift that being with her gave him. Then there had been the wretchedness of those poor children. Jamie was worried about Walt. The great bear of a man seemed to have had the stuffing knocked out of him when he'd seen them. Both Jamie and Winter had believed him when he had said he hadn't known about the illegal testing and the end-results. Winter had assured him that he couldn't be expected to be everywhere with his finger on the pulse in his huge empire. He was taking it far too much to heart, they both told him repeatedly. But Walt was not in the mood for listening to their attempts to buoy him up. Jamie could sympathize with Walt's decision to give up the hunt. Dieter sneaking off the way he had, stealing the plane from them, had been not just unsporting but downright dangerous. What if the Indians had chosen the same moment to skive off too? How long would they have lasted in such a hostile environment? And then there was the business of the car exploding in Germany, killing the poor chauffeur. It had been a long way from the fun this expedition was supposed to be and, he presumed, Guthrie had planned. He wasn't so far from giving up himself. But it was Winter who had pushed him to continue. He smiled as he thought of her, seeing her standing in the middle of Walt's vast drawing-room, hands on her slim hips, flicking her long blonde hair off her shoulders in a defiant gesture, her attractive face mobile with fury, a belligerent look in her grey eyes that made the colour deepen to a pretty shade of slate . . .

'Don't you dare give up, Jamie – you're going to let that little creep Dieter win? Walt can't go now, you can see that, it's up to you, Jamie – you've got to win for the rest of us.'

He could have scooped her up in his arms there and then, he wanted to badly enough. But he didn't, he liked Walt, he liked his straightness. Walt, he felt, was turning into a reliable friend. He couldn't cheat on him, not now. Walt was obviously in love with Winter; he treated her differently from the other women Jamie had seen him with.

Before moving on, Jamie decided to stay a couple of days in New York and Walt invited him to be his guest. He had sleep to catch up on and he had to organize himself. He got his clothes cleaned and shirts laundered and shopped for a thing or two. He did wonder if he was idling, delaying his departure so that he could see more of Winter. Or was it because he too had lost much of his enthusiasm for this game?

Jamie was buying some trousers when he bumped into Twerp, in New York for the week on business for the bank he worked for. Twerp suggested they meet up later that evening to take in a club since he had a dinner engagement. Jamie dined alone at the Friar's Club. It was, however, difficult to dine completely alone in New York where he knew so many people and a steady stream of acquaintances came up to his table to say hi and to wish him well on the new project.

When Jamie arrived at the crowded and newly fashionable club where he'd arranged to meet Twerp, he was shown to a table where he sat waiting for him, watching the dancers gyrating on the underlit glass dance floor. Then his heart lurched for he saw Mica – tall, lithe, supple, beautiful. Her movements were so unselfconscious, she was like an exotic animal, he thought. Her eyes were closed and she was oblivious to everybody and everything in the crowded room except the relentless beat of the music. He had known it was inevitable that they would bump into each other at some point, it could only be a matter of time. But he had been dreading it happening nevertheless, wondering what his reaction would be. He found he was watching her with a pleasure tinged with regret for lost happiness. He suddenly realized that their relationship, or rather his with her, was a mirage of his own making. Seeing her, knowing it was over didn't hurt him nearly as badly as he had anticipated it would. They had been mismatched, it was obvious now. It was better for her to be without him, to find another man who could make her truly happy – she deserved that.

He sat up at that thought. But what did Mica deserve? If he was honest, the years with her had been empty years. He could truly say he'd tried with her; could the same be said of Mica? If he was really honest, the only times he'd been happy were in her bed. She was like a wonderful work of art to him, he enjoyed the fact that she was his – Winter was right. What else was their relationship built on? And why had he not seen it before? It could never have lasted, not on that basis. He knew why it was so clear to him now – Winter. On the sandbank Winter had shown him what friendship was possible between man and woman. Sex was not enough. How immature he'd been to think it was. If he couldn't have Winter then he'd search for someone like her . . .

The music stopped and Mica bent her long elegant neck, laughing with her companion. She stepped off the raised dance floor, her arms around her friend and then Jamie saw that the friend was female, another famous model. The reasoning of a moment before left him, and he felt a surge of anger, pain and humiliation as he was suddenly aware of many of the other customers slyly glancing in his direction to see what his reaction would be. Mica wasn't just with a friend; the way they held each other, the way they looked lovingly at each other, allowed him no escape from the truth. Mica had a new lover, and one of her own sex!

Jamie felt as if his stomach had turned into a punch-bag. He hadn't expected this – another man, yes, but Mica a lesbian? It had never crossed his mind before. All that steeling himself for seeing her on the arm of another man was for nothing. This was far worse and he didn't under-stand why. He stood up quickly before she could see him, before, in a way, she could see his shame. He left the nightclub hurriedly, hailed a cab and scuttled back to Walt's.

Winter was still up when he came in, sitting writing at a rather pretty escritoire; a large pair of imitation tortoise-shell spectacles gave her a studious, but very feminine, air.

'Jamie, you look awful, what's happened?' She slipped the glasses down her nose and peered anxiously over them at him.

He sat down and ran his hands through his hair. 'Well, a rather odd thing, it was a bit of a shock actually. You see, I saw my wife with another bird and it's upset me.

Stupid and old-fashioned of me, I suppose. It's just that I wasn't expecting it.' He spoke quickly, not looking at Winter, knowing full well that should he let her see his pain, if he had even a remote chance with her, he would most certainly lose her for ever.

Winter laid down her pen. 'Of course you're upset, Jamie. How grim for you. Was it somewhere public?'

'Yes, the Pelican Club – it was crowded with my friends.'

'Oh, even worse in front of people you know. They've probably known it's been going on since the very beginning,' she said sympathetically.

'So you don't think I'm over-reacting?'

'Of course not, it must have been a dreadful shock.'

'I felt so angry. I can't fight that, I thought. But then why should I think that? Why can't I be happy for her?'

'Jamie, she's humiliated you. It's like, well, you lost her and now it's as if she's pointing out that she never really wanted you and you're confused, naturally so. Why, it must be the ultimate betrayal to a man to lose his wife to another woman. You don't understand it, you can't, and you certainly wouldn't know how to fight it, or her, not as you would another man.'

'Yes, that's it. You're absolutely right. That was my reaction, but Winter, I thought I'd come to terms with it being over. I really wanted her to find somebody else but tonight when I saw them . . .'

'Maybe they were being just, you know, over-friendly? You know what these arty models are like.' Winter watched him, thinking what a fool Mica was and how sad he looked. She felt such anger for the woman who could do this to him – and did all this mean he was still in love with his wife?

'No, I know Mica. She doesn't like to be touched, you see, and this woman was touching her. No, she's in love – good luck to her. She deserves it.'

'Of course she didn't know you would be at the club, did she?'

'No, that's true.'

'And you'd have had to find out sometime.'

'You're right – male over-reaction.' He managed to laugh.

'That's better.' She smiled and he marvelled at how calming her influence was.

'Still, enough of me . . . how's Walt?'

Immediately the smile left Winter's face and she frowned. 'I'm worried, Jamie. I mean, he's functioning and everything, he's working hard, that's why I'm still here working at this hour. He's going ahead with his plan to launch the new hospital at Santa Anna and maybe a couple more. He's like a dynamo, as usual, with his plans for it. He really is the most generous man I know. The public has no idea how much he gives to charity. He's been to the laboratories where that drug was manufactured and he's interviewed certain scientists, and he's sacked them in no uncertain terms. They'll never get work again in any respectable company. Everything's just normal for Walt – except it isn't.'

'How do you mean?' He crossed to the drinks cabinet and poured himself a whisky. 'Walt won't mind my helping myself, will he?'

'Walt mind you drinking his whisky? Don't be so silly, Jamie. It's like he's lost. He seems to have shrivelled inside. Does that sound over-dramatic?'

'No, I know exactly what you mean. When he was sitting on the bank of the river just after we'd been to that awful place, he seemed to shrink before our very eyes.'

'Exactly. I think I should stay here for a while longer at least until his wife gets back, she's away staying with friends while her leg mends. He refuses to let me contact her – he doesn't seem to care if he sees her or not. I promised I'd stay here in the apartment for a couple of days to help him sort this Brazilian hospital thing out, but quite honestly, Jamie, it's to keep an eye on him.'

'I feel happier you're here. It's odd, you know, I've known Walt for years but never really trusted him. I thought he was a rather hedonistic, ruthless businessman who'd kill for a dime, but he isn't, is he? It's that big rugged exterior that makes you think he's like that. He's really quite a softie inside.'

'I adore him,' she said.

Ah, well, thought Jamie. He stood up abruptly. 'Still, I've got an early start, if you'll excuse me, Winter, I think I'll go to bed.'

And he did, though it was the last thing he wanted to do. He wanted to stay with her, talk to her, get to know even more about her. He lay in the dark for a long time, wishing things could be different. Winter was just what he needed – a woman who could be a friend, one who was logical and could understand him. Look how swiftly she had calmed him down over Mica – that had been pride, that was what his reaction amounted to. Pathetic, he told himself. There'd be other Winters in his life, he consoled himself . . .

Now he sat on the plane, his goodbyes said, and from his pocket he took Guthrie's envelope and puzzled over the clue again. '*Where Principe's deed ignited a continent, the flames burn still,*' he read. So, he thought, a deed was a deadly-sounding thing to do. Had this Principe bloke bumped somebody off? And the continent? The man's name was European, it sounded Italian, so the continent must be Europe. Ignited a continent . . . could that mean war? So what man's deed had caused a war in Europe? Second World War? No. First? He sat upright in his seat. That was it! What the hell was the Christian name of the man who killed that Austrian Archduke, the act that started the First World War?

'Oh, shit!' he said aloud, and the respectable English

dowager sitting beside him was not amused. 'I do beg your pardon,' he said. She stared at him and sniffed audibly as she stood up and loudly asked the stewardess to seat her elsewhere. 'Oh, Christ,' he said, more quietly this time. 'It's bloody Sarajevo. There's a bloody war on there!' The dowager glowered angrily across the aisle at him.

'I suggest, Lord Grantley, you keep your foul language to your filmic acting,' she said haughtily, and Jamie apologized again, most shamefacedly.

When Dieter arrived back in Munich, he did not go home. He felt hurt, betrayed and far too demoralized to face Magda. Seeing her and Gretel together had been bad enough. Having to hear Magda say she loved her was too daunting a prospect for him to face. He knew that if he saw and heard her he would break down. No one was going to see him in that condition, not even Magda. Instead, he busied himself with his plans. His Excellency's consignment of arms was safely en route, he could relax about that and stop looking over his shoulder for the possible assassin's bullet. He might as well continue with the treasure hunt. He would use his contacts in the arms-dealing world this time to transport himself to areas now difficult to enter. It would be the easiest way to get into the war-torn part of what had once been Yugoslavia.

In New York Winter's concern for Walt grew. As she had told Jamie, he was working normally but it was as if he was an automaton, as if Walt himself was not there any more.

'Would you like me to try to contact Mrs Fielding for you?' she asked him again one night, over the dinner they had just shared.

Walt laughed at this. 'What on earth for, Winter?'

'I'm sorry, Walt, I've not said anything before but I'm worried about you. You seem so distant and sad. I think you need to talk to somebody, and who better than your wife?'

Walt looked at her for what seemed an age before he spoke. 'There's just one small problem with that, Winter, I don't love my wife. She's the last person I would ever talk to about anything.'

She looked away. How often had she heard that particular line from men in New York, she thought bitterly. They're all the same, even Walt. She'd been proud that, given his reputation, he hadn't made a pass at her. His unsavoury reputation had upset her when she'd heard about it. She liked Walt, had even admitted to Jamie that she loved him, but he was married and if Winter had a rule, it was not to mess with other women's husbands.

'I've never loved my wife, Winter.'

'*Mr Fielding*, perhaps it's better if you don't talk about such personal things to me, after all I only work for you.' She emphasized the use of his surname.

'No, Winter, you know that's not true. You know you mean more to me than someone who just works for me. Don't worry, I'm not trying anything on. I'd have done that weeks ago, if that was all I wanted. Winter, it's more serious than that, I think I love you.'

'Oh, Mr Fielding, please . . .' She held up her hands as if pushing him away from her.

'Please, don't call me that, call me Walt again.' He felt despondent. He should not have said anything, he'd ruined everything now.

'You don't understand, Walt, I love my job, I don't want to lose it, I don't want any complications between us. I've heard about . . .'

'You've heard about me and my womanizing.'

'Well, yes. I mean, everybody at work knows about it,

it's common gossip.' And I've no intention of becoming just another of your statistics, she thought.

'Gossip?' He half-smiled. 'Winter, may I explain myself to you?'

'There's little point in that, we'd just end up embarrassed . . .' But still, she had to admit to herself that in the time she'd been with the company, she'd seen no such evidence of his womanizing.

'But I need to explain. Yes, I'm aware of what's said about me and it's probably only half the truth that you hear. I've deserved my reputation. But do you know what it's like to live in a relationship where there's no warmth and no love, Winter? Do you know what it was like, as a young man, day in, day out, to feel nothing for the person who shared my bed?' Winter looked embarrassed and didn't answer. 'And the relief, yet the emptiness, when we chose to have separate rooms? That's how my life's been for too long. I know I've used women, I admit that, but I've always been fair with them and I've been generous with money if not myself. Even then it's something I regret, but it was something necessary for me at the time, don't you see? I could forget the loneliness for a while in their arms.'

'And now?'

'Now I know it's not enough. Ever since you joined us I've been haunted by you, Winter. I've tried to interest myself in other women but I can't – not any more. I never expected, at my age, to fall in love. It's made matters worse. Fearing I can't have you has made me lonelier.'

'Walt, I'm sorry. I don't understand. You keep going on about being lonely, but how can you be? You have all your colleagues and you have lived with your wife for years. Heavens, if it was that awful a marriage, why didn't you divorce her years ago? You could afford to,' she said rather waspishly, still unable to forget the rumours, afraid he was like all the others, wishing that he'd said nothing and they could have gone on as they were. She stood up, about to leave the room.

'My loneliness, Winter, started the day I killed my father, and was made worse the day I confessed to my mother and alienated her for life.'

Winter sat down, aware that she had a stunned expression on her face. Walt gave a short, bitter laugh.

'You didn't expect me to say that, did you? Not Walt Fielding, respected member of society.' He laughed. 'I've lived with this since I was eighteen. Sometimes the guilt is unbearable, sometimes I'm lucky and it fades away for a while, but in Brazil it tumbled back into my mind with a terrifying intensity. Seeing those children, knowing I'd maimed them, killed others, then the images of my father's death returned in all their stark horror. I killed my father,' he repeated, as if to make certain she understood. 'My life has been burdened, and fairly so, with that knowledge, and so it will continue. Sometimes, Winter, the prospect is too bleak to contemplate. Some days I wonder why I bother to continue . . .'

'Walt, don't talk like that, please. Look, I think I know you, Walt, better than before. I see you, under that bluff exterior, as a kind and generous man. If you killed your father then I can't believe that there weren't extenuating circumstances. There has to be a reason for what you did.'

As an avalanche starts with one small snowflake, so Walt began to talk. He told Winter of his father and his brutality, of his mother's pain. He talked bitterly of Charity's part in it all. He didn't know why he spoke to her or why, after all these years of secrecy and silence, he should choose this young woman, a woman he knew he loved and one he must be alienating with his confession. But he could not seem to stop talking, he felt compelled to tell her about it in far more detail than he'd ever gone into with Gubbie, but then Gubbie and he had long since stopped discussing his deed. It was something from their past, long buried. But tonight, as each secret was divulged, he felt his burden lighten in some mysterious way, even when he knew that by telling her he had lost her for sure.

'So now you know I'm a murderer, you won't want to work for me any more.' Let alone love me, he thought sadly.

'Yes, I do, I'm honoured that you should have chosen to tell me all this. But I think you should do something about it, Walt.'

He looked at her questioningly. 'What? What can I do? Go to prison? Even after all these years, no doubt that's where I would end up.'

'You don't know that. I think you should make a clean breast of it. I think you should go to the law and tell them what you did all that time ago. I think you should go and see your mother and ask her to bear witness for you that your father was an intolerable bully and that you were driven to distraction. Heavens, you were a child.'

'And Charity?'

'Has Charity ever loved you, or does she love possessing you? It seems to me she could never have loved you or she would have let you go, years back.'

'God knows! But some days I think I hate her. I didn't always, I tried once to love her. I owe her a great debt, you know. She worked hard for me so that I could study when I was young. It was she who helped develop the company. I shall always be grateful for all that, but when she turned her back on our son, I could not forgive her. Something died that day, I gave up trying and I think that's when hate entered my soul.'

'And how long are you to be thankful to her? For the rest of your life? No doubt she did what she did because she wanted to. You didn't make her, did you?'

'No, in fact there were times when I wished she wasn't so ambitious – there wasn't much time left for fun.'

'And now what are you going to do?'

'I don't know . . . I just don't know.'

'Well, for a start, Walt, I think you must go to your mother. Try to find her forgiveness. Think of how she must have suffered too.'

'She won't see me.'

'Then make her see you.'

'Why should she? I'm a bad man, Winter.'

'No, Walt, don't say that. Misguided, but not bad.' She put her arms around him and as he leaned against her he knew she was right, knew what he had to do.

8

Dieter looked about him. He could not see one building that was not damaged. Some were gutted by fire, some had huge shell holes in them. The crackle of sniper fire was in the air, the stench of charred wood, the worse stench of burning bodies. It was cold, bone-numbingly cold, and Dieter felt he had stepped back in time. He stood in the street afraid, and felt again as he had as a small child in Germany, when every hour could have been his last. He shuddered. Why on earth had Guthrie brought them to this hell on earth? A man shouted at him in a language he did not understand but he did not need to for the urgency in the man's voice was sufficient to tell him to duck. A shell whined through the air and landed a hundred yards away with a sickening crump, there was a momentary silence and then the screams of the wounded filled the air from the market-place where the shell had landed amongst a group of people who had been shopping for what little food was available. He had seen no dogs, no cats. He doubted whether any such animals had survived, given the gaunt and hungry look of the people.

'It's not funny, is it?' the young man beside him said.

'Perhaps we'd better take cover for a while.' He led Dieter down some basement steps and into a cellar full of people. Dieter found himself reeling back from the stench. 'You get used to it.' The young man grinned as he found a plank for them both to sit on.

Dieter already liked Joe. He had been met in Belgrade and handed from one group to another as he was passed along the line further into the war zone. He had rendez-voused with Joe about fifty miles from here and it was he who had guided him through the final phase of a nerve-racking journey which had brought him to this town which he had never known existed, and whose name he could not even pronounce.

'It's dreadful,' said Dieter. 'You see the news reports on television but nothing prepares you for the reality of it.'

He searched his mind for words to describe his abhor-rence at what he saw, his shock at the cruel reality of a town under siege. 'You speak excellent English,' he said instead, and thought how prosaic conversation could still be, even in the most extreme conditions.

'I should hope so. I've lived in Milwaukee all my life.' Joe laughed. 'I've only been here three months, but you learn quickly. My parents were from here and my mother insisted that I keep up my mother tongue. Now it's come in handy.' Dieter wondered how he could be so cheerful at the sight of the destruction of his ancestors' home town and he remembered the anger and pain he had experienced when he saw his father's Berlin mansion in a pile of rubble.

'So do you feel Yugoslav or American?' he asked out of curiosity.

'Oh, American, but I felt I had to come and help.'

'Who sent you to meet me?'

'The doctor in charge told me to go and collect you. What are you here for? You're not a journalist, are you? And you're not a celebrity — we used to get a lot of them before the shelling got so bad. Are you a politician?'

'So you don't know Guthrie?' Dieter asked, ignoring the questions, for how, in view of what he saw, could he explain that he was here because of something as futile as a treasure hunt concocted in a luxury hotel in Cannes.

'Guthrie? No, should I? I was just told to find you and to bring you back to the orphanage.'

'Orphanage?' said Dieter. 'Oh, no, not more children.'

'I'm sorry? Don't you like children?'

'No, it's I who should be apologizing. It's just that only last week I had to see something relating to children that was distressing. Somebody seems intent on pointing me in the direction of poor, suffering children.'

'Then you've come to the right place. There's plenty of them here for you. Sometimes I think there isn't a child left here with any joy in its soul.'

'Is any aid getting through?'

'Spasmodically. Depends on who's in control and who's allowing stuff through, and how long yet another cease-fire holds and how much we can bribe the sons of bitches.'

'Will you stay here much longer?' Dieter asked.

'I didn't want to at first. As soon as I got here I wanted to get out, back to safety and sanity. I thought I couldn't take it. But now I'm not sure, now I think I'll stay. You feel so helpless when you see all the misery that you feel you have got to do something. I just don't think I could turn my back on the kids. Someone's got to look after them.' Dieter looked at the handsome young man, and suddenly felt very ashamed that he, when young, had not thought to help others, and indeed had never done so, for it was something which had never crossed his mind before.

The current bombardment ceased and they emerged into the street. Dust filled the air from the newly battered buildings and the stench of explosives lingered.

'We've got to cross that street over there, the one where that crowd's gathered. The shells have stopped, but we've still got to watch for snipers. You see that break in the street where that building's collapsed? They're firing there, that's the safest crossing place – relatively speaking.' Joe laughed. 'We'll have to wait our turn.'

'Isn't there another way?' Dieter asked.

'Only if you really want to be killed.' Joe grinned.

Dieter stood and watched as middle-aged women with shopping bags in their hands and men wearing suits and carrying briefcases as if bravely pretending to a normality which no longer existed, crouched behind a piece of corrugated sheeting. Their faces were alert, listening. There would be a rattle of fire and the group would duck low. In the space between the rattling of the fire, presumably while the gunman was reloading, three or four of them would run across the space and then the shooting would start again. Dieter stood with them, breathing deeply, rhythmically, to calm his nerves. What the hell was he doing here? He must be mad. Why didn't he just turn round and go back the way he had come? He didn't have to be here. What was he putting his life on the line like this for? There was a scream, a woman had been hit as she ran across the gap. Three men, one of them the young American, dived down, crawling along the pavement on their bellies to get to her, and dragged her back to safety.

'That was an incredibly brave thing to do, Joe.' Dieter clapped Joe on the back.

'It was nothing.' Joe shrugged. 'In a way, I guess, I quite enjoy the danger. It's different, let's face it, to life in Milwaukee.'

Their turn came, they ran across the gap, Dieter felt his heart pumping with excitement as well as fear. And once on the other side they both hugged each other with elation.

'It gets a bit better now,' Joe assured him. 'But you'd be wise to keep your head down.'

Dieter needed no second bidding as they dodged through the streets and buildings until eventually they came to a large, anonymous-looking cement-fronted building. It looked as if it had once been a school but was now empty; the windows were boarded up, the glass had long gone. Only stumps of trees remained in the playground – the wood had been taken to keep fires going. Joe opened a door that led down into a basement and Dieter followed him. Below was pandemonium. It was difficult in the dull light from a single unshaded bulb to see how many people were congregated there, but judging from the noise the majority were children.

'This is our orphanage,' said Joe, almost proudly, Dieter thought. 'Not that we know for sure that they really are all orphans. Some we've found wandering in the streets, others in ruined houses. Some of them have been here six months, some only arrived an hour ago. Come.' He led the way to the large underground room and through to the back where a young nurse was standing, patiently boiling a saucepan of water in which Dieter saw some kitchen knives and a couple of pairs of scissors. He wondered if she was sterilizing them and if so, why kitchen utensils?

'This is a hospital too?' he asked.

The young nurse turned to him. 'I suppose you could call it that. It's safer here in lots of ways. The hospital has become an obvious target. We deal with the children as best we can and the least badly wounded we can manage ourselves. We take the really seriously ill to the hospital but today we can't – the shelling's too bad. The doctor couldn't get through again, Joe.'

'Shit,' said Joe. 'How's the little boy?'

'He died, Joe. I'm sorry.' She put out her hand and touched him. 'You tried your best.' Joe looked away from them.

'You only take children?' Dieter asked, to cover Joe's obvious distress.

'Yes, I'm afraid adults must fend for themselves. We concentrate on the children, there's got to be a future somewhere down the line,' she said. Dieter did not compliment her on her English — such social niceties seemed out of place here. Joe and the nurse showed Dieter into the next room. Around the walls and down the centre were rows of mattresses, so tightly placed together that passage between them was difficult. On each mattress there were two, sometimes three, children. They looked at Dieter with large, blank eyes. Eyes that looked dead, eyes with no expression.

'These are our worst cases. The other children in the other room, they don't look like this,' the nurse said, as if reacting in tune to his thoughts.

Dieter walked slowly along the mattresses, looking at the dirty bandages, observing the children's fear, sensing their pain. He swung round.

'It's their eyes,' he said with anguish. 'They're not the eyes of children.'

'They've seen things no child should see — people killed is the least of it. They've seen their families tortured, their mothers and their sisters raped. Some of them are so traumatized they can't even speak to us,' the nurse explained.

'But these wounds will get infected if you use bandages this filthy.' Dieter pointed at one child's leg encased in a dark grey bandage.

The young nurse laughed. 'That's all we have,' she said.

'I think I can get you more,' Dieter said.

'Oh, we've masses, we just can't get hold of them, that's the bastard of this little confrontation, they won't let the aid through.' She went to one mattress, knelt on the floor and began to remove the dressing on the leg of a little girl who could only be three. 'Shrapnel,' she said to Dieter in explanation. As she began to unwind the bandages, the child began to whimper. No tears came, just the strange keening, whimpering noise. She tried to draw her body away from the nurse's hands. The blank expression in her eyes was exchanged for one of fear. 'Could you hold her?'

the nurse asked. 'They sometimes thrash around a bit.' Gingerly Dieter put his arms around the skeletally thin child.

'You've no pain-killers, then?'

'A few, but we have to reserve those for the really badly wounded.'

'Really badly wounded? Dear God, what's this?' He looked down at the pus-encrusted sores on the child's leg. 'Will she keep it?' he asked.

'God knows,' said the young nurse.

'How do you do it?' Dieter asked. 'How can you deal with her pain?'

'Someone's got to,' she replied.

The child's whimpering increased. One small hand clutched at Dieter's jacket. He held her tight, wishing the pain could be transferred to him.

'What's your name?' he said softly. Of course she could not understand him and did not reply.

'She doesn't know her name, she's forgotten it. She was found in a cellar in a village not far from here – her dead mother was lying across her, she must have shielded her from the bullets with her own body,' the nurse said so matter-of-factly that it made the telling of the tale more chilling.

'Dear God!' said Dieter. 'No name, eh?' He smiled down at the little one. 'Then I shall call you Katja, such a pretty name. I wanted to call my daughter Katja one day.' He talked in a gentle monotone to the child. 'Would you like me to tell you a story? Of course you would. Once upon a time there was a pretty princess called Katja . . .'

The nurse continued to work, cleaning and rebandaging her wounds.

'Thanks very much . . . Dieter, isn't it? I've never seen her that quiet before. Odd, wasn't it, almost as if she understood your story?' The nurse tidied up the few instruments she had.

'Do you need other helpers?' Dieter, to his astonishment, heard himself say as he still held on to the child. He was loath to let her go.

'Oh, yes, please. Any help we can get, that would be wonderful. Thank you so much.'

'I'll just hold her until she goes to sleep,' he said and rocked the child gently as he told her another tale of knights on wild white chargers.

Dieter worked in the orphanage for three days, helping to clean, helping to sterilize the few precious instruments they had, even at one point boiling a pile of rags which the nurse fondly called bandages in a precious can of water, on a Calor gas-operated stove. Even in the basement the noise of the shelling continued so that the children were constantly reminded of the terror above, and they cried. When they slept they dreamed and screamed.

Any spare time he had he tended to spend with Katja, holding her, trying to comfort her and always worrying about her. He wondered why he concentrated on this one small scrap, and what it was about her that had made him single her out. He thought he knew the answer – he could not help them all, and to lessen his feelings of inadequacy he had chosen just one to give all his need to help. A need which had taken him by surprise.

The next day a rumour reached them that a new load of aid from their own particular charity had been released at Sarajevo and was waiting at a roadblock twenty miles away. Someone had to go and get it before it was stolen. Joe stepped forward immediately.

'I'll go with you too,' said Dieter, though he was unsure why he'd volunteered so promptly without thinking, pretty certain that he was likely to regret his action later. But deep inside him he knew the reason – if there were antibiotics to be got to help Katja he was determined to get them. The car they climbed into Dieter regarded as totally inadequate; rust had eaten away at the underside, the passenger door fitted badly and he sat holding on to it grimly, feeling certain it was about to burst open and sweep him into the road.

'Where do you get petrol from?' he asked.

'Contacts,' Joe said monosyllabically.

They were fortunate in their trip to the rendezvous which, given where they were, was uneventful. But once at the depot the delays were frustrating, for chaos reigned, no one seemed to be in control and no one was willing to take responsibility. It was made worse when they realized that they could see the two packages they had come to collect. Dieter's patience, never strong, was quickly lost, which only exacerbated the problem since, faced with his anger, the authorities became even more intransigent. Seeing the way of things, Joe begged Dieter to wait in the car while he negotiated. He had to argue, plead, barter and finally bribe to get the precious packages.

Dieter had not been impressed by the young American's driving on the way to the aid centre and insisted that he would take the wheel on the way back. No sooner were they on their way than they were stopped by yet another patrol who informed them that because of snipers it was too dangerous to continue on the next stretch of road unless part of a UN aid convoy making another attempt to get through to the beleaguered town. There was a further delay as they waited for the convoy to form. But when they set out they felt safe, protected by the large white armoured cars with the blue flashes of the UN upon them up ahead. They could only have been travelling about twenty minutes when suddenly there was a cracking noise and the windscreen shattered into a frosted maze of glass. Dieter immediately punched a hole in his side so he could see where he was going.

'What the hell was that, a stone?' Dieter asked, turning to his companion.

Joe sat bolt upright, a surprised expression on his face. 'I think I've been hit, Dieter. I've been shot.' Dieter stopped the car.

'Oh, my God!' exclaimed Dieter. There was the sharp cracking sound as a second shot rang out. Dieter instinctively ducked, hitting his head on the steering-wheel. 'Don't worry, Joe. Don't move. I'll get us back,' he said with rising panic. He let the clutch in too quickly as he put the car into gear and stalled the engine. He swore as he turned the ignition, time and again; he was flooding the engine as he pushed his foot too hard on the accelerator.

'Dieter, not so fast, you'll flood the carburettor,' Joe said hoarsely.

'I know what I'm doing,' Dieter snapped, feeling anxiety mount as he saw the safety of the convoy disappearing round the bend in the road. They were sitting ducks. His hands were shaking but he forced himself to take a deep breath, counted to ten and then tried again. This time the engine fired. He kept his head low and advised Joe to do the same as they drove along at speed in pursuit of the convoy. The steering-wheel began to feel sticky; Dieter looked down, and saw that it was covered with blood which was dripping on to his thighs. He glanced at Joe to see where the blood had spurted from but Joe was sitting quietly, ashen-faced, holding his stomach. Dieter looked back at the wheel. He saw that his hand was bright scarlet, the blood was dripping down his own arm on to his hand. It was his blood! He felt queasy at the sight of it. Where had he been shot? He hadn't felt anything. He looked again and saw that blood was pouring from the sleeve of his jacket – he had been hit in the arm. The moment he identified that he had been shot and where, the pain began. Like a fast-moving brush fire, agony rippled down his arm into his hand and his fingers. He had to release the steering-wheel and his arm flopped lifeless on to his lap. By now Joe was groaning and Dieter could see he was barely conscious. Blood was oozing between Joe's fingers – he'd been shot in the stomach. Dieter realized that such a wound must be dangerous. He had to control his own pain, learn to ignore it and to concentrate on keeping the car on the road and getting his companion back to the orphanage as quickly as possible. It was a nightmare drive and one that he would never forget, for the road was rutted with shell potholes and at every bump and turn his arm jolted and the pain shot through him like razors tearing him into shreds.

It was almost dark when they finally arrived back at their destination. Dieter stumbled out of the car and down the steps, holding his wounded arm with his other one, and as he ran, pain shuddered through his body at every footfall. He pushed open the door and called out for Anna, the young nurse. 'Joe's been hit,' he yelled, then collapsed in a heap on the floor and, almost with relief, allowed the blackness of unconsciousness to relieve him of all responsibility.

A week later Jamie finally arrived in what had once been Yugoslavia. He was not surprised to be told by the man who materialized at his hotel in Zagreb that Dieter was already there, he'd had a head-start on him anyway by taking the plane in Brazil. Jamie was still seething about that and he was looking forward to seeing Dieter: there was a lot he wanted to have out with the treacherous German. This time he'd really give him a piece of his mind.

It had taken Jamie some time to get here. Travelling to Yugoslavia was one thing, getting into the battle zone was more difficult. Tourists were hardly welcome. He could not think how to pull it off until one night, watching the news on television, he had hit upon the idea of becoming a journalist for the duration of this trip. The television teams seemed to have no problem getting there and moving about the place. Unfortunately newspaper editors were not as keen as Jamie on his brilliant idea that he, as a film star and a peer of the realm, should go to Yugoslavia and send them back a report which their readers would be keen to read. While aware that he might be killed, which of course would make a good lead story, they could also anticipate the questions which might be asked if he was. Since he had never done any journalism in his life before, they were deeply sceptical about his ability to file anything. But after a very, very long drunken dinner with one editor, Jamie was presented with his credentials. Even then, it had taken him days to get here, and when he had his guide would not take him to Sarajevo which was where he presumed he should go. Instead he was taken to this city he had not even known existed, and seeing it he wondered why he'd bothered.

'What a mess!' he said, in the understatement of the year, as he was shown into the small room where Dieter was lying on one of the orphanage mattresses. 'The whole place is falling down,' Jamie said. 'Bloody hell, Dieter, you look dreadful,' which wasn't exactly the scathing introduction he'd planned on the journey here.

Dieter managed a weak smile. 'Thank you, Jamie, your concern makes me feel much better,' he said through parched lips.

'Congratulations, Dieter, that was almost an English joke.'

'Yes, I thought so too.'

'What happened? Are you in pain?' Jamie's innate good manners and concern triumphed over his anger.

'Well, a sniper bullet smashed my arm. It does hurt somewhat. Unfortunately it's gone septic, that's what's making me feel and look rather ill.'

'Have they any antibiotics here? Painkillers? I gather there's a dreadful shortage of everything.'

'Yes, there is. But Joe, a young American aid worker here, and I managed to get some in. I told them to use them on the children first, though.' Dieter spoke with difficulty.

Jamie's initial reaction was to say, 'You did what?' with total amazement at Dieter's uncharacteristic unselfishness. Instead, he said nothing but patted the hand of the man he did not like. 'We'll soon get you sorted out, Dieter.'

'Have you heard how Joe is? He was wounded too – in the stomach. They managed to get him to the hospital in a lull in the shelling but I haven't heard anything today.'

'He's doing fine. Soon be playing baseball.'

'You're not just saying that, Jamie?'

'No, honest. That pretty little nurse told me. They just heard. The wound looked far worse than it was, you know. It's you they should have taken to hospital, not him.'

'It's hell on earth here. Have you seen the children?' Dieter asked.

'No, not yet. I wanted to see you first when I heard that you'd been hurt.' He marvelled at how quickly his anger had turned to pity at the sight of the fever- and pain-racked Dieter.

'I warn you, Jamie, it's very upsetting. The poor kids, no one should do this to children, no one, ever.' He coughed from the effort of speaking.

'If there was an arms embargo they wouldn't be able to, would they?' Jamie said coldly at the hypocrisy of the man, and he wished he hadn't been so nice to him. If people like you didn't sell such things, it would be a better world, he thought, but decency winning again, he kept the thought to himself.

Dieter looked at him out of eyes glazed with fever. 'I know what you're thinking, Jamie, don't you think I've been thinking the same? I lie here regretting so much. It's one thing to set up deals and to send shipments of arms to anonymous people and anonymous countries, it's an entirely different matter when you see what the bullets can do.'

'But you must have realized, don't give me that guff.'

'Once I saw it, a long time ago in Africa, but I was young then, it was an adventure, and they would have killed us if we hadn't killed them. I never thought further – of what happened afterwards. Of women, of children being maimed and hurt. It was just a business to me.'

'It must have helped you enormously, having such a selective thought process.' Jamie looked away from Dieter with an expression of disgust and wished he hadn't given up smoking again.

'There's nothing you can say to me, Jamie, that I haven't thought about myself while stuck here.'

'Have you?'

'You don't believe me?'

'Well, look at it this way, Dieter, it's a rather sudden conversion, isn't it? Maybe once you're better it'll disappear – your conscience, I mean.'

'No, Jamie, it isn't like that.' His good hand grabbed at Jamie's sleeve. 'It won't change. It's not because of me. I've not been lying here thinking I might die and setting myself right with God. It happened before I was wounded. When I saw the kids, the suffering, I cried. My heart went out to them, I experienced such remorse . . .'

Jamie still looked sceptical and wished he hadn't come.

'I've been involved in an evil business, Jamie, I've caused great suffering. I realize that now. When – if – I return, I'll never do the same again. The money I've made I shall use to help kids like this. Believe me, Jamie,' he said urgently, and Jamie couldn't understand why his believing should be so important to Dieter.

Jamie didn't know quite what to say or where to look

because he didn't really want to look at Dieter. It had taken him long enough, too long in Jamie's book, to reach this simple conclusion. He wished Dieter was confessing to anyone but him. 'We've got to get you out of here,' he said with forced brightness.

'Yes, but I don't see how, do you?'

'You leave it to me, Dieter, I'll sort something out,' Jamie said confidently, not in the least sure how he was going to arrange it.

Dieter had not exaggerated. Jamie could not believe the state of some of the children nor the conditions they were living under, with no drugs, little food and water. He felt a huge block of misery descend upon him at such inhumanity, and total frustration at his own apparent inability to do anything about it. He had his article to write but he doubted if it would do any good. Who'd listen to him when far more articulate professionals had been pounding their senses with the bestiality of this war for months now. Anna, the young nurse he had met when he first arrived, was now, since the only doctor had been killed, in sole charge. She could only have been about twenty, he thought. Too young for such dreadful responsibility.

'Do you know who I should contact to try and get Dieter out of here?'

Anna looked at him, a frown on her face, as if she half remembered him, but wasn't sure from where. He wasn't surprised she did not fully recognize him, for he was dirty and unkempt, something that Jamie Grant, constantly in the list of the top ten best dressers, never normally was. 'The problem is, will he go? We found him a place on a plane a few days ago but he refused to leave the children.'

'Honestly?' These good deeds of Dieter's were almost unbelievable.

'He's been wonderful, turning his hand to anything. And he's so good with the children, calming and comforting them, playing with those who can play. I've missed his help since he's been wounded. I shall miss him when he's gone.'

'Really?' And this time Jamie's astonishment was palpable; perhaps Dieter had learned something after all.

'I think if you can, you should try and get him out. It's hopeless here. I can't treat him and, quite honestly, I don't have the time with all the children. Put bluntly, I don't think he's going to live if you don't get him out soon.'

If there was one advantage to Jamie's position, it was the fact that everybody felt that they knew him. It was a rare person on this planet who hadn't seen him starring in the Peter Ascot films, either in the cinema or now, often as not, on television. Certainly every Christmas it had become a sort of modern tradition to have a James Bond film on one television channel and Ascot, Private Eye, on the other. So even here, in the midst of civil war, once he'd washed his face, shaved and tidied himself up, people recognized him and doors opened for him.

They were in luck. Yet another group of fact-finding Western politicians had flown into Sarajevo and their leader was a particular fan of Jamie Grant; also his popularity in the opinion polls at home was slipping and he would welcome a photo opportunity with such a world-famous star. There would be a place on the plane leaving in two days' time, and transport had somehow miraculously been laid on to get Dieter to the airport. It would be a dangerous and uncomfortable ride, and no one could guarantee if they would get through, but Jamie could see no other option.

While they waited for the time of their departure Jamie sat beside Dieter's stretcher, talking to him when he was awake. He stopped mentioning the pending escape, for Dieter had become very agitated when it was first mentioned, saying he could not go and leave the children. There was not much Jamie could do to make him comfortable apart from helping him drink a little of the precious water and eat a little watery soup which was all the orphanage had to offer. When he was asleep Jamie helped Anna and her few helpers as best he could. He dreaded doing it, finding the children's fear and their withdrawn state, let alone their cries of pain, almost too much to bear. He knew that for the rest of his life he'd be haunted by those screams. He wished he could whistle up a bus, pile them in and, like the Pied Piper, whisk them off to green grass and sunshine and fun.

The shelling of the city grew worse. Jamie began to wonder if either of them would get out. Odd to think that this was where he might die, where all the foolishness would end. He wished he'd seen more of Fiona now. God, how he did! Winter was probably right, he'd been avoiding her. When he got out of here – if he got out of here – he'd make damn sure he saw her. To die without telling her he loved her was a thought he didn't want to contemplate.

Dieter's condition worsened at an alarming rate. As he deteriorated so he began to ramble. Jamie sat listening to a strange monologue in German, French and English as Dieter poured out his heart to him. When he rambled it was so disjointed that he understood little. But then there were times when Dieter spoke with total clarity.

'Jamie, there's a little girl here, she doesn't know her name but I call her Katja – she's only three and very frightened and she's got to have an operation or she'll lose her leg. We've got to get her out somehow or other.' He sounded agitated. 'I'm so afraid she's going to die, can you get her out?'

'I'll see what I can do,' Jamie promised, and Dieter grabbed hold of his hand with surprising strength and held it tight.

'I mean it, Jamie, we've got to get that child out.'

'Yes, okay, okay, leave it with me.' Dieter slumped back on to the dirty pillow and lapsed again into sleep or unconsciousness – Jamie was never quite sure which state he was in.

In the middle of the night Dieter woke.

'Jamie, are you there?' he called.

Jamie, who was asleep on the floor, was immediately awake.

'I love Magda, Jamie, more than words. Will you tell her, tell her what I said if I don't make it back?'

'You're not going to die, Dieter. Don't talk such rot,' Jamie said with false confidence.

'But you don't know all of it, Jamie. She must be told. I've failed her, you see. I've failed her dreadfully.'

'Oh, I don't think Magda would say that, she loves you. You only have to see the way she looks at you,' he said encouragingly.

'No, you don't understand. I've never been a husband to her, I can't. I can't do it with Magda.'

'Well, yes . . . there, there,' said Jamie, acutely embarrassed now. He patted Dieter's good hand, not knowing how else to deal with the situation. He'd come here disliking the man intensely and yet over these days and nights as he listened to him talk of his childhood, of finding his dead father, his illegitimacy, of his fight for survival in Berlin, Jamie began to understand him better and even to like him. If he'd learnt one thing it was that there had to be an explanation, buried deep perhaps but there all the same, for why grown men and women are the way they are. He hadn't minded listening to Dieter, taking his unhappiness on board in some strange way. But this? He supposed that if he hadn't known Magda it would have been easier, but he wished the man would shut up, there were some things one didn't talk about. And then he remembered how he had opened up to Winter, how much it had helped him. 'Talk it through, Dieter. I'll listen.'

'It's my mother, you see, Jamie. She reminds me of my mother and I can't do it.'

'Does she look like your mother?'

'No, not really. I think it's because I love her and I loved my mother. I worshipped my mother and she let me down. She became a whore, you see, so that we could survive, and I never forgave her and she's dead now. I've put Magda on a pedestal too and I'm afraid to touch her, in case I stop loving her. And if I stop loving her I don't know what I'd do for the rest of my life. Can you understand that, Jamie?'

'Yes, yes I can,' he said, and managed not to sound doubtful although he really wasn't sure what Dieter was talking about. But he knew, as he looked at him, that Dieter was telling him of another sort of hell, one, he thanked God, he knew nothing of.

Before they left the orphanage for their hair-raising drive to Sarajevo, Dieter was so ill that he was more dead than alive. At least he could not object as they loaded him into the makeshift ambulance. When they finally arrived at the airport after a journey of such gut-watering fear that Jamie decided he'd had enough excitement to last the rest of his life, a UN doctor immediately injected Dieter with some precious antibiotics which by now he was too weak to refuse. The plane was fuelled up and waiting for immediate take-off. On the journey back Dieter opened his eyes only once, looking anxiously, feverishly for Jamie. 'Is the little girl here?' he asked faintly. 'Katja?'

'Yes,' said Jamie, 'I managed to wangle her on.'

'Ah, good,' said Dieter, and this time he slept, and as he did he smiled.

9

The plane carrying the fact-finding mission, Dieter, Jamie and the little girl finally landed in Paris. Magda was there, waiting for them, with an ambulance for Dieter.

'You've got two patients, Magda,' Jamie said, grinning, but at the same time feeling a little sheepish talking to her since Dieter had confided in him about his sex life. 'He's brought a little girl back with him, she needs an operation rather urgently.'

'Thank God you were with him, Jamie. I'll take care of her, don't worry.'

'Where are you taking him?'

'I've arranged for him to be admitted to the American hospital, it's the best, and Dieter deserves the best.'

'Yes, he does,' said Jamie, and realized he meant it. 'Now I'm going to find myself a hotel and have a long, hot bath.'

'And the treasure hunt?'

'It seems to have fizzled out. We got there but could not follow up the last clue. Nor do we have the next one. It would have been impossible to find anyone there really, so I suppose nobody won – except Guthrie's pet charities. It's been a rum do all round,' he said in his usual understated way.

'Oh, what a shame, Dieter did so want to win.'

'Didn't we all?' Jamie laughed. With Dieter and Katja safely on board the ambulance, Jamie helped Magda climb in and he waved as it drove off, lights flashing. He silently wished Dieter luck.

'Lord Grantley?' Jamie swung round. It was one of the grey-suited, fact-finding mission team. 'I've something for you,' he called, and pounded across the Tarmac towards him. In his hand he had three envelopes which he waved at Jamie. 'I'm to give you these,' he said.

Jamie laughed. 'Good old Guthrie,' he said. 'Isn't he a marvel?' And he took the envelopes.

After his long hot bath and copious coffee which he had only been able to dream about in his time in Yugoslavia, he had a cigarette which he couldn't resist. After a hearty breakfast Jamie went to bed and slept through the rest of that day and night.

Walt had been causing consternation on the markets of New York. For Walt was selling in a serious way. The empire that he had spent the last twenty years building he was now dismantling in the space of a few weeks. He explained his reasons to only one person, Gubbie.

'The whole operation has gotten too big, Gubbie. Dealing with drugs we are dealing with people's lives. Had this business of mine been smaller, one where I could have kept my finger on every operation and subsidiary, then I'd have known about that disgusting field trial in Brazil. I could have stopped it.'

'But would you have, man?'

'Jeez, Gubbie, I hope to God I would. Do you think I'm so greedy I'd allow that sort of suffering?' he said with just a hint of his old belligerence. 'Shit, Gubbie, you of all people.' He turned away, his face a mixture of anger and hurt. 'No, I would not have.' He slammed one large fist into the other. 'I can't rely on anyone else – only myself.'

'Maybe so. But I don't see how you can blame yourself, man. Hell, look at the number of drugs that fuck people up – how many chairmen of the relevant companies resign or sell up?'

'That's with them and their consciences. I can't live with mine, it's loaded enough already without something like this to add to it.'

'But all your ambitions?'

'What use are they? I've money enough for the rest of

my life – but what sort of life is it? No one to really share it with, and my only child dying a cruel, slow death.'

'But what the hell will you do to fill the time, a workaholic like you?'

'I'll find something, gardening perhaps.'

'*You* a gardener! That I should love to see.' Gubbie laughed.

'You're not disappointed? I mean, if you want I'm sure I can help you find a position with one of the buyers.'

'Hell, no. The last few years I've only stayed on because of you. You've done me proud over the years, Walt. I quite fancy taking early retirement. I like the idea of buying Liz and me a condominium in Hawaii, and smoking dope and watching the waves.' Gubbie looked quite pleased at the prospect.

Charity, when she returned from her visit to friends and with a fully healed leg, was beside herself with rage.

'Why the hell are you doing this to me?' she asked, having waited up for Walt to return late one night.

'Because I have no further interest in it,' he said.

'Don't talk so stupid. You stand there saying you have no interest in your business any more, so you're going to sell it. You sound like a petulant child, Walt. What about me? What are we going to live on?'

'I shall get a very good sum for my businesses. I shall give you a hefty settlement, on the income from which you can continue to live in the style you choose. What I do with the rest is my own business.'

'Settlement? Settlement?' Charity latched on to the word, her face creased now with anxiety. 'What do you mean?'

'I want a divorce, Charity. As simple as that. I'll look after you, you've nothing to fear.'

'You can't divorce me, you know you can't. You know what I shall do.'

'Charity, you can do whatever you goddam like, I don't

care any more, do you understand? And I really cannot see the point in you and I continuing to live this charade of a life. I don't love you and you don't love me.'

'Walt, after all I've done how can you say that? I've loved you from the day I set eyes on you. I've never stopped loving you.'

'No, Charity, you don't love me. You love possessing me. I don't wish to be possessed any more.' He turned as if to leave her.

'Walt, don't go, please don't go. Why are you leaving? You've another woman, haven't you? You're leaving me for another woman.' She spoke in panic. 'Look, Walt, I know about those other women, it hurt me over the years but if that's what you wanted – anything to make you happy, Walt – I didn't mind because you always came back, but don't leave me now. Please, Walt, please,' she was pleading.

'No, I'm not going to somebody else. I could wish I was, but I'm not. I'm tired of our lifestyle, I'm tired of what I'm doing, I do not wish to do it any more. I have no desire to live with you any more, Charity, so do your worst.' And he shut the door and left her, sobbing, in the middle of her oh-so-perfect, beautiful living-room which she liked to call a salon.

Later that week, on his plane flying to Oregon, Walt sat deep in thought. He had consulted his lawyers; it seemed he could still face a prison sentence for the murder of his father all those years ago. But on the other hand, his lawyers had said, they felt there were certainly extenuating circumstances, most importantly his age at the time of the crime – he'd been just short of eighteen. Had his father died a few weeks later, things might have been very different, he was told. If his mother would be a witness in his favour, telling the court of his father's brutality to them both, then they felt that Walt might probably be able to use a plea of manslaughter and receive a suspended sentence – in other words, get away with it. But as he sat on the plane he wondered if he wanted to 'get away with it'. He had begun to think that if he was punished for his crime with a hard prison sentence, maybe some of the guilt at least might disappear. But then he wondered what would happen if it didn't and he'd rotted in prison for nothing? He had decided he would see his mother first, and this time he would insist that she speak to him. Maybe she would decide for him.

His car drew up in front of his mother's house. His childhood home never ceased to amaze him, for it still looked the same from the outside as it had always done, if a little smaller than he remembered it. He knew from his lawyer that it had changed beyond all recognition on the inside but as he approached it and climbed the steps of the wooden verandah and rang the bell, he felt as though he really was returning home. There was a long delay in the door being answered and he knew the reason. His mother would have heard the car and seen him approach. She would have watched him get out of the car and would know that it was her son who stood waiting on the doorstep. He rang again, determined to see her this time. Eventually the door opened. He had prepared himself not to recognize his mother for she was old now, but still within the wrinkled face and beneath the grey hair Rosamund's face looked up at him. A great surge of love for her filled him. He longed for her to put her arms up to him, to hold him again and to tell him she loved him. But he realized from her stern expression that this was unlikely to occur.

'I never thought to see you again, Walt. I thought I'd made myself perfectly clear all those years ago.' She spoke in a firm voice, not at all that of an old person, and she spoke with a determination that made his heart sink.

'I know, Mother. But things have changed. I have changed. I need to talk to you now.'

She held the door open for him to enter. He stood in a spacious hallway with a highly polished floor and a fine mirror on the wall, and she led him into a comfortable, beautifully furnished sitting-room.

'It looks nice,' he said, for want of something to say.

'Yes, I've got it how I want it,' she said, 'thanks to your grandfather.'

'Yes, good old Grandfather. We've both a lot to thank him for.'

'You wish to talk to me – then talk, Walt.'

'I've come to give myself up to the authorities, Mom. My whole life I've never been able to escape from what I did that day.'

'Good,' she said simply.

'One should be punished for what one has done, so I'm quite prepared to go to prison, if necessary. I'm only human, Mom, I would like to go to prison for the smallest amount of time possible, and my lawyers tell me that if you will tell the court the truth of our life with my father I might get a lighter sentence.'

'You might also get off, you were only a child when you killed him.'

'Yes, there is that possibility.'

'Then you wouldn't be punished.'

'Not in a conventional sense, no.'

'What has your life been like, Walt?'

'Not particularly happy, Mom, if it's any consolation to you. You can't get away from guilt, it tinges everything, even the glossiest of lives.'

'This guilt you talk of, it's always with you?'

'If I forget, it's only a momentary thing.' He realized she was smiling at his reply and such a reaction chilled him.

'Your son, he's still alive?'

'Oh, yes, he could stay the way he is, in a twilight world, for ten, fifteen years more. He no longer knows me,' he said, sadness tinging his voice.

'And no doubt Charity blames you and says it's a punishment from God.'

'Yes, she did as a matter of fact.' He looked surprised that she should know.

'Stupid woman, I always thought she was stupid.' Rosamund sat down and indicated he should too. 'I think you're rather stupid too, Walt. What would be the point of confessing now? All that rubbish in the papers, having old wounds open up. And do you for one moment think I want my dirty linen washed in public, for the whole area to gloat over? So the answer's no – I wouldn't stand as a witness for you.'

'I see, Mom. Well, that's it,' he said and stood up and turned towards the door.

'Sit down, Walt. I haven't finished. I think you've suffered enough. I think God has punished you, if society hasn't.'

He turned round at her tone and sat down feeling for the chair, not taking his eyes from her face. 'I've thought a lot over these years, inevitably so. I couldn't help loving your father, he could be a good man, but he could be an evil man too, I admit that. He *was* cruel to you and I was weak not to help you more. And I was blinded by my love for him. I'm not excusing what you did, I could never do that, but at the same time, Walt, I don't want to see you in prison. You are my son and I find I still love you.' She sat there, a small woman cloaked in quiet dignity. He wanted to rush over and enfold her in his arms, but he didn't know whether he dared. Large, rich and powerful as he was, this tiny old woman had the ability to frighten him still.

'Did you say "love", Mom?'

'Yes, it's true what they say. No matter how hard you

try, you can't stop loving your son. And I did try. Those few times you came here and I saw you I had to fight myself not to open the door to you. I wanted to hate you so much – but I found I couldn't. It's an easy thing to say I won't see you when you're far away. But now, with you here, in this room . . .' Her voice trailed off as her eyes filled with unshed tears so that she had to blink to see.

'Christ, Mom, I've missed you.' He shook his head.

'Me too, son . . .'

Later they sat at the pine table in the brand-new kitchen, paid for by Walt, unknown to his mother, as she sliced into a newly baked angel-food cake. 'Your favourite, if I remember.' She smiled at him.

'Yup, no one ever baked a cake like yours, Mom, everyone said that.' She poured them both coffee.

'So what do you intend to do?'

'Well, I've told Charity I want a divorce and I'm willing to settle money on her. She'll be rich, which is what she enjoys, but of course she may go to the police.'

'Who'll listen to her? A middle-aged woman being discarded by a wealthy husband. No, they'll think it's the spite of a scorned woman.'

'Do you think so?'

'I know so.' She chuckled, for the first time.

'I want to move back out here, Mom. I want to find a house and bring my son here and live with him until he dies. All my life my goal was to be rich, but what for? It doesn't make you happy, Mom, not if there's no one to share it with. I own a pharmaceutical company near here, I'm going to keep it and sell everything else.'

'Everything?' she said.

'Yes. I want this company to concentrate on new drugs that maybe we can still save from the rainforest, before it's too late. And a laboratory dedicated to a cure for Huntington's Disease – they renamed it, so maybe with a new name we can find a new cure. I have to do that for my boy.'

'And? There is an "and", isn't there, Walt? There's something else you're going to do.'

'Yes. From the money I raise from selling my businesses I'm going to set up a foundation to help the natives of Brazil,' he said simply. 'It's the only way I can think of to get rid of another load of guilt.'

'Have you met somebody else? Is that what has galvanized you into asking Charity for a divorce?'

'I have. I love her very much. I made the mistake of telling her so but only managed to embarrass her. I'm afraid she's fallen for someone else.'

'Poor Walt,' his mother said.

'Poor Walt nothing, after what I've seen just recently I'm very fortunate. This is a new start, and how many people get given the chance of a new start?'

Dieter, once he had recovered consciousness in the hospital, and once he had begun to feel better, had told the nurses he didn't wish to see his wife. But Magda was made of sterner stuff than Dieter had ever realized, and on the third day of his stay in hospital she refused to take any notice of them and pushed her way into his room.

'I know what you're thinking, Dieter, and you're wrong. Gretel was in bed with me because I was worried and afraid for you. She was there just for company, there was nothing else, you know.'

He looked at her stonily. 'I didn't even know that you knew Gretel,' he said.

'When you didn't turn up and the police were looking for you I tried everyone to find you. Eventually I had to call her – we waited together.'

'That must have cost you dear, to call her.'

'I knew her, I had done for some time. But she's a sweet woman and she loves you dearly. I trust her more than I'd trust the others.'

'What others?' he said.

'Oh, come on, Dieter, don't play games. I've known all along about the other women. When they were silly little affairs that lasted a month, I could manage to deal with it, but Gretel was harder.' She was pacing nervously about the room, and he wished she would stop.

'And you didn't mind?' He should have been pleased that she had not minded; instead it made everything seem bleaker in an illogical way.

'Of course I minded!' she snapped at him. 'I love you, Dieter, I always have. It's hard to be a woman and to know you're not exactly what your man needs and to know he goes to others to find it.'

'Oh, Magda, it's not you, I know it's not you. I have always said it was me.'

'Still, it is as it is. We can't change things.' She suddenly sat down on his bed and looked wildly about her as if in panic. 'But while you were away . . . Now hear me out.' She held up her hand, forbidding him to interrupt as he so often did. 'While you were away, Gretel told me of your dream to have a son. Now, I thought if Gretel had your baby we could perhaps adopt it and then you'd be really happy and you'd never leave me.' She began to cry and Dieter held up his good hand to her.

'Oh, Magda, my darling, what pain I must have caused you for you to even suggest such a thing. Can you ever forgive me?' And with a searing pain he had to acknowledge the awful selfishness of his ways.

'Sometimes I wish I couldn't, sometimes I wish I hated you, but it seems that if you love someone as I love you, there's nothing you can do about it, and on every other count you've been a good husband.'

'Magda, while I've been ill, I've made a lot of resolutions

and one is that the women cease, all of them, including Gretel.'

'Oh, poor Gretel, she does love you so much, you know.'

'But, you see, I don't love her, it's you I love, Magda. And we have no need for Gretel's baby, we shall adopt Katja and we shall live happily ever after with her.' But even as he spoke he wondered if it would be possible. Would too much of his past come with him to haunt his future? But he knew he needed Magda — when he thought he had lost her he had felt an unhappiness that nothing else in his life had equalled. Nothing else mattered; what did his money, his title, his position count for if she was not with him to share it?

Jamie waited five days before he visited Dieter in hospital after having checked he was able to receive visitors. Already Dieter was looking a lot better. And after Jamie had gone through the niceties of inquiring after his arm, he produced Dieter's envelope.

'Dieter, we've got the next clue. I'm pretty sure I know the solution, but I think I should wait until you're better before I go. When you think how you got wounded, it would hardly be fair if I took advantage of it.'

Dieter smiled. 'Oh, the English, always so correct in these matters. You know very well if you'd been wounded I'd have taken advantage of you.'

'Would you, Dieter? I doubt it, things are a bit different now.'

'You're going straight on with it, then? Not going back to England?'

'No. There's nothing there for me.' Jamie looked away from Dieter so he couldn't see his face and the uncertainty in his expression. He wanted to go to London to try to see Fiona but, he had found, he was too much of a coward to do so. Mica's rejection was enough, he didn't want another. 'Nice flowers,' he said, to fill the silence that had fallen.

'Did I talk to you, Jamie, when I was ill?'

'A bit.'

'I'm sorry, then. One shouldn't burden others with one's own stupid problems.'

'They weren't stupid problems, Dieter. They were very serious problems. But you know, I've got a feeling you're going to be able to sort them out.' He knew he spoke with the infuriating bonhomie which the healthy adopt when dealing with the ill.

'I hope you're right, Jamie. I certainly feel different about everything, about my whole life. It's quite a thing to come to terms with. I'm not going on with the treasure hunt. I've decided that as soon as I'm out of here, which the doctors think will be in only a week to ten days, I must organize some aid into that country. I can use my contacts, but aid must be got there to those children. I couldn't go back, you see, to my life before, not now.'

'I know what you mean, it's put everything else in perspective, hasn't it? It's made the way we all live seem futile and stupid.'

'Oh, not you, Jamie, you've given enormous pleasure to people with your films, something concrete. You must continue with them.'

'I've got to continue acting if I'm to keep a roof over my head.' Jamie laughed.

'Oh, you'll win the treasure now.'

'If there is any treasure. I mean, this has been the most peculiar treasure hunt, if you think about it. We haven't had to work particularly hard at solving the clues, so I begin to wonder what the treasure is or even if it exists. I think Guthrie's been playing God, if you ask me.'

'Maybe, maybe he has. Maybe it was just a game to him to see how we would act. The man's an enigma. But

I've no regrets, have you? I've learnt a lot, but best of all – thank you for rescuing Katja, Jamie. I'm indebted to you. How did you manage it?'

Jamie looked at the door to make sure no one was listening. 'The paperwork beat me, Dieter, if you must know. In any case I hate anything to do with bureaucracy – it brings out the worst in me. I mean, I don't understand these people, kids keep dying for lack of drugs and food, no parents to care for them, rape babies no one wants to know and yet they insist on hanging on to them, and in those conditions. We weren't going to get her out if we went through all the regular channels so I got the nurse to give her a sleeping pill and I put her in my bag. She was small enough – one of those big, long bags, you know? I covered her with my clothes, she had air to breathe, and I just carried her on to the plane as hand-luggage – no one was checking at the airport – we were covered by the diplomatic immunity of those pompous fact-finders. Once we were in the air I unzipped my bag – you should have seen their faces!'

'Good for you. We'll make a criminal out of you yet.' Dieter laughed. 'Magda and I have decided we'd like to adopt her but we know nothing about her, so how do we get the authorization?'

'I guess you're going to have to bribe a few more people, Dieter.'

'I guess we are.'

A week after returning home to Germany Dieter still tired easily after his illness and had gone to bed early. He lay with an unread book on the covers. He looked up as Magda entered the room bringing him a brandy – he'd rather that than pills, he'd told the doctor.

'There, are you comfortable?'

'Yes, fine,' he replied. She leaned across him to

straighten his sheet and as she did so her full breast brushed against his hand. He felt a jolt of pleasure flash through his body. Without thinking, he grabbed at her hand. 'I love you,' he said, suddenly hoarse. 'I want you,' he cried out, almost with anguish, and pulled her down towards him, his mouth feeling for hers as his hands searched the softness of her breasts.

'Dieter,' she sighed as his hands touched her nipples and teased them, making them quickly erect. He cupped her breasts in his hands, holding them gently, and then his mouth closed on first one and then the other, sucking at her hungrily as she called his name.

Her sexuality so long held in check was released. She tore at her clothes, pulled back the sheets, ripped at his pyjamas and pushing him back on the bed she mounted his body. He felt fear shoot through him, he turned his head away. 'What's the use?' he cried out.

She did not answer him but instead sat astride him and he felt the warm velvety soft wetness of her vulva rubbing against him, gently at first and then with a greater urgency. He felt a stirring beneath his scrotum and then with a rush it was as if molten metal was racing upwards, uncoiling him like a spring, making him large. With a triumphant little cry Magda impaled herself upon him and as she moved her body rhythmically up and down his shaft she began to laugh and to cry as they rocked to a climax – too soon, too fast, too quickly over.

They both sat up and looked at each other in astonishment.

'Oh, Magda . . .'

'Oh, Dieter . . .' They spoke in unison and then they both began to laugh and hold each other tightly, as if like this they could keep the moment a little longer.

'Perhaps we should try again,' Magda said, taking the initiative once more.

'Maybe we should.' He tried to sound confident.

It was slower this time, more relaxed, more sensuous. And he need not have worried. Whatever had stopped him before had disappeared in the smoke and horror of the war.

10

'Due South of Ariadne's Pool . . .'

With no reason to hurry since he was the only one left in the treasure hunt, Jamie decided to linger in Athens for a couple of days. He'd been drinking a coffee and leafing through the English language newspaper when he saw in the social column that his mother was in the city. He was surprised, for March was not the time of year he'd have expected a socialite like her to visit Greece – he wondered what she could be doing there. On a whim he called her, it was years since he'd seen her and he did not know why he bothered. But now, suddenly, he felt he wanted to.

Poppy, when she welcomed him at her luxury villa outside Athens, was a sad sight. Her hair was peroxided far too blonde for one of her age and she had fallen into the trap of a face-lift too many. Her tautened skin had a strange, shining, marbled look and her eyes were slightly slanted into an expression of permanent surprise. As she was in her sixties now, the bright, short-skirted pink dress was not the happiest of choices. Why she was in Greece soon became apparent when a new fiancé was produced, an old but very rich Greek millionaire. Jamie had to smile at his mother. What number husband could this be. Five?

The villa was full of people, as he had expected it to be. As always with his mother, life was one perpetual party. She was warm in her welcome and without a hint of criticism that he had been out of touch for so long.

He wondered if he'd come because he wanted to talk to

her about Mica and Winter and Fiona. If this was so, he didn't. There was never the right moment for they were never alone. And he doubted if they could ever talk on such a level — why had he thought they would? There never had been any intimacy between them, why should he think it could suddenly be? And as he watched her flitting excitedly about her guests, seeing to their needs, joking, gossiping, he thought how stupid it had been of him to think she'd even want to hear.

He felt like an observer as the house-party ebbed and flowed about him. There was nothing unfamiliar to him here — this was very much his sort of place, his sort of people, and his kind of entertainment. Normally he'd have been having a wonderful time. But now? He felt isolated, he found difficulty in making small-talk, he found the other guests less than amusing. He'd even found himself refusing to take part in a possibly lucrative game of backgammon; the idea no longer attracted him. He realized he no longer belonged here.

After two days and a fond farewell to his mother, he left and took the boat from Piraeus to the island of Naxos in the Aegean Sea. And as the ship, half-empty at this time of year, set sail, he felt an intense feeling of relief to be leaving the mainland.

Once again the clue had been an easy one for him to solve, even if he did not know what lay due south of Naxos. Years ago, when he was young, and a comfortable bed and excellent restaurants had not been the priorities they now were, he had been to Naxos with a friend. It was long before the island had surrendered to the lure of the tourists' money and they had spent a happy holiday there. They had slept and eaten in a simple taverna, got drunk every night, and when their money was beginning to run out they had slept on the beach. Those had been magical nights, he remembered, as he stood on deck and watched the lush green island approach. They had been nights of intense companionship when he and his friend had talked in an uninhibited way, as they would never have done at home. Nights when the sky was not black but a deep, comforting inky-blue like the Madonna's robe. A sky where the stars appeared to be so close that he dared to think that perhaps man was not alone in the universe. The smell of wild thyme had filled their nostrils, the incessant chirp of the crickets their ears, an experience never to be repeated. Not now, when he'd ache in the morning from sleeping on the sand and hadn't a friend he'd want to share such confidences with – except . . . No, best not to think of Winter.

The boat docked and it was a short walk to where he remembered Ariadne's pool was situated, where local legend said she had bathed while waiting for her disorganized Theseus to return. It was a deep rock-pool which he'd enjoyed all those years ago when the water was always as warm as a bath. It was smaller than he remembered it and perhaps not as romantic. The narrow channel which led under an overhanging rock out to the sea must be the point from which he measured due south, he presumed.

The one advantage of the influx of tourists was that it was not difficult to find someone who spoke English and whom he could use as an interpreter with one of the old fishermen. Due south were other islands, of course, in this sea scattered with so many, and their virtues were extolled and argued over a bottle of retsina by everyone in the bar – Naxos was best and he should not weary himself with further travel, was the consensus. Eventually, after several more bottles of retsina, he elicited the information that if he meant *exactly* due south then he must be looking for Kovos. Judging by their expressions, nobody thought much of Kovos . . . it was small, he was told, a mere pebble thrown out in anger by the gods. It was almost barren, the wine was undrinkable, the bread poor, the olives shrivelled, the people were unsociable, the women ugly – nobody went there. What for? Better, he was told, to stay on Naxos . . .

The following morning, with a sore head, he found a boatman willing to take him to this unfavoured place. The fisherman was puzzled by his insistence not to be dropped off at the cluster of houses by the sea which constituted the island's fishing village, but instead, to land on a small rocky beach, the one due south of Ariadne's pool on Naxos. It was barren, certainly, in comparison to that other island which, fortunate in its water supply, was more lush. It lacked mountains, and there was only one hill that he could see inland. The olive trees were sparse, it was not pretty. It was no wonder, he supposed, that it had been left alone by the tourists.

He stood in the spring sunshine looking about him. 'Thanks, Guthrie,' he said aloud. 'North, south, east or west, which, you old prat?' It could not be north for north was the sea. West, he could only walk a hundred yards and would again be in the sea. East or south? He did what any gambler would do, took a coin from his pocket, tossed it in the air and it came down heads. 'South,' he said aloud, and set out.

He had to walk across scrubland before joining a road which was more of a track and wound inland from the sea. It was leading him to the hill. Now he could see a large village. The houses were built in terraces in the rock which made it look as if they were tumbling down the hill. Jamie reckoned it was a good two miles from the sea. As he began to ascend the hill he paused and looked about him. There appeared to be little on the island, no marina, no pedalcraft in the bay, no gleaming yachts moored. Compared with the other islands of the Aegean, Jamie supposed, it was rather an ugly duckling. For all that, he liked its barrenness, its simplicity; it was refreshing to find somewhere so unblighted by civilization.

The climb up the hill to reach the village was steeper

than he had expected from a distance, and even though it was late March he still had to keep stopping to get his breath: give up smoking, he told himself – he'd started again – and drinking, an inner voice said. It might be a good idea to do so, he thought, as he set off again, not just for his health, though at forty-three he was most certainly about to enter the dangerous middle-aged reefs and dangerous currents of heart and lung disease if he didn't do something about it. Giving up both would serve another purpose, it might improve his looks, make him less haggard in the morning, give him something less to worry about. His vow to do both deepened when half-way up the hill he was overtaken by two old women, both carrying heavy baskets. Judging by the wrinkles on their faces, they must have been twice his age. They nodded their greeting, smiled and quickly passed the puffing Jamie.

'Shit,' he said to himself. 'Jet-propelled grannies.' And he laughed and plodded on up the hill.

Although the island was barren, on the slopes below the village the fields were green and lush with crops and vegetation. The village was like a dozen others he'd seen, white buildings entered by steep staircases with small secretive alleyways, a place of light and shadow. In the central square were a small church and a rather ramshackle taverna, with chairs and tables on the pavement. There was, as far as he could see, no post office, no police station. He sat down, ordered a beer and looked about him. The place was bustling. There was none of the indolent somnolence of the usual Greek village and he noticed how spruce everything was, no peeling paint, no litter about. It was a veritable model village. He'd learnt that so often these villages were almost deserted, the young having left to go to sea, or to Athens in search of work and entertainment. But here, as a bell rang, a crowd of children appeared, running excitedly from the school, and groups of youths were in evidence. It was not a place where only the very old were left, there were people of all ages. A high proportion were elderly, wrapped up against the March chill. Old women bustled about with their shopping, but were not bent and infirm, they walked upright and swiftly. He wished he knew some Greek so that he could talk to them and ask them the secret of their mobility.

His drink finished, Jamie did what he often did in a village, he went to the graveyard. It was, he always claimed, the only good reason for having learnt Latin, for at least he could read the tombstones. Here it wasn't so easy as everything was in Greek, but he had sufficient ancient Greek to be able to decipher the inscriptions. He began to become extremely interested in the fact that here, everyone seemed to die at a very advanced age. A hundred and ten, a hundred and fifteen – seventy was rare on a tombstone. He began to feel excited. Maybe Guthrie had not been playing games with them. Maybe his elixir did exist after all. For why else should this village be so full of active old age pensioners, and the graveyard be full of centenarians? So what was it? Had they access to some drug, some little-known herb?

He retraced his steps and went back to the taverna where lunch was now being served. Was it their diet, he wondered, peering as discreetly as possible at the plates being served around him, but it looked like the normal Greek food – lamb stew, feta salad, someone was having fish, another keftalia. The old men were drinking retsina, he was pretty sure, and on the table was the customary carafe of water. Being unable to speak Greek, how was he to find out their secret? Perhaps there was an English-speaking doctor who might be able to point him in the right direction. But then, if there was something here, other people must have found it, so why hadn't it been exploited before? Or maybe it was something that could not be marketed.

'Excuse me, are you Jamie Grant, the film star?' He turned and looked up into the dark brown, amused eyes of a priest dressed in long black robes, with a beautiful ornate crucifix hanging on his chest.

'Yes, as a matter of fact I am.'

'I thought you were, I thought I recognized you. We have your films here, you know – in the square in the summer we put up a screen, they are very amusing films,' the man said in heavily accented English. 'May I?' He indicated the spare chair.

'Of course, some wine? How fame travels.' Jamie smiled.

'And you follow your fame. What brings you here? We get very few tourists, even the boats don't stop. We're not glamorous enough for tourists.'

'Perhaps that's a blessing,' Jamie said.

'Perhaps.' And the priest smiled.

'You speak very good English,' Jamie said, thinking it was probably expected of him.

'Thank you, I was at Cambridge many years ago but unfortunately I never acquired a good accent. We do find it difficult to rid ourselves of our Greekness, I suppose.' He grinned. His full mouth nestled in his flowing brown beard.

'Everyone seems to live to a fine age here,' Jamie said, trying not to sound too curious.

'Yes, we are very fortunate, we have many years to enjoy God's beautiful earth.'

'Why do you think it is? This is a veritable Shangri-la.'

'Oh, hardly, surely in Shangri-La everyone stayed young and beautiful? You cannot call the majority of us beautiful. Age so rarely is.'

'I don't know, I think there is a great beauty to be seen in an old face,' Jamie said politely and untruthfully, dreading, as he did, his own face ageing. It might be fine for peasant farmers or fishermen but not for film heroes. 'It's the way everybody moves so lithely, they seem so fit,' Jamie said admiringly.

'Perhaps it is the simplicity of our life. We have no bus, so if people want to go to the village by the sea for fish, they walk or cycle. We have two cars – one belongs to the doctor and the other belongs to me. No doubt the doctor and I will die young!' And he laughed.

'Is it your diet?'

'Who knows? Maybe with a healthy diet it is possible to live longer, is that not what the wise doctors say?'

Jamie felt he was getting nowhere fast. 'I noticed,' he said, 'that everyone here in this taverna is drinking large amounts of water. That's not usual, not with the Greeks, surely – aren't you afraid of cold water, don't you think it's bad for you?'

'No, of course not, water is good for you,' the priest said.

'Then maybe there's something in the water, a mineral or somesuch that makes for all this longevity.'

The priest attracted the waiter's attention to order food and wine and did not reply. Jamie wondered if he had not answered on purpose.

'Tell me, do you know Guthrie?' Jamie asked when he had the priest's attention again.

'Ha! Doesn't the whole world know dear Guthrie?' The priest laughed. 'Yes, I know Guthrie. We were at Cambridge together.'

'Were you now? Aha! I see. Then it is you he has sent to point me towards what I am looking for?'

'Has he? Am I? But what is it you search for? Perhaps I can help, perhaps not,' the priest said enigmatically.

'Guthrie sent us in pursuit of the Elixir of Life,' Jamie said with a self-conscious grin, as he usually did if he mentioned the word elixir, or even when he thought of it, for even now, this far on, he felt it could not possibly exist. 'A treasure hunt.'

'An elixir, something that prolongs life indefinitely. I see, quite a task.'

'Yes, it has been quite a task.' Jamie leaned forward, an eager expression on his face. 'Is it your water?'

'Is it my water, our water, what?' the priest said innocently.

'Is there a property in your water which makes everyone here live so long?' Jamie said patiently. 'Or is there something else which is causing it?'

'Who's to say?' the priest answered infuriatingly. 'Is it the sun, is it our lifestyle? We are content.'

'Have you ever had it analysed by a chemist in Athens?'

'No, why should we? It's pure, nobody dies from drinking it.'

'But have you never been curious?'

'Why? What would be the point?'

'The point is, you could bottle it and sell it and be rich,' Jamie said, but uncertainly.

'What for? We have everything we need here, we are happy with our lives. We do not need many of the things that you and your civilization think are necessary, or even what the islanders on the next island think are essential. We have peace and tranquillity, we amuse ourselves. Those for whom it isn't enough leave, but those who remain are content. We love each other, you see, all of us. We are a very loving community.'

'You don't think it is the water, do you?' Jamie said, disappointed.

'I didn't say that, I just know that certain circumstances have occurred here that make us as we are. But,' he said, his voice changing, 'I thought there were to be three of you?'

'There were, but two left, dropped out if you like. In a

strange way I think they found themselves, they didn't need the elixir.'

'And you do?'

'Well, I've got a roof that's continually springing leaks,' said Jamie, 'and some extra money might help in that quarter.' He laughed, but then, seeing the priest's sober expression, stopped. 'Maybe I haven't found myself, maybe I haven't been as fortunate as the others,' he said seriously.

'I see. Well, young man, there is no mysterious secret in our water; if you wish, I will show you our source. Only you can decide what you wish to do then.'

Jamie and the priest set out from the village and climbed further up the hill. There was no road, only a rocky path that led around the side of the hill. They eventually stopped at an opening into the hillside, guarded by a luxuriant creeper, which the priest hooked back, revealing the wide opening. They entered. The priest had a large torch with him and handed Jamie a second. Bent double, they stumbled through a long, dark, dank passageway hewn in the rock, until suddenly it opened out into a high-ceilinged ante-chamber and then they stepped into a cavern which seemed to Jamie as huge as a cathedral. He looked down into a wide, still, underground lake.

'You see? There is it – our water supply. By any stretch of the imagination, it's a miracle. Even here in the arid heat of summer it never dries up. Where it comes from we have no idea, we just thank God that he gave it to us.'

Jamie sat down on a ledge above the water. There was a fissure in the rock high above him and the sunlight cascaded in on to the water, making it appear as blue as turquoise. Was it the water or was it the rocks? He did not know, he only knew that he was looking at something of incredible beauty. White rock formations hung from the roof of the cavern like the pipes of a giant organ. Others sprouted from the floor of the cave but they were deep down in the water, like a ghostly drowned city. It was very peaceful in the cavern and Jamie sat there for a long time, mesmerized by the water, unaware that the priest had bustled off to attend to some task. He knew instinctively that he had reached the end of the journey, even if he was unsure what he should do now.

9 The Conclusion

1

Jamie arrived at Guthrie's château outside Paris exactly on time. It was eleven o'clock in the morning of 6 April, three months to the day since they had set off on the treasure hunt. So much had happened, so many different experiences; he had learnt much and been puzzled by more. He had returned confused.

The château was greatly changed. Already spring flowers were in bloom in the garden which had been spruced up beyond recognition. And wherever he looked there were children, playing on swings and slides and a large inflatable fairy castle. At intervals throughout this trip, it seemed children had been involved. There had been a little girl running symbolically on the battlefields of the Somme, the sad, silently weeping chidren in Brazil, the wracked and suffering children in Yugoslavia. At each stage they had all been moved by them. Strange, when you thought about it – Dieter with none, Walt with his son who was ill and would die young, and Jamie with the daughter he never saw and whom he now realized he was afraid to seek out for fear she would reject him again.

The door of the château was opened by Guthrie's flat-faced servant, who, Jamie now realized, was a Brazilian Indian. Jamie asked for Guthrie and the man showed him across the large hall, still unfurnished except for a long table with chairs lined up on either side. Guthrie was in his study where they had had their last meeting.

'Jamie, how wonderful to see you, dear boy. And as punctual as one expects an Englishman to be.' Guthrie was sitting behind his desk. 'Buck's Fizz do you?' He indicated the tray with a champagne bottle on ice, a jug full of freshly squeezed oranges and, he noticed, only two glasses.

'One can always rely on you, Guthrie, for a Buck's Fizz.'

'Perhaps they should put it on my tombstone, sweetness,' Guthrie said as he mixed the drinks.

'Maybe.'

'You're the only one here?'

'Yes, but you know that.' He nodded towards the two glasses. 'I presume you know what happened? You've been like an unseen magician all the way along this trip.'

'I have a fair inkling. I just want you to confirm it.'

'Those kids in Brazil shook us all, Walt especially. He didn't know about those drug trials, you know, I'm sure of that. Okay, it was his company and I suppose one can argue that the buck stops with him, but he would never have countenanced it. Finding out shattered him, I'd go as far as to say it changed him. That's when he dropped out, he couldn't go on, you see. He had to go home and sort things out.'

'He's selling everything, you know – the whole bang shoot. He knocked Wall Street sideways. He's keeping one laboratory in Oregon, I hear. He's setting up a foundation for the Brazilian Indians – isn't that perfectly sweet of him?' Guthrie grinned. 'And Dieter, dear, proper Dieter? Tell me about him.'

'As I'm sure you know, since you seem to know everything,' Jamie said with an edge to his voice, 'the last time I saw him he was vowing to give up the illegal arms trade and was going to start using the same system, routes and people with the same bribes and commissions, to get aid into countries that needed it. What we saw in Yugoslavia would have made the devil weep. All he could think about were the children. He nearly died too – he was wounded getting medicine for them.'

'Yes, that was most unfortunate. But who would have thought dear Dieter would ever put himself at risk? But then he didn't die, did he? Instead he's a reformed little Kraut and he's setting up an enormous trust for orphans of war-torn countries, using his ill-gotten gains – nice touch, that. Highly commendable. And to top it all he's adopting a little girl – he called me to tell me that. Sweet! So, dear heart . . .' Guthrie lumbered to his feet and crossed to the safe, dialled the combination and removed the cheques that had been placed there three months previously. 'I am to congratulate you, the money's yours fair and square, I suppose – if you've found the elixir. Have you?'

'I think so.' Jamie looked at the cheques on the table. His hand resting on the desk would have liked to reach towards them. He consciously controlled it, and took a deep breath.

'If I have won then I don't want the money, Guthrie. I've been thinking, you see.'

'Really?' Guthrie said flatly, no hint of surprise in his voice.

'Yes. I'd like you to keep it. Give it to UNICEF.'

'Would you mind if I kept it for myself?'

Jamie looked at him expectantly. 'Well, if that's what you want, I don't suppose I mind.' But he realized he sounded disappointed. 'Let's face it, I didn't put any money in, so I haven't any right to it really, nor any say in what should be done with it.'

'I don't want it for me, dear boy, if that's what you're thinking. No – I want it for my little kiddiewinks here. Did you notice the children as you came in? Sweet little things, aren't they? Running around full of the joys – a mite noisy, but then they can't help it, can they?'

'I couldn't help but notice them. How many are there?'

'Twenty-five, and we've room for another ten. It's my new project, a place for children who need escape and rest. Not an orphanage, no, more a sort of jolly holiday home. A short-term thing, to heal them.'

'That's commendable – to use your favourite word. But if you don't mind me saying so, Guthrie, rather an odd thing for you to do. Why?'

'For fifty years I've done nothing but enjoy myself – lived the life of a hedonist, as you might say. I've decided that for the next fifty years, I shall be less selfish and less self-indulgent.'

'Are you giving up your villa and everything?'

'Good God, no, dear boy. I couldn't live with the little luvvies – never!' His large frame shuddered at the idea. He poured them another drink. 'Nor could I give up the old champers. I've no intention of slumming it into my dotage. No, everything chugs along as before, I'm just spreading the loot about in different directions, so to speak.'

'And having decided to reform yourself, you thought you'd do something on the same lines for us, for Walt, Dieter and me? Show us the error of our ways?'

'Gracious, did I do that?' Guthrie chortled.

'A bit arrogant of you, wasn't it?' Jamie was not laughing.

'Oh, come on, Jamie, where's your sense of humour gone?'

'I lost it en route. Quite honestly, Guthrie, who the hell do you think you are?'

'Why, Guthrie, of course – good old lovable Guthrie, but if you've other ideas I'm all lugholes, sweetheart. Fire away.'

'You had no right to do what you did. Do you remember what you said the reason for this was? "*Something to relieve the tedium of winter. To amuse you, dear boy.*"' Jamie gave an expert imitation of Guthrie's voice. 'Some fun! You've almost destroyed one man – Walt. He's a shadow of his former self and he's a good man, not what we imagined. You could have killed Dieter. As it was, he was desperately ill. He'll take months to recover. And what do you know about him? Sod all. What do you know about what his childhood was like? What made him the buttoned-up, inhibited individual he is? And Walt? What do we know about what happened to Walt to make him the ruthless businessman he became?'

'Bah! Childhood as an excuse, spare me, do, Jamie. We've all been fucked up by our parents – it's called life,' Guthrie flashed back.

'Don't give me that crap, Guthrie. Nothing that happened to you or me in our cosseted world as children could equal what happened to Dieter. Did you know he found the father he worshipped dead? With the back of his head blown off – what do you think that did to him? And living in Berlin at the end of the war, and finding out his mother had prostituted herself so that they could eat? Christ, a kid like that today would be besieged by social workers and psychiatrists sorting him out. But he had no one – he had to sort himself out.'

'Well, he's gone and done that now, hasn't he? And if you want to know about dear, kind-hearted Walt – word has it he murdered his father. Now there's a little surprise for you, Jamie boy.'

'I don't believe it.'

'Then don't, dear heart, if it upsets you. But 'tis the truth.'

'How? When?'

'Oh, years ago when he was a golden-haired cherub! Apparently his father was an unpleasant soul who beat him up and, plop, Walt popped him on the head and drowned him – can't say I blame him.'

'God, that's awful. How do you know?' asked Jamie suspiciously.

'A little bird told me.'

'What's that mean? That you had us all investigated? Shit, you're an arrogant sod, Guthrie.'

'I had my reasons.'

'Poor Walt, can you imagine living with a secret like that and then someone like you blundering along and finding out?'

'My my, what a forgiving little soul you've become, Jamie.'

'Leave the sarcasm out, Guthrie. All I know is that Walt's okay. If he did kill his father, he's suffered over the years. I won't stand in judgment. As for you, Guthrie, I don't know if I'll ever forgive you for what you've done. It was just a game to you. I can assure you it wasn't to us. You had no right to set us up like that. Standing in bloody judgment. Playing God. You've been a bastard. Two wrongs don't make a right.' Jamie realized he'd probably blown the film now, speaking out as he had, but he found he didn't give a damn. He'd had to say something to Guthrie, had to, for all three of them.

'Tut, tut, Jamie, cliché,' Guthrie said in a sing-song voice. 'Lecture over?'

'Oh, what's the point? You won't listen to anyone anyway. Everything's got to be a giggle to you.'

'My turn now, Jamie. Let me tell you a few home truths. I wasn't playing games – I was serious. If you have wealth you have responsibility – those two had neither. They deserved what happened to them. You've met Jose, my Brazilian servant? He and his wife were simple, trusting Indians – the white man knew best, they thought in their innocence. His wife was one of Walt's victims – that's how I came across the whole sorry story. They had three children and were too poor to afford more. She took the drug in desperation and in all innocence. Their baby was born with no back to its head but alive. So she took it into the forest and she killed it and then full of shame and remorse she killed herself. I wanted Walt to see the consequences of his actions.'

'But for Christ's sake, haven't you been listening? He did not know.'

'He should have known – as you said, the buck stops with him.'

'Now who's talking in clichés? Couldn't Jose have just sued?'

'A simple Indian? Don't be naïve, Jamie. How could he, how would he know where to start? In any case he didn't want money, he wanted his wife. And hitting Walt for money wouldn't have hurt him, he's got too much of it.'

'It was a complicated bloody charade, why didn't you just tell him?'

'Would he have gone to see for himself? A busy man like that? I very much doubt it.'

'So what's poor Dieter done to you to be punished?'

'Do you remember, about two years ago, there was a mysterious plane crash over the Pacific Ocean? All three hundred passengers were killed.'

Jamie found that the world was always so full of such catastrophes that it was difficult to remember specific ones. 'Yes, I think I do,' he said.

'It was a bomb – the president of a certain African state was rumoured to be travelling on that plane and it was blown from the skies by his political rivals, and the innocent passengers with it. Inconveniently the information had been incorrect, the president wasn't even on the plane, but a young friend of mine was blown to pieces in it. He was a talented boy, just starting out in his career as a singer – an opera singer. He had a wonderful voice which is now lost to us. He had just married and his wife was pregnant, but sadly, upon hearing the news, she had a miscarriage – she was left destitute. To Dieter the arms business was well-named "toys". You say I play games but I'm not alone. Dieter plays too – it was just a game, an excitement. He's successful in so many other fields, he did not need to dirty his hands in this way. It was a game motivated by avarice only. You might say again, why did I not tell him? But what use would there have been in that? He knew we all knew and disapproved of what he did, but did that stop him? No. Sterner action was required.'

'So you had been planning all of this for some time?'

'Yes, I wanted them to suffer. I'd been investigating them for some time. It was, however, just sheer chance that they were staying in the same hotel in Cannes. I was tipped off about that too.'

'And me? What have I done to earn your attention?'

'But, dear Jamie, nothing, you're perfection. There is nothing to punish you with. I might wish you didn't gamble quite so foolishly but all your friends think that. And who have you harmed? Only yourself. No, you just happened to be there and it would have been ill-mannered to exclude you from the trip. And then I thought perhaps it was a good idea if you did go with them. You could perhaps be useful in helping Walt out when he needed it, you can't expect an American to solve riddles set in Europe, now can you? He did start with a bit of a handicap. But maybe I was wrong and you did acquire something from it. You've turned down all this money for a start. And what about the film, you wanted to invest in that?'

'There's backers galore fighting to invest now that you've got yourself involved in it, you know that. My money wouldn't be needed.'

'But you're always so pushed for cash. Why don't you want this?'

'There really is more to life than money, Guthrie. But, if you must know, I wouldn't be happy with this money – it would be wrong to use it for pleasure after what I've seen. It should only be used for good.'

'Do you still want to make this film? Or are you suddenly turning into a monk or something?'

'I'd love to make the film. I've still got debts – the Elysium Club for a start. And then there's the upkeep of my house – I really need to work. But I suppose there's fat chance of that now, not now I've shouted my mouth off to you.'

'Don't be so silly, Jamie. I love a good old barney, you know I do. You're probably right, I did over-reach myself, *un peu* – I always was a meddling old fart.'

'You old rogue, you win.' Jamie smiled, aware that he could not stay cross with Guthrie, nobody could.

'Oh, good. You've got to think about Grantley, your wonderful house, the house you love above all else. Let's face it, you wouldn't be whole without it.'

'If I get a second chance at a career, hopefully I can earn enough to keep it going. But I've decided that if I can't, then it goes. It's only a house, after all, people and relationships are more important. Perhaps that's something else I've learnt.'

'So you met my friend Panos the priest. He liked you very much. He said he thought you were better-looking than in your films, isn't that nice?'

'He's a very charming man, yes, I met him.'

'And having met him, what's your conclusion?'

'It's not the water, is it, Guthrie?'

Guthrie looked at him. 'Isn't it?'

'No. I didn't bring any with me but if it were analysed I think we'd find that it was just water with a few added minerals, as good for you as Perrier or Vichy.'

'That is so. I did once have it analysed for Panos. But all the same it is excellent water and you could have been on to something very big. It still could be a source of revenue, I'm sure – bottled Greek water from the Aegean. Why weren't you interested?'

'I thought about it . . . I'll admit, for quite some time.

But at what cost? Those villagers have it made, Guthrie, I couldn't be the one to alter their life. No, if there is an Elixir of Life then I think it is within us. I think those people on that island live as long as they do because they are content. If we started a bottling plant there, and made them rich and affluent, how long would they stay content? How long before they started dying off at three score years and ten? I wouldn't like that on my conscience, Guthrie.'

'So you think it's just contentment that keeps them that way.'

'Yes, but then there was something else the priest said, I thought it was odd at the time, now I'm not so sure. He said that they all loved each other and maybe that is where it all springs from. I mean truly loving, nothing sexual, a spiritual love. Loving other people more than you love yourself,' he said thoughtfully.

'What a nice idea. Let's hope you're right, Jamie, dear boy. More champagne?' Guthrie handed over the champagne flute. 'But tell me, Jamie, it was fun too, wasn't it?'

'Oh, yes, I'll give you that. Sometimes scary and sometimes sad, but yes, you're right, it was fun – not that I'd want to repeat the exercise.' Jamie laughed.

2

On the flight back to London, Jamie sat deep in thought. He had to face it, something had happened to him as well. He was usually scrabbling about for money, yet he'd happily turned his back on a fortune. And then twittering on to Guthrie about love and contentment, something he would never normally do. I must be going potty in my old age, he thought. But he smiled to himself because, for the first time in a very long time, he did feel very much at peace with himself. He was looking forward to the filming beginning – and not just for the money. It would be a good film with a good part, he already knew he would get immense satisfaction from doing it as well as he could. Most important, he realized, he was not set on doing it for the fame and adulation it would bring him – he knew now how empty, ephemeral and unimportant fame was. Of one thing he was sure – he would never gamble again as long as he lived. Not after what he had seen, when the amount of money he could lose in one night could keep the orphanage in Yugoslavia going for a year. He'd been a fool where money was concerned. He would not be foolish again. He'd said this before, but this time, in some strange way, he knew he would keep his promise to himself.

From the airport he took a taxi to his flat and, as always, good-naturedly and patiently discussed the Ascot films with the cabbie. He shouldn't complain, he told himself, those films had served him well. Without them he wouldn't have been up for this part. At the apartment block the lift was in use, so he wearily mounted the stairs, his weariness caused not by fatigue but rather by the prospect which he dreaded – entering his flat for the first time since Mica had left.

Would her presence still be there? Would the old longing for her return? He hoped not, he wanted, needed, to rid his life of her. He knew who he did want, even though he knew he could not have her.

He pushed the front door open and bent down to pick up the accumulated mail – it was inches deep. So Mica hadn't been back at all since he had left. He didn't know if he was pleased by that or not.

The flat had the oppressive silence of an empty house and as he stood in the small hallway he was sure he could hear every creak and movement of the large building. He paused before switching on the electric light for he knew what he would see. He steeled himself as light flooded the long central corridor of the flat. On the deep red walls from one end to the other were large photographs of Mica by many world-famous photographers. Twenty Micas in various poses, her lovely face set in different attitudes, stretched before him. He dropped the mail on the floor and began to walk quickly down the corridor removing the portraits one by one. He then bundled them into the hall cupboard – out of sight. He felt a mite better when he had done that.

In their bedroom he could smell the lingering trace of her perfume. He crossed to the dressing-room and, as he feared, her wardrobe was still full of her clothes. The scent of her here was almost unbearable. He'd have to clear them out . . . but not yet, he couldn't face that, not now. He needed a stiff drink first, then maybe he'd be able to do it.

For Dieter those two acts of love, which had doubtless occurred because he was so mentally exhausted that his mind had not been quick enough to tell his body it could not perform, led naturally on to others. All the love he had held dammed in his body was released and he and Magda were like young lovers faced with the joy of learning about each other's bodies and what gave their partner pleasure. There was only one cloud in their lives and that was Gretel – how to tell her what had happened, and what to do.

There was no need to face her. Gretel saw them walking in the garden. She stood at her bedroom window and watched the way they looked at each other, and she knew. She clutched at the curtain, swayed against the wall. She felt dizzy. They had used her, both of them. She tugged at the curtain and it crashed to the floor. In her jealous anger she systematically wrecked the room before packing and rushing from the schloss for ever.

*

Walt had soon found a suitable house. It was large — necessary if his son was to have his separate accommodation with quarters for his nursing staff and a gym and heated indoor pool to help his poor stiff limbs. The experts told him that Hank would not be aware of the pool and the equipment in the gym. Walt was not so sure, and went ahead with his plan.

Until now Charity had always decided where they lived. This was the first house he had chosen for himself and he had liked the old house on sight, surrounded as it was with trees and with a luxuriant garden which he hoped he would now have the time to tend. Best of all, it had a view of the sea from every window.

It was over fifty miles from his mother's house and twenty from Westlake and his remaining laboratory. He had chosen the distance from his mother purposely. He still could not quite believe their reconciliation, he felt instinctively that it might be a far more fragile thing than was, at first, apparent. If they were to live too close the temptation to see her, impose himself upon her, might be too strong. She had said she loved him, now he had to give her time to forgive him.

Surprisingly, after all these years, he felt a strange comfort in being home in his own state. He'd heard people talk of their roots and had always set it aside as sentimental rubbish. He was no longer so sure. Maybe there was something here, in the soil, that would keep him and comfort him.

With the speed at which he did everything, the deeds of the house were quickly in his possession, and he had organized the workmen to renovate and decorate it before he left for New York.

His mother had been right about Charity. She had not gone to the police — his secret was safe. And after talking to his mother he was sure it was not his imagination that his guilt was less.

Once Charity had realized the size of her settlement, which included the Park Avenue apartment and a house in Connecticut, she had seemed surprisingly happy and when last heard of was back, once again, in the social swim.

The process of divesting himself of his business interests was moving apace. Walt had calculated that he needed just under a year to tidy everything up and to have his Brazilian hospital foundation up and running. He did wonder if he'd be sufficiently occupied when it was all over, with just one laboratory to run. But he'd face that problem when he reached it — already he had wondered about taking up gardening, he could fish again perhaps. One thing he knew now, he wouldn't miss the endless socializing which he and Charity had pursued. He wondered now if they had done it to cover the emptiness, the sterility of their relationship.

In an ideal world he would have liked to have had someone to share his new life with, preferably Winter, but then who could have everything, he asked himself. He wasn't really surprised to find a letter of resignation from her on his desk when he returned to his office, he couldn't blame her. He had no right to burden her with his confessions. She'd go to Jamie now, he supposed. He hoped she'd be happy but he felt achingly sad that he would not see her again. However, he told himself, he had a lot to look forward to in his life. Caring for and loving his son, for one. And he felt a strange sense of liberation. He was not afraid of loneliness; looking back, he saw that he'd lived his entire life alone.

Jamie had had a busy day. The jungle drums of London gossip had been busy and the phones had been ringing all day. Friends had been welcoming him back from his long trip, invitations were pouring in. He'd forced himself to pack Mica's possessions. The cases stood in the spare bedroom, and Jamie had arranged for a carrier to pick them up in the morning. He had the film to do and he would fill his life with work and books to keep the need for her away.

He poured himself another drink and slumped into an easy chair. God, he wished Winter was here – she'd have been the cure for everything. He wished now that he'd had more guts, had spoken up and told her how he felt instead of wimpishly leaving the field clear for Walt. Always too much the gentleman, he snorted with laughter at that notion.

The door-bell rang. He wasn't expecting anyone, certainly not at six in the evening. He padded along the soft carpet in his bare feet.

'Yes?' he said to the young woman standing in the shadow outside.

'Hello, Dad?' she said diffidently and tried to smile, but her nervousness set her lips in a rigid grimace.

'Fiona!' he said. 'What a wonderful surprise.' He grinned, which seemed to make her relax a little. He didn't know what to do. In the circumstances kissing her seemed over the top, and shaking her hand far too formal. Instead he put his hand on her shoulder and squeezed it and said, 'Come in, come in, do.' He led the way to his drawing-room and she stood awkwardly in the middle of the room.

'This is nice,' she said, rather gauchely.

'A drink?' he asked, since it was always his refuge in any situation he was unsure of.

'Vodka, if you have it.'

'No problem – your father always has everything in the drinks line. Ice?' He was glad she said yes, which meant a trip to the kitchen to fetch it. He needed to be alone for a few moments for he found his hands were shaking and he was clumsy trying to move the ice from its tray. He couldn't believe she was here. After all this time and after she had said she wanted nothing to do with him . . .

They talked of inconsequential things – the weather, his collection of modern art, the porcelain soldiers he also collected. And all the time he was watching her, assessing her, fully aware she was doing the same to him. She was beautiful, he thought proudly, and there *was* more of him in her face than her mother, he thought happily.

'How's college? Anthropology, isn't it?' he asked.

'You knew what I was doing?' She sounded surprised.

'Oh, yes. The family lawyer always kept me posted.' He needed to change the subject, talk of lawyers sounded too cool. 'I've just been to Brazil – saw some Indians – just up your street.' He knew he was making this light sort of conversation because he was afraid to know why she had come, what she had to say to him.

'It's more modern anthropology – you know, our own society, why our marriages break up, that sort of thing.'

God, he thought, she's going to be a social worker, how grim. 'I see,' he replied. Then they sat for a couple of moments in an awkward silence. This was ridiculous, he thought, they would get nowhere this way. 'Look, why did you . . .' he started to say.

'Look, Dad, I've got to say . . .' She spoke in unison with him.

'You first . . .' he said, after they'd stopped laughing at themselves.

'Mum's dead.'

The laughter stopped immediately. 'Oh, Fiona, I'm sorry. When?' he asked, while thinking how odd it was to feel absolutely nothing at the news of the death of someone he'd once known so well, had lain with, and who had carried his child.

'Ten days ago. She had cancer.' She spoke so matter-of-factly that he wondered if it was because she was keeping her emotions reined in, or for some other reason.

'That explains the phone call,' he said, remembering the call – was it before Christmas or after? He couldn't remember now. Had she been calling to say she was dying? Had she wanted to make amends?

'Did she say anything . . . you know, about me?'

'No, nothing.' She sounded as if she was sorry, he thought.

'I tried to call her back but there was no reply, then I had to go away and, well, to be honest, I forgot about it.'

'Why should you remember? Perhaps she called you before she was rushed to hospital.'

'Perhaps.'

'I had to go through her things – sort them out – I think it's better if I sell the house.' She spoke disjointedly, as if wanting to say something but not sure how to begin.

'Of course. That must have been awful for you to do, I'm glad I've never had to sort out the effects of someone I was fond of. But couldn't your stepfather have done it for you?' he said, with a fleeting flash of anger at the insensitivity of the man.

'He left last year. He'd stuck it for so long and in the end he couldn't live with Mum, you see. I didn't blame him, she wasn't the easiest person to get on with. I missed him dreadfully after he left. He didn't know she was ill. None of us did – it was very quick.'

'That's a blessing,' he said, feeling it was not politic to say how difficult he himself had found Sally.

'Fiona, about me. I expect you feel pretty hurt by the past. That you think I deserted you. But I've never forgotten you, you know . . . It was just . . .' And he stopped, for how could he explain to this young girl the complications, the paradoxes of his emotions.

'You thought it best for me if you didn't see me, that's it, isn't it? You didn't want me to be too badly hurt.'

'Why, yes, that was the reason. And . . .' He thought for a second of Winter and his conversation with her. 'I have to be honest. I think I was protecting myself too. When I had to say goodbye to you on one of the access visits it tore me up. I hoped that one day you'd understand. I do realize it's difficult for you. I know why you refused to speak to me the last time we met. It's just, Fiona, I'd give anything, do anything for you to give me a chance.' He knew he was begging, somehow it didn't matter.

'I hated you. I felt so bitter . . .' She paused as if controlling herself. His heart sank at her words. 'When I saw your pictures at the cinema, or when I saw photographs of you in the newspapers, I loathed you. I never admitted to anyone that you were my father – at school I used to say that it was just coincidence that my name was Grantley and that if I looked a bit like you that also was a coincidence.'

'I understand.' The despair was in his voice and he felt blank inside.

'But . . . Dad, I'm so confused. I've learnt the truth. In the last few days I discovered Mum has lied to me about you all my life. She told me, you see, that you'd deserted us, left us with nothing. She said that you didn't want me born, that you wanted her to have an abortion and that when I arrived you didn't want anything to do with me. And then, after she died, when I was going through her papers I found these.' She opened a large handbag she was carrying and took out a flat bundle of letters tied with a blue ribbon. 'She must have been very mixed up. I mean, look at this ribbon, you tie love letters up with ribbons, don't you? And back at the house in a packing-case in the attic I found scrapbooks of your career. Loads of them – every photo and interview you've ever done, all neatly pasted in. And yet she said she hated you. I don't think she could have, it's really sad, I think she must have always loved you. Anyhow, these are your letters to her over the years. They explained everything to me; why you went, your feelings about me, money matters. I didn't even know it had been you supporting me all this time, that it was you who set up that trust fund for me; she told us – me and my stepfather – it was done in my grandfather's day by him. And then in the attic – that really upset me – I found boxes and boxes full of presents from you, all unopened, all still in their wrapping. I cried when I saw them. That was such a wicked thing to do to a child. It was an evil thing to do to you. I so wish she was alive so that she could know that I'd found out the truth. I'm so angry with her.'

Jamie had listened to her with ever-increasing excitement, he had no room for anger. 'Don't blame her, Fiona. I was a pretty lousy husband, you know, that bit was true. I was feckless and a gambler and your mother longed for a conventional life and I'm not a conventional person. I don't seem very capable of the husband role.' He laughed at that and she joined in, a small, tentative giggle. 'God, I'm glad you've found out the truth, though. It hasn't been fun knowing I've been made out to be an ogre.'

'Why didn't you come and tell me? We've wasted so much time.'

'I was afraid to. I didn't have much luck when I tried.' He smiled his lop-sided smile.

'You're better-looking than in the films . . .' she said shyly.

'And thinner?' He grinned.

'You know, I remember you taking me to the zoo. You always made me laugh. You were always such fun.'

'Perhaps we could have fun again. I'm still me.'

'I'd like that if you don't think it's too late. If the hurt hasn't destroyed everything.'

'Fiona, my darling, it wasn't you. None of this had anything to do with you. My love for you remains, it always has, locked away in my heart.' He looked at his hands and then his feet, and then almost shyly, as diffident as any swain, he said, 'Are you doing anything tonight? Perhaps we could have dinner together?'

'I'd like that, we've got a lot of catching up to do, Dad.'

'Too right.' And then he allowed himself to hug her and she was clinging to him like a limpet and he was grinning and laughing and crying all at the same time and the future suddenly seemed one hell of a lot rosier than an hour ago.

Walt, once again in New York, reverted to his Sunday visits to his son. He sat in the pretty room of the nursing-home, so unlike a sick room, and held Hank's hand. The nurses had warned him that the boy was having a bad day. Hank was thinner than when he'd last seen him four months ago and had a slight chest infection. A normal child would have thrown it off in a couple of days, but for Hank it meant bed, antibiotics and constant monitoring so that it did not develop into full-scale pneumonia. The nurses had called it a bad day but what was a good day for the lad? Could being strapped to a wheelchair and placed in front of a constantly playing television set be classed as a 'good day'?

As if suddenly aware of the television set, Walt got up and turned it off. There was no response from Hank as to whether he had been enjoying the programme or not. Walt was annoyed. He had had a five-disc CD player installed for his son and had asked the staff that music be played constantly upon it for him. He'd tried all sorts of music to stimulate the boy, from symphonies to opera, pop and heavy metal. He would have to speak to somebody about the television set. He was not going to have his son sitting mindlessly in front of it.

He put on one of Simply Red's discs – he always did each time he came, and once, several months before he'd gone away, he'd been sure Hank had squeezed his hand while it was playing. The music on, he settled back in his chair and once more took hold of his son's hand.

'I've bought us a house, Hank. You're coming to live with me. No more nursing-homes. Maybe one day soon we can go fishing again like we used to. Remember? And you'll see the sea and migrating whales from your room . . .' And for nearly an hour he talked to his crippled son. 'I'll never leave you again, Hank. Never. We'll spend the rest of our lives together, won't we?'

What with the noise of the music and his own concentration on his son, he had not heard the tap on the door nor the soft footfall cushioned by the carpeting. He jumped when a hand touched his shoulder.

'Hello, Walt – I hope you don't mind me butting in like this.'

He swung round. 'Winter!' he exclaimed. 'This is a surprise. How did you know to find me here?'

'But it's Sunday, Walt. You're always here on a Sunday,' she replied simply and smiled, and Walt longed to put out his hand and touch her beautiful lips.

'I didn't expect to see you again, Winter. Not after . . . I did understand your decision to resign. I'd made things impossible for you, I see that. I gathered you'd cleared your office . . . This is the last place I'd expect to see you.' He knew he was gabbling, knew he must sound half-baked, knew he must talk of mundane things otherwise he might make a fool of himself with her again.

'I changed my mind – if you'll have me back.'

'Of course I'll have you back, but there won't be a job much longer for you, Winter. I meant it, I'm giving everything up. I've found us a house. Hank and I are moving back to Oregon. I've kept a laboratory there, I'll continue my research – did you know they've isolated the gene for Huntington's? Maybe future generations will be safe. Now I have to work to help those afflicted. Maybe with that to concentrate on and back with my roots I'll find some sort of peace.'

She touched his shoulder again gently. 'I didn't mean I'd changed my mind about work, Walt.' She was standing straight, an almost defiant expression on her face as if she was steeling herself to speak. 'Is your offer still open?'

'My offer?'

'You said you loved me. I wondered if you still did or if it was something you said on the spur of the moment.'

'Oh, I meant it. I've never said that to another woman, ever.' He was standing now, but with his legs braced against his son's bed with one hand holding on to the head-board as if he was afraid to let go, as if he'd topple over if he did.

'Walt, I know it now. I love you too, I need to be with you. I've been so sad these last few weeks while you've been away in Oregon. I had finally to face that it was because I was missing you. I guess, deep down, I've known for some time that I loved you but I wouldn't accept it. I kept denying it to myself. I suppose I was afraid to because I didn't trust you totally.'

'But—' he began.

'No, Walt, let me finish or else I might chicken out. I was wrong to deny myself this chance of happiness. I fell in love with you as you are – not some idea of you. I know it's a foolish woman who thinks she can change her man. I know now that I'd rather have you as you are than not have you at all.'

'Winter,' he said, almost as a sigh.

'And then I got to thinking that you had no idea how I felt, I reckon I kept it secret – too secret, probably. And having quit the company – you might have found someone else by now. And I realized if I didn't find you to tell you, if we didn't try it together, then I'd know I'd spend the rest of my life being miserable, trust or no.'

'But, Winter, I have changed already. I'm the real me now. I don't want anyone else but you – that's the magic of you.'

'Walt, I've got to say, though,' she continued, as if she

had not heard him, 'there's one thing . . . I don't want to be just another mistress, it wouldn't be enough, nothing like that. I want to mean more to you. I suppose what I'm trying to say is, if we do start something then don't take me up only to drop me, I couldn't bear that.'

'God, what must I have seemed to you?' He took hold of her hand. 'Listen to me, really listen, Winter. I don't want another mistress. Once I'm free I shall ask you to marry me.'

'I want to be your wife, Walt,' she said simply.

'Oh, Winter, I can't believe I'm hearing this, I thought I had blown it once and for all. But my lifestyle will be different – a quiet life in Oregon, no more jet-setting.'

'I want a quiet life in Oregon.'

'Why, I thought it was Jamie you had fallen for and wanted.'

'Dear Jamie – could you imagine me living his lifestyle? The country house, being lady of the manor and wife of a mega filmstar with all that glitz . . . Walt, that's not me.' She laughed at the idea. 'I think Jamie thought he loved me but he hasn't got over his wife yet, he has a long way to go before he can really love again. Jamie's a dear friend and one I hope I shall know and cherish for the rest of my life. But that's not love. To love someone means to feel incomplete without them, as I do without you. No, Walt, it's you, I need you.'

'Oh, my darling, you've got it all wrong. It is I who need you.'

And from the bed they both heard an almost imperceptible sigh.

'Hank!' they both exclaimed.

'He can hear us! I always said he knew what was going on.' Walt hugged Winter to him tightly as if afraid she would disappear. He released her and put his hands on each side of her lovely face and stood silently looking at her as if studying her, almost as if he was memorizing how she looked at this moment.

And then slowly he bent and his mouth was upon hers. Her lips parted slightly and Walt sighed as the kiss he dreamed of and never thought would happen became reality.

Anita Burgh
Distinctions of Class £4.99

Jane dared to dream as she grew into a beautiful woman in a dead-end world of mean streets, but she never dared dream that one day she'd be the laird's lady, wife to Alistair Redland, future Earl of Upnor.

When that impossible dream became real, she had to wake one day and find her love-match wrecked on rocks of class pride and social prejudice.

So in cloistered Cambridge and elegant Italy, Jane built her life anew. Always desirable, wherever she went there were men who knew just how desirable.

Until her star of destiny drew her north again, to the Highlands where a twist of fate lay ready to seize again her dreams and test her courage . . .

Anita Burgh
The Azure Bowl   £4.99

For Alice Tregowan, daughter of a wealthy mine owner, the Cornish
estate of Gwenfer still holds the dreams of a past long buried: the
wealth and privilege she sacrificed in her fight for freedom . . . and
love.

But for Ia Blewett, daughter of a drunken and penniless miner and
Alice's childhood friend, Gwenfer is the symbol of all that she could
never have; and all that she will struggle to gain in her relentless quest
for wealth and vengeance.

From the sweeping landscape of rugged Cornwall, to the brothels of
Victorian London and the grim tenements of turn-of-the-century New
York, theirs is a story of passion and conflict, of courage and desire.

Anita Burgh
Love the Bright Foreigner   £4.99

Ann had built her life around marriage. But the sudden death of her husband proved how vulnerable her world really was. Then a chance encounter unlocks the door to the prison of her grief, sweeping her into the world of a magnetic and mysterious foreigner . . .

But still the past haunts her, a past inextricably interwoven with her own tragic first marriage and her lover's sinister secret. Gradually the truth begins to emerge, threatening to destroy her new-found happiness and shatter her world for ever . . .

Love the Bright Foreigner sweeps from Cambridge to Athens, London to New York – it is an unforgettable story of love triumphant in the face of despair.

All Pan Books are available at your local bookshop or newsagent, or can be ordered direct from the publisher. Indicate the number of copies required and fill in the form below.

Send to: Pan C. S. Dept
              Macmillan Distribution Ltd
              Houndmills Basingstoke RG21 2XS

or phone: 0256 29242, quoting title, author and Credit Card number.

Please enclose a remittance* to the value of the cover price plus £1.00 for the first book plus 50p per copy for each additional book ordered.

*Payment may be made in sterling by UK personal cheque, postal order, sterling draft or international money order, made payable to Pan Books Ltd.

Alternatively by Barclaycard/Access/Amex/Diners

Card No.

Expiry Date

_____

Signature

Applicable only in the UK and BFPO addresses.

While every effort is made to keep prices low, it is sometimes necessary to increase prices at short notice. Pan Books reserve the right to show on covers and charge new retail prices which may differ from those advertised in the text or elsewhere.

NAME AND ADDRESS IN BLOCK LETTERS PLEASE

. . . .

Name _____

Address _____

_____

_____

_____

6/92